Praise for

"A beautiful, **meticulously researched story** that will keep you on the edge of your seat until the very last page"

USA Today bestseller, Genevieve Graham

"A **triumphant, unforgettable tale of sacrifice, hope, and second chances** … with a twist that will have readers holding their breath"

Renee Ryan, author of The Secret Society of Salzburg

"**Readers of historical fiction, don't miss this one!**"

USA Today bestseller, Andie Newton

"A **winning and memorable tale** that boasts a perfectly-judged grasp of historical detail, **wonderfully nuanced characters**, and a **narrative arc that never falters**"

USA Today bestseller, Jennifer Robson

"A rare novel that is **both heartbreaking and heartwarming** at the same time. Prepare to fall in love"

Soraya M. Lane, bestselling author

Since 2006, *New York Times* bestseller Donna Jones Alward has enchanted readers with stories of happy endings and homecomings that have won several awards and been translated into over a dozen languages. She's worked as an administrative assistant, teaching assistant, in retail and as a stay-at-home-mom, but always knew her degree in English Literature would pay off, as she is now happy to be a full-time writer. Her new historical fiction tales blend her love of history with characters who step beyond their biggest fears to claim the lives they desire.

Donna currently lives in Nova Scotia, Canada, with her husband and two cats. You can often find her near the water, either kayaking on the lake or walking the sandy beaches to refill her creative well.

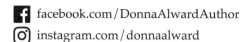

www.donnajonesalward.com

facebook.com/DonnaAlwardAuthor
instagram.com/donnaalward

Also by Donna Jones Alward

When the World Fell Silent

SHIP OF DREAMS

DONNA JONES ALWARD

One More Chapter
a division of HarperCollins*Publishers*
1 London Bridge Street
London SE1 9GF
www.harpercollins.co.uk
HarperCollins*Publishers*
Macken House, 39/40 Mayor Street Upper,
Dublin 1, D01 C9W8, Ireland

This paperback edition 2025
25 26 27 28 29 LBC 5 4 3 2 1
First published in Great Britain in ebook format by
HarperCollins*Publishers* 2025

Copyright © Donna Jones Alward 2025
Donna Jones Alward asserts the moral right to
be identified as the author of this work

A catalogue record of this book is available from the British Library

ISBN: 978-0-00-873987-4

This novel is entirely a work of fiction. The names, characters and incidents portrayed in it are the work of the author's imagination. Any resemblance to actual persons, living or dead, events or localities is fictionalised or coincidental.

Printed and bound in the United States

All rights reserved. No part of this publication may be reproduced, stored in a retrieval system, or transmitted, in any form or by any means, electronic, mechanical, photocopying, recording or otherwise, without the prior permission of the publishers.
Without limiting the exclusive rights of any author, contributor or the publisher of this publication, any unauthorised use of this publication to train generative artificial intelligence (AI) technologies is expressly prohibited. HarperCollins also exercise their rights under Article 4(3) of the Digital Single Market Directive 2019/790 and expressly reserve this publication from the text and data mining exception.

Chapter One

April 10, 1912
Southampton

HANNAH

"Oh, Lou, isn't it simply magnificent?" I spun away from the glorious sight of the *Titanic* and beamed at my best friend, Louisa Phillips, who, like me, was standing in awe of the veritable palace resting at Southampton's dock. Her blue eyes were alight with an excitement that mirrored my own. I reached out and clasped her gloved hand, giving it a squeeze. "Oh, this is absolutely tremendous," I bubbled. "I can't wait to get on board and see our cabins!"

Lou was three inches taller than me and far more self-possessed than I was at this moment. Her blond hair was precisely curled, tucked, and pinned beneath a cream confection of a hat that was wider than her shoulders and more than adequately adorned with silk ribbons and diaphanous netting. And while her face held a certain enthusiasm, her bearing was one of elegance and, well, presence. She was the kind of woman who walked into a room and owned it. Heads turned her way and never failed to admire.

I, on the other hand, often felt like a rambunctious little puppy, or perhaps a kitten, sometimes adorable, more prone to get a pat on the head than admiring respect. It had always been thus, since the day we first met at St. Hilda's School in Exeter. When I couldn't find my pencil, she'd plucked it out of my hair and handed it to me. We'd been closer in height back then, but I'd kept more of my baby fat while Lou's figure was already willowy with bumps in all the right places. Lou hadn't cared a bit. She'd announced we were to be best friends, and we were – the jolliest of friends for nearly fifteen years now. It didn't seem to matter how different our lives were. Through thick and thin, we always said.

"It is exactly as you say, Han. Magnificent." Lou squeezed my hand back and her smile widened as her eyes twinkled. "Oh, we are going to have such fun on this crossing!"

"Not too much fun," came a grumbling voice beside me, and I sighed on the inside. Charles could be such a wet blanket.

Lou was undeterred, though. "Oh come, Charles, even you have to admit the *Titanic* is built for pleasure." She let go of my hand and slid her arm through mine, and we all looked up at the massive ship. I was stuck between the two of them, which felt rather appropriate, considering. My husband was always the steady, rather dull one, which often appealed to my quieter side. But then there was Lou to my right, elegant, confident, and always ready for a party. If not for Lou, I'd probably be a recluse. Whenever I needed a dose of fun, I looked to Lou. She could lighten the darkest of moods with her charm and easy laugh. And I'd needed that over the last year or so, while I made a return to the land of the living.

Charles smiled a little, looking slightly pained. "You're right of course, Miss Phillips." He never called her by her Christian name, which made her somewhat cross, and he knew it. "There is no end to the delights promised on the *Titanic*. It should be a pleasant crossing."

Out of the corner of my eye I saw Lou roll hers, and I stifled a smile. *Pleasant* was such an innocuous word, like *nice* or *amenable*, which required no commitment one way or another. Still, I looped my left arm through Charles's as we made our way through the chaotic throng to the gangway for first class. "It's going to be marvellous," I decreed, raising my voice in the din, calling forth the small flicker of hope I held that perhaps getting away from our day-to-day humdrum could somehow improve my marriage. If I could just shake Charles out of his rut, maybe we could share the kind of relationship we'd once had while courting. He'd smiled more then. He'd brought me flowers and we'd gone for walks and danced at soirées. That had all disappeared over the last two years. Neither of us was the same after—

I shook away the painful memory, determined not to let it ruin what was bound to be a momentous day. All around us, voices cluttered the clear, salty air. I was simply transfixed by the sheer size of the ship, all white and black and gold, regal and yet ostentatious, settled firmly at the dock with an attitude of blatant superiority. The noise was horrendous; it felt as if all of Southampton and indeed most of Hampshire had congregated to watch the spectacle. Workers scurried along the docks like industrious ants, preparing for the departure; reporters called out rapid-fire names as they sought to pluck a new, juicy tidbit for their stories. Nets of trunks and baggage swung over the deck to be loaded into the hold, including our belongings. Except what we would unpack in our cabins, of course. A shout went up as men guided the cargo to the deck. Horns from motor cars punctuated the air with their brash calls.

A frisson of excitement fizzed in my veins once more. One week from now I'd be in New York City, something I'd never even dared to dream of. And while on board the *Titanic*, I'd be dining on the finest food, listening to music under sparkling lights, dressing in beautiful, eye-wateringly expensive frocks. Charles, for all his reticence, was not stingy. He'd taken us to London for four glorious days of shopping before herding us onto the Waterloo Express this morning. I had new outfits to wear and the filmiest of lingerie, not to mention a brand-new scent, *Quelques Fleurs*, that I'd fallen in love with. I was most excited about the Paul Poiret ensemble, though. It was by far the most modern thing I owned, and I hoped it would knock Charles's eyeballs out.

Charles urged us forward. Lou dropped my arm as we navigated our way through the crowd, and she kept a tight hold on the plain brown valise she had insisted on carrying, saying she didn't trust her personal items to be delivered correctly. That surprised me, because I was the one who tended to worry about those sorts of details, while Lou generally waved a hand and cared less. Still, every woman was entitled to her own personal privacy. If she wanted to carry her own bag, so be it.

Being Mrs. Charles Martin has its advantages, I thought, as we threaded our way through the throng to where the first-class passengers would board. My husband wasn't titled, but he was influential, at least in Devon society. He'd made his fortune in mining, and at only thirty-three, had a bright future ahead. And Lou ... well, Lou's family held a baronetcy in Exminster. She was a "miss" and not "Lady" anything, but the Phillips's manor house and the four-hundred-year history behind it gave her a pedigree I lacked as a solicitor's daughter. After several years of marriage, I was still not used to how crowds parted to let us pass and felt somewhat awkward about it.

The procedure to board for first class seemed much easier than steerage, too, with no pesky checks for lice, which made me shudder just thinking about it. We simply walked across the gangplank and entered the ship, greeted by a smiling steward who said he would show us to our cabin.

"This way, if you please. May I take your bag, miss?"

Lou lifted an eyebrow at him. "I'm perfectly capable, thank you."

The perplexed steward looked at Charles, who merely shrugged. "This way, then," the steward repeated, and we set off.

Here we were, stepping inside the grandest ship in the world, the scent of fresh paint still hanging in the air and the white halls pristine and unblemished, without marks in the paint or scuffs on the floors. We were the first passengers to tread these decks, the first who would eat off the elegant Spode china and drink from the cut crystal. I looked over at Charles and squeezed his arm, attempting a smile. Our marriage had become so stale and lifeless. I desperately wanted to change that. "Darling, this is so exciting," I said for about the tenth time in an hour. "I'm so glad we've come."

He patted my hand and smiled. "Good. I say, it would have been a boring crossing without any company. It is a chance to combine a little relaxation with business."

Hope fluttered in my chest. "Exactly." We kept going through a maze of corridors that had me quite disoriented, but I kept on, undaunted. "I heard there are Turkish baths on board, and an orchestra, and the papers called it an 'ocean palace.'"

"And there's a gymnasium," Lou said from behind us.

Charles half turned to look over his shoulder at her. "That's hardly suitable, I shouldn't think."

The steward piped up, "Oh, there are special morning hours just for the women, sir. Entirely appropriate."

Lou snickered behind me and Charles's neck went a little pink. I knew he wasn't Lou's biggest champion. He found her outspoken and entitled, two things I actually adored about her. Most of the time, anyway.

"I think I shall want to try it out. Maybe even wear trousers. So much more comfortable. I did pack some, you know." Louisa knew how to be scandalous and get a reaction. Charles, unfortunately, went for the bait.

"Yes, of course, and while you're at it, smoke a cigar and run for Prime Minister." I could practically hear him rolling his eyes, and I was torn. On one hand, I knew Lou was being deliberately provocative and trying to niggle at Charles. But on the other, I was amused and even agreed with her. The constrictions around women's clothing and suitable activities were ridiculous. We shared the opinion that a man would never tolerate having to truss himself up in a corset every day or walk around in stockings and skirts.

"Here we are, sir." The steward opened a cabin door to our right, breaking the tension. "Miss, yours is just next door, here," he said, and took Lou a few steps down the hallway and to her cabin, which adjoined ours.

It was just Charles and me now, and I let out a breath as I peeled off my gloves. I loved my bedroom in our house at Lamerton and thought it quite grand. But as I stood in the centre of the *Titanic*'s first-class cabin, I marvelled at the sheer opulence of my surroundings. Stunning oak panelling covered each wall, the elegant carved patterns repeated in the bed posts. I liked the lines of the furniture, too – straightforward and clean, unlike the fussiness of our furnishings at home, which Charles had pointedly informed me were *Louis Quinze* as he apparently set store in that sort of thing, though I wouldn't have cared either way. The bed had a velvet canopy held back by sleek ties; the spread was of the same rich material in a dark red. Four fluffy pillows graced the top, promising good rest while aboard. There was a large washstand with a double basin in pink-veined marble, a long, upholstered sofa perfect for lounging, and a table and chairs with an electric lamp and a massive bouquet of flowers, the heady fragrance overpowering the tinge of fresh paint. A second bed was against the opposite wall, smaller but with the same luxurious bedding. I eyed it suspiciously. Did every cabin have two beds? I had hoped that perhaps by sharing a bed, Charles and I might … reconnect. It happened so rarely these days. Perhaps he'd *requested* a cabin with two beds. The thought put a definite damper on my mood.

Still, I turned in a circle, determined to not let such thoughts ruin my excitement. It seemed as if all our comforts were taken care of. There was even an electric heater! Two windows, both with etched and stained glass, let in the light. Dark blue paper covered the top third of the walls. I adored the rich colours that reminded me of sparkling jewels – gold adorned with rubies and sapphires. Jewels similar to the ones I travelled with: some that I had kept out to wear during the voyage, some to be entrusted to the purser on C Deck for when we reached New York, and the brand-new earrings Charles had bought me on Bond Street two days ago, emeralds surrounded by five pearls, like milky-white petals of a flower. I loved them, but I would have traded them in a heartbeat for more than the polite regard with which he treated me.

"What do you think?" Charles asked, holding his hat in his hands and puffing out his chest. "B deck is supposed to have the best cabins. Do you like it?"

I glanced at the door to my left, then back at my husband. "It's beautiful. I love it. There's so much space. Everything is perfect, Charles."

"Of course it is. The *Titanic* is the best ship ever built, not just the biggest. Over forty-six thousand tons with six decks and four stacks. Three engines, my dear. Think of how much coal it takes to power twenty-nine boilers. It's a marvel of engineering, I tell you."

I'd heard these numbers before, but I indulged him because Charles was actually quite handsome when he was passionate about something. His grey eyes lit up and the customary severe expression gave way to one of wonder. It was a shame that a hulk of iron and coal seemed to excite him more than his wife, but I appreciated that he had interests that fuelled his brain. Besides, his enthusiasm was what had made him rich. He was always talking about learning and innovating. It was why we were on this trip to begin with – so he could meet with other powerful men and learn about silver mining in America. As his wife, I was so proud of all he'd achieved and happy to be on his arm.

"The ship is so large, I doubt I'll even be able to feel it moving," I replied, running my hand along the silky-smooth post of the bed. "While we wait for our things to be delivered, could we go out on deck to watch the departure?"

"If that's what you'd like. We have a whole week to enjoy the ship." The ship. Not each other. But in an unusual display of affection, he took my hands and looked into my eyes. "You're certain you and Miss Phillips will be all right in New York? Perhaps you should come with me. I don't know about leaving you alone in a strange city."

"Don't be silly," I said, pleased at his concern but determined to dismiss it. "Lou has been there before, remember? And you don't want us along on a business trip, getting in your way. I shall like to shop on Fifth Avenue and have tea at the Plaza. Perhaps even take in a play on Broadway."

He frowned.

I laughed. "Nothing racy, darling, I promise. Lou might be a little unconventional, but she does have a sense of propriety. She won't lead me astray. Besides, then we have the return journey home to relax, and you'll be able to tell me all about your travels."

The wrinkle in his brow smoothed, and once again I got that surge of hope in my chest. Maybe what our marriage really needed was a holiday, away from the concerns of business interests. I swallowed against a lump in my throat. I felt in my heart that we needed to be on more solid footing before I broached the subject I knew would poke at a very sore wound. Besides, things had been odd with Lou lately as well. The customary ease we had with each other had been a little strained. I was looking forward to a week in New York with her, a bit like old times with just the two of us.

"Shall we head up to the promenade, then?" Charles asked.

"Let me check with Lou, then we'll go." I was saved from knocking on Lou's door, however, when she knocked on the adjoining one first and then opened it without waiting for a response. "Darling," she said, "I have my own bath. I think I'm in heaven."

LOUISA

Even the thought of putting up with Charles Martin couldn't put a damper on the relief I felt having bought myself a good month away from home and the pressure to become Mrs. Arthur Balcombe, second son of a viscount with "excellent prospects."

The *Titanic*'s departure was a huge spectacle, and I let the excitement of those on shore and around me slide through my veins as I shook off the lingering feelings of resentment at my parents for their unrelenting pressure that drove me to such lengths. I was twenty-six. I'd hoped they had given up on matrimonial hopes for me, but no such luck. They had been horribly angry when I'd turned down a proposal from a promising young scholar from Oxford who came from a good family – never mind that he was four years younger than I and still wet behind the ears. Father had actually threatened to cut me off if I didn't "come to my senses." Well, Father had no idea what I was capable of, or how his plan was going to backfire. In the meantime, I planned to enjoy every moment I got to spend with my best friend on the *Titanic*. And if that meant tolerating her dullard of a husband, too, then I was more than willing. If my parents thought they'd got the best of me, they had another think coming. I was more resourceful than they knew.

I closed my eyes for a few moments and soaked in the sheer vibrancy of the commotion, letting the chaotic energy of it fill me and chase away the ennui that had plagued me for weeks, replacing it with a renewed purpose. The breeze stung with the scents of coal smoke and salt, and the calls of passengers and spectators was drowned out intermittently by the raucous blast of the ship's horn. A celebratory feeling hung in the air, and I wasn't immune to the excitement. It wasn't every day a woman got to cross the Atlantic on a luxury liner's maiden voyage. Years from now I would look back and say *yes, I sailed on the* Titanic *during her first crossing. I ate the finest food and listened to music under glittering lights and was surrounded by money and jewels*. Because, as my mother once warned me, there was only one first time. *Oh, Mother, if you only knew.*

I looked over at Hannah and Charles, standing at the railing and looking down at the hundreds of people below waving the *Titanic* off. Sometimes the two of them seemed like chalk and cheese, but right now, elbow to elbow, they looked right. Happy, even, and I was glad of it. That marital bliss thing was not for me. I'd never been interested in settling down or settling for anything. But Hannah... It was what she wanted. To be honest, part of the reason I was excited to go to New York was so that we could have a week to spend together as friends. Like we used to before Charles.

But if Hannah ever asked me if I were jealous of her husband, I'd deny it. Instead, I told myself I was happy for her. Right now, her face was beaming as she stood by her husband and waved at the crowd on shore. How could I want anything less than happiness for my dearest friend?

On the decks below and aft, second- and third-class passengers were waving to those on shore as well. I thought of those in steerage in less glamorous surroundings. This was no holiday for them, was it? Most would be emigrating in search of a better life, and for a brief moment I thought I might know how they felt. I certainly wasn't happy or even contented with my life and was utterly frustrated that somehow my worth was wholly tied up in a husband. It wasn't like I had a surfeit of choices, was it? But then, I did not have to worry about paying rents or putting food on the table for my family. I straightened my shoulders and turned my face into the wind, putting my moment of self-indulgence behind me. How could I compare my dissatisfaction with real poverty and a struggle for survival? Many of those people would probably never see their families again, would they? How selfish of me to feel sorry for myself. Especially when I had the means and talents to change the trajectory of my life. And I meant to change it, make no mistake.

"I have no idea why you're frowning so," Hannah said beside me, nudging my arm. "I for one am beyond excited."

She'd used the word *excited* – or some variation of it – so often this morning it was starting to grate on my nerves, but I smiled anyway because it was impossible to be annoyed at her hopeful, happy face.

"Honestly, I was just thinking of those in steerage," I admitted. "And the reasons they might be leaving everyone they love behind. They won't just dash back across the ocean for a visit to loved ones, you know? This is truly a last goodbye."

"Oh, for heaven's sake, don't be so dramatic," grumbled Charles. "I'm sure the accommodations in steerage are far better than usual and miles better than they have at home. This week will be like a holiday for them, too."

I pasted on my polite smile. "Perhaps. But it might have taken their whole savings to simply purchase a ticket. They don't have the freedom and choices we're blessed with. There's nothing wrong with thinking of people less privileged than we are, Charles."

He scoffed and turned away, and Hannah sighed. Frustration bubbled inside of me, and I uncharacteristically bit my tongue. For Hannah's sake, I immediately felt guilty for creating friction, even though I was just voicing my beliefs. But Charles could be so … blind! Ugh, he was such a *man*. How many people were trapped, never daring to dream of something better for themselves because of our social structures? How glorious for him to always be able to do what he wanted or cast his vote to make decisions for all of us.

I kept my lips closed, though. If I said as much, Charles would be calling me a radical, and I wasn't here to make things worse for Hannah. I loved her more than probably any other person in the world. Not once had she ever let me down or made me feel I needed to be anyone other than who I was.

"I'm sorry, Han," I murmured. "I know you're trying to make things better with Charles. I'm probably going to be little help in that regard. We do seem to rub each other the wrong way."

"You're very different people, but I do not want you being less you," she said firmly, a smile on her lips. "Just maybe don't march around the corridor shouting, 'Votes for Women!' That might not go over so well."

I snorted. Hannah could have a decent sense of humour when she relaxed, and despite Charles's dour mood, she seemed happy. I wanted that for her so much. She deserved it. Her last few years had been difficult ones. She seemed to see something in Charles I couldn't, so if this was what she wanted, I wanted it for her too, even if it meant we couldn't be quite as close as we used to be. I didn't understand what she saw in him, but he wasn't a bad sort … for a man. Truly, his greatest transgression was being a bore. It could be so much worse.

"I promise," I said, knowing it would be an easy one to keep. I'd save my marching and shouting for rallies and protests. While we were in London, I'd only *mentioned* meeting Mrs. Pankhurst and Hannah's eyes had widened with alarm and perhaps a little awe. "Though I do wonder… If I marched along the promenade with a placard, do you suppose they'd throw me in the brig without any supper? Put me in handcuffs?" I held out my hands as if waiting for them to be clapped in irons and wiggled my eyebrows. Protesting was hardly the greatest of my transgressions, though Hannah didn't need to know those details. She definitely wouldn't approve of some of my activities.

"Don't even joke about that," Hannah whispered, though she

chuckled, and nudged her shoulder against mine, affection for her filling my heart.

Another series of blasts and the slight vibration beneath my feet intensified. We were sliding away from the dock, leaving England behind for a new adventure. I stood at the railing beside Hannah and took a deep, happy breath, feeling hope for the first time in weeks. "Thank you for letting me come along," I said to her, truly grateful she'd said yes. It afforded me a rare opportunity, and I was determined to capitalize on it. Even though my travel plans hadn't worked out *exactly* as I'd hoped, I was sure I'd have a grand time. How could I not?

"Thank you for suggesting it," she replied, lifting her hand and waving at the people below, even though there was not a soul there who knew either of us. "Instead of a dusty old train and dirty mines, I get to spend a week in New York with my best friend."

"I know you want to fix things with Charles," I admitted, feeling that I was indeed cutting in. "And now I'm dominating a week you might have spent repairing your marriage." I kept my voice low. Charles wasn't paying attention, but he wouldn't take kindly to us discussing their matrimonial discord so casually. He was a very private man.

"And I shall. We have this crossing and then the return." She dropped her hand and faced me, and the serious look in her eyes troubled me. Her problems with Charles didn't simply have to do with the fact that he was preoccupied with work and never seemed to have time for her. In my opinion, they were not in love, and I suspected Hannah felt it, too. If this trip didn't work as she hoped, she also knew that the rest of her life lay before her, empty and loveless. Seeing my friend try so hard and get nothing in return only strengthened my resolve to avoid such a marriage. I certainly didn't love Arthur Balcombe. I didn't even know him. Marriage, in my mind, was severely overrated.

"I'm sure it'll work out splendidly," I lied, putting my hand on hers on the rail as we moved further away from the dock. "How could it not, when you're simply the loveliest person I know?" That, at least, was the truth. Hannah was such a good person. Perhaps too good, when it came down to it. If she had any fault, it was probably that she was the most accommodating person I knew, always caring for the comforts of others over her own.

We stood silently after that, during the slow progression away from the dock and into the harbour. We stopped for a few minutes, when there was a tremendous commotion as the steamer *New York* broke its moorings due to the wake from our ship. But thanks to a few tugs, all was soon well again, and we were on our way, down Southampton Water toward the Isle of Wight and the Solent. Later this afternoon we would stop in Cherbourg for more passengers, and tomorrow a stop in Ireland – and then the vast ocean.

Once we were truly on our way, Hannah and Charles decided to go for a short stroll along the promenade and then to tour the first-class amenities. They invited me along, but I declined. I would see the ship later, on my own time. Right now, I simply wanted to enjoy the freedom of the sea ahead, the wind in my face, and the luxury of being alone without maid or companion. It happened so rarely. I could stare at the coastline or observe all the comings and goings of the other passengers to my heart's content if I wanted.

When the chill finally seeped through the fine wool of my suit, I turned away from the sight of the coast slipping by and looked for the exit. The crowd had thinned now, but my gaze caught on a man around my age, standing with companions at the railing, perhaps thirty feet away. He wasn't looking at the scenery. Instead, his dark gaze met mine and held it, and something unexpected fluttered low in my belly at his steady regard.

I lifted one eyebrow in cheeky response.

A slow smile curved the corners of his lips, and he lifted a finger to the brim of his Homburg before turning his attention to his companions. He knew just what to do to make himself intriguing and mysterious. I should know. I'd played the game often enough.

I spun from the rail and made my way to the entrance inside, instantly enveloped in warmth and comfort. But as I traversed the corridor to the first-class lounge and then ordered myself a brandy to ward off the chill, I kept thinking back to his teasing eyes and knowing smile, and the way he'd deliberately turned away, leaving me wanting more.

Perhaps this crossing was going to be interesting after all.

Chapter Two

```
April 10, 1912
   Titanic
```

HANNAH

The afternoon with Charles had been ... pleasant. We'd strolled the promenade while he pointed out different parts of the ship. I'd nodded and smiled, pretending to be interested. We'd visited the first-class lounge, discovered the location of the sumptuous Reading and Writing Room (for the ladies, he said) and the Smoking Room, and then we'd gone down the massive Grand Staircase all the way to D Deck and had tea in the Reception Room. I hadn't eaten much at all in the morning, so the hot tea and finger sandwiches were just what the doctor ordered. I couldn't deny that our surroundings were eye-poppingly extravagant. It really did feel like being on a floating palace, just as the papers had said.

With Lou entertaining herself, I'd rather hoped Charles and I might sneak away to our cabin for some private time. But when we finally got back, he was more interested in unpacking our things than in being intimate.

"Charles, surely we can call a steward to do this later," I'd said. "I rather hoped we might ... well ..." I'd faltered, unsure of how to broach what had been on my mind for months. How did one proposition one's husband? I took a deep breath. "Charles, don't you ever wish our marriage was something ... more?"

He'd paused his unpacking and stared at me. "What do you mean, more?" He swept a hand to the side. "Look at us, on the *Titanic*. What more could we possibly want? Are you not happy? Do I not provide for your every need?"

"No. I mean, yes," I amended, trying to reconcile his meaning with mine. "Materially, our life is lovely. I couldn't ask for more."

"I'm a rich man, darling. You'll never want for anything, I promise."

"That's not what I mean, though," I tried, willing him to understand. Things had become so formal between us. No, not formal. Sterile. There was nothing bad about his behaviour. It was just ... perfunctory. Polite.

He flapped a hand at me. "We should finish unpacking. Without a maid, you'll take longer to get ready for dinner tonight. A little work now will free up time later."

I couldn't give a fig about efficiency. He was right, though, that Lou and I had decided to travel without servants and would, instead, help each other with dressing, ringing for a stewardess when we needed assistance. It was clear to me that Charles wasn't in the mood for talking about our relationship, and I decided to let it go for now and pick my moment. We'd only just departed England, after all. There was plenty of time.

Now, a few hours later, the three of us – Lou, Charles, and I – were being led to our assigned table in the dining saloon. The bugler had announced dinner with a rendition of "The Roast Beef of Olde England" and we'd taken the lifts instead of the staircase to D Deck.

There'd been time for a cocktail, so Charles and I had mingled, meeting several of the passengers. We said hello to Mr. and Mrs. Tyrell Cavendish, who were traveling to New York to visit Mrs. Cavendish's parents. We met the Futrelles, both authors, whom I found quite intriguing, but Charles was uninterested as he placed little importance on reading for pleasure (though he didn't seem to mind that I enjoyed it immensely).

Lou seemed to be searching for something, or perhaps someone, but her attention was diverted when we came upon the Fortune family from Canada: Mr. and Mrs. Fortune, their three daughters, and their son. Lou took an instant liking to Mabel, whose vibrant energy seemed a match for hers, and the two of them chatted at length while I spoke with Ethel and Alice. Charles Fortune, in his teenage enthusiasm, found a rapt audience in *my* Charles, and excitedly relayed bits and pieces of trivia about the ship once he realized he had a captive audience. I was far more interested in my companions. Ethel was engaged and had gone to Europe with the family not only for a vacation but to shop for her trousseau. When she said she'd purchased items from Worth, I mentioned my shopping excursion with Lou and we were off, comparing Worth to Poiret to Lucile, the fashion house of Lady Duff-Gordon. Truthfully, I was disappointed when the call to dinner came, but we all agreed to meet up again.

We were nearly at our table when I realized Lou was no longer behind me.

I turned and saw her closer to the entrance, standing beside one of the tables. A dark-haired man was next to her, speaking as he held her hand in greeting, and for the first time in memory I detected a blush on her cheeks. The man's companion remained seated, though I noticed his gaze followed the Fortunes as they entered. Alice's head turned ever so slightly in his direction. Interesting.

"Darling, we're waiting."

The steward was holding my chair, but Charles had seemed to forget Lou was part of our party as well. "Let me get Lou. She's been waylaid."

I slipped over to where she was still standing, though thankfully the gentleman had let go of her hand. "Louisa, our table is ready," I said, offering a smile.

"Oh, of course." Her blush deepened. "May I present Mr. Reid Grey?"

"Mr. Grey," I said politely, and held out my hand. "Mrs. Charles Martin, and Miss Phillips's best friend." I added that last bit with a touch of sharpness. Not that I didn't think Lou could handle herself; of course she could. I said it so he'd know that I was watching for impropriety. Lou was fiercely independent and slightly scandalous, but we always looked out for each other. Lou would never admit it, but she needed looking after, too. Sometimes I wished she didn't always cause a stir wherever she went.

"This is Hannah," Lou added.

I looked pointedly at Mr. Grey's companion, a handsome man in his late twenties, I guessed. The one who had been so intrigued with Alice Fortune. Mr. Grey hastily made introductions. "Ah, yes. Miss Phillips, Mrs. Martin, this is my friend, William Sloper."

"Mr. Sloper. I smiled, but my expression was far cooler than Lou's. Warning bells had started to ring in my head. We had only been on the ship for a matter of hours, and there seemed to be something here that was not quite proper, though I couldn't say what. It was in the feeling, rather than the actions of the moment. Mr. Grey was being far too familiar with Lou, and she didn't seem to be discouraging him. I knew Lou was a little more ... well, adventurous than I, but he seemed rather forward to me. "Louisa," I said quietly, "Charles is waiting."

Annoyance twisted her lips for a brief second, so quickly I barely noticed it, and then she smiled again. "I must go. Good evening, Mr. Sloper." Her gaze clung to Mr. Grey's a bit longer. "Mr. Grey."

He nodded politely, and I pulled Lou away. "What are you doing?" I whispered as we headed toward the table where Charles now waited to seat us. I could tell he was put out at our tardiness. Honestly, I appreciated his penchant for punctuality, but he could be awfully rigid sometimes, and I felt his disapproval. I even shared it a little, not that I would say that to Lou.

"I'll tell you later," Lou whispered back, then put on her most charming smile. "Charles, thank you for waiting. I'm so sorry I was delayed coming in. I met Mr. Grey earlier, on deck. He was just sending his regards."

"Yes, well." That was all Charles said, instead of finishing an actual sentence. But he did seat us and then plopped himself down in his chair.

The dining saloon was gorgeous, with glossy white walls and pillars leading to the sculpted ceiling. The brightness of the white was broken by the red and blue tiles of the floor and the solid oak furniture. Dark green leather covered the chairs, and the table linens were snowy white. It was hard to believe we were even on a ship, as the portholes were covered with leaded windows, providing the impression that we were in an exclusive restaurant instead of sailing across the Atlantic. Uniformed wait staff slid through the room unobtrusively, catering to passengers' wants and needs in a seamless manner.

What followed were ten courses of delights, though I waved off any mention of oysters, as I'd never acquired the taste for them and the mere sight made my stomach turn over. Wine flowed freely, but sadly, conversation did not, and we busied ourselves with tasting and sipping while all around us voices chatted and laughed. Finally, I took two bites of my vanilla éclair and declared myself stuffed, and Charles wiped his lips with his napkin and then took a sip of his wine. "Delicious," he decreed. "I'm not sure my waistline can bear eating like this for a week." He smiled at me. "I noticed you enjoyed it as well, Hannah."

I saw Lou frown from the corner of my eye, and I ignored her even though his comment made me self-conscious of the slimmer silhouettes of the latest fashions. "Oh, I did, very much," I agreed. "Other than a few sandwiches at tea, I didn't eat much today. I'm sure tomorrow I will be much more moderate." I was full but still looked longingly at the remains of my éclair.

"Well, I intend to stuff myself with every delicious morsel for the entire week," Lou said, patting her stomach. "Such creations are meant to be enjoyed by the palate, not just the eye. The asparagus tonight was perfection, and so was the beef. I've never had anything so tender."

A little anxiety tightened in my belly. Why did Lou always feel like she needed to challenge my husband? I knew she thought she was standing up for me, but all it did was put me in the middle and make me want to constantly smooth things over. She was not Charles's favourite person. Nothing she said was going to get a warm reception from him.

For the first time, I wondered about us taking this trip together. It wouldn't do for things to be awkward for the entire week we were on board. The time in New York would be no problem at all. It was Charles and Hannah together that created tension, with me caught firmly in the middle, defending one to the other.

Charles stared at Lou benignly, and then said, "One day, Miss Phillips, your passionate nature is going to get you into trouble."

She laughed. "Oh heavens, I do hope so," she replied, and I couldn't help it. A tiny snort came out of my nose. If Charles knew half of what Lou got up to with her committees and protests, he'd forbid me from associating with her at all. My husband, for all his qualities, could be an absolute stick. I admired his morals, of course, and I didn't always approve of Lou's methods, either. But he'd become quite uptight over the past few years.

He frowned, then looked at me. "I thought I'd go to the Smoking

Room. May I escort you to the Reading and Writing Room perhaps, my dear? I hear the ladies are going there to socialize."

"Actually," I said, "I thought I might stay to hear some of the music in the Reception Room. It won't go too late, and Lou will be with me, won't you, Lou?" I looked at her helpfully. "It's been so long since I listened to an orchestra."

"Of course. I promise we'll have one after-dinner cocktail, listen to a set or two, and then head to the comfort of our cabins. I'm dying to try out the bed. It looks like I'll be sleeping on a cloud."

Sometimes Lou caused friction, but other times she came through like a trick. I breathed out a sigh of relief.

"If you're certain, darling. I could stay."

For all my wanting to spend time with Charles, the idea of being stuck beside him for the better part of an hour or more, trying to enjoy the orchestra while he was bored to tears, was not my idea of a fun end to the evening. I also knew him well enough to know that clinging to him every moment was not the way to rekindle his affection. No man liked to be caught in a noose. "Go," I said, smiling. "I know you're keen to meet some of the other men. I'll see you later, in the cabin."

He escorted us out of the saloon, and as we passed by Mr. Sloper's table I noticed it had already been vacated. Lou didn't even look, and for some reason, I was glad. I had an uneasy feeling about Reid Grey. He seemed a bit smooth for my liking. My misgivings weren't helped by knowing that Lou was in a rebellious mood. I knew very well that she was avoiding making a decision about Balcombe. Her parents had made it quite clear that there would be no money if she put off marriage any longer. Lou didn't have extravagant tastes, but she was certainly used to her independent lifestyle, and she used her allowance to fund her causes, too. It was hard to imagine her saying no to Balcombe and then needing to work as a shop girl or something, but Lou was positive her parents meant what they said. I couldn't help but think that she was concocting some sort of plan – one she hadn't shared with me.

We made our way to the reception room where the orchestra was playing "Salome" and other passengers were mingling. I saw new faces that had perhaps joined first class after our stop this evening in Cherbourg, but I realized quite suddenly that I did not recognize any of them. Lou, on the other hand, procured two fresh glasses of wine for us and, after handing me one, whispered that the couple to our left was Sir Duff-Gordon and Lady Duff-Gordon, Cosmo and Lucy respectively. I goggled. Lady Duff-Gordon had her own design house, and her Lucile gowns were in demand. Both Lou and I had gowns she'd designed, and I'd spent a ridiculous amount on intimates as well. I rather had the thought that it might help bring back the light in Charles's eyes, reignite his desire for me that had diminished to barely a flicker.

"And that," whispered Lou, close to my ear, "is Ben Guggenheim. He's American, and that woman he's with is not his wife. That's his mistress, Ninette Aubart. She has her own cabin, but I'll bet you your entire allowance that it's just for show."

"How brazen," I murmured, lifting my glass and taking a healthy sip. I was quite shocked, actually. Of course I knew affairs happened, but since when did men openly travel with their *amours*? "Lou, how in the world do you know all this?"

"Darling, you really are behind in your gossip rags." She smiled and then nudged my arm, giving a laugh. "Seriously, though, I read the first-class pamphlet. There's a list of all the passengers. J. J. Astor and his new, very young wife are on board. They just joined us."

Even I knew about the Astors, and I rarely paid attention to American gossip. I angled a look at Lou. Sometimes she could be such a puzzle. She was vocal about women's independence and marched for the vote. She handed out pamphlets and much to her parents' chagrin, had been known to carry a placard during demonstrations, raising her voice and pumping her fist. She hadn't yet landed in jail like many of the suffragettes, but it was only a matter of time, a fact that prompted her father to repeatedly demand that she "stop this nonsense."

She also loved a juicy tidbit of gossip and an even better party. She adored champagne but would happily swallow a gulp of whiskey, and I'd even seen her smoke a cigar. All in all, Lou was scandalous – in all ways but one. Not once had I heard of her getting into scrapes of the romantic kind. She'd once told me that she would never let a man control her virtue. Was she outrageous? Very, but in some ways she was also the most principled woman I knew. Our friendship wouldn't have survived this long if she were not.

Sometimes I wondered why she was still my closest friend. I'd always felt so in her shadow. But that was another question in the mystery of Louisa Phillips. Since our days at boarding school, she'd been loyal to a fault. She'd been by my side during my darkest days, never once leaving me to suffer alone. I knew without a doubt that she loved me, and I loved her in return, despite our differences.

We saw the Fortunes again, and they were joined by Mr. Sloper and Mr. Grey, who both nodded in our direction. Mr. Grey's gaze clung to Lou for an extra few seconds, and when I looked up at Lou her cheeks had flushed as she broke eye contact with him. "Lou," I cautioned, then took her elbow and steered her away. "I do believe that man is trouble."

"Oh, I hope so," she responded, draining her glass and beckoning for another. I frowned. We'd had cocktails and then wine with dinner. I had taken two or three sips from my glass, and it was still three-quarters full. I'd lost count of Lou's libations.

"Lou, what's going on with you?" The musicians were playing a jaunty ragtime tune now, which practically begged for dancing but alas, there was no dance floor. I wondered why. In all the opulence and majesty, why was there no room for dancing?

"Nothing, darling. Look, Reid Grey is a handsome flirt, and that's all. Surely you're not going to deny me a harmless flirtation while on board?" She received her fresh drink and took a gulp, but her gaze evaded mine.

"I'm not sure a man like Reid is harmless, Lou." I looked up into her face, noticing her smile had fled. "I get a strange feeling about him."

She blinked slowly, a small smile touching her lips. "And I appreciate your concern, Han. I truly do. I don't intend to be reckless, so please don't worry. I know you want to spend time with Charles during the crossing." She winked at me. "A girl has to have something to occupy her time."

"Lou—"

She reached down and squeezed my hand. "You're a total darling, but I promise I'm not looking for trouble." She met my gaze, her expression serious and honest. "I also know it when I see it. Don't worry, Han."

She was right on that point. Lou could sniff out a bounder better than her father's hunting dogs on the trail of a fox.

"Come on, then." She drained her glass and lifted her chin. "It's late. Let's head to our cabins, get out of these corsets, and have a good gab before bed like we used to do in school."

That was the Louisa I loved, and so with a happy nod, I put my glass on a nearby empty table, and we walked to the trio of lifts together.

LOUISA

Bless Hannah, she really was the sweetest of souls, but she was so ... naïve. Of course I was looking for a little trouble, or I'd be bored to tears for the next six days. Reid Grey was just the kind of trouble I needed. A flirt, certainly. Charm and mystery. But he was harmless. All flash, a little substance, but not a drop of menace behind it. Exactly the kind of no-strings man I liked. Men like Reid liked to think they were searching for the perfect woman to settle down with, but I knew his kind. Once the chase was over, they got bored and moved on. I didn't intend to let him catch me. Or at least … not right away.

Hannah and I went back to our cabins and changed into nightgowns and peignoirs, then sat on my bed, our legs crossed beneath the billowy fabric. For half an hour I endured silly chatter, waiting for her to tire, and thankfully it didn't take long. She yawned and said she was going back to her cabin to turn in. Admittedly, it had been a long day, and it was after eleven. She wanted to be in her own bed for when Charles returned. And I wanted her in her own cabin so I could slip into regular clothes again. My night wasn't yet ended.

I didn't bother with corsets or the appropriate layers. I simply pulled a skirt and blouse on over my combinations and stockings and covered it all with my wool coat. I didn't bother with a hat, either, but I did pull on gloves before gently opening the door and closing it with the quietest of clicks.

The hallway was quiet, and I saw no sign of Charles or anyone else I might recognize. With a shake of my head and a roll of my shoulders, I sauntered down the hall toward the exit and the stairway that would take me up to A Deck. It was nearly midnight; most passengers had gone to bed as the entertainment died down after eleven. That nearly worked to my detriment, however, as I was more likely to be noticed amongst the stragglers than if the area had been teeming with people chatting and enjoying themselves.

I nodded to a few men, feeling a strange twist in the pit of my stomach as a lone woman wandering the ship late at night. Being aware of my surroundings was second nature to me now; a lot of people didn't take kindly to suffragettes stirring up trouble at political meetings. It always paid to know where the exits were and who you had to get through to get there. I had learned that the hard way, but never again.

In this case, though, I wasn't exiting to get away from someone, but to get *to* them.

I stepped outside on the starboard promenade, my shoes making a dull sound on the wooden floor. The air was brisk, and I inhaled deeply of the sharp cold, instantly invigorated. I was early by a few minutes, but I didn't mind. I began walking aft, rather than waiting right by the entrance. The further away from the grand staircase I was, the less likely I was to be seen.

I was glad to have the time alone, to be honest. It happened so rarely, and I stepped up to the white rail and placed my hands upon it, the cold from the iron seeping through my gloves into my fingertips. We were on our way to Ireland now; we'd be at Queenstown before noon tomorrow for our final stop. Then, once the coastline was behind us, I could truly breathe with ease. The first part of my plan would be complete, and I could enjoy the crossing before having to worry about what came next.

I sucked in the fresh air, letting it restore me. The wind brushed my ears along with the rhythmic shushing sound of water against the hull as the ship sliced through it. I closed my eyes, letting all of it wash over me, breathing out my stress and worry until the muscles in my shoulders started to unwind and the tension in my face dissipated.

"You are a picture," a man said from behind me.

I didn't turn right away. Instead I let the deep timbre of the voice envelope me. Reid Grey was dashing, but there was an innocence in his countenance that was deceptive. He absolutely looked like someone you could trust. He was also the kind to suggest a midnight rendezvous that would wreak havoc with a girl's reputation.

I smiled at that thought and finally turned.

He'd put on his overcoat as well; it really was too chilly to flounce about in dresses and tails. But he too had come without his hat. And he held his gloves in his hands, rather than wearing them.

I stared at the black leather encased by his strong, pale fingers, and the itch began. His boy-next-door look didn't fool me. I knew of his reputation for breaking hearts.

"Mr. Grey," I said solemnly, and was delighted when I caught a dark twinkle in his eye.

"Miss Phillips. Whatever are you doing out here alone this late at night?"

I smiled, feeling warm and soft all over as his approving gaze slid over me. "Oh dear, the air was just so cloying inside. I thought I should faint."

He laughed, a low chuckle that slid deliciously over my spine. Then he came forward, and instead of taking me in his arms – which was what we both wanted, anyway – he too leaned against the cold rail. I wasn't the only one enjoying the chase, willing to let it play out slowly.

"You are not the fainting type," he said, leaning onto his forearms. "Unless it suits you."

I laughed, feeling lighter than I had in months. "You are right about that," I agreed. "But not everyone enjoys my brand of femininity."

"And what brand is that?"

I looked over at his profile. "You know. The kind that eschews corsets, rides astride instead of side-saddle, believes women should have the vote as well as a hundred other rights denied to us because of our gender."

He turned to face me, his expression one of such tenderness my heart skipped a beat. *That* wasn't part of the plan. Oh, he was good. I could see how a woman could get swept up in his attention.

"You should know that I love those things."

"Do you? Or are you just saying that to further your cause?"

"Whose cause, exactly?" he asked, and that low, seductive chuckle rumbled on the air again. He was so close now I could feel his warmth, even though he had yet to touch me. Even though I desperately wanted him to. I'd been practically living like a nun for the past two months at my parents' house in the country, missing London horribly. But Papa had decreed that renovations to the house in Mayfair had to be done and that I needed to vacate while it was "teeming with workmen." My argument that I could oversee things had fallen on deaf ears. A single woman remaining there in such circumstances was inappropriate. For God's sake.

I lifted my chin and smiled up at him. "Rather cheeky of you, tipping your hat to me when we departed Southampton."

"Louisa—"

I stopped him with a hand on his chest, resting on the heavy wool of his coat, though I was certain I could feel his heart beat beneath my palm.

"And stopping me at dinner to give me that silly note."

"You're here, aren't you?"

"Maybe I shouldn't be."

"You don't mean that."

I didn't.

"Reid…"

I meant to say his name in a way that would hold him off a little longer, draw out the anticipation. But instead it was breathy, full of longing.

He put his hand over mine, resting on his chest, and looked down into my eyes. "It has been too long, Louisa. And you knew I wouldn't be able to resist when you sent me that letter."

Ah, yes. The letter sharing my news that I'd be sailing to New York on White Star's brand-new ship, on her maiden voyage no less. I couldn't help the silly grin that widened my lips. "I was simply making conversation, darling, you know that. I share my news in every letter."

"You might fool some with that innocent tone, Miss Phillips, but not me. You and I both know exactly what you meant." He was smiling too, and then he stepped back. "How've you been, Louisa? Really? London has been terribly dull without you."

My smile faded and I turned back to the railing again. Oh, why couldn't he have just kissed me instead of ... of talking? The teasing banter was light and fine. But his simple question had a very complicated answer. It was true I shared my news in every letter, but I never shared my secrets. I was very selective in who got to know what about me.

"I've been incredibly bored, languishing in Exminster, and would have much preferred London," I said, trying a light laugh that fell a little flat. "Truthfully, I'm tired. Tired of just about everything."

He nudged my arm with his elbow. "Oh, come now. When we were together in London last year, we had a grand time. Sparkling lights and lots of champagne and dancing. Granted, you always managed to slip away, leaving me wanting. But I suspect that's exactly how you planned it."

He'd got it exactly right, and I sighed and shook my head. "You see far too much. And understand too much. I'm not sure I like that."

"Ah yes, the woman who longs to be understood but hopes she isn't. And they wonder why men can never seem to understand you lot." He slid his right hand over and put it on top of mine. "Louisa, I do see you, you know. Hell, I spent a lot of money paying for passage for the chance at six days with you. I don't even care to go to New York."

I was flattered. I was. More than that, I was surprised. He hadn't told me of his plans, even though he'd written a reply. I hadn't known he was going to be on board until I saw him at our departure. And then, of course, his name in the pamphlet.

"And your friend, Mr. Sloper?"

"We just met, actually. He's an American stockbroker who has developed something of a crush on one of the Fortune sisters. He was actually supposed to go home on the Mauretania."

I hesitated. We were alone on the deck. It was late and cold and anyone who'd decided to take a midnight stroll had gone inside. I looked over at his profile. "I didn't expect you to come, you know."

He turned his head and met my gaze. "Does that mean you didn't want me to?"

There was much that was complicated about this crossing. Things he didn't know. Things Hannah didn't know. He could be a perfect distraction, when it came down to it. I'd indulged in distractions before. I couldn't put my finger on why this felt different. And normally I'd play coy in this moment, and say something flippant, but instead I opted for the truth.

"I'm very glad to see you, actually." More than glad. The itch was still there, the one that wondered what it would be like to take him to bed. But there was something else, too. A comfort I hadn't expected. For all his flirting, Reid Grey was a solid sort of man. It was why I'd found myself exchanging letters with him. Nothing serious, but we'd kept in touch.

"Glad. Hmmm." He turned fully and slid his arm around my waist. "Glad is a very bland term, Louisa. It's right up there with 'nice' and 'pleasant.'"

I couldn't stop a little laugh from escaping my lips. Hadn't I just thought something similar about Charles today? "What do you want me to say, Reid? That seeing you makes my heart go pitter-patter?" I tried the light-hearted reply, but the pressure of his hand increased and he pulled me closer. I had the unreasonable urge to snuggle up against him and feel his arms around me, safe and secure.

Which was ridiculous. That was something that Hannah would think, not me. And certainly not with a bona fide flirt like Reid Grey.

"Does it?" he asked, his voice husky against my ear, making me shiver. "Make your heart go pitter-patter?"

I was about to come back with a saucy reply when I tilted my chin so I could look in his eyes, and anything I was going to say disappeared on the ocean breeze.

In all the months I'd known Reid, we'd flirted and danced and snuck little touches, but we'd never slept together, never even kissed other than bussing our cheeks upon greeting. But tonight – this morning, rather, now that the clock had passed midnight – all that changed.

He lowered his chin so that our mouths were level, our breath mingling, creating frosty white clouds in the air between us. My eyes slid closed in anticipation, and I waited for him to claim my lips. But he didn't. He touched his mouth ever so gently to mine, not quite asking, but not demanding, either. The pressure was sure and confident but remarkably gentle and…

And tender. That was the second time tonight I'd thought of that word regarding Reid and it made me uneasy. At the same time, I responded, accepting the contact, reciprocating. Because the truth was, I liked Reid Grey. I always had, from the moment we'd met at a house party in Wiltshire a year ago September. At the time I'd been having a blazing affair with Royden Clarke, a young stockbroker who ran with a rather fast set. That had fizzled out as quickly as it had ignited.

I did have a rule that while affairs were permissible – even necessary – I only ever indulged in one at a time. And it had to be discreet.

Reid pulled back, just a little, his chest rising and falling as he caught his breath. I was breathless myself, and more than happy with the feelings elicited by his kiss. There had to be chemistry, and you couldn't always tell that by flirting. But the way my pulse throbbed and my body tingled told me well enough that we'd be suited in bed.

If that was where I wanted us to end up, of course. I wasn't going to rush. I had a week to scratch this particular itch, and I also liked playing the game.

"Mmm," I hummed, running my tongue over my lips. "Nicely done, sir."

"Nicely done?" he sputtered, then laughed. "If it is only nicely done, I need to up my game considerably."

"I look forward to it," I replied, and my limbs were antsy at the thought of wrapping around him. "For now, though, I should sneak back to my cabin. In the morning, Hannah will wonder why I'm so tired."

"I could genuinely wear you out," he suggested, with a gorgeous lift of one eyebrow. It nearly made me want to say yes. God, I loved a man with a sense of humour.

"Not tonight." I stepped back from his embrace. "No need to rush things, is there?"

He surprised me by smiling softly in the starlight. "None at all. We've all the time in the world, Louisa. You're worth the wait."

I left him there and slipped back inside, sneaking back to my cabin as quietly as I could. But sleep was a long time coming. A part of me took his parting words and held them close, soft and warm in my heart. I was worth the wait? Since when? And what did he mean, we had all the time in the world? I had pegged him as a man who loved the chase, but what if he meant something more?

I flipped over and punched my pillow, closing my eyes as I pulled the coverlet up to my chin. An affair was all I had time for. I had much bigger plans – ones that definitely did not include love, or Reid Grey.

Chapter Three

```
April 10, 1912
Titanic
```

HANNAH

I was nearly asleep when Charles returned to the cabin. He entered, smelling faintly of brandy and cigars, a scent I'd grown used to. He was quiet when he entered, as if trying not to disturb me, but the truth was, I wanted to be disturbed. I wanted us to have a real conversation, to connect somehow beyond polite niceties. I wasn't sure how, though. Every time I tried to broach a topic that was about us, he changed the subject or brushed it off.

He undressed in the darkness, shuffling sounds as he navigated the inkiness of the cabin. I imagined him taking off his tie, shrugging out of his waistcoat, laying them over a chair, perhaps. There was a thump and a muffled curse. He'd run into something, and I smiled at the uncharacteristic rough language. Then I rolled to my side so I was facing the room, and said softly, "Hello, darling."

Endearments. Did we even mean them anymore? A cold pit of trepidation opened in my stomach, afraid of being turned away once again, as if I were an inconvenience.

"Oh goodness, Hannah. I didn't mean to wake you. Go back to sleep."

"I wasn't asleep," I said, sitting up and leaning back against the soft pillow. "I was waiting for you. You can turn on the light if you like."

A few more shuffles, and then the cabin was encased in a warm glow. I swallowed a laugh. Charles was in a funny state of undress: in his shirt and underwear and his hair mussed. "Oh, goodness."

He looked down at himself and smiled a little. "I didn't mean to be out so late. I met an interesting fellow with several mining interests. John Weir. We might have had one too many drinks." His earnest eyes met mine. "Despite his advanced age, I couldn't keep up with him, nor did I want to try."

I'll say this for my husband: he was moderate in his vices.

"It's all right," I replied, patting the bed beside me, urging him to sit. Perhaps chat a little longer. "Lou and I had a good talk. I haven't been in bed very long."

He poured himself a glass of water from the pitcher provided to the room. "We really should turn in and get some sleep," he suggested, putting the glass back in its place. "So we can be up for breakfast." I watched as he took his pyjamas from a drawer and slipped the shirt over his head.

I didn't know what to say. I was trying, dammit. Trying to reach him and he was being deliberately distant. Determined to keep our conversations polite, on the surface. Nothing too intimate. Nothing … real. I wasn't sure if I wanted to scream in frustration or cry. Both, if I were being honest.

And yet how could I blame him? I had shut him out for months, unable to tolerate the gentlest of touches. Now there was nothing I wanted more than to be in the safety of his arms.

He put on the bottoms before turning out the light and I scooted over, waiting for him to slide beneath the soft covers, glad I'd warmed the bed for him. But there was a shuffle and a sigh and then a murmured, "Goodnight, Hannah," from the other side of the room.

He'd chosen the smaller bed. Chosen it instead of sleeping with me. I curled into myself, wondering when I'd become so repulsive, knowing the answer in my heart. Two years ago. Two years ago January, to be precise. Hot tears slid from the corners of my eyes, but I didn't sniff, didn't sob. I didn't want him to know that he'd made me cry.

April 11, 1912

When Lou saw me the next morning, she looked me straight in the eyes and frowned. "You've been crying," she whispered, pulling her cabin door shut behind us. I'd gathered my clothes for the day and told Charles that I'd dress in Lou's cabin, so she could help me with buttons and such, and vice versa. She took the articles from my hands, dumped them on the bed, and took my hands in hers. "What happened?"

"Nothing," I replied, sinking down into a chair, my nightgown billowing out around me. "And that's the problem. Oh Lou, he slept in the other bed. Am I so repugnant?"

Her lips hardened into a thin line. "No, you are not. Oh, I'd like to give that man a piece of my mind. This is not your fault, Han. You're the loveliest person I know. Ugh, he is such a … a cold fish!"

I snorted. I couldn't help it. I knew Lou had paused because she had been thinking of a very different word, and she tried to tame her language around me. "You can say whatever words you want, you know. I'm not going to need smelling salts or anything."

She grinned back, and my world seemed right-side up again. Mostly, anyway. I rolled my neck from side to side and stretched, feeling my back release with a satisfying pop. "How did you sleep? The beds are extremely comfortable, don't you think?"

"Like a baby." She disappeared to her wardrobe and then came out again, carrying a smart suit on her arm. "What do you think of this for daytime? Too austere?"

Lou had such a smart sense of style. The suit was navy faille, draped at the side, with a silver belt and buckle caught up on the left and a small lace yoke at the neck. It was one of the Lucile items we'd purchased on our trip. Other than the lace, it was on the plain side but was striking in its simplicity.

"Not austere. Simple and stunning. It makes a statement. I thought I'd wear my grey cashmere this morning. Charles likes me in lighter colours." I hadn't given up on reaching him somehow, even after last night's rejection. Reviving our marriage was more important than even Lou knew.

"That is one of my favourites of yours, even if it isn't brand new." Lou skipped over to the bed and began sorting through my things. She held up my corset. "I swear, these have got to go. Or at least become more comfortable. I'm not opposed to a flattering shape, but Lord above, I do like to breathe and be able to eat more than a mouthful without feeling ill."

I shrugged. "I've taken to not lacing mine so tightly," I said. I rose from the chair and went to the bed, taking the item from her fingers.

"I wondered at that." Lou looked me up and down with a critical eye. "You look like you've put on a little weight finally. You were skin and bones there for a while, Han. I was worried."

Heat rose in my cheeks and I busied myself sorting through the garments on the bed. "Well, we're never going to make it to breakfast if we chat all morning in our night clothes."

"And I'm starving," Lou decreed, and we set the topic aside and got down to the business of dressing and helping each other with our hair and hats. Both of us lamented our hair-styling skills, which did not match those of our maids, but our broad hats with their ostentatious trimmings covered our sins. We did agree, however, that we would call a stewardess each night before dinner to help us with the more intricate styles. Lou promised to arrange it all after breakfast and that I wasn't to worry about a thing.

I was just relieved that she had tightened my corset and hadn't commented again on the thickening at my waist, after mentioning my weight gain. Truthfully, I'd been too thin for months, not eating properly, not caring. I'd wondered if Charles was turned off by how thin I'd become, but now I wondered if he was repulsed by the weight I'd put back on.

A knock sounded on the door to the hallway, and Lou went to open it. My thoughts scattered when Charles appeared on the other side, looking bright eyed and handsome in his morning suit. There wasn't a wrinkle or crease where one didn't belong, and he'd shaved, his skin glowing from the fresh blade. I smiled widely, happy that I still found him attractive despite our troubles. "Is that a new suit?" I asked. "The cut is perfection."

"Thank you." He gripped his lapels and smiled. "Good morning, Miss Phillips. Are we all ready to go down to breakfast?"

"We certainly are," I replied, stepping toward the door.

"I'll catch up with you by the lifts," Lou said, standing back. "I just want to tuck a few things away."

She'd unpacked completely, and the bag she'd been so possessive of when boarding was nowhere to be seen. But I knew for a fact that Lou was travelling with some of her nicer jewellery. I'd saved out some of my own to wear during the passage, and the rest – with the money that Charles had brought for the trip – was secured with the purser. I wondered if Lou had done the same, or if she was keeping everything in her cabin. I'd never known her to be overly cautious, but perhaps if she were keeping her valuables in her cabin, she felt the need to be more vigilant.

Charles held out his arm and we proceeded down the corridor and through a doorway, reaching the area around the Grand Staircase and the lifts in short order. We waited there for Lou, standing to the side in our own little bubble, Charles nodding to the odd person or group that passed us by. "Charles," I began hesitantly, "you know there is no need for you to sleep in the smaller bed. The other is big enough for us both."

His head swivelled in my direction, his eyes alarmed. "Hannah. We do not need to discuss this here."

"No one can hear us," I disagreed. "And it needs to be said. Please don't put me off. You're my husband. I know we have our own rooms at home, but don't you..." I faltered, my throat tightening. "I miss you. Don't you want to share a bed with me?"

I was whispering, and I saw a muscle tick in Charles's jaw. I knew he disapproved of my timing and where we were – in public.

"Anyone could hear us here. This is something to talk about in private."

I stood my ground even though it made me horribly uncomfortable. Confronting him so directly was Lou's style, not mine, but we only had six days to try to mend our marriage. That was not a lot of time. Sharing a bed was, in my view, the bare minimum. "Why?" I asked. "So you can put me off again? We never talk, Charles."

He looked over at me. "Don't be ridiculous. We're talking right now."

"No, I'm talking and you're prevaricating. And soon you'll change the subject. Sometimes I wonder if you want to be married at all."

Shock blanked his face at my blunt declaration. He was not used to me speaking my mind or being so direct. I couldn't quite believe I'd said it myself. That I decided to speak my feelings in such a manner without thinking first was truly a testament to how tired and upset I was.

"I can only assume that your forthrightness is a result of spending time with Miss Phillips. She's far too outspoken."

That irritated me and also prompted me to defend my best friend. "Lou has nothing to do with this, and perhaps we could all learn from her candor." My voice was sharp, and I immediately took a mental step back. I didn't want to argue. I wanted to reach him, desperately. I softened my voice and pleaded, "Charles, don't you want to fix what's wrong between us?"

"Apologies for taking so long." Lou came up behind us, her face wreathed in a smile and an aura of vitality surrounding her. It was no wonder she turned heads. It wasn't just her uncommon beauty but the energy that surrounded her that was so attractive. I was always glad to see Lou, but her timing just now left a lot to be desired. Charles was saved from answering and my heart sank as I realized that for once he looked happy to see her, as if she'd just rescued him from something horrible. I felt like crying. Nothing about this was going the way I wanted.

"Shall we go down?" he asked, holding out his arm for me, but I didn't feel like taking it. I felt ill, actually. Not because of anything he said, but because of that single expression of relief that had crossed his face when he was spared from answering. Perhaps he didn't want to fix us. Perhaps he really did want a polite marriage of two strangers who showed up for social occasions together but lived separate lives.

Perhaps I needed to start reconciling myself to that possibility.

Still, I was peevish about it. If I took a gentle approach, I was easily brushed off, and if I were more direct, I was told I was too much like Lou. Well, if that were the case, I could indulge him in that assessment. I took a page from Lou's book and swept forward without his arm, moving toward the staircase. I didn't need to take the lifts down two decks. I had perfectly good legs and could avoid being trapped in a lift, surrounded by uncomfortable silence. My throat clogged with unshed tears. Who was I trying to fool? My exit was far more about running away than it was about making a statement. I had ruined everything ... as usual.

A quick glance behind me showed Charles looking puzzled and Lou shrugging her shoulders before following me. I slowed, but didn't wait. I trailed my hand on the glossy railing and lifted my chin as I descended the wide, curved stairs with sure steps, my skirt flaring around my feet with each one. I had done nothing wrong, had I? I didn't deserve to be punished further for something that had been out of my control. I was trying, after all. It couldn't be too late—

Lou caught up with me. "Hannah, what's going on? You walked away from Charles, leaving him standing there like ... well, I think he felt like an idiot. Did you quarrel?"

"No," I said, and smiled weakly, nodding at a passing couple I recognized from the previous evening. "I'm just hungry."

We reached the bottom of the stairs and Lou stopped me with a hand on my arm. "You have always been a horrible liar. Wait for Charles. You can tell me what happened later. I'm worried about you, Han."

I looked at her but closed myself off from feeling anything more than my righteous indignation, which for the moment was serving as a very thin armour. "Nothing happened. Nothing at all," I replied, which was painfully truthful. When Charles came up beside me, I didn't look over at him, either. Instead, I schooled my face as we walked, the three of us, to the entrance of the saloon. I would try again later to get through to Charles, but for now I was too annoyed. And beneath the annoyance was fear.

Maybe I should just tell him we were having a baby. The thought of going through my pregnancy alone, with a husband who refused to share it with me, opened up a chasm of loneliness that I was afraid would suck me into a world that was cold and grey and lifeless. That frightened me more than anything, more than even the finality of darkness. I never wanted to go back into that horrible, dark prison of my mind again. If anything went wrong, I wasn't sure I had it in me to come back a second time. And that was precisely what kept me silent: I needed him to come back to me now, when he didn't know about the pregnancy. I needed to know he loved *me*. Just me. Then, and only then would I feel like I could face the future.

"I hear there are fresh strawberries," Lou said behind me, oblivious to the bleak turn of my thoughts.

Fresh strawberries. Champagne and music and gowns and jewels. How insignificant they felt in this moment.

Chapter Four

April 11, 1912
Titanic

LOUISA

I had no idea what happened between Hannah and Charles, but I did know that I hated getting out of my bed this morning after last night's rendezvous. It wasn't even that I was out that late; it was that I couldn't get to sleep afterward.

Reid Grey was supposed to be a distraction. A diversion. I hadn't had many affairs over the years, and I was always careful, but they had always, *always* been about fun. Flirting. And yes, perhaps the exhilaration of a bit of danger. More than once I'd considered that if a scandal emerged from one of my liaisons, I would be able to escape the pressure from my family to marry.

But that would also affect what I truly wanted to do with my life. I wanted to make a difference. I wanted to champion rights for women, I wanted to help other women who didn't have the small but veritable clout of a baronetcy behind them. I couldn't do that if I were easily dismissed because of indiscretions and amoral behaviour. Women rarely had any credibility. Loose women even less.

I dipped my strawberry in a little sugar and popped it in my mouth. Oh, if they – meaning society – only knew the half of it. I was very, very good at keeping secrets. The plan I was working on right now, one that would really take off once I returned to England, would ensure the future I wanted.

I frowned when I considered that Reid Grey had the power to get in the way of that.

The atmosphere at breakfast was awkward. Charles and Hannah wore matching placid expressions and ate mechanically, but there was no conversation. I was hungry, so I ate the fruit and managed a few bites of coddled egg until I couldn't stand the silence anymore. "If you'll excuse me," I said, putting down my napkin and rising. "Hannah, shall I see you at luncheon?"

She looked up, startled, and two dots of colour rose on her cheeks. I could only think that she'd realized the extent of the awkwardness and that it was chasing me away, which was mostly true. "Oh. I was thinking of finding a book and going to the Reading and Writing Room after breakfast. I thought you might join me."

It sounded dull as dirt, but I also knew many of the women would socialize there, so I gave her a smile and nodded. "That sounds lovely. I'll meet you there later."

Charles looked up. "Miss Phillips."

"Charles." Ice dripped from my lips. It was the way he said my name. It always put my back up.

I nodded and then turned to depart the saloon, a sense of relief washing over me the further I got from the pair. I was sure Hannah would fill me in later, but clearly whatever she was trying to do to connect with Charles was not working out as she hoped.

I was still hungry, so I took the lift up to A Deck and went to the

Verandah Café. This atmosphere suited me much better: wicker furniture, windows looking outside, palms and trailing plants giving it a light and bright feel. My mood immediately improved. The port side of the café was non-smoking, and while I didn't often smoke, a quick check showed a handful of children and their caregivers inside. I shuddered at the very thought. Instead, I went to the starboard side, was seated at a table, and soon had a cup of coffee and a decadent pastry in hand. This was more like it.

I was just sipping at my second cup of coffee when Mabel Fortune came in. I'd liked her immensely yesterday. She seemed perfectly happy to defy convention, within reason, and without digging too deeply I got the impression we had similar thoughts about women's roles and, well, the idea that perhaps we were capable of running our own lives. I lifted a hand and waved, and she smiled and waved back. Seconds later, she slipped into the chair opposite me. "Good morning, Miss Phillips! I'm delighted to find you here." She leaned forward and lowered her voice. "I have escaped my mother for the time being and am dying for some time away from my sisters," she confessed. "I love them dearly, but my word. We've been together for over a month and now we're sharing a cabin. Sometimes there can be too much togetherness."

I laughed as Mabel rolled her eyes and a cup of coffee was procured. "I am also tired of tea," she whispered.

This was a woman I could be friends with.

"Please, call me Louisa, I said, lifting my cup.

"Then you must call me Mabel," she replied. "Now, tell me all about yourself. We barely skimmed the surface yesterday."

While I relayed my basic predicament of trying to escape the marriage knot, Mabel told me how she was in love with a jazz musician and how the trip was her parents' attempt at separating them. "It hasn't changed my mind a bit," she declared, reaching for an iced bun and biting into it with an enthusiasm I admired.

"Nor I," I replied with a smile, leaning back in my chair.

"Honestly, I just want to be left alone. Let my parents give me my dowry – I won't even get into that archaic tradition – and leave me to my causes."

Mabel eyed me curiously. "You don't want children?"

I shrugged. "If I ever do, I'd like to have a say in who with. And when."

"I agree with you there."

After our coffee, I mentioned that I was to meet Hannah in the Reading and Writing Room, so we left the casual comfort of the café and strolled through the first-class lounge to the space intended to be a female domain in which to socialize, similar to the men's smoking room but far more "ladylike" and appropriate.

We stopped in the doorway of our destination and Mabel gave a little gasp of delight. "Why, this is beautiful."

"Isn't it?" I asked, gazing around me, feeling my own sense of wonder. I was no stranger to elegance and extravagance, but this room was perfection.

My nose caught the slight, sharp scent of paint from the white panelled walls, while my feet stepped on soft, plush carpet. On one wall was a stunning coal imitation fireplace with a mirror above it, and straight ahead were tall windows looking out over the promenade with heavy draperies the colour of claret precisely tied back so every fold was evenly matched. There were a few potted plants that spread their leafy foliage, and sconces lit on the wall, adding a touch of coziness. Tables and chairs, armchairs and settees filled the space, about a quarter of them occupied by other ladies dressed similarly to myself: elegant suits for daytime, polished shoes, and ostentatious hats that extended to the width of their shoulders. There were even a few writing desks for those inclined to pen letters or write in diaries, I supposed, but at the moment these remained vacant. I spied Hannah, sitting alone, a book in her hand. She looked lonely, and I momentarily felt guilty for abandoning her this morning. Of the two of us, I was the gregarious one, and she, reserved. Her behaviour before breakfast was puzzling and made me realize she must be feeling truly desperate if she had abandoned her customary, and sometimes infuriating, restraint.

"There's Hannah," I said, smiling at Mabel.

We joined Hannah, and before long Mabel had her laughing with tales of her trip to Egypt, Hannah's book forgotten beside her. We sat and enjoyed a half hour of chit chat, much more relaxed than last night had been in the dining saloon. "What are your plans for New York?" Mabel asked. "Where are you staying?"

"The Belmont," I answered. "And we're going to shop, and have tea at the Plaza, and I'm going to take Hannah to the theatre. It will be her first time, but not mine."

"I wish I could join you," Mabel lamented. "It sounds like such fun. We're going back to Winnipeg, however."

I hadn't ever heard of the Canadian city, and while Mabel was telling us about her life there, laughter captured my attention, the kind of laughter one didn't generally hear in a room of gentle-bred ladies. Oddly enough, it made me smile, and I dipped my chin and put my finger over my lips to hide my amusement.

"That's Mrs. Brown." Mabel leaned forward, her voice a conspiratorial whisper. "She boarded last night in Cherbourg and we met at the concert after dinner. The woman with her is Helen Churchill Candee. Quite a firebrand, from what I understand."

I looked closer at the woman, scouring my brain. "I know that name," I said, pursing my lips. "Is she English?"

"American," Mabel responded. "A writer and a decorator and a very outspoken proponent of women's rights."

"That must be it," I replied. "I myself am a member of the Women's Social and Political Union."

Hannah's eyes widened. "You are?"

I shrugged. "Of course."

I sensed her disapproval. It wasn't that Hannah didn't agree with the cause; we'd been talking about it for years. No, it was that she didn't like the tactics, and that was exactly why I'd kept this from her. Hannah was so ... genteel. She would be the type to go to the Prime Minister and say, "I'd like to have the vote, please," and expect results.

But rights were not something that should be doled out. Rights were, by nature, unalienable. I was no less human than a man. I deserved to have authority over my life and a say over our society. It was a fine line I trod with family and acquaintances. Not too outspoken, or I'd be cut off, financially and socially. I did a lot for the cause in the background, however. And for that I needed money.

"I heard the Astors boarded as well," Hannah murmured, trying to change the subject. It was her way. Not to argue but to avoid hot topics and any sort of confrontation. To keep the peace. Which was why her behaviour this morning had been so surprising. It was unlike her to square her shoulders and walk away, and I wondered at the change. Something big must have happened to rile her so.

"They did. The Astors are friends with Mrs. Brown as well, did you know?" Mabel asked. I was beginning to realize she enjoyed her gossip, as her eyes twinkled at me. "They say Madeleine is in a delicate condition. Gracious, he's old enough to be her father."

Hannah gave a small shrug. "I've heard it's a love match, though," she said quietly, her voice soft and surprisingly sweet. Clearly her fiery irritation at Charles had mellowed in the hour since breakfast. "Apparently he dotes on her. Have you met them?"

"Not yet," Mabel replied. Another burst of laughter came from Mrs. Brown. "Would you like to be introduced to Mrs. Brown?"

She didn't wait for an answer but stood and gestured to us to follow her. "Oh, Mrs. Brown, how delightful to see you again!"

Mrs. Brown and Mrs. Candee sat in club chairs upholstered in a soft floral fabric, and Mrs. Brown stood as we approached.

"Miss Fortune, good morning." Mrs. Brown offered a congenial smile. She was a solid woman, with expensively cut clothes but without the air of gentle elegance I had come to expect from first-class ladies. I liked her immediately. She struck me as a woman who knew how to accomplish things, someone who knew how to get her way, and there was nothing I admired more.

"May I present my new friends, Mrs. Hannah Martin and Miss Louisa Phillips?"

I turned to shake Mrs. Brown's hand. It was firm and confident, and as I met her gaze my smile grew. This was someone I felt good with, and that happened so very rarely I knew I needed to take note of it. "Mrs. Brown. A pleasure."

"Likewise. Come, join Mrs. Candee and me. She was just telling me the funniest story about when she was decorating the White House."

"Now, not the whole White House," Helen replied, nudging Mrs. Brown's elbow. "Hello. Don't you all look young and fresh this morning. No sea sickness worries, I gather."

I guessed her to be around fifty or so, with lovely dark hair and intelligent eyes that seemed to see everything. I held out my hand. "It's a pleasure to meet you, Mrs. Candee."

"Please, you must call me Helen," she answered, shaking my hand firmly and letting it go again. "Now, come join us and tell us all about yourselves. That'll be far more interesting than the two of us old ladies blathering on."

We all took seats at a table, a nearby steward procuring an extra chair so we could all sit together. I looked at Helen and smiled. "I wouldn't call either of you an old lady," I said with a smile. "And I rather think you're the interesting ones. You've lived so much more life than we have."

Margaret Brown looked at Helen and grinned. "I like her."

As we chatted about light topics, getting to know each other, I scoured my brain for where I'd heard Mrs. Candee's name before. There were suffragist demonstrations happening everywhere; America and Canada were having their own movements. It dawned on me that I'd seen a book years ago, perhaps when I was just finishing school, that had been somewhat scandalous. "Mrs. Candee," I said, when a break in the conversation fell, "did you write a book on working women?"

"Dear me." She sat back, surprised and yet looking pleased. "I did, over ten years ago now. *How Women May Earn a Living*. It did not make me popular in some circles."

"I bet not," Margaret said, chuckling. "There is nothing more fearsome to a man than a woman who doesn't need him."

Mabel piped up, "Like yourself. I quite admire you both. You are unafraid to live your own lives. How liberating!"

Margaret's expression softened. "It can be, I suppose."

"And I wouldn't say unafraid is the best word," Helen joined in. "Sometimes, necessity breeds invention. I had to support my family, so I found a way to do that."

I was so very intrigued by these women. They were twice my age, but successful, rich, even. They were self-possessed and happy. That was all I truly wanted. To be able to decide what I wanted my life to look like and to pursue it. I wondered if this trip – and what I hoped it would yield – was worth it. But then I looked at Mrs. Brown and Mrs. Candee and I knew that whatever I did would be justifiable. I would not become dull Mrs. Balcombe and live with a man who was no more than a stranger, just to appease my parents. If Helen Candee could support her family, surely I could support myself somehow.

Hannah had been soft-spoken compared to our animated conversation, but she spoke up unexpectedly. "Mrs. Brown, you remain married, do you not?"

Margaret Brown nodded. "Yes, Mrs. Martin, I am. We lead … well, independent lives."

"And that's been satisfactory for you?"

There was an awkward silence. It was a horribly probing question, aimed at a woman she'd just met, and as if she suddenly realized it, her cheeks flushed and she bit down on her lip. "Oh, my goodness. That was so impolite. Please forget I asked."

But Margaret leaned over and put her gloved hand over Hannah's. "My dear girl. There is so much to be gained by women talking to other women. I did not marry J. J. thinking that we would go our separate ways. We're different people, is all. And it got to a point where our differences made it impossible to go on as we were. We're happier apart, really. And we remain close. Probably *because* we went our separate ways, truthfully."

Hannah nodded, but her eyes remained troubled. A heaviness settled on my insides. Hannah was so sweet and lovely, and I had known her intention for this trip was to mend things with Charles. But the look on her face, the question she'd just asked… Perhaps she was considering something far more drastic. Like she was afraid her marriage was over. If not legally, in practicality. As much as I didn't understand her preoccupation with hearth and home, my heart ached for her. She deserved so much happiness, growing up without her mother, wanting nothing more than the warmth and love of a family. And she'd nearly had it once. Before everything had been ripped away from her.

Well, I determined, if something happened and Hannah left Charles, she could live with me. We could bump along just fine together, and I'd be her family. We were as close as sisters anyway. Or at least, as close as I imagined sisters being, seeing as I had none of my own. It just meant that I had to be even more calculating in my plans.

I looked over at Helen Candee and Margaret Brown. These were two women who managed to live life on their terms. They had money. A certain level of prestige, though I knew what my family would say about "new money." As far as I was concerned, money spent the same way whether it was new or old, and I rather respected the new as it was a product of industry and hard work rather than the privilege of inheritance.

That perspective didn't do me any favours in my parents' set, that was for sure. I could just imagine saying such a thing at Mama's annual spring garden party. But right now, on the *Titanic*, just off the coast of Ireland and soon to be headed across the ocean, I was a tiny bit freer to be "rebellious."

And speaking of rebellious, I had yet to see Reid this morning. That I'd looked for him in the dining saloon and again on my way to the café was perhaps troublesome. I needed to make connections with the women on board, not spend my time seeking his attention.

"We thought we might go out on deck while we're at Queenstown," Helen said. "Would you three like to join us?"

Hannah agreed readily. "I would. I quite like spending time outside and it should be interesting. I've never seen Ireland before, and I hear the coastline is stunning."

"Me as well," I said. "Mabel?"

"I'm off to find Mother, unfortunately. We agreed to meet for luncheon later."

It was only just past eleven, but Mabel was free to do as she wished. I was not averse to spending more time with Mrs. Brown and Mrs. Candee. In particular, I wanted to talk to Mrs. Candee about her suffrage efforts. I knew little about what was happening with women's rights across the Atlantic.

It was cool and breezy as we stepped out on deck, and I put my hand to my head to check my hat was still firmly anchored. Clouds scudded across the sky, and the *Titanic* loomed large compared to the smaller boat approaching from the harbour. I breathed deeply of the fresh, salty air, and looped my arm through Hannah's as we followed the other two women to the rail. Neither of them ventured to the section of promenade that was enclosed, sheltering passengers from the elements. It was as if, like me, they wanted to feel the wind on their faces and the sun, capricious as it was, on their skin.

A few people would disembark, one being Father Browne,

who'd spent his twenty-four hours on board snapping photos. I'd seen him after our departure from Southampton, out on the promenade and then around the ship with his camera. He'd even convinced Captain Smith to have his photo taken. For such a short journey – England to Ireland – Browne was leaving the ship with countless photographic treasures.

While a handful were leaving, over a hundred more were coming on board. They were mostly third class, with a smattering of first- and second-class passengers. I looked over at Hannah and grinned. "Another hour or so and we'll truly be away," I said, anticipation fizzing through my veins. "New York, here we come."

Hannah laughed. "You're so good for me, Lou." She squeezed my arm. "No matter what happens, I'll always be glad I took this trip with such a dear friend. A sister."

My eyes stung, and not from the wind that buffeted my face. I hated keeping secrets from Hannah, especially when she said such things. The last thing I ever wanted to face was her disapproval. I think I dreaded that even more than angering my parents, perhaps because I'd already felt their disappointment for so long. If she knew the truth about my trip, she'd be so very angry with me, and rightfully so. She could never discover the real reason I'd wanted to travel to New York; it wasn't all to do with avoiding Boring Balcombe. Or rather, it was much more than that, and she would never approve.

"Isn't it gorgeous, ladies?" Mrs. Brown rested her gloved hands on the railing and leaned forward. A lighthouse lay off to our right, a beacon of safety to those navigating the rugged coast. Green hills rolled inward above the harbour, an emerald carpet only dimmed by the clouds as they blotted out the sun.

I let go of Hannah and moved to stand beside my new companion. "It's beautiful. I've never been. It almost makes one want to get off and go exploring."

Margaret laughed. "You are a free spirit, aren't you, Miss Phillips?"

"I'd like to be," I admitted, patting her hand. "But sadly, convention still must be adhered to, at least in appearances."

"Ah. A subversive." Helen overheard what I'd said and chuckled. "A woman after my own heart. You're quite right, Miss Phillips. Even in our rebellion we must maintain certain ... sensibilities. If we're to be credible at all."

Hannah gave a light laugh. "Oh my. I've found myself amidst revolutionaries."

"Join us, Han," I dared her. "It's great fun."

"I believe in your cause," she agreed readily. "And yet I do not yearn for the independence you've gained or seek."

"Ah, yes. Marital bliss." Helen smiled at her warmly. "I do believe in such a thing, Mrs. Martin. Even if I myself did not have it."

Hannah blushed. "I'm so sorry—"

Helen flapped a hand. "Heavens, dear, don't be. It was years ago, and my life looks just as I want it. I wish the same for you."

"You are all so very lovely," Hannah replied. "Honestly, I was feeling like the odd one out."

"Don't be silly, Han." I rubbed her arm. "I know I go on about not wanting to be married, but truly it's because I don't want to be wed for the sake of being wed. If I fell truly, deeply in love, I might reconsider."

What bothered me in that moment? I meant it, and I didn't like it.

We were watching the tenders – the *PS Ireland* and the *PS America*, fittingly enough – make their way to the ship when a discreet cough sounded behind us.

I turned to find Mr. Reid, without Mr. Sloper this time, but in the company of two other moustachioed gentlemen I recognized but didn't know. "Miss Phillips, good day," Reid said, as polite as could be, a twinkle in his eyes.

"Hello, Mr. Grey."

"And Mrs. Martin. A pleasure to see you again."

Hannah nodded, but she looked rather guarded. Instead of putting me off, her suspicion settled over me like a warm shawl. Hannah loved me and in her way was trying to protect me. For all our differences, that was something truly special.

The other two gentlemen doffed their hats, and Helen's smile was particularly warm. "Miss Phillips, Mrs. Martin, let me introduce my friends, Colonel Archibald Gracie and Mr. Francis Millet."

"The artist?" Hannah asked, and I turned my head in surprise.

Millet looked rather pleased to be recognized. "One and the same, madam."

Reid stepped forward and shook the hands of Helen and Margaret, pausing a little and sharing a laugh with the latter, something I couldn't hear. All in all, the three of us were of one generation and the other four were of another, and together we made a rather gay party. Colonel Gracie was chivalrous and entertaining, and he and Millet had an easy way about them that made us all comfortable in their presence. For my part, I was painfully aware of Reid just to my right. He was ever so proper today, in his coat and top hat, but when he glanced in my direction the heat in his eyes was undeniable.

It did things to me, things I didn't expect and was usually able to keep a tight lid on. Maybe it was because we were away from the usual rollicking parties and social engagements. Perhaps it was because the possibilities for flirtations and trysts on board were plentiful. It had been a very long time since I'd indulged in any romantic endeavours.

While the time spent outside had brushed away the cobwebs and refreshed my mind and body, the chill of the air began to seep through the wool of my coat. The tenders began their return journey to the harbour, having divested themselves of their passengers, and we'd soon set sail again.

"You're cold." Reid's voice was low and close, and I turned my head to find him watching me with concern darkening his eyes. I felt something strange, as if his consideration and care wrapped around me like a hug. I shook it off, uncomfortable with the notion. Hugs, metaphorical or otherwise, were not a currency I was accustomed to. I smiled instead and shook my head.

"I'm fine. Truly."

"We could go inside..." He gestured toward the exit, where it would be warm and out of the wind. Tempting, but again I shook my head.

"Call me foolish, but I want to remain out here. To slip away and say goodbye to *terra firma* before heading across the ocean."

Hannah had slid up beside me. "Me too," she said firmly. "It's beautiful, is it not?" We stood shoulder to shoulder, and I got a sense of her remaining close to protect me, which was sweet, though I had no need of her protection. But there was more to her tone. For all Hannah's gentle tenderness, I was reminded of how much steel she held in her spine. How could I have forgotten the ways she had suffered in her life, and yet remained soft and loving? Tender and hopeful? She was all the good things I was not. Her suffering had gentled her edges and had given her compassion. Mine had only given me anger and a nagging need for justice.

"Ireland's coast is truly stunning," Reid said to her, offering a smile. "It's wild and yet welcoming, beautiful green hills and valleys and unforgiving cliffs and waves. I wonder at those who are leaving it. It must break their hearts."

I was touched at his insights, and I saw Hannah soften a little as well. "I think of them often," she admitted, "the people in steerage. Lou said, quite rightly, that most of these people will never see their homeland again. We are so very fortunate."

Reid looked at me. "Your friend does you credit, Miss Phillips.

She has a compassionate heart. Not many in our set spares a thought for those eking out a living."

I raised an eyebrow. "Mr. Grey, you're in banking. Not exactly a profession for championing the masses."

"True enough," he responded, then paused. "But that doesn't mean we can't think of our fellow man with empathy."

"And does this empathy extend to the plight of the opposite sex?"

Hannah snorted beside me, and then I heard another chuckle. Our exchange had caught the attention of our companions, and Mrs. Candee's eyes gleamed at me. "Oh, well said, Miss Phillips," she said, pumping her fist.

"Hear, hear," agreed Mr. Millet.

Hannah nudged my arm. "You have found your people, Lou," she said softly.

"And what about you, Hannah? Will you join us?"

She hesitated for a moment, then met my eyes. They were soft and perhaps a little sad, but not without a spark of hope. "I shall join you in spirit, but first, I must find my husband. We're meeting for luncheon, and I'd like to freshen up first. Shall I see you there, Lou?"

"I don't think so," I answered, disappointed, then turned to the left so I could face her better and say the next bit more privately. "Go have lunch with Charles and try to mend what's between you. I can see it is wearing on you."

She nodded, a bit too quickly, letting me know I had hit the nail right on the head. Storming away from Charles, treating him silently, was not her nature. I just prayed that Charles was not such an idiot as to turn her away.

"Mrs. Martin," called Margaret, "you and your husband are welcome to join me for dinner tonight, in the restaurant. As a matter of fact, you're all invited. We'll have a grand time."

"Thank you." Hannah smiled, and I wondered for the millionth time how Charles could be so cold. She was an angel. Certainly a better person than I, and beautiful to boot. "I'll ask Charles if he's made any plans. It does sound fun."

"It's settled, then."

The ship began to move, all forty-six odd tons of it slowly nudging forward. On open sea, we'd speed along the waves at more than twenty knots, but for now it was the slight vibration beneath our feet and the smallest awareness of the view shifting an inch at a time. Hannah said her goodbyes and slipped away, and the older friends engaged in a conversation all their own. That left me standing at the rail with Reid, staring at the coast, knowing that after this moment there was truly no turning back. I could not undo the things I'd done in my past, nor did I truly want to. It was up to me to make sure that I used what I'd done to shape my future. The *Titanic* was an odd place to be in this moment – a liminal space between the past and the future I longed to create for myself. One of independence and autonomy. And yet, even with that determination, I was drawn toward the man beside me, wanting to remain close to him.

I wished I'd never written him that letter and surreptitiously invited him along. I desperately wanted to be flippant and carefree, but I found I couldn't. That was a new and disturbing development. I'd never had a problem keeping my flirtations light and fun before.

Reid looked away from the Irish coast and captured my gaze. "William is otherwise engaged for lunch," he said, a small smile playing on his lips. "Would you care to join me?"

Everything in my head screamed no, that I should stop this right now before it went further, before something silly like my heart got involved. It told me that I hardly knew Reid, other than our encounters in social situations over the past year or two. Who really was he, and could I trust him? I trusted no one, really, except Hannah. I heard all these warnings in my head but my heart wasn't listening, and my lips betrayed me by answering, "I'd love to."

Chapter Five

April 11, 1912
Titanic

HANNAH

Charles met me in our cabin at twelve thirty, just as the *Titanic* began to leave Queenstown. The last of the passengers were aboard, and we were officially on our way to New York. I'd spent a few moments tidying my appearance, especially my hair since the wind on deck had mussed it, leaving strands loose around my face. Even the elaborate hats couldn't protect the most precise hairstyles from the brisk sea breeze.

"Ah," he said, coming inside, "you're here. Lovely." He smiled, but there wasn't much feeling behind it. I could see he was making an effort to put us back on an even keel, though, which was what I wanted as well. I didn't know why I'd thought being more forthright – as Lou might have done – would work. It wasn't like me to be snappish and storm off. No wonder Charles was treading carefully.

"I thought to freshen up before luncheon." I gave my hat a final adjustment, then turned to him. "Charles, I'm sorry about this morning. I was angry and didn't behave well by walking away like that."

He shifted and slid a finger under his collar, but to my surprise, met my gaze and gave a little nod. "I'm not sure how to answer your questions, Hannah, and you've been pushing. I just don't know why."

I didn't want to argue again, so I stepped forward and took his hands in mine. "I just want us to have a nice crossing. To enjoy each other's company."

"Don't we do that already?"

"Of course." I didn't want to disagree with him, but instead wanted to make him see that there could be so much more. "I-I miss the way we used to be, before—"

"Hannah, please."

The sharpness of his tone nearly deterred me, but I was determined to break the pattern of me broaching the topic and him shutting it down. I wanted us to talk calmly, rationally. "Charles, we have to say it. Have to talk about it at some point. The way things were before I lost the baby."

He pulled his hands away from mine, but it didn't quite feel like he was freezing me out. Especially when he took a deep breath, and I heard how shaky it was.

"I know you were devastated." I kept my voice soft and prayed for patience. "As I was. But we had a good marriage."

"I know I haven't been … fun," he conceded. "I've focused on work, providing us with a good life."

"And you have done a marvellous job. I'm so proud of what you've accomplished. I just … wish there was room for me in there, too. I'm lonely. And every time I've tried to talk to you about it, you've put me off. This morning I was simply frustrated. I'm sorry for how I acted."

He came to me and took my hand. "I know. I don't like us being at odds. I'm sorry, too. Let's try again, shall we? Let's go to lunch. Will Miss Phillips be joining us?"

I shook my head. "She has other plans. It's just the two of us."

"Good. I'm glad."

"She's my best friend, Charles." I hated feeling like I had to constantly defend her. We were different people, but she was a good person. She'd been there for me for years. That had to count for something, didn't it?

"I know." He sighed, then squeezed my hand. "But perhaps it's a good thing that I'm happy to have lunch alone with my wife?"

My heart warmed at his words, and hope surged through me. This was a better start. Even though I wasn't entirely pleased with how I'd acted earlier, if it had made him stop and consider and helped bring us to this point where he was at least willing to talk, I was a little bit glad I'd done it. This was a good step.

But things were far from resolved. There were so many bigger issues to deal with, so much at stake. I wasn't at all convinced that he would be as amendable to really pulling apart the strands of everything that had gone wrong. He was a "look to the future" kind of man, but how could we do that when the past kept interfering?

I was determined to take this one small step at a time. Luncheon was a relaxed, enjoyable affair. I didn't press talking about that horrible January morning, and instead focused on Charles: looking into his eyes, smiling, laughing lightly at his subtle wit. Flirting with my husband of four years was, I realized, surprisingly fun. As we dined on creamy soup and tender chicken, I tried to remember what I'd done in those early days when we had been courting, before he'd asked my father for permission to marry me. It was easier, I realized, without Lou between us. Lou always seemed to put Charles on edge.

She was a unique flavour, of course, and not for everyone. But she was kind and funny and she loved me, all reasons why Charles should like her.

We had nearly finished our main course when Charles gave a little scowl. I might not have noticed except I was paying rather close attention. "What is it?" I asked, putting down my fork and blotting my lips with my napkin. "You look displeased. Is the chicken not to your liking?"

He blinked and relaxed his lips, not quite smiling but not frowning, either. "I see Miss Phillips has found a luncheon companion, that's all."

I turned in my chair and saw she was sitting with Mr. Grey at his table. They looked to be in animated conversation. "Lou is free to eat with whomever she wants," I said lightly. "It's given us time to eat alone, hasn't it?"

"It has, my dear." He took a drink of water and put down the goblet. "I'm sorry. I didn't mean to spoil the mood."

"You didn't. This has been really lovely, Charles. At home we rarely eat together except at night. And you look more rested, even after just a few days."

Lou's laugh rang out behind us, and Charles scowled again. I couldn't help it; I sighed. "Charles, please. She's having a good time and a laugh over lunch. Forget about Lou. I don't know why you dislike her so much, anyway."

His grey eyes held mine. "Because she's loud and opinionated and because … because she thinks the rules don't apply to her."

"What rules?" I was genuinely confused.

"Leave it, shall we?" He balled up his napkin and put it on the table.

"No, I don't think so, dear." I held his gaze. Charles hated a scene and wouldn't make one here in public; nor would I act as I had this morning and rush off in a huff. "She's been my best friend for over fifteen years, Charles. I love her. I do wish you'd at least try with her. She has a kind heart, I promise you."

"She runs roughshod over you, Hannah, and takes advantage. And you're too sweet to realize it. Like insinuating her way onto this voyage."

Was he jealous of Lou? Now that was something that might make sense. He shouldn't blame Lou, though. "Don't blame Lou. We were talking about the voyage, and she sounded so keen, especially about New York. I'll be honest, I thought a week in New York City with a friend would be more pleasurable than a dusty train west and then waiting around for you while you worked. Not because of you, please understand that," I rushed to reassure him. "I felt I'd be in the way. So I asked if she'd like to come. Her parents are pressuring her to marry Arthur Balcombe, Charles. She hardly knows him."

"He's a nice enough man."

"You've met him what, twice? That's once more than she has. And just because someone is nice does not mean you should just up and marry them. This felt like the perfect solution, but I'm truly sorry you're not happy with the arrangement. If I'd known you were this much against it…"

Charles waved off any pudding and sighed. "You would have what, Hannah? You presented it as a *fait accompli*."

Silence fell over the table. He was not wrong. I had gone to him with it all arranged except for the purchase of her ticket. Which I had insisted he pay for. *My treat*, I'd said.

I loved Lou. I would be loyal to her until the day I died. I also wanted to save my marriage. It was awful, being stuck between the two people who meant the most to me, and them not liking each other.

Moreover, I wasn't sure if I was truly in the wrong or not. Charles had been so frosty to me of late. Yes, I wanted to repair what was between us, but this was, at its heart, a business trip and he had responsibilities. This was not just a holiday for him. Was it wrong of me to want to spend time with my cherished friend rather than sit around waiting? I'd done so much of that, and it was a horribly lonely place to be.

"I did, yes. I thought I was making everyone happy."

His shoulders dropped, and some of the tension dissipated. "I know. It is what you do, really. That's why I didn't make a fuss. It's harder when she's in our orbit all the time, though."

The whole topic made me both anxious and sad. Neither Charles nor Lou knew about the baby I was carrying. I truly had no idea how Charles would react to the news, and Lou would smother me. That I knew for sure. Beneath the table linens, I rested my palm against the tiny bubble just forming beneath my corset. I was worried about their reactions, but the truth was that I was terrified. I would need both of them in the months ahead, and how could I do that if they were always at odds? No matter how they would feel about this pregnancy, I was the one utterly terrified.

In a rare display of affection, Charles reached over and took my other hand in his. "I will try harder," he promised, meeting my gaze. "I know she's important to you."

Relief and affection flooded me at the warmth of his gaze and his words. "Thank you, Charles."

We were nearly ready to leave when I remembered the invitation for dinner. "Oh, darling, I nearly forgot. Mrs. Brown has invited us to dine in the restaurant tonight. I'd like to accept, if possible. She and Mrs. Candee were so very nice to me this morning."

"I don't see why not." Charles rose and held his hand out to me. "Is it to be a party, or just the three of us?"

"A small party, I think" I replied. "Mrs. Candee, of course. Colonel Gracie and Mr. Millet, you know, the artist?" At Charles's blank look, I kept on. "And Mr. Grey and Lou."

His jaw tightened, but then he smiled. "I did say I would try harder, didn't I?"

I smiled back at him, truly hopeful for the first time in days. Perhaps, instead of just reaching Charles's heart, I needed to find a way to bring the two of them together. Perhaps there was some sort of common ground that could put a halt to the friction between them.

LOUISA

"If looks could kill, Charles Martin would have me dead on the spot," I said, laughing, sliding out of the soft sheets and walking naked to the table where a crystal glass of Scotch waited.

I was determined to not regret going to bed with Reid, especially since just last night I'd decided a slow seduction was best. It was just sex, after all. Very, very good sex, as it happened, and if I had prolonged the anticipation I would have missed out on a glorious afternoon. I took a sip of the drink, then ambled back to the bed, handing him the glass and getting under the sheet again, against his body that was both hard and warm. I wasn't sure what he did to keep himself fit, but his was no soft banker's body. Lucky me.

He downed the liquor, reached over and put the empty glass on the floor, then pulled me close so that I was lying over his chest, my breasts pressed against him.

"Charles Martin is a stick," Reid said, running his fingers down my arm, making all the fine hairs stand up. "He has a beautiful wife, and I can guarantee they are not spending the afternoon in as pleasurable a way as we are."

I snorted. "No, indeed. Though I rather wish they would. Hannah needs an attentive husband. No, not needs. Deserves."

"And how about you?" He dropped a soft kiss on my shoulder, sneaking a taste of my skin with his tongue before pulling away. "Do you want an attentive husband?"

My insides froze, but I kept the smile on my face. "Good God, no," I said. "Why would I when all the pleasure I could want is just here?"

Reid gave a wicked smile, then pulled my head down for a slow, seductive kiss. "Louisa," he said, when our lips parted, "may I just say that the reality of you is better than anything I've imagined?"

"Likewise." I slid away and rolled to my back, wishing for a cigarette. I hadn't planned to capitulate so easily. It was only meant to be lunch, a little more flirting, leaving him wanting more. A girl needed a way to entertain herself between trying to avoid the noose of matrimony and fighting for her rights. But golly, we'd laughed so much during luncheon that I'd barely remembered to eat, even though the food was top-notch. Though many would disagree, I found laughter an effective aphrodisiac in the right situation. I loved when a man was smart enough to make me laugh.

Then there was the encounter with Margaret Brown. I still had mixed feelings about that. She was a powerful woman, and a kind one, too. I felt a twinge of guilt, taking advantage of her generous nature. Sharing a laugh with Reid had erased the uncomfortable thoughts from my head and replaced them with something far more exciting. We'd escaped to the first-class lounge on A deck, under the auspices of borrowing a book from the lending library. But Reid had passed by me, grazing his fingers along the hollow of my waist. I'd blindly turned pages in whatever book I'd picked up from the shelf, pretending to peruse while his touch lit little fires along my spine. And when he'd disappeared out the door and down a hallway, I'd waited a few moments and followed.

It had felt dangerous. Exciting.

I didn't have to go far. He stood, one shoulder leaning on the wall, waiting as if he'd been sure I would follow. I didn't quite like that he knew me that well. It might have been nice to have him wonder if I'd meet him or not; I never wanted to be a sure thing for any man. He'd given me that half-sweet, half-saucy smile and merely turned and walked a few more steps to his cabin door, opening it and ushering me inside.

I still could have said no. Being alone with a man in his cabin was certainly scandalous enough, and Reid was a rogue. But he did have honour, and if I'd changed my mind I knew without a doubt that he wouldn't have pressed.

I hadn't said no, though, not after the first kiss had stolen my breath and melted my bones. He'd been a most thorough lover. Carefully undressing me, placing my clothes piece by piece over a chair, the care and attention more seductive than any rushed disrobing. But once I was in his arms…

Well, I was a thoroughly satisfied woman, whose body still hummed with the aftershocks of pleasure. I hadn't realized how much I needed the release until now, stretched out, feeling loose and limber.

"I'm glad I exceeded expectations." Reid grinned. "And I much prefer this to playing shuffleboard or getting trounced by William on the squash court. It's far more stimulating and tons more satisfying. You really are head and shoulders above Sloper in every way."

He was teasing me and damned if I didn't like it.

I shifted until I was shamelessly astride his hips, the tips of my breasts touching his chest. "Darling," he murmured, the corner of his mouth curling in naughty pleasure. "You are most unexpected."

"Heaven forbid I be predictable," I replied, nipping at his lip, teasing. His hand slipped over my hip, warm and possessive, while his gaze dropped to the pendant dangling from a gold chain, swaying between us as I experimentally rolled my hips.

"This is lovely." He reached up with his free hand and captured the teardrop-shaped ruby, a round diamond at the tip of the drop. "Unique. Like you."

"I didn't know you were interested in jewellery." I bit down on my lip as, with his fingers still wrapped around the gems, he dipped his head and swiped his tongue over a nipple.

"I'm interested in beautiful and rare things," he murmured, tugging on the pendant and pulling me down closer until my neck was even with the soft heat of his lips. "I love touching them. Feeling the warmth of them in my fingers." He kissed my neck, sending shivers down my spine and goose flesh over my skin.

I wasn't sure if he was talking about my necklace or me, but I ceased to care when his hand left my hip and slipped between us.

Forget distraction. Reid Grey was dangerous. And damned if I didn't fly to him like a moth to a flame.

Chapter Six

```
April 11, 1912
   Titanic
```

HANNAH

I hadn't been in the à la carte restaurant yet, and when I first stepped onto the luxurious carpet, I realized it was perhaps the most glamorous room on the ship. It felt as if everything was gilded somehow: the French walnut panelling, the fluted columns, even the ornate moulding on the plaster ceiling was outrageously intricate. Axminster carpet cushioned my feet while Aubusson tapestry graced the chairs in a pink rose damask.

I held Charles's arm but looked over at Lou and widened my eyes. She grinned in response. This wasn't just first class; it was practically palatial. Neither of us was used to such a setting, though Lou had always been able to pull off the type of bored nonchalance that marked the premier set. I usually ended up feeling utterly provincial.

I was doubly glad I'd worn my blue silk Lucile gown and my diamond necklace with the aquamarine accents. Lou sparkled all over, from the jewelled pins in her hair to the topaz earrings dangling from her lobes. Her dress was a warm gold charmeuse, with gold embroidery and the barest black netting over the skirt, paired with long black gloves. It suited her colouring and the honey of her hair perfectly, making her look like a glowing candle amidst the dull and drab tones of tailcoats and even several of the frocks. More than one head turned as the four of us – me with Charles, Lou with Mr. Grey – stepped up to the podium. They weren't looking at me, and I couldn't blame them. Lou was absolutely radiant, and I could say that without an iota of envy.

We were greeted and Charles gave our names, and then we were led toward a long table set for a party. Margaret was already there with Mrs. Candee and, to my surprise, a couple I instantly recognized as the Astors. My stomach did a little nervous turn. I was utterly intimidated. What would they think if they knew I was simply a solicitor's daughter from Devon? Oh, I'd learned the proper etiquette at a dining table and there was nothing amiss in my wardrobe, but I watched as Lou smiled, spoke, shone. These were her people, not mine. Money bought entrée, but not class.

J. J. Astor stood as we approached and adopted a pleasant smile, and I noticed Colonel Gracie and Mr. Millet doing the same. "Jack," Margaret said clearly, "this is Mr. and Mrs. Charles Martin."

"Mr. and Mrs. Martin. How lovely you could join us this evening."

"Thank you. We were delighted to be asked." Charles turned toward Margaret. "Thank you for the invitation, Mrs. Brown."

"Of course. We have things in common, after all."

Charles smiled. "Ah, mining. I'm familiar with Ibex, of course."

Margaret smiled at the mention of the company that had provided her family with their fortune. "Well, yes, I suppose.

Though I rather meant your beautiful wife. It is easy to see why you are so taken with her. I've taken quite a shine to her myself."

"Of course, of course." Charles reached over and patted my hand. I hadn't realized he knew of Mrs. Brown's background, but I should have known better. My husband was a smart man.

"And this is Miss Louisa Phillips, and Mr. Reid Grey." Margaret rounded out the invitations. "This is J. J. Astor and his wife, Madeleine. Dear friends."

Lou and Mr. Grey said their greetings and moved to take their seats. "Hello," I said to Madeleine, who seemed a little bit shy. I could relate.

Madeline Astor smiled softly. "Hello," she replied, giving me a slight nod. "Your dress is beautiful, Mrs. Martin. And your necklace is exquisite."

I put my gloved hand to my neck, resting it against the heavy stones. "A wedding gift from my husband." I kept the smile on my lips, remembering the day before our wedding four years earlier, when he'd had it delivered. Those breathless, exciting days when my life seemed laid out before me, golden in its perfection. How naïve I'd been.

Mrs. Candee joined the conversation, and we spent a pleasant hour of dining. I remained mostly quiet, watching the dynamic of those around me. A trio played just outside, and the soft music filtered in, adding to the ambience and providing a background to the tinkling of crystal and silver. We dined on the finest of food in what people were calling the "Ritz" of the ocean, with delectable selections of lobster, quail, and lamb. The wine flowed freely, though I noticed Madeline exercising restraint and so did I, and I wondered if the rumour I'd heard that she was pregnant was true. The rich food was already a lot on my stomach, and the sip or two I took of the red wine tasted heavy and almost syrupy to my tongue.

I spoke occasionally, but for the most part was content to listen to the conversations around me. Lou and Helen were speaking animatedly of the previous year's tragedy in America, the Triangle Shirtwaist Fire. I had no idea that such an event had even happened, but Lou had not only heard about it but knew several details. They moved on to the issue of women owning property, with Lou lamenting that she still needed to marry, and that rather defeated the purpose.

Reid lifted his glass and said dryly, "You could always hope to be widowed."

Chuckles sounded all around, and Lou sat back, her face relaxing into a smile. "As you can tell, I'm a bit passionate about it all. And I'm certainly not against marriage. I simply don't think that I need a husband in order to know my own mind."

"No danger of that," Charles muttered, then, as if suddenly realizing he'd voiced his opinion, he tried a smile. "Miss Phillips, you have been my wife's closest friend longer than I've known her. I think it's safe to say that you know your own mind more than any woman I've ever met."

It was one of those moments when no one could tell if he was paying a compliment or offering a backhanded insult, and Louisa smoothly replied, "Why, thank you, Charles."

The response created an awkward conversational vacuum, however, and it was Margaret who bridged the gap. "Mrs. Martin, I was just admiring your necklace. Madeleine here says it was a gift from your husband. You have lovely taste, Mr. Martin."

I reached up and touched the heavy gems. "It's one of my favourites that I saved out to wear during the sailing."

Margaret nodded. "I think we all did the same, didn't we, ladies? I'm a bit furious with myself, though. I had on a cherished bracelet today, and somewhere on my travels around the ship, I lost it."

"Oh, no." I put down my fork. "Do you remember the last time you were wearing it?"

She nodded. "I know it was still on my wrist when we were in the Reading and Writing Room. But then we went out on deck, and after that, I did a fair bit of walking and then into luncheon. I didn't notice it missing until I went back to my cabin to change in the afternoon."

"What did it look like?" Lou asked, before placing a morsel of tender quail in her mouth. "Maybe we can keep an eye out for it. Or perhaps you can check with the purser? Surely if someone found it, they'd turn it in."

"Oh darlin', I checked there first thing. The ship's so big it's probably lost forever. It's gold with six amethysts in oval settings. I should have double checked the clasp. It's always been a little finicky."

"I didn't notice it this afternoon at tea," Madeleine said quietly. "I'm so sorry you've lost it."

"It does sound beautiful. I hope it turns up," Reid offered. "Gemstones are such a good investment, don't you think?"

Margaret met his gaze. "You're thinking as a banker, and of course I appreciate that. But this piece was a personal favourite. It is worth far more than dollars and cents."

"Or pounds and pence," Millet quipped.

I thought back to when we were all on deck, performing introductions. Had the bracelet come off then? The only person Margaret hadn't known at that point was Reid, and they'd shaken hands. Surely he would have said something if the clasp had come loose and the bracelet had fallen.

The talk of missing jewels and the worth of gems continued as we nibbled on pudding, which for me was a delightfully light dish of peaches in Chartreuse jelly. When the last dish was removed and conversation dwindled, Margaret asked us all to join her to listen to the after-dinner music on D Deck. I'd found the previous night's entertainments so lovely that I was happy to have a repeat performance. But I sensed Charles's reluctance, and remembered he'd spoken of having drinks again with this Weir fellow in the

Smoking Room. When Astor agreed to stay for the music, Charles agreed to stay for a short while. One did not just cut out when socializing with the richest man on board.

Charles lasted precisely twenty minutes at the concert before rising to make his excuses. "I'm afraid I must go. I have a previous engagement in the Smoking Room," he explained, offering a smile. "This has truly been enjoyable. It was wonderful to meet you all."

Colonel Gracie rose and shook Charles's hand. "Let's make sure it's not the last, shall we?"

Even Astor smiled at Charles. Despite that one awkward moment during dinner, his manners and general affability had gained him the regard of some powerful people. I discovered I was quite proud of him, actually. It could be argued that he'd bought his way into their attention, seeing as we were all sailing first class, but just as money didn't buy class, neither did it buy respect. Charles was a hard-working, ethical man, and even if our marriage was struggling, I couldn't deny he was, at his core, an extremely good person. Perhaps that was why the chasm between us felt so wide and cut so deeply. It would be easier to dismiss if he were a brute or odious in any way. Other than being a bit of a fuddy duddy, he really had much to recommend him.

"If Mrs. Martin would like to stay, she's more than welcome to remain with us," said Madeleine, and I looked at her in pleasant surprise.

"We'll see she gets to your cabin safely," Margaret chimed in.

"Are you sure, darling?" Charles asked, reaching for my hand. "I can certainly escort you now, but if you'd like to stay, you're in good hands."

"Don't forget, my cabin is just next door," Lou reminded him, and true to his word to try, he met her gaze and smiled.

"Of course."

"I shan't lack for chaperones," I laughed, patting his hand. "Go enjoy your brandy with Mr. Weir."

I stayed for another two numbers. I was increasingly tired, especially after remaining awake waiting for Charles last night, and then lying in the dark feeling sorry for myself sleeping alone. The past month or so fatigue had crept up on me as well, which I assumed was due to my pregnancy. I looked over at the young Mrs. Astor and longed to ask if she was expecting and perhaps have someone to talk to about it, but we'd only just met, and I wouldn't presume to ask something so personal.

The wistful bars of *Chanson de Nuit* washed over me, leaving me inexplicably tearful. The melody of the violin tugged at my heart, making me wish for happiness even more intently. The piece sounded lonely, as I was, but made me envision what I wanted most of all: a deliciously pink, healthy baby cuddled close, with my husband's arms around me. A family. All of us together. I just wanted to be … loved. I blinked as hot tears blurred my eyes for a few moments. I'd spent so much of my life longing for that very thing. Would I ever find it? No, not find it. I'd had it. But could I keep it?

"If you'll excuse me, I do think I'll turn in," I said, standing as the last notes faded and polite clapping filled the air.

J. J. stood as well and offered me a small smile. "We shall ensure you're delivered safely," he said, and I rather liked his face in that moment. There was kindness and understanding behind his gentlemanly manner. Indeed, when he smiled this way, I understood perhaps why Madeleine was drawn to him, despite his age.

"Oh, there's no need," I replied. "I've learned my way quite well and I'm safe as can be on the *Titanic*, am I not?"

"I'll go with you," Lou said, though I could tell she did not want to leave Mr. Grey's company. Besides, I was feeling the need to be alone for a while. Not even Lou could help with this. I had to find a way by myself.

"Please, stay and enjoy the music, Lou. There's no need. I'll see you in the morning for breakfast."

Margaret spoke up. "Are you certain? It's no trouble."

"Very." She'd stood as well, and we embraced and bussed each other's cheeks. "Thank you so much for the wonderful evening. I've enjoyed spending time with you all." I nodded to the group that had been most enjoyable companions for the evenings. The only company I wanted right now, however, was that of my husband, and he was three decks above me, smoking and drinking with Mr. Weir.

"Goodnight, Mrs. Martin."

I left them all behind and turned toward the direction of the lifts. Back on B Deck, I let out a sigh of relief. I had made it through the evening just fine. And now I had a little time to myself. To breathe, to think, perhaps even have the cry that had been brewing behind my eyes and nose throughout the evening. I was the pragmatic one, but lately my emotions rode closer and closer to the surface. Maybe by letting it out, I could regain some of my equilibrium.

The cabin was dark when I entered, and I turned on the lamp. Everything in our cabin was spotless and perfect; not a wrinkle on the linens or a ring left from an afternoon teacup on the table. I found the ship to be on the cool side, even when inside, out of the elements, but the heater in our cabin created a cozy warmth that fought against the raw chill of April on the North Atlantic.

I sat on the edge of the bed, taking stock of what had led to this moment in my life. Rich, Lord, I was richer than I had ever dreamed of being when I was a child. I was traveling across the ocean in unparalleled luxury. I had a husband. A child on the way, even though their very existence was a secret I held close to my heart until the right time. And yet I felt so very adrift. How was it that I was still somehow that lonely, motherless child who wanted nothing more than her father's love and attention?

I lifted my hand to my mouth. Oh, goodness. Was that it, truly?

Was Charles like my father, then? After Mama had died, father had withdrawn. He'd worked; he'd made sure I had a stable home with food and clothing and opportunities and education, but he'd held his heart back from me. Just as Charles was now. I was chasing that affection with my husband now and feeling utterly lost without it. And angry, because I felt like I deserved to be loved. Didn't I? Didn't everyone?

I was a fine lady in a fine dress in a fine house and had no real reason to complain other than I was so very, very lonely. The cure for which no money could buy. Perhaps there was something about me that was unlovable. Some ... deficiency. Was I not pretty enough? Smart enough? What was it about me that made it easy for people to leave me behind?

With that depressing thought, I set about undressing. I took the pins from my hair and shook it out, combing through the curls with my fingers before retrieving my brush and pulling it through the strands with long, steady strokes. Then I tried to unbutton my dress, but I couldn't reach all the buttons along the back, and I realized that trying to get out of my corset was going to be an issue, too. Maybe I should have let Lou come back with me.

I couldn't always rely on Lou to make everything right though, could I? She couldn't always be a buffer between me and the harsh realities of life, though it was easy to rely on her because she'd always been there whenever I called.

Even if it was just for six buttons on the back of my dress.

I rang for a stewardess instead, and a lovely young woman named Violet came to my rescue. In no time at all I was whisked out of my elaborate frock and into my nightgown, and she'd hung and folded every piece of clothing until nothing was out of place. I pressed a generous tip into her hand before she left, and then I got in bed under the covers to consider what I wanted to do next. My eyes were heavy, but I knew Charles would be along soon. He was aggressive in business but moderate in his vices. I was certain he'd return before midnight.

When I woke, the cabin was dark, and I heard Charles's light snuffle coming from across the room. I sighed, angry at myself for falling asleep instead of being awake for when Charles returned. I hadn't even heard him come in, or undress, or realize that he'd turned off the lamp. I was sure I had left the light on, hoping it would keep me awake. Despite the rough beginning to our day, it had ended so very nicely. Until I'd fallen asleep and ruined it all.

I shivered against the chill in the room and pulled the coverlet up to my chin as I stared at the shadowed ceiling overhead. I thought about what Lou would do in this situation and shook my head; Lou would never be in this situation. She would rise up and demand nothing less than she deserved. Where she got her resolve, her confidence, had always baffled me. Both of us had been raised in families where we were largely ignored and occasionally deemed in the way. And yet we couldn't be more dissimilar.

As Charles's deep breathing created a rhythmic sound in the cabin, I placed my hand where our child rested. I couldn't find it in me to blame myself after the first baby had died. I'd nearly died, too. I'd spent weeks in bed, recovering, mourning. Of course I had been entitled to that.

It was the aftermath that kept troubling me, poking at my heart and telling me how wrong I'd been. I couldn't blame Charles for shutting me out when I'd so clearly shut him out first. I had been a living, breathing person, but I'd been dead inside. I had not been a good wife to him, so how could I expect him to be a good husband?

And that was the crux of it. I needed him to come back to me so I could stop blaming myself for how everything had gone so wrong.

There'd been moments, of course, where things had been better.

The occasional night when he'd come to my room and we'd reconnected, but even that had broken my heart a bit each time, for it was a meeting of bodies and not of spirits. Yes, I wanted him close to me physically, but it was his heart I craved.

I slid out of my bed and tiptoed across the floor to the smaller bed on the opposite wall. My heart beat torturously with fear I would be turned away, but why was I here, in the middle of the ocean, if I wasn't prepared to take a risk? I pulled back the covers a little and slipped beneath them, my front pressed against the warmth of his back. My entire body gave a little cry of relief at the connection – the aliveness of his body, the heat, the familiarity.

"Hannah?"

Charles's voice was muffled from sleep, and he shifted, but I didn't want him to move, not really. This much, just this much touch and I felt like a drowning man who'd been thrown a life preserver. "Shh," I said softly. "I was cold."

"Hannah, I— The bed's too small."

"Please don't tell me to leave, Charles. Please."

There was a tense moment where everything in his body, in the air around us, felt taut with indecision. Then he let out a deep sigh and rolled onto his back, sliding his left arm beneath my head so I could curl up against his side.

I nearly wept. I had been so starved of physical touch, I realized. Taking his arm for a stroll, giving Lou a hug… It wasn't the same. It wasn't the same as letting out a breath and letting go of the weight of everything pushing me down. I didn't want to cry, I wouldn't, because I didn't want to jeopardize this tenuous moment by being overly emotional. Instead, I held myself so tightly I thought I might break, barely breathing, wanting this moment to go on forever.

"Better?" he asked softly.

I nodded against his shoulder.

He moved his hand against my shoulder, wrinkling the fabric there, a gentle gesture that gave me hope. He was right that the bed was incredibly small for two people; he was up against the wall and if I rolled to my back, I'd be in danger of rolling clear off to the floor. The result was that I had to be close. It was unavoidable.

"Get some sleep," he suggested. His voice was oddly hoarse. "You need your rest."

I nodded against the soft spot where his shoulder met his chest. And then I relaxed into his embrace, my lip quivering, and closed my eyes.

Chapter Seven

```
April 12, 1912
Titanic
```

LOUISA

I hadn't dared spend the night in Reid's cabin, nor had I let him come back to mine. I was too concerned that Hannah or Charles might hear something or run into him in the corridor. Nor did I want to be sneaking back to B Deck in the middle of the night. He'd escorted me to my cabin – I'd shown massive restraint in making do with a single kiss at my door – and then I'd somehow managed to get myself out of my gown without dislocating my shoulders.

Morning sunlight filtered through the lead glass window and I stretched, basking in it, the sheets caressing my skin. I hadn't even bothered to put on a nightgown last night, instead enjoying the simple, sensual pleasure of sleeping naked. There was no maid to interrupt me, and Hannah would not intrude unless invited.

Besides, all I needed to do was throw on one of my new silk kimonos and I would be adequately covered.

I did not even feel like going to breakfast this morning, which was unlike me. I usually wanted to be where people were, but somehow, after last night, I needed to retreat for a little while. Drop the façade for ten minutes or two hours or however long it took for me to feel ready to face the world again.

Yesterday afternoon's tête-à-tête had been perfect for blowing away the cobwebs of doubt and, well, worry. I closed my eyes and went back there for a few moments, but when I got to the part where Reid said I was worth the wait, my eyes opened again, distracted.

Reid Grey was a flirt and known for dalliances. He was nice, rich, but when all was said and done, he was just a bit of fun. Or he was supposed to be. He'd seemed far too serious yesterday, and I had fallen right into the trap like a bee drawn to nectar. I wanted to desire him. Enjoy him. But I did not want to care for him. He was making that exceedingly difficult.

I rang for morning coffee and when the stewardess arrived, I answered the door in my kimono. I requested she come back in an hour and also asked her to deliver a note next door, telling Hannah that I would meet her for luncheon but was resting this morning. I drank two cups of coffee, then put myself to rights as best I could until the young stewardess returned and helped me dress. It was all done with quiet, polite efficiency, and honestly, it was lovely to not have to make conversation as I would have with Hannah.

I was feeling rather guilty, because I wasn't accustomed to avoiding my friend or keeping things from her. Yes, Hannah and I were planning a week of fun and excitement in New York, but I was there for another purpose, too. One she would not approve of. The funny thing was, I could live with myself and my choices. It was thinking about her disapproval that stopped me up every time and made me revisit my plan and consider—

Consider what? Consider going along with my parents' wishes? Saying the hell with my parents and live on others' charity? I would not, could not, do either of those things. Both options required me to relinquish any control I had over my own existence.

Not even Hannah – sweet, principled Hannah – could get me out of this one. It had gone too far already. And I didn't need her to rescue me. I was perfectly capable of looking after myself. Sometimes, though, being around her quiet perfection illuminated my deficiencies a little too brightly.

I finally felt ready to face the day around ten thirty, but before going up to the promenade for fresh air, I went down a level first, to the Purser's office, and deposited my bag. I no longer felt safe keeping it in my cabin and wanted it – and its contents – secured until I reached New York. Walking away moments later, I felt lighter. The damn thing had been an albatross around my neck. The bag would stay secured until we were ready to disembark in New York. By the end of my week there, I would not have to worry about it. Nor would I need to worry about marrying Bumbling Balcombe. Problem solved.

I had clearly missed breakfast, but luncheon wasn't for another few hours so once again I headed to the Verandah Café for a little sustenance. I didn't need a full meal, nor did I need the more formal setting of the Café Parisien. Oddly enough, I was relieved to find I didn't know anyone else present as I took my chair. I was a social person, but today I craved solitude and space. Outwardly I was fun, slightly outrageous Lou Phillips. For weeks, though, as I put together my plan, secrets had piled on top of secrets and it was starting to wear on me. I hadn't confided in a single soul, nor could I without endangering my reputation or my position within society. There were things one just didn't do. Lines a person didn't cross, man or woman.

But dammit, if I were a man I would not be in this position

anyway. So what if I did what I needed to do to secure my own independence?

Once I'd finished my snack, I decided to wander up to the boat deck and the uncovered promenade there. While the enclosed sections on the A Deck were lovely to keep out the wind, today was mild and spring-like, and I craved the air and the openness of it all.

A number of passengers had the same idea, including those who had brought their beloved dogs on board. I had only been walking for a few minutes when I met an entire family walking their pups.

There was something lovely about seeing a family all together. So often, especially among the richer set, children were cared for by nannies or shoved off to a playroom somewhere. They were to be seen and not heard, perfect little miniatures of adults with perfect manners. How refreshing to see a family strolling arm in arm, smiling and engaged in conversation as if they actually *liked* each other.

I also looked longingly at the dogs, which were attached to leashes and were walked by the children – perhaps twelve or thirteen years old, at my best guess – rather than servants or crew. The lead dog pulled on its leash as if wanting to come say hello. It was all the invitation I needed.

"Oh, an Airedale!" I put out my left hand for a sniff, then rubbed the top of the pup's head. I stepped forward and smiled. "Good morning. I'm Louisa Phillips. Your dogs are adorable." Indeed, a smaller spaniel wagged its tail and looked up at me with large brown eyes.

"William Carter," the man said, "and this is my wife, Lucile, and our children Lucy and Billy."

"Good morning," Mrs. Carter offered with a smile. "A pleasure to meet you."

We chatted briefly, but I couldn't resist. I knelt a little and held out my gloved hand to the spaniel. It nudged up against my glove, looking for pats, big doggy eyes innocent and trusting.

I'd had a dog as a small child, a terrific companion as my brother was away at school and my parents had as little to do with me as possible. I told all my secrets to Millie, and she'd tolerated me putting ribbons around her neck and brushing her soft fur with my hairbrush – at least until Nanny caught me doing it and sat me in a corner for an entire afternoon for using my brush on a dirty animal.

But Millie wasn't dirty. She was my only friend. One of the stable boys found me a brush I could use and every day I ran it over her glossy coat until it shone. Nanny continually checked my pearl-backed brush, but never did find any dog hair.

When Millie died, my father had declined to get another, not wanting the "aggravation." Only hunting dogs were allowed and never in the house. As the Airedale came over to get in on the attention, a little corner of my heart warmed and opened. "Well, hello, you lovelies," I murmured, a smile growing on my lips. "Aren't you both adorable?"

I could just imagine my mother remarking that I'd soil my gloves, and I gleefully added more pats to my and the dogs' delight. A warm chuckle came from above me and I looked up to find Mr. Carter grinning down at me.

"Ah, you are clearly a dog lover, Miss Phillips."

I reluctantly stood, and the Airedale stuck its head beneath my hand and nudged, still seeking attention. "I'm an animal lover in general, but I haven't had a dog since I was a girl. How wonderful you are all able to travel together."

"The children insisted," Mrs. Carter said, smiling. "But truly, our pups are part of the family."

"The Astors took their Airedale, Kitty, with them to Egypt! And Mrs. Rothschild has the sweetest Pomeranian." Lucy spoke up, quite the young lady herself.

I suddenly missed home with a fierceness that took my breath. Or rather, not the home I'd had but the one I'd always wanted. Hannah and I, we'd had the same cold, lonely childhood even though our situations were vastly different. It made perfect sense that she'd seek to create a warm, loving home with a husband and children, just as much as it made sense that I vowed I would never perpetuate the horrible tradition of loveless marriages. At twenty-six, my father didn't even seek to gain any sort of advantage in my marriage. He just wanted me to be someone else's responsibility.

I rose to my feet and smiled again. "It is such a beautiful day. Enjoy your walk. I'm sure I'll see you again. And Miss Lucy…" I leaned forward, and in a stage whisper, said, "A little bacon fat will make your spaniel's coat extra shiny. That and a good brushing did wonders for my Millie."

"Did you have a King Charles Spaniel too?" She looked at me with wide, inquisitive eyes.

"A different spaniel, but with the softest ears. She was my best friend when I was your age." I smiled, my heart softening. I desperately wanted this young girl to feel seen and heard. Important.

"Thank you, Miss Phillips! Did you hear that, Daddy?"

Mrs. Carter sent me a small smile. "Come now, let's finish our walk before luncheon. It was lovely to meet you, Miss Phillips."

"Likewise," I said, and I watched as they continued on their walk, the little dog taking twice as many steps to keep up as the slower, aging Airedale.

"I never would have guessed you were a dog lover," came a deep voice behind my shoulder.

Reid was dressed in perfect finery today, from his impeccable morning coat to his perfectly brushed top hat. The sight of him made my mouth water, because beneath the perfectly tailored accoutrements was a bit of a rogue. It was what drew me to him: this sense that he was not a bounder, that he wasn't a bad man, but he could be, if he let himself. I wouldn't want to associate with anyone who was truly horrible, but I couldn't deny that the possibility of danger was a bit thrilling.

"There's a lot you don't know about me," I replied, sending a flirtatious smile and then turning my back to him again.

"Ah, but I'd like to fix that." He stepped up beside me and we began to stroll. I was happy to see him; how could I not be? And only a little disappointed to miss out on a solitary walk to clear my head.

"I intend to remain an enigma." We passed a couple walking arm and arm, and I nodded while Reid touched the brim of his hat.

"Despite yesterday's activities, you are indeed a mystery," he said, leaning closer as not to be overheard.

My cheeks heated even as the cool breeze brushed my cheeks. "Reid," I chided softly.

"You surely cannot blame me." He took my hand and placed it on his arm, so we were not strolling merely side by side but as a couple. "For wanting more, I mean. I'm entranced by you, Louisa."

My heart surged, but I merely smiled. "Those are very pretty words."

He laughed. "God, I like that about you. You are not easy."

"That's the nicest thing you possibly could have said." I beamed, then stopped, looking out at the sea past the bulky mounds of the lifeboats secured on the deck. There was a bench behind us and Reid led me to it.

I couldn't see as well once we were sitting, but the wind was a little less brisk and I closed my eyes, basking in the spring sunshine. "So," I said, changing the subject, "where were you all morning?"

"Ah, let's see." He lifted his hand and began ticking things off his fingers. "I had a fantastic shave after a hot bath. Divine, by the way. Then I went down to the saloon for breakfast, very disappointed not to see you there, by the by."

"Hmmm."

He grinned. "After that, I wandered around, fairly aimlessly, really. I ran into Colonel Gracie again. He's a fun chap to chat with.

And I saw your friend's husband having breakfast. Expected to see you there, actually."

"I had a lie-in. It was glorious." I was concerned that Hannah hadn't been with Charles, however. I hoped they hadn't had another row.

"Ah. Anyway, I thought about going to the gymnasium, but men's hours are in the afternoon. So I came up to the boat deck and voila! Here you are. Great stroke of luck."

"Is it indeed?"

He stopped and put his hand on my arm. "Miss Phillips, you are playing coy this morning."

I frowned and realized he was right. Not the fun kind of flirtation we'd indulged in yesterday, or even the first night on board. But the kind that was like swatting at an unwelcome insect. Partly a game, partly irritated. None of which was Reid's fault.

"I'm just out of sorts this morning. Pay no attention to me."

He squeezed my arm before letting it go. "Now that I cannot do. What's bothering you?"

"Nothing of consequence." I did not want to make Reid Grey my confidant in any way. We were lovers, I supposed, though it had only been one afternoon of pleasure. That was how I wanted to keep it. When I'd written him about the trip, lovers was what I'd envisioned, and I intended to stick to that plan.

"Where did you go after you left me last night?" I asked, changing the subject. He'd seen me to my door at ten thirty, and while most entertainments finished by eleven, I very much doubted he'd gone to bed that early.

"I found a card game." He grinned. "Low stakes. There are a few others popping up here and there, but they're too rich for my blood. Cardeza likes high stakes." He shrugged. "Saw our pal Colonel Gracie for a few minutes, but he didn't play and didn't stay long. What are your plans for the day?"

We resumed walking toward the stairs. Soon it would be time for me to head to D Deck and the saloon for luncheon, and my stomach growled thinking about it. "Not much, I suppose," I answered. "Luncheon with Hannah and Charles. Then I will probably read until tea-time. I reserved a deck chair, actually. I would much prefer to be outside."

"I never pegged you for an outdoor girl," Reid said, holding out his hand and leading me inside.

I had to admit, I never failed to be awed by the Grand Staircase. At the very top, light glimmered down through the massive glass dome, making the oak and mahogany shine. The elegant iron balustrades and carvings were stunning, and on the A Deck landing, a statue of a cherub holding a torch marked the end of the handrail. But my favourite was the carved clock that watched over all at the very top, crowned by two women, Honour and Glory.

"No detail missed, eh?" asked Reid, noticing my lingering stare at the clock.

"I find it interesting," I replied. "We talk about Mother Nature and Father Time, but here it's the women who have provenance over time, who are crowning it. But not just any women. They are winged. Angels. Beautiful and benevolent. Even… Look at their faces, Reid. They look happy and maybe even … carefree."

He chuckled. "It's a clock, Louisa."

"Oh, but it's not just a clock. That's a clock carved by a man, which has elevated the female form, but clearly Misses Honour and Glory are not of this world. Women would never have such power in the real world."

His gaze settled on me. "Are you sure? Because you certainly had me under your spell yesterday."

I did not roll my eyes. I knew he didn't understand, because no man could. But women didn't really hold any power. That was going to change, though, if I had anything to say about it.

Which I could only do if I avoided marrying Beastly Balcombe. I knew his type just as well as I knew Reid's. He wanted a wife on his arm and then hidden away in the country when she wasn't of use. Balcombe was an intellectual of the worst sort as far as I was concerned. He used knowledge to serve his own purposes, casually disregarding our collective responsibility to those he considered beneath his notice, notably the poor and those of the female persuasion.

But instead of delivering a speech, I looked at Reid, arched a brow, and said, "I am glad to hear it. Perhaps you can now use your influence to help us gain the vote and better working conditions."

"Let me know how I can help."

He did not say it in jest. There, with the clock at our shoulders as we faced each other, he met my gaze as seriously as I could ever remember a man doing. "You actually mean that, don't you?" I asked.

He nodded. "Of course I do. Why shouldn't you have a say in your own future? It's ridiculous. I know a lot of women who are smarter than most men of my acquaintance, and yet they cannot just go out and buy a home or even make the same wage as a man." He frowned. "I know I'm incredibly privileged to live the life I do, and I'm not always fond of the methods that some of these groups use, but I do agree with the message."

I was so dumbfounded I didn't know how to respond. It was incredibly forward thinking … for a man. Reid grinned. "My word, but I think I've rendered you speechless. I didn't think that was possible."

What was possible was that I was coming to care for him very much. There were alarm bells ringing in my head, but they were drowned out by the immense regard I felt. "You have far more substance than I gave you credit for," I replied. "It's a surprise."

"Louisa, I knew why you sent me that letter. I knew what I was getting into. You were looking for a dalliance. A fling. And I was – and am – willing to oblige. But you must know, I care for you as well. I always have. The way you smile, the way you laugh – it lights up a room. I like how you make me laugh and the way we joust with words. I like you, Louisa. And I respect you."

I snorted. I couldn't help it. No man had ever used the word respect with regards to me. Hurt flashed across his face and I suddenly realized he was being completely in earnest. "I'm sorry. I just… This is hard to take in, that's all."

It was nearly time for luncheon, and more passengers were taking the stairs past us and down to the A Deck lifts. We had been in our own little bubble, but this was far too intimate a conversation to risk being overheard.

Reid tugged on my hand and pulled me a bit closer, leaning in. "Don't worry. I know what this week is and what it isn't. I just wanted you to know that I like *you* as much as I like the fun bits."

"Likewise," I whispered back.

He stepped back and gave a nod. "Miss Phillips. Enjoy your luncheon with your friend. Perhaps we shall run into each other this afternoon. Around, perhaps, three o'clock."

My face heated. I knew what he meant, and he knew I would show up. With a final saucy wink, he touched his hat and turned on his heel, taking the stairs to A Deck and then turning a corner, out of sight.

I descended the stairs in a much more measured and contained way, though feeling less composed on the inside.

I could not fall for Reid Grey. Liking him, liking the sex … that was one thing. But this soft feeling that kept coming over me when he said pretty things? Dangerous. And they weren't even that pretty! He didn't compliment my hair or my dress or compare my eyes to the stars in the heavens. There was no lovely poetry or verse he quoted to woo my heart. Instead, when faced with my convictions, his answer was "let me know how I can help."

If it didn't scare the daylights out of me so much, it could make me cry just thinking about it.

Would I show up this afternoon? Of course I would. Yesterday's "exertions" had been sublime.

But would I fall in love with him?

Of course not. I'd make sure of it. Because if he truly knew the real Louisa Phillips, he wouldn't ask to help.

He'd run for the hills.

Chapter Eight

```
April 12, 1912
   Titanic
```

HANNAH

I awakened still held in Charles's arms, the soft linens pulled up to my shoulders, snug as a bug. It was the best sleep I'd had in months, deep and restful. I tried not to stir, as I didn't want to wake my husband and have this fragile moment end.

Carefully, I shifted my head so I could look up at his profile. A day's worth of stubble darkened his jaw, and the furrow that often marred his brow was smoothed in slumber. Even his moustache seemed relaxed, resting on his upper lip, perfectly groomed. I longed to touch it, for I knew the hair was deceptively soft. But that would mean moving, and it would likely wake him. Instead, I took my fill of him with my eyes.

Last night's acquiescence was another step in the right direction, but I knew we had a long way to go. I felt guilty, not telling him about the baby, but I needed to know he cared for *me*, and not just because I carried his child. I wasn't even sure the news would be welcome. Anytime I brought up children after losing our first, I was met with a scowl and a change of subject. If he did say anything, it was "let's not talk about that right now." He came to my bed so rarely it was surprising it had happened at all.

He had been away on a business trip to London and had left me behind, and when he'd come back four days later, he'd spent the evening in his study with a bottle of brandy. I'd never asked why; I was too afraid to know the answer. All I knew was that he'd come to my room just before midnight and the next morning he hadn't wanted to speak of it.

Our child had been conceived out of a liquor-fuelled liaison and not a coupling of hearts. And yet I could not find it in my heart to be sorry. I was afraid, certainly. Losing our son had been the worst thing I'd ever experienced, far worse than losing my mother. The grief had nearly killed me. Of course I was terrified to try again. But I couldn't stop the flare of hope that leaped through my heart at the thought of a second chance. I wanted a family. I wanted to be a mother. Was it selfish to want a happy marriage as well? I didn't think so. My parents had been happy, at least what I remembered. There'd been laughter and smiles for certain. And we'd done things together, too, as a family. I wanted that so keenly it hurt.

Was it wrong to want to know that he cared for me, and not just because of a baby? I didn't want him to know yet. I wanted us to find our way together first so that during the months ahead we could rely on each other.

I remembered hearing my father talk to my uncle after my mother died. "She was my beating heart," he'd said, his voice broken as they sat at the dining table with a bottle between them. "We faced everything together. I don't think I can do this without her."

I so wanted that with Charles. Not the devastation, but facing things together. We'd been tested once and failed. This was our second chance in so many ways.

His eyes fluttered and then opened, staring directly into mine, making my heart leap with hope.

"Good morning," I whispered, offering a small smile.

"Good morning." He frowned a little. "Rather tight quarters."

"Cozy," I corrected, though his observation cooled the warmth I'd been feeling inside.

"It was rather cold," he admitted, rising up on one elbow. I was on the outside of the bed, so he couldn't really get up until I did, and I wanted a few minutes longer. Beneath the warm covers. With his body closer to mine than it had been in weeks.

"I slept so very well once you warmed me up." I curled up against him, felt him stiffen. Why, oh why did he react this way? It made my heart want to weep. "You're so lovely and warm, Charles."

He let out a breath. "Yes, well, I suppose we should get up and get ready for the day."

"Do we have to?" I touched his shoulder, lightly but intimately. "There is nothing pressing today. We're on holiday, remember? At least until we reach New York. We could ... spend the entire morning in bed if we wished."

His cheeks flushed. "Hannah..."

"We used to, remember? When we were first married?"

I remembered those days. Our love had been new and fragile, but we'd taken the time to let it grow. Charles had never been one to declare his feelings by shouting from the rooftops, but there had been stolen moments when we'd wanted nothing more than to spend time together.

"Couples are supposed to do that on their honeymoons," he answered, smiling a little.

"Then perhaps this can be a second honeymoon for us." The finger I'd been running along his shoulder slid over to his chest, which was covered in the thin material of his pyjama shirt. His breath hitched, a subtle but real reaction. "Wouldn't you like that?"

"Hannah, please stop this."

"Stop touching you? But you're my husband."

He pulled down the covers and scooted over me awkwardly, getting out of bed. There was a telltale tent in his pyjama bottoms that said he'd been affected by my touch, at least. He turned away and reached for his dressing gown.

We were on our third day now and I felt as if I were getting nowhere. We'd have good moments that gave me painful hope and then it would all be dashed as he withdrew. I gave him openings so he could talk to me about his feelings, which he either ignored or deliberately misinterpreted, proceeding to change the subject entirely. I didn't want to give up, but the back and forth was exhausting. I was tired, I finally admitted to myself. Tired both of trying to make something out of what probably no longer existed, and tired on such a basic physical level from the changes happening inside my body.

I thought of Lou, in the cabin next door, and wondered what Lou would do. She was made of such strong stuff. She wouldn't have fallen apart like I had, spent months in a fog of grief. She would have taken some time, of course – anyone would – but then she would have bucked up and got on with it in her own inimitable way.

Charles had moved to pour a glass of water from the pitcher and I stared at him, the weight of inevitability pressing down on me. This trip that I'd been so sure would mend the rifts between us was no miracle excursion. It was possible that the damage was too great. Beneath the coverlet, I touched my belly, thinking about the baby inside.

"I had drinks with Weir again last night," Charles said. "He has some interesting ideas. He's got a lot of experience. His friend

Henry joined us. Great Irish bloke, with a lot of metallurgical experience. Oh, and Miss Phillips's friend Mr. Grey was there."

Business. He was changing the topic to business. I didn't know whether to be absolutely incredulous or horribly annoyed. Or both. I did know I was frustrated beyond belief. I was tired and slightly nauseated, as I was every morning, but tried to ignore it as it usually rectified itself with some tea and food. But this morning, after I'd got my hopes up and had them dashed, I bit back.

"John Weir associates with Guggenheim, you know. And that man is travelling openly with his mistress. Is that really appropriate company?"

My snap took him by surprise and his face flattened. "It's business. I do not care about their personal lives, and neither should you."

"Fantastic," I replied calmly, throwing off the covers and rising from the small bed. "If you have no such qualms about Ninette Aubart, then you can hardly object to my close relationship with Louisa, who is beyond reproach."

He snorted. "She's a suffragette."

"So is Margaret Brown, and you don't seem to mind her friendly overtures."

Stymied, Charles went to the wardrobe and began removing clothing for the day. It was his classic response: to turn away and busy himself with something else to avoid talking. I slid my feet into my slippers and followed him. "Also, Louisa isn't openly sleeping with a married man. So I expect you to be the very soul of amiability around her for the rest of the journey."

His lips twisted in consternation. "Really, Hannah, is this conversation necessary?"

I took a deep breath. It wasn't like me to argue or poke or prod, and the fact that this was the second time I felt pressed to do so spoke volumes about my level of irritation. "You changed the subject, not I." I reached around him to pluck a skirt from the wardrobe. "You refuse to talk to me about us, so this is sadly the consequence."

"I don't like quarrelling." He held a snowy white shirt in his hands, and his gaze met mine. "I don't know why you're so irritable lately."

"Don't you?" I sighed. "Charles, I have wanted to talk to you about our marriage for days now. We are on the grandest ship in the world for the better part of a week and you insist on being polite and then talking business rather than about anything important." I took a deep breath, in for a penny, in for a pound. "I miss the man I married. I miss the couple we were. But it does seem as though that has changed and we cannot get it back. Correct me if I'm wrong."

He flinched, as though my words had struck him, and I felt badly for it. I never wanted to hurt anyone, but cajoling, fawning, pretending ... nothing was working. As Lou would say, sometimes only honesty would do, even if it hurt. Of course, she'd said that to me when she'd particularly disliked a shade of silk I'd chosen for a new dress, but the sentiment held water, in my opinion.

"Of course things have changed," he replied, his jaw tightening. "How could they not? If you think we can go back to before what happened happened, you're a fool."

I hadn't actually expected him to admit it. He couldn't even say the words "before the baby died." That horrific event was now reduced to "what happened." I nodded my head infinitesimally, absorbing what he'd just said.

A wave of nausea washed over me, stronger than usual. I must have paled because Charles's hard expression softened and concern filled his eyes. "Are you all right?"

"I'm just queasy," I admitted. "But do not trouble yourself. I don't feel like breakfast today, Charles. You go on without me. I think I shall rest a bit."

"You shouldn't be seasick," he reasoned. "The crossing has been so smooth."

"There are a lot of things I shouldn't be." I tightened the belt on my peignoir. "I'll be fine. You go."

He hesitated, as if considering, then sighed. "Very well." He wasn't even going to fight for us. Even after being mostly honest with him, he chose to walk away than face our problems.

I got back into my bed as he finished dressing, and then he spared me a glance. "Get some rest. Ring a stewardess if you need anything at all, or send a note to find me."

"I won't," I murmured.

A pained expression crossed his face, and for a moment I thought he was going to say something more. That traitorous flicker of hope fluttered awake in my breast, but Charles turned and walked away, out of the cabin, shutting the door quietly but firmly behind him.

Tears stung my eyes, and I curled into the covers. I didn't cry often, but I indulged myself in this moment, because I truly couldn't see a way out of my predicament. Charles had never been further from me.

I must have fallen asleep, because it was late morning when I opened my eyes, gritty with unshed tears. There was still no sign of Charles, and with tears shed, I was left with an emptiness that felt even worse. I got out of bed, rolled my shoulders, and, not caring how I looked, went to Lou's door and knocked three times.

"Coming!" she called from the other side, her voice faint.

A few moments later she opened the door, looking perfectly put together. There were roses in her cheeks, and a sparkle in her eye that told me she had perhaps run into Mr. Grey already this morning. Her face fell as she met my gaze. "What's wrong?"

I shut the door between our cabins, then turned to her, lifted my chin, and finally told the secret I'd been holding close for weeks now.

"I think my marriage is over, Lou. And I'm pregnant."

Chapter Nine

April 12, 1912
Titanic

LOUISA

"Oh, no." I immediately wished I could take back the words. In an instant Hannah bristled, her nostrils flaring in an uncharacteristic show of anger. I rushed forward, taking her hands in mine. "That's not really what I meant," I said, while a million thoughts and feelings raced through my head and heart. "I think what I should have said was, 'oh dear, what a mess,' because, well, it is. I mean, if having the baby is what you want. Dammit, I'm making a hash of everything. I'll shut up and let you explain."

What I didn't expect was for Hannah to burst into a flood of tears.

Hannah was the steady one. She wasn't prone to bouts of

emotion on either side of the spectrum. She didn't rage, neither did she weep. She had a remarkable capacity for control and "just enough" passion for someone to realize she felt deeply without it being a show. She was the soul of propriety. For her to cry so now told me without question that she was at the end of her pitiful rope.

"There," I soothed, holding her in my arms. She pressed her cheek against my shoulder as sobs quaked her body. "Get it all out, darling. Oh my, this is why you've been so intent on fixing your marriage. How long have you known?"

"A-a-a few m-m-months," she hiccupped, catching her breath.

"And you didn't tell me?" I held her by the shoulders and pushed her back enough that I could look into her tear-stained face. "Oh, poppet. Why ever not?"

I was hurt. I probably shouldn't have been, but Hannah and I had always said through thick and thin. I had been by her side the last time, week by painful week. I could only imagine how alone she must be feeling, but all the same, it stung knowing she hadn't trusted me with this news. The fact that I was keeping my own secrets poked at me, sitting uncomfortably behind my breastbone. How could I judge Hannah when I wasn't even close to being honest with her? And what did that say about our friendship?

"I-I wanted to be sure," she replied, scrubbing her hands over her face. "I thought what if I lost it again or... I knew you would treat me like glass, and I didn't want that. I wanted to feel normal."

She was right. I probably would have babied her ridiculously. I was right to be afraid for her; it wasn't just the baby who'd been in danger that night, but her as well. She'd lost a shocking amount of blood. Cold settled over me at the thought of this happening again.

"You're right. I would have fussed and hovered, and I shall probably do that now, too."

"You mustn't." She sniffed and I went to fetch her a handkerchief. She blew her nose and then looked at me with narrowed eyes. "You really mustn't, Lou. I am not an invalid."

"Come." I took her hand, led her to one of the chairs by the small table, and took a seat opposite her, pulling the chair close. Her nose was red and her cheeks a little blotchy, but she looked as determined as I'd ever seen her, and that was a relief. "Han, if I get protective it's just because..." Tears welled in my eyes. I didn't cry often, but the memories of those horrid days would never leave me. "I almost lost you that night. Not just your little one, but you, too. It frightened me so badly. It still does. It lives here." I pressed my hand to my heart.

"I know. Charles and I certainly weren't trying to do this again. Not that I didn't want to. It's just that since then, he barely touches me."

I wrinkled my nose, perplexed. "What do you mean, barely?"

She shrugged, her gaze sliding away.

"You mean you aren't intimate with each other? Ever? Clearly you were once."

Hannah swallowed and then bit down on her lip. "Only a few times."

I got up from my seat, hands on my hips. "Wait. You're telling me you've only slept with your husband a few times in the past two years?"

"My God, Lou, not so loud. Oh, I shouldn't even be talking about this. It is so improper."

"Poppycock." I sat back down and took her hands again. "Who can you tell if not your best friend?"

"My very *unmarried* best friend."

"Dearest, I know how these things work." Knew better than she could imagine, not that I was about to divulge that bit of information. My word. Hannah was having a baby.

I brought my thoughts back in line. "All right. Let's start at the beginning. You are expecting a baby... When?"

"Late October, I think," she answered.

"And this trip, this attempt to heal your marriage..." It all sank in. What she hadn't said but had to be true. "Charles doesn't know."

She shook her head. "Of course not. I had wanted to take this trip so that we could maybe"—she gave a sharp inhale, then let it out on a shaky breath—"get things back to where they were before."

"Before the baby died," I clarified.

Her gaze held mine, and in her eyes I saw relief, not pain. "Thank you for saying it that way. I'm so tired of dancing around it, using words and phrases that cushion the reality of it. My baby died. I'm pregnant again. My marriage is a mess, and I desperately wanted to fix it before embarking on this a second time."

"You must be so terrified." I was terrified for her. I couldn't imagine how she must feel.

"I am," she nodded, squeezing my hands and then letting them go. "But Lou ... I'm more afraid of the loneliness eating me up until there's nothing left of me. I know you don't like Charles, but when we were first married, we were really happy. It was a quiet life, but we talked and laughed and spent time together. We slept together every night. After the baby died, he said he would stay in his room because I needed my rest. He never came back. And what I needed was him."

Rage filled me so that I was burning with it, but I tamped down the fire. It was not what Hannah needed right now, not from her best friend. There would be time to rage later, and I would, make no mistake. "I take it things haven't improved," I said, trying to tread carefully.

She shook her head. "Oh Lou, I've tried everything. I tried being kind and thoughtful and pleasant. I tried to be perfect, in all the ways that he likes. I invite him in, but he turns me away. He won't talk to me about the baby. He changes the subject every time I bring up our relationship, and this morning..."

She broke off, her lip wobbling. Seeing her trying not to cry over it only fuelled the fire burning inside me. "What happened this morning?"

She shuddered, then cleared her throat. Bless her, she was trying. I was so very glad she was finally talking about her troubles. Keeping it all inside was never good. I only had to look at myself and the stress I carried each day to know that.

"Last night he came in and went to bed in the small bed," she confessed. Her cheeks turned pink again. "I tried to sleep, but then I went over to him and said I was cold and got in bed with him."

I held my breath. Clearly something had gone wrong, and I didn't want to interrupt. Hannah was about to share something deeply personal, and I worried that if I said anything she might not reveal the whole story.

"It was so nice, Lou. To know he was there next to me, to feel his warmth and hear him breathing. Even the odd snore." She smiled sadly. "This morning, when we woke, I thought for a moment we might…" She broke off, blushing yet again.

"Reconnect," I supplied, providing a rather banal euphemism.

"Exactly. But when I touched him, he couldn't get away from me fast enough." Tears welled in her eyes, but they were not just tears of sadness. I recognized the glint behind the moisture. She was angry, too. Of course she was. How humiliating.

"The bastard," I muttered.

"Lou, really." A wrinkle formed between her eyebrows. I had heard Hannah swear possibly twice in her life. If "bloody" even counted as swearing. I had to remember to curb my tongue around her.

"I know you don't like it when I curse, but Charles is a damned fool," I declared with a firm nod. "You're lovely. You really, really are. I ought to shake some sense into him."

The idea must have struck Hannah funny as she began to laugh. "Oh Lou, if I thought it would do any good, I'd let you have a go at him. But it won't. I need to face it. He doesn't love me anymore, not in the way he used to." Her lip wobbled again. I could see she was trying not to cry, and my heart broke for her just as surely as my outrage burned.

Stupid Charles bloody Martin. How dare he? Effective or not, it would be eminently satisfying to let him have it. Right in the bollocks.

"He does not deserve you," I said instead.

She gave a soft snort. "You have always been my biggest champion. Oh, I do feel loads better for having told you. But Lou, what do I do?" She placed her hand on her abdomen. "I am terrified. I don't know if I could survive the same devastation again. Not without him."

"First of all, you have me. That will never change." Even as I said it, I knew I couldn't offer guarantees, and guilt wound its way around me, squeezing like a snake crushing the life out of its prey. I pushed the thoughts aside to be dealt with later, keeping Han as my main focus. "You feel all right? Things have been okay?" At her nod, I let out a breath. "Good. There's no reason to think this will happen again, is there? What has the doctor said?"

Hannah got up from the chair and walked over to the sofa, picking up a pillow and needlessly fluffing it. The cabins were lovely but there really was nowhere for her to hide. Though I suspected she wished to.

"Han?"

"I confirmed it with the doctor," she said, avoiding my gaze.

I wanted to smack my head. She absolutely should have told me sooner. This was foolish, and to not ask about the risks? That was Hannah in denial. "Confirming you're expecting and discussing the risks you might face are two very separate things, dearest. Listen, I understand that you don't want to hear if something's not right—"

"It must be all right." The firmness of her tone set me back for a moment. This wasn't something she could control, but she was trying her damnedest.

"You need another appointment. If you don't want Charles to know, you can see a specialist in New York. It'll all be quite confidential."

She nodded, and I realized something more: Hannah needed someone to take control of the situation, just a little bit, because the burden had become too much for her to bear alone.

I got up and went to her, wrapping her in another hug. "Darling, you asked what you're supposed to do, and I don't have all the answers, but what I do know is this. You are a strong woman, stronger than you think. You are not alone, either. Charles, for all his faults, would not consider divorcing you even if he has fallen out of love. No, listen," I insisted, as she shook her head at that last awful truth. "He will see you housed, clothed and fed. Material things don't feed the heart, but they do keep you in comfort. You will have this baby, and you will love it so much you'll want to kiss its tiny fingers and toes every hour of the day. His or her Auntie Lou will spoil them rotten, and you as well. And you will build a life, and it will be a good life."

Hannah nodded, her eyes brimming.

"I am so sorry it has come to this," I offered, wishing yet again that I could crown Charles for being such an idiotic man. "Please do not let what's happened with Charles define your entire life, darling. You have so much to offer. Besides, I cannot possibly do without you. So we'll muddle on together."

"You as Mrs. Balcombe?"

I gasped and put my hand to my chest in a dramatic gesture. "Never!" I laughed. "We'll save *that* topic for another day. Right now, you need to wash your face, get dressed, lift your chin, and go with me for coffee and the most delicious pastries you've ever eaten. Forget the dining saloon, I'm taking you to the Verandah Café for lunch."

Hannah squeezed me tightly. "What would I ever do without you, Lou?"

"We'll never know, now, will we?" I said, squeezing back and then letting go. But as I went with Hannah to choose her clothing for the day, I knew that if she had even an inkling of what I was planning, she might not want to be my friend at all.

Chapter Ten

April 12, 1912
Titanic

HANNAH

Lou made sure I was turned out beautifully. This morning I decided to go with lighter colours and a fresh appearance to perk up what had become a rather heavy mood. Lou was wearing a green skirt with a broad sash that nipped in her white lace blouse and accentuated her trim waist. Her hair was in a loose roll that gave it a slightly softer look and before we left, she topped it with a straw hat with silk roses and a green ribbon that matched her skirt.

I chose a skirt of soft, pale peach, with a snow-white blouse perfectly fitted across my shoulders and breasts, which had recently become larger in pregnancy, a fact that I did not complain about as I'd always been rather lacking in that department. I dressed up the blouse with a pink and cream cameo at my throat, one of the few pieces of jewellery I'd kept of my mother's. We selected a straw hat for me as well, one with flowers a slightly darker shade than my skirt and a romantic trail of white tulle cascading over the back of the brim. I had to admit, the soft, pinky-peach hues set off my complexion beautifully. As Lou helped me with buttons and bows, she noticed that my corset was fitting a bit looser than normal, and there was a little bubble at my belly.

"Look at you," she said softly, as I pulled on the skirt over my petticoats. "You're glowing, Han. Even if this isn't exactly how you wanted things, I'm happy for you."

"Thank you," I said, smiling a little. "I feel better now, having told someone." Indeed, it was as if a weight had been lifted off my shoulders. "It's like that old saying: a burden shared is a burden halved, or some such thing."

"Of course you feel better. You must have been feeling so alone. You needn't. Not ever, you understand? All you ever have to do is send for me, and I'll come. Always, Hannah."

I squeezed her hand, feeling closer to her than I had for weeks. Something had been standing between us, and I didn't want to think it was my secret, but perhaps it had affected our friendship more than I'd anticipated. Either way, it felt like old times as we chatted and laughed on our way to the A Deck and the café.

"Look, the Fortunes are here," Lou said, and we stopped by their table to say hello. At another table was Renee Harris and her husband, Henry, theatre owners from New York. Lou introduced us, and when I mentioned we would be staying at the Belmont, Mrs. Harris immediately invited us to dinner and a Broadway show at one of their theatres.

"Do you know everyone?" I whispered to Lou as we moved along toward an empty table.

"Hardly, darling. But I do make the rounds during the day. You realize the whole idea is to see and be seen, yes? You can't do that always hiding in the Reading and Writing Room."

"You're far more gregarious than I," I whispered, as we took our seats.

Now that the morning nausea had abated, I realized I was starving. We ordered pastries and coffee and tea and I asked if there were any strawberries, as they would taste especially good.

"Well done," Lou said, after the steward had departed.

"It's just strawberries," I replied, fiddling with my linen napkin.

"It's not," Lou protested, "Hannah, you have always been the 'go along to get along' girl, never asking for anything extra or wanting to put anyone out. I know why. We both felt in the way as children. Lord knows we both craved love and affection. You never ask for anything because you try to please everyone. And I'm the opposite. I don't care to please anyone but myself. Does that make me selfish, do you suppose?" She wrinkled her nose.

"Not selfish, exactly," I said, though it didn't sit quite right with me. How did one go through life without caring what others might think, or wanting to make things better for them? And yet Lou did care for others. I knew that by the way she supported me, by the way she tried to improve the world for other women. It was a bit confusing, when all was said and done. "We just act differently, that's all. There's been many a time I wished I was more like you, Lou."

She laughed. "Likewise. My mouth is always getting me into trouble. Maybe that's why we're such good friends. Maybe we balance each other out."

I put my hand over hers. "Now that's a lovely thought." It was certainly much better than thinking we were drifting apart because of our different perspectives. I didn't want to lose Lou; she meant so much to me. That didn't mean she wasn't occasionally frustrating.

Our tea and food arrived, and for a few minutes we were busy adding milk and taking first bites of light-as-a-cloud pastries. Lou had just started on her second when she let out an excited scream. "Elsie!" she called, lifting her hand, a smile lighting her face. She turned to me, her eyes dancing. "I knew Elsie Bowerman was on board, but our paths have not crossed until now. That's her mother with her, I think. Edith."

They came in our direction. "You'll love Elsie," she said. "She's a suffragette, like me. Stupendously smart. She got a second class at Cambridge."

My eyes widened as the women approached. Lou made introductions while I felt horribly intimidated. Elsie Bowerman reminded me of Lou, actually, full of vigour and passion and a youthful energy I was quite envious of. She, too, was a member of the WSPU, and for several minutes the two compared "notes" of recent happenings. When it became clear they were dominating the conversation, Lou sat back and deftly shifted the topic to other things: the *Titanic*, New York, and then we shared a few stories from our days at St. Hilda's. Our laughter attracted others until we were quite a party, and we moved to the first-class lounge where we could mingle and socialize more easily. It was, I realized, the most fun I'd had on the ship thus far, made more enjoyable by the spontaneity and freedom of it all.

Lou leaned over once and murmured, "This is how it should be, Han. These women ... they support other women. Not just the Elsies and Mrs. Pankhursts of the world, but women like Renee Harris and Helen Churchill Candee and the Fortune sisters. There's a sisterhood out there waiting for you. I promise."

"Won't they think I'm dull?" I asked, being serious. "My life is not exciting at all. I haven't done anything important. The women you're describing ... they're all trailblazers." I didn't want to admit that trailblazing was not the life for me. It was just ... so much.

"You have time to do something, if that's what you wish. But Hannah, you're charming and lovely and welcoming and fun. God knows we need women like you." She turned to face me. "Darling, you are the type of woman that makes us feel less alone. You're needed. I need you."

Ship of Dreams

I was going to cry, right here in the middle of the first-class lounge around all these wonderful people. Lou sensed it and so backed off, nudging my arm in a teasing motion. "All right, enough wibbling. Come on. I see Lady Duff-Gordon and I am going to introduce myself shamelessly and tell her I adore her designs."

Before I could form a response, she had taken my gloved hand in hers and started tugging me along to an immaculately dressed woman with glossy dark hair, an impressive string of pearls, and the most spectacular hat. My straw boater was darling but looked provincial in comparison.

I hung behind Lou as she made introductions. For a few moments, Lady Duff-Gordon's face reflected boredom and, well, it was clear to me she was looking down her nose at Lou. I would have been happy to move on – one should not perhaps meet their heroes, I thought – but then Lou said something witty and Lady Duff-Gordon's face softened and a smile flirted with her lips.

Gossip was, of course, the order of the day, and while I tuned out a lot of it, my attention was drawn back by the words "jewel thief." I stepped closer to Lou, curious.

Lou was nodding seriously at Lady Duff-Gordon and a few other ladies who had joined the circle. "You know," Lou said, "Mrs. Brown lost a bracelet. She thought she lost it while we were on deck at Queenstown. Now I wonder."

"A few other items have gone missing, too," someone said. "I heard Mrs. Allison asking the purser if anyone had found a necklace. Apparently the clasp had a tendency to fail."

Lady Duff-Gordon nodded. "Cosmo said that last night, one of the men in the Smoking Room was missing his pocket watch. Weir, I think he said."

I perked up at that. Charles had been drinking with Weir. "And he never found it?"

"I haven't heard," she said, apparently enjoying the gossip but otherwise unconcerned. "I don't usually pay attention to what the men get up to."

"Amen," came a voice, and a few others joined in soft laughter.

"Still, we ought to be on our guard if someone is targeting our valuables." This came from Renee Harris. "I suppose keeping things at the purser's office makes the most sense. Locked up safe and sound."

A watch, a bracelet, a necklace. We'd only been on board a few days and things had gone missing. For at least two of those items, I knew of one person who had been present. Reid Grey. Charles had mentioned him being in the Smoking Room last night. I looked askance at Lou, whose face was alight with interest at the gossip but showed no concern at all.

"Excuse me, if I might borrow Miss Phillips for a moment," I said, then pulled her aside.

"Are you all right?" she asked, her smile slipping. "Feeling all right?"

I sighed and rolled my eyes. "This was also one of the reasons I didn't tell you," I whispered. "I knew you would hover and fuss."

"Sorry. What's the matter, then?"

I wasn't sure how to broach the topic, so I tread carefully. "Lou, how well do you know Reid Grey?"

Her cheeks coloured, which was unusual. I had never seen her blush over a man before. "Why do you ask?"

I hesitated, knowing I really had no grounds to accuse someone based on the flimsy fact that he was merely in the right place at the right time. "I just... I have an uneasy feeling about him, Lou. There's something I don't trust. I don't want to see you get hurt—"

"I won't." Her response was clipped and short.

"I know you can take care of yourself," I admitted. "But as this morning showed, we do worry and care about each other. It has to go both ways, you know."

She dropped her shoulders. "I know. I'm sorry for bristling like that. The truth is, I find myself caring for Reid more than I intended. It was supposed to be a simple flirtation, but I quite like him, Han." Her eyes were wide and truthful, the smile on her face a bit self-deprecating.

Her confession did not assuage my concerns; in fact they only increased. "I ask because... Hear me out, please. The other morning when Mrs. Brown lost her bracelet, I thought back to when we were all together. Out on deck, the only person to shake her hand was Mr. Grey. She knew everyone else. Last night, Charles was in the Smoking Room with Mr. Weir, and he said Mr. Grey was there, too. And now Weir has lost his pocket watch." I twisted my hands nervously. "I just..." But I didn't finish the sentence, because I realized how foolish I must sound.

"Reid Grey is far too principled to be a jewel thief, and I'm not that gullible, Hannah. It's a coincidence, nothing more." She waved her hand as if swatting away a fly.

"Well, how long have you known him? The way he looks at you, I don't like it. How can you be sure you can trust him—"

Lou silenced me with a sharp look. "You can't start accusing people of a crime just because you don't like how they look at someone," she said firmly. "I've known Reid a few years, I suppose. Socially. That's all. And he has no reason to steal anything. He's got his own fortune."

She said it and then got a distant look in her eyes that I couldn't quite place. It was all quite worrisome. Especially her staunch defence of him. "Are you in love with him?" I asked.

"Will you leave it, please?" she snapped, her voice barely above a whisper. "You need to trust me, Hannah. Reid Grey is not a jewel thief. Now, could we please try to enjoy ourselves?"

After our earlier closeness, I felt thoroughly chastised, though I probably deserved it. Reid was a sore spot, I could tell, but I wasn't helping Lou by poking at it. I'd made her uncharacteristically cross, which only worried me more. Just when

I thought we were getting closer again, I said something that fractured that peace.

Lou straightened and smiled brightly, her countenance completely changing before my eyes. The effect was staggering. I knew she had an ability to mask her emotions, but I had never quite considered how thoroughly she could adopt a persona. "Hello, darling!" I heard her say, as she stepped forward to greet Mabel Fortune again with a kiss on the cheek. "We got separated there for a time. Let's have a proper chat."

Without her saying one more word, I understood that the subject of Reid Grey was closed.

It did absolutely nothing to dispel my misgivings.

Chapter Eleven

```
April 13, 1912
   Titanic
```

LOUISA

I laid awake in the dark, listening to Reid breathe deeply and rhythmically beside me. He had an inside cabin, and without a window, I missed the first weak rays of dawn that must be lighting the April sky. I couldn't be sure of the time. What I did know was that we'd still been awake at midnight, and after a fitful sleep, I'd now been awake for what felt like at least an hour, thinking. There were no sounds of people in corridors or any sort of bustling about. Honestly, it was a bit claustrophobic in here. I wondered if I could sneak out of the bed and back to my own cabin before most people awakened. It would be a chance, as there was bound to be one or two passengers who liked early morning strolls on deck. But perhaps better now than later.

The bigger problem was that despite feeling constrained, I didn't actually *want* to leave. I could not ignore the fact that Reid Grey was not the simple diversion I'd hoped he would be. I was in real danger where he was concerned, and it was something that I'd said when talking to Hannah that had provided a brilliant yet terrifying solution to my problem. It wasn't what she'd said about him being a jewel thief; that idea was utter tosh. It was the reasoning I gave for his innocence: that he had more than enough wealth of his own. As soon as it left my mouth my brain had kicked in and said, "Why not marry Reid? Then you won't need your father's money and this ridiculous plan of yours could simply … disappear."

The fact that it was so tempting sent alarm bells pealing madly. Marriage was definitely not on my agenda, and I didn't love Reid. I couldn't possibly. We had met a handful of times prior to this week, flirted shamelessly, and obviously had thought about each other as I'd sent the call and he'd answered, booking himself a ticket for a trip he didn't need. Chemistry we had in abundance. But love?

He snuffled and rolled to his side, his calf sliding deliciously alongside mine.

What kept me lying awake was not remembering the sex – which I had to admit was very, very satisfying – but the way he talked with me, looked at me. He was interested in what I had to say, and perhaps it was just talk, but he even supported my ideas. We spent at least as much time talking about the silly and the serious as we did in bed.

In short, I was having feelings. Big ones.

The kind that made me reconsider everything.

The kind that were so unlike me I felt utterly knocked for six.

Reid's breathing changed. He was waking, and I lay quietly, unsure if I wanted him to know I was awake or not. He curled around me, sliding a hand around my waist and sliding it up to rest on my breast, and I sighed with pleasure. Why, oh why, did he have to feel so *good*?

"Good morning, love," he murmured against my shoulder, and I shivered. His lips curved – I could feel the smile against my skin – and then he kissed the soft spot just below my neck. I wondered what it might be like to wake each morning like this. Then I thought of women like Helen, Margaret, Elsie. All fighting for women's rights without husbands or the protection of marriage. Did thinking about those things, marriage and such, make me somehow less dedicated?

And then I thought of Emmeline Pankhurst, married to a man who supported her causes, and knew there was no one more fervent about our rights than she.

Of course, there were a few other obstacles in my way. Like the original plan to avoid needing to wed at all, the means of which were now safely secured in the purser's office. And the fact that Reid also understood that this trip was for an affair, a fling. Love, marriage, was likely the last thing on his mind as well. As Royden once told me, I was a great girl for a lark, but men married women like Hannah.

It wasn't the truth of it that stung. It was that a week after he'd said it, I discovered he'd proposed to a lovely second daughter of an earl and they were going to be blissfully happy. I didn't mind affairs, but I drew the line on affairs with committed men, married or otherwise. Their wives and sweethearts deserved better.

"You're thinking awfully hard for so early in the morning," he murmured against my neck, and I shivered again, not sure if I was aroused or amused and realizing it was probably a bit of both.

I certainly wasn't about to admit to my feelings, but we had become closer over the past few days. He'd taken me to dinner at the à la carte restaurant last night, where we'd drunk champagne and lingered over the most decadent, beautiful food under glittering lights. We'd dined intimately *a deux* while gazing into each other's eyes and anticipating the night ahead. Our time together also kept me out of Charles's orbit, which was probably a good thing. I was still hugely annoyed at the man and my mouth was likely to get me into trouble. I didn't care about vexing Charles, but I did not want to cause Hannah any anxiety.

I realized, in hindsight, that Reid Grey had been wooing me. The concept was so very sweet I didn't quite know what to do with it.

"I was just thinking about what happens next," I admitted, rolling over to face him, even though I couldn't really see him in the darkness. "After New York, I mean. I plan to have a marvellous time with Hannah while we're there. She deserves some excitement."

"You love her very much."

"Like a sister, only maybe better. Without the sibling rivalry or rows."

He laughed, pulling me close and twining our limbs together. "That I understand. My brothers and sisters and I drove our nanny and our parents crazy with our bickering. We get on well now, though."

"My brother is older than I am, and dull as ditch water," I confessed. "Anyway, when we return from New York, I need to have a serious conversation with my parents."

"About Bossy Balcombe."

I chortled at the new incarnation of the nickname. I'd told Reid about the pressure to marry Balcombe and how his very conservative expectations of a wife were absolutely unacceptable. As if I ever planned to truly obey anyone.

"Yes, about that. I'm sure he'll make someone a rather good husband, or something. But that person is not me. I am dreading the conversation, though. My father threatened serious repercussions if I didn't settle down and behave." I rolled my eyes even though Reid couldn't see them.

"He'll cut you off financially."

"Yes, exactly."

Reid propped himself up on the pillows and then tucked me in against his shoulder. "I'm assuming you have a plan."

"I do. Nothing I can share right now, but—"

"Can I help?"

"I doubt it."

He was quiet for a long moment, and then his voice came, husky in the darkness. "What if you married me, instead?"

I stilled, flooded by a dichotomy of emotion that put me even more off balance than my earlier thoughts. Traitorous elation that he'd asked – sort of – and deep disappointment that he'd done something so predictable as to try to rescue me.

"That long silence isn't encouraging," he said softly.

"I'm sorry." I pushed away and sat up, holding the sheet to my chest. "Dammit, can you turn on the lamp? It's so dark in here."

He sighed, then rose and a few moments later a soft glow filled the room. Now that I could see, I stared at his naked form as he came back to bed and got under the covers with me. I was normally comfortable with nakedness, but right now I felt exposed and vulnerable. Since we were in his cabin, the only clothes I had were the ones I'd worn last night. I really should have snuck back to my cabin. Treading the decks in last night's attire was sure to create comment.

"I'm sorry," Reid said, interrupting another thought that had not quite taken root in my brain. "I know this was not what you planned for us on this trip, and I didn't either. I came for a spot of fun and adventure, really. But now that I really know you, Lou, I realize how much I care for you. I like you, so very much."

Like, not love. I wasn't sure if I should be relieved or disappointed.

"And I like you too, Reid. You're not entirely wrong, you know. We've become rather close, and not just in bed."

He lifted his hand and brushed a lock of hair behind my ear, the gesture so tender and sweet my heart gave a little lurch. "You're an incredible woman. I would be lucky to have you as a wife."

"You say that until you have to come get me out of jail when I've been arrested for chaining myself to the House of Commons," I quipped, half serious.

He laughed, the rich sound rippling over my skin. "Darling, you should know by now that I like a bit of scandal and adventure. That's why I'm here, isn't it?"

Scandal and adventure. Very early on, I had dismissed the idea that creating a scandal was a solution, that if I wanted to be taken seriously I needed to cling to at least some of my respectability – being involved in the movement was enough scandal all on its own. But the longer I thought about it, the more I had reservations about my original plan. Making connections in New York was key, but it certainly meant forsaking any sort of moral high ground. Then there was the question of Hannah. How would I explain my absences? What if my efforts didn't produce the kinds of results I needed?

"I suppose," I mused, "that getting caught walking out of your cabin in last night's gown would cause a stir. Certainly, if it reached Balcombe, any thoughts of a wedding would be off."

I was teasing, because ruining my reputation would definitely solve the marriage problem but not the "what would I live on" problem. Reid, however, was uncharacteristically unamused. His face tightened and his nostrils flared just a little, and I realized he had been serious in his proposal, even if his words had been slightly flippant.

"Sorry," I murmured, unsure of what else to say.

"I suppose I am good enough for a fling, but not good enough to marry," he said, a sour edge to his tone.

He wasn't angry. He was hurt. I understood that defensive tone; I'd used it enough myself. I slid out of bed, feeling horrible that I'd hurt him, and reached for his dressing gown, which I wrapped around myself. It smelled of his soap and skin.

"I thought you were teasing," I said weakly, going to a nearby chair and sinking into it. The silk upholstery was slippery against the robe, and I struggled to get comfortable.

Reid got out of bed and pulled on a pair of trousers, leaving his chest bare. Stubble shaded his jaw; he was in need of a shave, but I liked this slightly rough look. A knot of anxiety centred in my stomach at the way he looked at me. Not with anger, but with love and hurt.

I shook my head. "Reid, we've been on board three days. This is ridiculous, don't you think?" Couldn't he see that we were a long way from even considering something serious? Besides, hadn't I made it clear that I was not interested in marriage?

"You might think so, Lou, but we've always had a connection, you and me. And not just sexual. We've exchanged letters for months."

"I—" I faltered, tensing. "That was … entertaining."

"Men and women don't write to each other for no reason, Lou. I've been falling in love with you from the start."

He'd said it. He'd said the word love. No, no, no.

He loved me.

And now he was standing before me, in trousers and mussed hair and a day's worth of stubble, telling me so, after asking me to marry him in a non-traditional way in the middle of the ocean knowing very well there was nowhere I could run.

Panic bloomed in the centre of my chest.

"I can't," I said, my words strangling on their way up my tight throat. I got up from my chair and started gathering my things from the floor of the cabin. They were strewn everywhere, a fun game at midnight when we'd swigged from a champagne bottle and flung items of silk and cotton far and wide in our haste. I found my combinations and stockings, tried my best to put them on while still being mostly covered by his dressing gown. "Why did you have to ruin something so lovely by talking about love? You don't even know what that is."

He came to me and put his hand on my arm, stilling my frantic motions. "I do know," he said softly. "And so do you. That's what's got you so afraid."

I scoffed. "I am not afraid of anything."

God, what a horrible liar I was. I was afraid of everything and had spent years acting as if I wasn't. It had worked well for me, up until this moment.

Reid turned me by my arm until I was facing him and tilted up my chin with a finger. "You are terrified, darling. Promise me you'll think about it. We could be so good together."

Me, married to a London banker, probably living in Mayfair or some other posh neighbourhood. Maybe neighbours with my father, wouldn't that be a gas? I wouldn't want for anything. I could shop at the best stores. I would run my own household. And Reid had hinted that he wouldn't mind my extracurricular activities – like staging a female revolt.

No, it was all too perfect. Fairytales did not exist. Look at Hannah and Charles, for God's sake. Lovely people, lovely marriage, then boom. Tragedy, heartbreak, a perfect marriage shattered. Hannah's heart was broken. Though all our talk of the other wonderful parts of her life had cheered her, we both knew the truth: this was a wound that would never really heal for her, and I'd be damned if I'd go through the same.

"I don't want marriage," I said clearly, stepping away. "I thought you understood that."

"Every woman wants marriage," he scoffed, scowling at me. "Honestly, Lou, if you could get out of your own way for two minutes, you'd see that we have something special. Not just chemistry, but affection and fun. Conversation and ideas."

But I shook my head, reaching for my corset, struggling to put it on, determined to manage somehow without him touching me. "Not every woman wants to get married, Reid. That's an asinine statement to make." Everything was a mess as I floundered with my dress, finally getting it somewhat straight. I couldn't reach the last buttons, but if I put my wrap around my shoulders, it would hide the ones undone. Reid didn't offer to help. I think he knew I would only refuse.

I had to get out of here. I pulled the silk wrap over my shoulders and shoved my feet into my shoes. It wasn't far, if I could be fast. Down the grand staircase, across the open area of the first-class entrance, through the doors and down the hall. Maybe no one I knew would see. Maybe they'd all be aft, at the café, or outside catching the morning air.

"Lou," Reid said, a final plea in his voice. "Don't go."

"I have to." I knew how tempting his offer was, how part of me wanted to scream yes, and how he was right: I was terrified. I did not know a single, happy society wife. That sort of union represented everything I did not want to become.

He stepped back with a nod. "It's been fun," he said, a final jab that went right to my heart.

With tears stinging the backs of my eyes, I went to the door and cautiously opened it. Then, cheeks blazing, I scooted down the hall.

I walked down the stairs and through the entrance area as if I owned the place and was dressed in an appropriate suit for morning wear and not an evening gown with pearls…

I touched my neck. My pearls were not there. I closed my eyes as I reached the baize doors leading to the hallway and cabins beyond. My grandmother's pearls, and now they were with Reid. They had to be. Because last night he'd commented on loving me wearing those pearls and nothing else.

Dammit.

I entered my cabin and shut the door with a quiet click. It was barely half-six; I'd got three, perhaps four hours of sleep before getting into it with Reid. I was exhausted. I'd worry about the pearls later. Right now I just wanted my bed, and I pulled down the covers and fell into it, fully dressed.

Chapter Twelve

April 13, 1912
Titanic

HANNAH

The voyage was half over, and it felt as if so much had happened and yet nothing had happened at all.

I knew I should be lapping up all this luxury. Fine china, beautiful music, glittering lights, beautiful dresses, sparkling jewels. It was all something out of a fairytale, really. Everyone seemed happy and gay and carefree, floating on this palace of iron and coal. For my part, I was trying not to be miserable. Nothing was going as I'd hoped.

Currently, I was preparing to take tea with Mrs. Brown again. She had proved to be a bright spot and delightful company, her candor refreshing and her warmth making up for what some might consider rough edges. We were to meet in the reception room outside the dining saloon in ten minutes, but I was early. Charles and I had not spoken of our row since yesterday morning. This afternoon he had decided to take advantage of the gymnasium, as this was the time reserved for the men. I didn't want to be relieved, but I was. Our conversations were polite and stilted. We spoke of the day's weather, how fast the ship was going, and what entertainments we might like. When the highlight of your conversation was discovering there were wagers being laid on the *Titanic*'s daily speed and distance covered, you knew your marriage had moved firmly into the realm of polite strangers. I was trying to come to terms with that.

Mrs. Brown descended the stairs to my left and I put on a smile. I was doing my best not to be sad and instead focus on what I could make of my life rather than what I had lost. Lou's boundless energy and optimism had guided me in that direction. I had gaffed there as well, though. She hadn't liked my questions about Mr. Grey, and last night the two of them had eaten in the restaurant rather than the dining saloon. I hadn't seen her today, either. My knock on her door this morning had gone unanswered, and I'd called a stewardess to help me dress and fix my hair.

All in all, I was feeling a great amount of dissatisfaction as Margaret Brown approached and held out her hands.

"Mrs. Martin," she said, her voice projecting into the cavernous space. "I'm so glad you could join me."

"Me, too," I replied, trying to shake off my doldrums.

She gave my hands a squeeze and peered into my face. "Well, now. You're looking a little down in the dumps, dear. Let's get some tea and cakes and set the world right again, hmm?"

How could one resist the force that was Margaret Brown? If I could imagine Lou in twenty years, she'd be much the same. Confident, unapologetic, and kind. I hated that we were at odds right now.

The tea was scalding hot and the sandwiches and cakes

perfection, but the true enjoyment of the afternoon was the company. I felt as if I were making a true friend as Margaret shared stories of her humble beginnings and what it was like moving to the upper crust of Denver society. I reciprocated by admitting I often felt a fraud in this sort of environment, as a solicitor's daughter. "We certainly weren't poor, and my father was able to send me to a nice school. But even Lou, as unconventional as she is, flourishes amongst the nobility, and her papa is only a baronet."

"Don't let titles intimidate you, Mrs. Martin. You know, I've never understood the British fascination with titles and rank, as if they were somehow one's accomplishment for the simple act of being born. I'd take ten of your husband for any baronet or earl or prince. He's a good man. Smart, and hardworking. He's made a success of himself."

Pride swelled in my chest. The fact our marriage was changing didn't stop me from loving Charles or being proud of his accomplishments. Hearing him praised by others was a lovely thing.

"He has," I agreed, popping a *petit fours* into my mouth. I dabbed my lips with my napkin and took a sip of tea. "Mrs. Brown—"

"Margaret, please."

I smiled. "Then you must stop calling me Mrs. Martin. Hannah will do."

"Agreed."

"I wouldn't normally do this, but I … I don't know who else to ask, and your situation being what it is…" My cheeks heated. Was I really considering airing my dirty laundry to a stranger? And if not a stranger, a new friend? This sort of thing was always kept private. No one talked about marital troubles. It just wasn't done. It was one of those things you gossiped about with others but never revealed yourself.

"Hannah, you can ask me anything and I promise it will go no further."

I looked down at my lap but then forced myself to look up. If I were going to be honest, I must also resist feeling shame.

"How did you know it was time for you and your husband to … to lead separate lives?"

Surprise flashed through Margaret's eyes, but then they softened with compassion. "Oh, my dear. I never would have guessed things were troubling you both. I thought you were just showing that famed English reserve."

I tried to smile. "English reserve? Have you met Lou?"

Margaret laughed. "Good point. She's a firecracker."

"Sometimes I wish I were more like her." I reached for my tea, hiding behind the cup.

"Why?"

I looked up, surprised at the question. "She's beautiful and articulate and passionate and commands attention. Who wouldn't want to be a dynamic creature like her?"

"That's all well and good if you want to command attention. But why should you be anyone besides who you are?"

I didn't know how to answer that. I'd always felt so lacking. So … grey against her vibrancy.

"Mrs. Martin— Hannah, sorry, here's what I've learned about confidence. It's the result of something, not the cause. When people are self-assured, it's because they know, deep down, who they are and what they stand for. It's right in the term, self-assured. Assured in themselves. When that happens, confidence radiates. Now, there are those who inflate their sense of importance, and that's not confidence. That's arrogance. You only have to be Hannah Martin. You only have to be true to what is important to you, in here." She put her hand to her heart. "You do not need to be another Louisa Phillips. The world already has one of those. You just need to be you."

I let the words sink in and tried to accept them as truth.

"As far as your question," she continued, brushing some scone crumbs off her lap, "I don't know if there was ever one thing that led us to the moment we made the decision. I find it hard to believe, though, that this is the life you want for you and your husband."

"It's not," I admitted. I chanced a look around the room. Others were taking tea, smiling, laughing, nibbling on culinary delights and sipping from their dainty teacups. I couldn't imagine anyone having this private or serious a conversation in public, but perhaps it was the activity around us that provided a bubble of security. "Mrs.— I mean, Margaret, the truth is, I lost a baby two years ago and nothing has been the same since. I spent so long grieving that I ignored my marriage completely. And when I finally resurfaced, the husband I knew had been replaced by a polite stranger."

Margaret didn't reply. It turned out she was also a good listener.

"For the past several months, I've tried to talk to him about it, to get us back to where we were before, but he's not interested."

"He's said this?" she interrupted briefly, her brows pulling together.

"In every possible way I can think of," I replied. "But the problem is, I'm expecting another child. After the last time—"

I stopped, my throat suddenly too tight for me to continue.

"You poor girl," Margaret said, her strong voice suddenly soft with compassion. "You must be terrified. Does he not want the baby?"

I swallowed past the lump, took a sip of tea to wet my throat before answering. "I haven't told him. I was so hoping to get us back to normal before giving him the news."

"Hmmm."

She didn't say anything after that, which was unsettling. "Hmmm?" I asked. "Perhaps I should have told him the moment I knew, but is it wrong to want him to ... to love me, not just because of a baby?"

"Oh darlin', of course not." Margaret reached out and patted my hand. "And you might be right about your marriage. If you are, you'll just have to reach inside and corral all your inner strength. Hell, most women I know are in marriages where love has little or nothing to do with it. Not that I don't think you deserve those things, you do. I'm just saying, you're stronger than you think. We all are."

Lou would have said the exact same thing. She had, really, as well as insisting that she'd always be there for me.

"A practical marriage," I filled in.

"Exactly."

"Even if it's not what I want."

"Harder when you've had the real thing and it goes away, isn't it?"

I nodded.

The steward came by and cleared our dishes, so our conversation halted for a few minutes. When he was gone, Margaret leaned forward. "Hannah, it's my experience that men can be infuriating." I snorted a laugh because her eyes twinkled as she said it. "But I also know that much of the time, they prefer contracts and ledgers to talking about feelings. That doesn't mean they don't have any. I'm sure Charles had to grieve the loss of your baby, as well as watch you suffer in the months following. That has to be hard on any man who loves his wife, and you did say he loved you, yes?"

I thought back to those early days. "He did. I know he did." For once, I did not second-guess myself.

"Listen, dear, I don't know how you fix it, if it's even fixable, or how you know if you should move on. I wish I did. But the one thing I do know is that you need to tell your husband about the baby. He'll find out eventually," she said, giving a chuckle. "But tell him. Keeping secrets never helped anyone heal anything. My mama taught me that."

I nodded. While Lou had given me good advice and was a solid friend, Margaret had the wisdom of years behind her. "My mother died when I was small," I confessed quietly. "I have often wished she were still here to help me through this tangle. I hope you don't take this the wrong way when I say this afternoon felt like having a mother's guidance."

"Heavens no," she replied, beaming. "Indeed, that's a great compliment. Now I'm doubly glad I invited you for tea."

"Me, too," I said, relaxing in my chair. "May I also say that I am not sure I'll be able to fit in any of my clothes once I arrive in New York? The food has been simply splendid. We have a fantastic cook, but I've never eaten like this in my life."

"Hannah, you deserve all the good and lovely things in the world," Margaret said, her face warm with affection. For me. The idea wrapped around me like a cozy shawl. "I hope you get them all."

We chatted a little longer about the entertainments on board, about life in America, about New York in particular, all peppered with Margaret's ineffable charm. Before I knew it, it was going five and time for me to head back to our cabin. I wanted to check in on Lou, too. It was unusual to not see her at all during the day. If she were spending her time with Reid, so be it. I had tried to be a good friend and express my misgivings as I did not want to see her hurt. Truthfully though, in a matter of days we would be in New York and Reid Grey would be ... elsewhere.

Margaret and I departed with an air kiss beside each cheek, and I made my way to the lifts to go up to B Deck and our cabin. Her words had hit home, and I mulled them over as I ascended. Would it really be best to tell Charles about the baby? How would he react? He came to my room so rarely that I had come to believe he was no longer interested in having a family. What if he were upset? The last thing I wanted to do was create more discord while we were stuck on a ship with no escape.

When I got back to the cabin, Charles was absent, so I went to the adjoining door and knocked, firmly. When there was no answer, I knocked again, harder. Ten seconds later the door opened, and Lou stood in the breach, dressed in a plain skirt and blouse, her hair a tangle around her shoulders and her face devoid of any powder or cosmetics.

"Good heavens," I said, shocked at her appearance. More shocking was the telltale rim of red around her eyes. She'd cried today, which immediately got my attention. Lou never cried. At least ... hardly ever. Things had to be very bad for her to resort to tears.

"Come in," she said, stepping back. I went into her cabin, and she shut the door behind us. "I would rather Charles not interrupt and see me like this," she said, letting out a sigh.

"What on earth is wrong?" I took her hands in mine, rubbing my fingers over her cold ones. "Are you ill? You should have sent word. I would have come."

She laughed, but it was a mirthless sound. "My only affliction has been self-pity, Hannah. Don't fret. I've been feeling utterly sorry for myself all day long."

"But why?"

She shrugged. "I know you don't like Reid, so it's a bit of a touchy subject."

I pulled her over to the sofa and sat down beside her, turning so our knees touched and I could still hold her hand. "What's he done?" I demanded. "Oh, I knew he'd hurt you—"

"I hurt him," she interrupted, pulling her hand away. "He ... um, proposed."

I sat back, speechless. Proposed? They'd been inseparable the last few days, but marriage? It was laughable, really. Lou was so determined not to get married, and this had been a whirlwind romance if it could be called a romance at all. "He really missed the mark, didn't he?" I asked, shaking my head. "Anyone who knows you at all knows you're not interested in getting married."

"What if I were?" she asked, and I stared at her in shock.

"You never said yes," I breathed. Then I remembered the red

eyes and limp hair and clothes and reassured myself that she had not, indeed, accepted his offer.

"No, I did not. And then I came back here and hid in bed all morning. I finally made myself get up and have a hot bath and called for some coffee and a sandwich."

Hid in bed all morning. Came back ... here. I lifted a hand to her face and brushed away a tear, then tucked a golden strand behind her ear. "You spent the night?"

She nodded miserably. "I did. Oh Hannah, please don't give me a lecture."

"I won't." My conversation with Margaret was still in the back of my mind. She'd shown no judgment this afternoon, only empathy. I could certainly extend that to my closest friend, even if the idea of her in Mr. Grey's bed was ... well, it wasn't shocking, even though perhaps it should be. "I've suspected you've had a few affairs over the years. It's been the one area of your life we've never talked about."

"Nor shall we. I'm not a woman who kisses and tells."

"I'm glad you've been discreet, at least." I didn't want to know about the others. I also didn't want to pass moral judgments, but it was a fact that Lou and I saw very differently on this matter. Charles had been my first and only, and our wedding night had been my first time. I couldn't imagine sharing my body with another man without the benefit of marriage. While I was trying very hard not to judge, it didn't mean I approved. "All right. Why the tears, dearest?"

I listened as Lou told me about how Reid had proposed they marry instead of her marrying Balcombe, a solution to all her problems. "It's not that it wouldn't work. It would, of course. But how could he even suggest it if he knew me at all? Ugh! The only thing worse than marrying that odious little man is knowing that the man you married did it out of pity and as a way to rescue you."

I flushed, the heat climbing my neck and into my ears. Charles hadn't technically rescued me, and we'd cared for each other, but there'd also been an acknowledged truth in that I was in my early twenties, running my father's dreary household and desperate for a life of my own. Charles had provided me an escape and I'd been glad of it.

Lou, though, was the kind of woman who needed to create her own escape. She needed to do things on her own terms. I knew that came from living a life that was heavily dictated by her parents.

"Anyone who knows you at all knows that is the last thing you want. No white knights on trusty steeds for you, darling."

"Exactly." She let out a massive breath. "The problem is, you see…"

She stopped, and I waited. Whatever was coming was bound to be one of Lou's truth bombs. They weren't always bad, nor were they always good, but they were, every single time, the absolute truth.

"I think I'm falling in love with him, Han."

Nothing she might have said shocked me as much as that. She rested her elbows on her knees and put her head in her hands. "How could I have let this happen? It was supposed to be all fun and flirting! A way to pass the time. I wasn't supposed to have *feelings*. He wasn't supposed to be this wonderful!"

A part of me wanted to laugh. I had often wondered if Lou would ever fall in love or meet her match in that department. Now here we were. My laughter impulse, though, was quickly subdued, as I still had misgivings where Reid Grey was concerned. His proposal had done nothing to allay them. I didn't trust him at all.

"It's awfully fast, darling," I consoled her, putting my arm round her shoulders. "A whirlwind, really. We're in the middle of the ocean, for heaven's sakes. No one would blame you for being swept away in the romance of it all."

"I've told myself the same thing."

Relief slid through me.

"But I don't think that's it, Hannah. I really don't. There's something about him. Always has been. Spending this much time together might have sped things up, but our attraction has always been there, simmering."

"Marriage takes more than simmering passions." I rubbed her back in little soothing circles. Here I was, thinking perhaps she'd come down with a cold or that her stomach was acting up from all the rich food, or perhaps it was her monthly. I'd even considered she'd been under the weather because of overindulging in the champagne last night, something that had happened a time or two before. But felled by love? I would never have guessed.

"I know," she wailed, and I rolled my eyes a little at how dramatic she was being.

She looked up from her hands. "He was right about something. We've been corresponding for months. Oh, just little letters full of inane stuff, but entertaining. We like each other. If it was just sex, I could dismiss it in a heartbeat. And I just hate myself for thinking maybe this *is* the perfect solution. Swap Balcombe for Reid, have a comfortable life with a man I quite possibly adore."

I sat back. "Lou, I love you. I admit I'm quite surprised at this revelation and the last thing I would ever want to do is make light of your feelings. But darling, the idea of you and a comfortable life? You'd be bored within ten minutes."

"I know," she wailed again, and then shook her head and gave a little growl. "Good God, what is happening to me? This isn't me. I don't get lovesick."

"Spending the day in bed is proof otherwise," I said calmly. Though I would not say it out loud, dealing with Lou's surprising trials of the heart allowed me to take my mind off my own, and gratefully. I got up and went to the water pitcher, poured her a glass, and returned to the sofa. "Here. Drink this. I'm going to get a cold cloth for your eyes."

She drank the water and then sat back, letting me place the folded cloth over her eyes and forehead. "That feels nice."

"I have never seen you so worked up," I said, walking about the room and picking up errant bits of detritus. I paused with my hands holding stockings and a single glove. "I mean, I've seen you full of avenging purpose as you head to some gathering or another to slay the patriarchy and demand women's rights, but never have I ever seen you fall apart over a man. I'm not sure if I should feel sorry for you or enjoy the moment for what it is."

She slid the cloth up from one eye, grabbed a cushion, and threw it at me.

I laughed.

She cracked a smile even as she covered her eye again.

The smile slipped, though, and she sighed. "I can't marry him, Han. You're right, of course. A comfortable life like yours would make me miserable. It's the very thing I've vowed to avoid. Look at us. What a pathetic pair we are, our love lives a complete and utter shambles."

I put the pile of clothes and a pretty choker necklace I'd found on the floor onto the end of her bed. Then I went and took the cloth, rewet it with cool water, and returned. Her last words unsettled me; I didn't want mine to be a complete and utter shambles. "Charles and I are nothing like you and Reid," I responded, still feeling the sting of her comment.

"Of course not. Though I've never understood what you see in a life in the country. Why you would choose that mundane existence for yourself."

I stared at her. "Ouch, Lou. I'm fighting to keep that life you insist is so undesirable."

She shook her head. "Sorry."

"I don't want the life you have." I left her with the cloth and went to sit in the chair, folding my hands in my lap. "I'm not even sure you want yours. Sometimes I think you do it just to spit in your

Ship of Dreams

father's eye. You always feel the need to rile him up so and then get angry when there are consequences."

Lou stared at me, the cloth forgotten in her hand. "What's got into you, Hannah? That was rather ... pointed."

"You want me to be more like you. But maybe I would like it if my dearest friend would settle down and we could raise our children together. I just don't say it because I know that's not what *you* want."

"Are we ... arguing?"

I sighed. "I don't know. I don't want to. And this doesn't mean I want you to marry Reid. I just think that sometimes you get in your own way with these things."

Lou stared at me for a few moments. "All right. I get your point, even if I don't like it."

"I don't want to argue either. We're supposed to be supporting each other."

She nodded, tears glistening again. "I'm sorry for what I said about your marriage."

"And I'm sorry you're hurting, Lou. That's what this is, you know. You're just so used to ploughing through and doing things that something like this knocks you for six. Now, here's what we're going to do," I said firmly, quite enjoying taking the reins for a little while and bossing Lou rather than the other way 'round. "You're going to call a stewardess to help with your hair, because it's beyond my capabilities. I'm going to bring my things in here, and we're going to get ready for dinner. Then you're going to dine with Charles and me. I know we're not the most invigorating company, but we're family, whether Charles knows it or not." I leaned over and gave her knee a pat. "What you need is a good meal, some delightful music, and stimulating conversation, which we'll undoubtedly find throughout the evening."

"Hmph," she responded, but there wasn't much annoyance behind it. It was her "I'm capitulating but pretending I don't like it" sound, one she'd used many a time in school when I'd come up with a plan to keep her out of trouble with the school head.

I reached over and removed the cloth, which was now somewhat warm. Her eyes looked a little soothed, and by the time we were ready for dinner, no one would know she'd spent the day in emotional distress. I worried, though, because I had no doubt that her dilemma was real. She did have feelings for Reid, and that was what made refusing his proposal so difficult.

"Give it time," I suggested softly. "If he really cares for you, he'll give you time to sort out what it is you want. He lives in London, right? You said you've been writing for months. There's no rush, darling. Give yourself space to feel all your feelings and think all your thoughts." I could never sound as wise as Margaret Brown, but my words were heartfelt and that counted for something. "If, when we get back to England, you decide Reid is what you want, then let him know. There's nothing wrong with not leaping into something headfirst."

Lou sat up quickly and enveloped me in a strong hug. "You are the truest friend that ever lived," she said, squeezing. "And that is such good advice. I spent the whole day feeling like I'd broken his heart, or that he didn't know me at all, or that I couldn't possibly be in love. I went in circles, Hannah. Horrible, dizzying, aggravating circles. But you are right. I do not need to know right now. If Reid Grey loves me as he says, he'll wait for me to sort out my mind. And heart."

"Exactly."

She gave a short laugh. "It comes as a slight relief to discover I have one."

"I never had any doubt."

"And I truly am sorry we quarrelled."

I was too. Not only because of what was said, but because it meant that we truly did value different things. I was determined, however, to not let it change our friendship.

"I'm going to arrange everything for dinner," I said. "You pick out what you're wearing. We don't have a lot of time to get ready."

She gave me a salute, and my heart lightened. The storm had passed, and she was on the upswing again. I slid into my cabin and found Charles already there. He took one look at my dress and lifted an eyebrow. "I heard your voices. I thought you were getting ready." He stood in front of the mirror, fiddling with his necktie.

"Sorry. Lou was under the weather this afternoon." I moved to the wardrobe to pull out my newest outfit, the one I'd bought to make the biggest splash. The Poiret number shimmered as I held it aloft, the work of thousands of beads painstakingly sewn into vibrant flowers along the hem of the tunic bodice and again along the edge of the slit that ran up the front of the cream silk skirt.

I turned to Charles, who was watching me curiously. I thought briefly about all that Margaret had said this afternoon, and then about my advice to Lou. Perhaps I, too, should think on my next steps and not rush to let the proverbial cat out of the bag. "Lou is joining us for dinner in the saloon tonight," I said.

"Just Lou?"

"Not Mr. Grey, if that's what you're asking," I replied, keeping my voice mild.

"I see."

"She has had a rough day, Charles. I was thinking a quieter, low-stress dinner might suit us all for tonight."

My wardrobe choice didn't exactly reflect that sentiment, but I didn't care. Charles was being distant; Reid was being stupid, at least in my view. Tonight was really about Lou, and me, and shining in our own right. Why shouldn't we? We could deal with the problem of the men later, in our own time.

"I'll be here to escort you both when you're ready."

Knowing his dislike of Lou, I recognized the generosity in his words. I went over and pecked his cheek, reminded of Margaret's statement that Charles was a good man. Just because our relationship had faltered did not mean he was not a man of character, and when the chips were down, he was steady.

"Thank you, darling. We'll try to be quick."

I gathered the rest of my things – shoes, stockings, and my new emerald and pearl earrings – and slipped back into Lou's cabin, to prepare for the night ahead.

Chapter Thirteen

```
April 13, 1912
   Titanic
```

LOUISA

I was never so glad to see my best friend in my entire life. The way she'd cared for me this afternoon – listening to my woes and even fetching a cold cloth for my eyes – had meant more than she would ever know. I had friends and acquaintances, of course, but no one I absolutely trusted like Hannah.

I didn't deserve her. I probably never had, but now more than ever, I knew that no matter the situation, Hannah would always act with a core of morality that was impossible to live up to. I loved her for it, but it did have the effect of making one feel rather awful about oneself. At the same time, I didn't understand how she could be so dedicated to a life where the dreams and achievements were not her own but her husband's. I might be smitten with Reid, but I would never be content to be in any man's shadow.

She must have said something to Charles, for I couldn't remember him ever treating me with such courtesy, even when I'd been to stay during the darkest days of Hannah's grief. His blue gaze had been exacting when we'd stepped from my cabin into theirs; I must have either passed muster or he felt incredibly sorry for me. I didn't really want Charles Martin's pity, but it did remind me that despite us not getting on, he was still a good person.

The dining saloon was not quite as glamorous as the restaurant, but that did not mean it was lacking in a single thing. I was, I realized, starving, and happy to partake of the evening menu's delights. The fish course was sublime, the roast duck succulent. Hannah spoke of her day; Charles, of the gymnasium. It was bland conversation but not unbearable. It was exactly what I needed to regain my footing. We nodded to new acquaintances; sent smiles to others we'd met during the past three days. It was, as Hannah might have said, very pleasant. While I often detested the word – I hated mediocrity – pleasant was exactly what the doctor ordered while my mind was in such a chaotic state.

I was perfectly at ease until Reid came in with Sloper and they sat at their table.

My insides froze as I looked at him. Instantly I remembered the earnest look in his eyes as he'd spoken of his feelings this morning and the hurt reflected back when I'd refused. The creamed carrots congealed in my mouth and it was difficult to swallow, but I managed it before reaching for my wine glass to wash away the suddenly bitter taste.

Hannah looked at me, turned slightly and saw Reid and his dinner companion, then turned back, reaching beneath the table linens to give my leg a reassuring squeeze.

I smiled faintly, appreciating her care and loyalty.

"You look stunning tonight, by the way," I said to her. "I knew you wouldn't regret the Poiret number."

"I'm terrified I'll get something on it," she confessed, but she sent me a sweet smile and her eyes gleamed.

"How much did that set me back?" Charles asked, popping a bite of squab into his mouth.

"Now, Charles, you should never ask that sort of question. It's like asking a woman's age. Whatever you're imagining, go lower, and everyone will be happier." I lifted an eyebrow.

To my surprise, Charles smiled and reached for his wine. "On the contrary," he said. "I was going to say it was worth every penny. You look lovely, Hannah."

"Oh, my." She pressed her hand to her chest. "I'm not sure I can manage all these compliments."

"You deserve them and more," I replied staunchly. "Why, even Madeleine Astor herself won't be dressed this fine tonight, you mark my words."

The white and ivory ensemble suited Hannah's pink-and-cream complexion perfectly, and the tunic top flattered her figure. But the true glory was in the details: the feminine drape across the bodice and shoulders, the vivid beadwork and colourful belt at the middle adorned with roses and leaves.

Charles reached over and took her gloved hand. "You're an angel, darling," he murmured. "Truly."

They gazed at each other so long that I felt as if I were intruding. I wondered if I should skip the final courses and disappear, but I didn't know where to go. I didn't want to be alone right now, and I certainly didn't feel up to making glittering small talk. I didn't even want to delve into political matters, something that usually sparked me right up. What in the world was wrong with me?

I cleared my throat. "I believe I'm in the mood for the French ice cream tonight. What do you think?"

Hannah looked over at me, her eyes shining. "I think ice cream is perfection."

We lingered a while, but after dinner, as we left the saloon and paused in the reception room, Hannah pulled me aside.

"Darling, I was wondering if... That is, I think this might be a good time to tell Charles about the baby." She had leaned close so she was almost whispering. "But if you want me to stay, it can absolutely wait. You've had a horrible day."

I didn't want to be alone, which in itself was a warning that all was not right in the world of Lou. But I also wanted Hannah to grab chances when she saw them, and I agreed with Margaret Brown: Hannah couldn't be sure of anything until Charles knew the whole truth. The fact that he'd seemed warmer tonight than in recent days meant she might have a good window of opportunity.

"I could use some fresh air after that dinner," I replied, squeezing her arm. "I won't be out late tonight, though. If you need me later, come knock on my door." I would certainly be there. My extracurricular activities had come to an end. No more sneaking around. No more late nights and risky moves. I would be the soul of discretion and respectability at least until we reached New York.

"You're sure?"

"I'm fine," I assured her. When we'd left the saloon, Reid and that Sloper fellow were still on their sixth course. I really could use the breeze on my face and the vastness of the sky to help me gain some perspective, because seeing him had been harder than I'd expected.

She kissed my cheek. "All right."

"Remember," I said, looking her dead in the eyes. "Knock if you need anything at all. And good luck, dearest. I think you're doing the right thing."

"If it all blows up in my face, I may end up bunking in your spare bed," she replied, a shadow passing over her face.

"And you would be most welcome. It would be like old times, just like it will be in New York. You just wait. We're going to order room service and have a grand time of things. And then I'm going to take you shopping and we're going to buy something splendid for the baby."

She looked over at Charles, who was chatting with another passenger I didn't recognize. Her face softened. "If he turns away, it'll break my heart, Lou. But I won't let it break me. Just you wait and see."

Brave words. I wasn't entirely convinced, but I admired her resolve. More than that, I hoped that Charles would dig the stick out of his posterior and realize what a gem he had in his wife.

We parted at the lifts for B Deck, and then I went up one more level to A and the promenade. Tonight I stayed on the starboard side and stayed toward the bow, close to the first-class lounge. I didn't want to wander far. I just wanted to feel the wind in my hair and have some quiet space to really think about my next steps, because this thing with Reid? It was making me reconsider everything I thought I knew. Everything I had planned.

It was cool, and I was glad I'd thought to bring my velvet opera coat with me to dinner, just in case we decided to venture out of doors. It wasn't heavy, but it did ward off the worst of the chill and the fur at the collar and cuffs added warmth. I turned my face into the wind and wondered how fast we were going; we seemed to cut through the waves like a hot knife through butter, gliding over the ocean with barely a dip or crest. Charles had filled us in on the current wagers for speed and distance. I knew now that we were cruising along at twenty-one knots at least and that yesterday we had covered over five hundred miles, a mind-boggling distance. Rumour also had it that Captain Smith had increased our speed and that we might even reach New York ahead of schedule.

I didn't care so much about it, but I could understand how others found it exciting. It wasn't the speed or the prestige of it that impressed me, it was knowing that the sooner we reached America, the sooner I could rid myself of what was in my satchel and breathe a sigh of relief as that part of my plan came to a close.

I was making a mental inventory in my head when a voice interrupted my thoughts.

"Good evening, Lou."

We'd quarrelled and I'd walked away, but that smooth, low tone still sent shivers down my spine. I closed my eyes, wishing I didn't want him so much. Wishing that this could have been just a bit of fun rather than awakening all these confusing feelings.

With a bright smile, I turned and said, "Hello, Reid."

"Have you forgiven me, darling?"

I raised an eyebrow. "Is there something to forgive?"

He huffed out a laugh. "Touché."

I sighed and turned away, facing the railing again. I didn't want to feel this warmth in his presence, like everything was somehow all right. It wasn't. If he knew what I'd done... If he knew that I'd chosen something illegal over marriage to him to move forward in my life, he'd regret ever confessing his feelings. He'd regret ever meeting me.

"Do you hear that?" he asked, coming to stand beside me. "Just the faintest strains. The music in the lounge. It's lovely, is it not?"

I could hear it, once I listened for it. They were playing a waltz I recognized, "A Thousand Kisses," and I found myself swaying a little to the melody.

"It does make one wonder," Reid mused. "Why they have such a fantastic group of musicians, and not one dance floor. I suppose it would be considered a waste of space, but it's the *Titanic*." He grinned. "Everything is big and ostentatious."

"It does make you want to dance, doesn't it?" I said, humming along a little.

"So dance with me, Lou."

That frisson of delicious nerves shuddered over me again. I wanted nothing more than to be in his arms, but that would only get me into trouble. I laughed lightly instead. "We're outside on the deck. Don't be daft."

"Who cares?" The song changed, but into another waltz, one I didn't recognize but with the same one-two-three sway that made my feet itch. I did love to dance...

He reached for my right hand and lifted it, curling his fingers around mine. It was the most natural thing in the world to slide my hand to his shoulder while his found my waist.

We stopped talking then, as if conversation would mar this perfect moment in time. Instead, we performed a truncated waltz, abandoning the sweeping turns and wide steps and instead taking shorter, intimate ones with our bodies close together. Once he lifted his hand and turned me in a circle beneath his arm before pulling me close again, and my breath caught in my throat as our eyes met. A million stars twinkled overhead, an inky, glittering ceiling above our pine dance floor.

I'd been swept off my feet more than once over the years, been the recipient of some grand gestures and glorious gifts. But nothing was as precious and beautiful as dancing on the *Titanic*'s deck on a cold April night with a man I was fairly certain I'd fallen in love with.

How had I let down my guard this quickly? How was it possible he'd worked his way into my very heart and soul?

"It's a mystery, isn't it?" Reid finally whispered, as the song ended and the dance came to a close. "How this happened. How we went from flirting to friends to... Dammit, Lou. You're the air that I breathe. You don't have to marry me. I fully understand what you said about being rescued, believe it or not."

"That's very enlightened of you."

"I have a grandmother who kicked her no-good husband out when he nearly bankrupted them." He shrugged. "She was the strongest, smartest woman I've ever known. You remind me of her, actually."

It was a tremendous compliment.

"But," he continued, "I'd be lying if I said I wasn't falling in love with you. I didn't come on this trip for six days of fun. I came because I thought it might be my chance to win you over."

"Reid—"

"It doesn't have to be today. Lou … please let me woo you. Let me show you what it's like when someone truly cares. Royden Clarke… That man was just after excitement with a beautiful woman. He was so beneath you. I wanted to knock out all his teeth every time I saw you two together."

This was the way the conversation should have gone this morning. Not an offer to save me but a declaration of devotion. Normally I would laugh at such a thing, but not with Reid. In the last three days he'd made me laugh more than anyone else had done in the last three months. He listened to me rattle on about my causes with proper seriousness, sometimes in full support and sometimes playing devil's advocate and asking, "what if." That comfortable life I was lamenting earlier still held a certain amount of appeal, because I didn't think life would be boring with Reid. He didn't just entertain me; he made me think, and I loved that about him. For the first time in my life, a man was treating me as if I actually had a brain.

"I don't know, Reid." I let go of his hand and stepped away a bit. "This is so fast and not what I expected at all."

"Then give me a chance to earn you," he persisted.

His choice of words only fed my doubts. Earn me? That made it sound as if he was putting me on some kind of pedestal, one from which I would topple in the blink of an eye if he knew some of the things I'd done. "You don't need to earn me," I muttered, shame sliding over me. "If anything, I need to earn you. You're too good for me, Reid Grey, and that's the truth."

"I don't believe that for a second." He reached out for my hand

and clasped it in his. The warmth of his skin seeped through my glove to my fingertips. "Will you at least think about it, Lou?"

I nodded, but already my mind was swimming. I had made my choices long before leaving England. Once in New York, those choices would bear fruit, giving me enough money to live comfortably for some time. When I'd boarded the ship, one path had been open to me and I'd known exactly what I had to do. But now I wasn't so sure, and not all of my misgivings had to do with my romance with Reid.

"I'll think about it," I agreed, because how could I not? "You need to give me time and space, though. If you're hanging about all the time, I won't think straight at all."

"Darling, you must stop giving me strategy tips." He grinned and came closer, until our bodies were brushing again.

"I'm being serious, Reid." And I was. Dead serious. "I need you to hear me when I say that I am done having my life dictated and coerced and nudged. As much as possible, anyway. There are limits, of course."

"For now," he agreed, brushing a strand of hair off my face. "But you're going to change things, Louisa. I just know it."

My old friend scepticism popped into my head once more. "I've never met a man so agreeable to the fight for women's rights. It's difficult to believe, really. Most men are terrifically frightened. Makes me wonder if you're really sincere."

"Ah. Well, it's flattering to be considered too good to be true, I guess. Perhaps I think you're not asking for much, really. A chance to have a say in your own government. The ability to live without having to rely on a man's handouts. It's quite simple, really. And that's why I realized rather quickly that I blundered horribly this morning." He smiled a little. "I was offering you a way out. My money and my protection, and yes, my heart, too, but the better thing would have been to offer you a choice. Deep down, Louisa

Phillips, I also want to be chosen because you love me, not because you need my money."

I stood up on tiptoe and pressed my lips to his, a gentle, soft contact that blossomed into something fuller, leaving me both satisfied and longing for more.

"I will think about it," I promised, giving him a nod. "But for now, I'm going back to my cabin to get some sleep. Tomorrow is time enough for you to start this wooing you speak of."

Reid stepped back, and then, to my delight, sketched an elegant bow. "Miss Phillips, allow me to escort you inside."

I took his arm and wondered, not for the first time today, what it would be like to have his arm forever. Not just now, in our youth, passionate in our beliefs and with each other, but at Margaret Brown's age, when twenty years had passed and we'd weathered many storms. Or Ida and Isidor Straus, in their sixties, always together with their regard for each other plain to see to anyone who cared to look.

Once inside, we paused at the staircase. He'd go right and to his cabin; I'd go down the stairs to B Deck and on to mine.

"Thank you for the dance, Mr. Grey," I said, giving a tiny curtsy while his lips curved in a just-for-me smile.

"May it be one of many," he replied, then lifted my hand and kissed the top, the contact burning through the silk of my glove.

My lips twitched. It wasn't going to be easy to put him off, and I wasn't sure I wanted to anyway. But I did need to think, and not just about whether or not I loved him. I needed to think about who I wanted to be. I wanted to know that I could look at myself in the mirror without regrets.

Reid stepped away, and I began the descent down the staircase. When I passed by Hannah and Charles's cabin, I heard voices from inside, and while I couldn't make out what they were saying, the muffled tone did not have the sound of happiness. My stomach clenched for the millionth time today. Why did everything have to be so complicated and … and difficult?

I went inside my own cabin and shut the door, then pushed the button above my bed to ring for a stewardess. I would not trouble Hannah tonight. I just hoped that in the end, things worked out with Charles. It wasn't the life for me, but she deserved happiness more than anyone I knew, and I would always believe that she should be able to choose what happiness looked like for her.

Chapter Fourteen

```
April 13, 1912
   Titanic
```

HANNAH

Once we were inside our cabin, I plucked at each finger of my right glove and then tugged it off, draping the white silk over a chair while I worked on the second glove. Charles loosened his tie, then turned his gaze on me. He stared so intently I wondered if I'd perhaps got ice cream on the corner of my mouth or a dribble of something on my dress. I looked down at the bodice, slightly frantic. This had cost a fortune, and I had no idea how to get out a stain before it set.

I didn't see anything, so I looked up again. "What is it?" I asked. "Do I have something on my face?"

He smiled, shook his head. "No, not at all. I was just thinking how lovely you look tonight. The dress, the hair ... you're even wearing the earrings I got you last week."

"Oh, thank you. They suited the dress perfectly, don't you think?" I said, warmed by the generosity of his compliments. "And this dress is a Paul Poiret. Lou made me get it. It's the height of fashion, she said."

"For once, I agree with Miss Phillips. Though I'll deny it if you repeat that," he added, lifting a finger in warning.

I laughed, and he chuckled, too. Oh, what a delight that was. To laugh together. You valued something when it was in particularly short supply.

"It shall be our secret," I agreed, then moved to a chair so I could sit and remove my shoes. I needed to be comfortable to tackle what was to come, and wished I could remove my corset, but I also wanted to remain in my gown for this conversation. I felt pretty and more confident in it, and I could use all the confidence I could get.

"I'm glad we came back right after dinner," I said, and patted the arm of the other chair. "It gives us a chance to chat. I've barely seen you all day."

A wary look came into his eyes, but he gathered my gloves, put them with his necktie, and laid them on the table before sitting. "Would you like some water?" he asked. The pitchers in the rooms were kept full at all times, and I sensed he was looking for something to do. Some way to avoid talking or at least change the subject.

"No, thank you. I'm perfectly fine." He'd got up to get himself a glass, and I made my voice a little firmer. "Do sit down, Charles."

He did, with a sigh. As if he couldn't run anymore after doing so for days, weeks even.

"Charles, the reason I've been trying to talk to you about us for so long is because there's something I haven't told you. I wanted for us to be ... well, fixed, I suppose, before I— before we— dammit."

His eyes widened, but otherwise he let my cursing slide. "A secret," he said, and then his brows pulled together as concern darkened his face. "Are you ill, Hannah? I know you saw a doctor a while ago. And you were so excited to come on this trip." He reached for my hand. "You called it a once-in-a-lifetime opportunity. Oh, darling. What is it?"

I blinked as hot tears had gathered in my eyes at his immediate distress. "I wasn't sure you still cared."

"Of course I care. You're my wife."

"I'm not sick, Charles. Not in the way you think. I-I'm pregnant."

He pulled his hand from mine and sat back. The concern of only moments ago was shuttered firmly back behind a wall of ice. No words could have communicated any clearer that he did not want a child.

"How?"

I stared at him. "The usual way," I replied, the words clipped as I wondered if perhaps he didn't even remember. He'd been drunk that night.

"But we..." His neck flushed, and then the pink climbed his face until his cheeks flamed. "I haven't been to your room in weeks."

"Months," I corrected. I'd been shocked to find out I was pregnant – the thought of going through again what I'd been through terrified me – but I'd not been dismayed. He clearly was, though. There was no seed of happiness ready to blossom into something beautiful and true.

He stared, then got up from his chair and moved away toward the window. There was only darkness beyond the thick pane, and I could only guess that he wanted to be as far from me as possible.

"That's all you have to say?" I asked, and all the frustration and anger I'd been holding in for months came bubbling to the surface, outweighing any fear or sadness. "It is yours, Charles. Never fear about that. You'd been liberal with the whisky that night, however, so perhaps you don't remember."

"Of course I remember," he snapped, turning to face me.

"I see." I paused, then shook my head. "Actually, no, I don't. Why did you come to my room?"

The awkward silence only amplified my fears.

"I'd been to London," he said quietly. "I... I was angry about something. When I arrived home, I reached for the whisky because —" He stopped, frowned. "There's no point in this."

"Go on," I said. "You reached for the whisky because..."

His jaw tightened. "Fine. I had very nearly started an affair, but I didn't. I couldn't do that to you. So I came home, hating myself, knowing you deserved better."

I wanted to believe him, but my brain stuck on "nearly started an affair." "So you came to my room because you wanted someone else? I mean, I suppose it's a 'men have needs' thing. We might as well face the truth. You stopped loving me a long time ago. We're polite strangers who happen to be married. We have become very good at pretending, but the moment I lost our baby was the moment I lost you." My voice rose and I didn't care. "Let's just finally be out with it, all right? Don't worry about hurting my feelings, because you can't possibly wound me any more than you already have."

"That's what you think?" He took one halting step forward, then ran his hand roughly through his hair. "Jesus Christ, Hannah."

I stood, too, feeling I needed to be at least close to eye level with him and not shrinking below him like a wilted violet. "Well. Cursing means that at least you have some passion in you somewhere, for more than your rocks and minerals and bank account."

His face flattened as his eyes registered the shock of my words. Momentarily, I felt guilty for being cruel. He was passionate about his work and he provided for us, and it was unfair of me to use that against him. I knew I should apologize, but I couldn't seem to find the words. Perhaps I did want him to hurt. Perhaps I wanted him to feel a tiny bit of what I felt every time he turned me away or acted as if I didn't exist.

"Why did you come on this trip?" he asked. "If my work is so distasteful?"

I lifted my chin, but stayed where I was, slightly behind the table, as if it gave me some sort of protection. Not that I ever expected Charles to endanger me; that wasn't his style. It was more of a mental barrier, giving me the strength to say the absolute truth. "I wanted to finally talk to you about the baby. Not this one, the last one. To work through whatever it was that had driven us apart. I wanted to fix us, Charles, so we could put the bad things behind us and so I—"

I halted, reconsidering the words that had almost left my mouth. I had been so close to saying "so I don't have to do this alone," but right now I did not want him to know how horribly frightened I was. He had already hurt me so much. His revulsion when I'd said I was pregnant was sign enough for me that I was going to have to find other support, within myself, even. And that was the scariest part, because I didn't know if I had it in me. It had broken me last time, but I'd healed. What if something horrible happened and I couldn't do it a second time?

I cleared my throat. "It's obvious you are not pleased about the baby, and we've appeared polite and happy in public. I'm tired, Charles. I'm so very, very tired. So let's just stop pretending."

We stared at each other for several long moments, and when Charles spoke, his voice shook.

"Are you saying you want a divorce?"

Did I? Not hardly. What I wanted no longer existed. "No," I replied. A hundred knives cut me as I spoke, sharp, stinging slices to my heart as I laid it bare. "Just to stop the charade. Lots of couples do it, right? We lead separate lives and my hope is to remain civil, as I do care about you so very much. For my part, I will try not to do anything to tarnish your reputation or spark gossip, and I'd ask you to do the same."

There it was. Together but apart. Sad, but at least I could stop trying so very hard to make him love me and then having to deal with his rejection again and again and again. God willing, I would have a healthy baby and would fill my life with motherhood, and it would be enough.

He said nothing. He did not blink. But as I faced him, sick to my stomach with the pain of it all, a tear slid from his lower lid and down the crest of his cheek.

"I don't know how to do this. I don't know how to do any of it." Anguish bled through his words, confusing my anger and waking my compassion. I didn't want to feel compassion right now. All my energy had gone into hoping his face would light up when I said we were expecting another child. Instead, he'd let me down. That hurt most of all.

"And I do?" I paced away, then back again, wishing the cabin were larger when it had seemed perfectly adequate so far. "We are married, Charles. But after the baby died, it was so very bleak, and you were nowhere to be found. You wonder at my devotion to Lou? Well, who do you suppose was with me during those dark days? It wasn't you. It was Lou. When I finally started feeling more myself, I thought perhaps things would return to normal, but you remained so distant and refused to talk about anything. And you know what the worst of it is? I've spent months – months! – going over every word, every possible thing that I might have done to make you stop loving me. Do you know what I came up with?"

His face was wet now, but my own floodgates had opened and I was letting everything I'd kept bottled up out into the open. "Nothing." I answered my own question. "I came up with nothing. I certainly didn't mean to lose the baby. I grieved, Charles. That was my mistake, I suppose. I grieved."

"Stop," he said, a hoarse command filled with pain. "For the love of God, stop, Hannah. I can't bear it."

I did stop, my chest rising and falling with my quickened breath, my heart pounding against my ribs. I had never spoken up for myself like this in my entire life. I had been pushed aside and just accepted it. Well, no more. If I were to be left behind, I would at least acknowledge it rather than melting away into the shadows as a meek inconvenience.

"I... I don't know how to do this," Charles said again, letting out a shaking breath. "You're so very wrong, and yet you're not, too. I have distanced myself. I told myself it was best."

"Best?" I gave a harsh laugh. "The darkest point in my life, and you thought disappearing was best?"

"It was dark for me too!" He whisper-shouted it, and I admired his restraint as I seemed to have misplaced mine. I didn't think Lou had returned to her cabin yet, but we had neighbours on the other side of us, and who knew who might be passing by in the hall?

I considered his words. There was no question he'd been upset by the loss of our baby. I had lost a lot of blood and was weak, but I remembered him sitting by my bed and crying – the only time I'd ever seen him do so until this moment.

"How would I know?" I asked. "Charles, when I was finally alert again, you were absent. You'd gone back to work. You acted as if nothing had changed at all."

"I tried to keep things normal. Steady. I buried myself in work because…" He went to the sofa, sank down upon it and put his head into his hands. "I was so devastated, and I'd been so afraid I was going to lose you as well as the baby. I didn't know what else to do."

I stepped back, struck by his admission. "You might have talked to me. We might have shared the grief."

"How?" He lifted his head, his eyes blazing. "You were so fragile, Hannah. When I looked in your eyes, it was as if there was no one there. I had all these feelings, in here"—he thumped his fist to his chest—"and I couldn't burden you with them. You were barely managing. You stayed in bed. Hardly ate."

He wasn't wrong about that.

"I had lost our baby and the future I thought we had. Then I felt I lost you. Of course I couldn't get out of bed. I didn't even want to live, Charles."

"Oh, God," he said, lowering his head again.

"We should have talked about this. We should have faced it together."

He nodded, and I saw two more tears drip from his face to the floor. I didn't want to soften, but I couldn't help it. I was glad. It was easier knowing he'd been hurting too. Not that I wanted him to feel pain, but because knowing it meant he hadn't just stopped loving me. At least not at first.

I went to fetch myself a glass of water, needing it now, needing to take a breath and think about everything that had been said. The water was tepid, curing my thirst but not really refreshing me. I put down the glass and went to sit next to Charles on the sofa. Now that my outburst was over, I sensed we might actually be able to talk and get to the bottom of everything. Not that it would change anything, but we might at least have an understanding.

I put my hand on his knee for a brief second, then removed it.

"When my mother died, my father was heartbroken. So was I. We'd been a close family. There'd been laughter and fun and love, especially love. I didn't know she was ill until a month before she died and she couldn't hide it anymore or get by with saying she was just tired. When she was gone, it was as if all the light went out of our house. No more laughter. No more fun. Father spent his time at his office, and I found my greatest solace in our cook, Mrs. Wilson. I felt utterly abandoned, Charles, and that was only made worse by the announcement that I was to be sent off to school. It was as if, once Mama was gone, my father couldn't stand to look at me."

Charles sat up, turned his head to look at me. I looked back, and it was hard to hold his gaze instead of looking away. Tough conversations were so difficult to manoeuvre. "I met Lou there. She hadn't been abandoned, like I had, but she was definitely neglected.

We were two unwanted girls who found each other and became as close as sisters. We became each other's family.

"Then school was over and she went on to new things and I went back to Father's. I might have helped him in his practice, but he only wanted me to run his household. He didn't quite ignore me, but he didn't really love me, either. And when the baby died, I felt exactly the same, only worse. I had this wall of grief I couldn't breach, and the person I wanted to be closest to had disappeared. Father didn't want me without my mother. You didn't want me after the baby was gone. I was not enough on my own. I want to be done with that, you see. It's a horrible way to feel and live. Like you don't matter. That your existence is only relevant when predicated on someone else's."

The fire within me had tempered. I no longer desired to lash out, though I couldn't say I was sorry I had. Now I was simply sad and trying to prepare myself to say goodbye to this era of my life and move on to something more … mine. I thought of the baby nestled warm and snug inside me. They deserved for me to persist, to thrive, so they could, too. I would do anything to make sure that happened.

Then Charles reached over and took my hand, threaded his fingers with mine, and a bittersweet ache spread throughout my core. The young, hopeful couple that had picnicked by the lake had come to this. Disappointments and recriminations.

"I am so sorry," he whispered, squeezing my fingers. "I didn't know what else to do. I had my own grief and then I nearly lost you and…" He sighed. "I nearly lost my mind, Hannah. I didn't know what to do with myself, so I shoved it all down and locked it up and threw myself into work so I didn't have to think about seeing you lying on that bed, covered in blood, so pale as if you were already dead."

The image he painted was so visceral that I understood it had left an indelible mark. I had slept and awakened for medicine and the tea and broth that Lou forced me to drink, but for a moment I put myself in his position and realized it would have indeed been a terrible shock.

"But I got better," I reasoned, squeezing back.

"I had done that to you," he continued, as if he hadn't heard my last assertion. "I kept saying how much I wanted a big family and it nearly killed you. The one thing I knew for sure was that I would never, ever put you through that again."

The implication of what he had just said sank in. I sat back, my brows pulled together in confusion. "Wait. Are you saying that you..." I hesitated, searching for the right way to express my suspicion. "You stopped coming to my room to prevent me from getting with child?"

He nodded, looking abjectly miserable.

It was, perhaps, a strange thing to reignite my resentment, but knowing that he had stayed away to avoid me getting pregnant infuriated me. "I thought... God, I'm such a fool. I thought you had stopped wanting me. Loving me."

"Never," he asserted, but that just made me angrier. As furious as I'd ever been in my life, full of fire and ash.

"Do you know how much of a waste this has been? How much time has been lost, how much damage has been done and how much pain I've gone through, when this all could have been avoided had you just talked to me?" I popped up off the sofa, put my hands on my hips as I stared him down. "Thinking the only way you could tolerate being near me is after you'd lubricated with alcohol?" I made a growly sound in my throat. "There are ... ways, Charles. Ways to ensure a pregnancy doesn't happen. Or you might have just talked to me about it. Instead you made these huge decisions about me *without me*." I was shaking now, I was so incensed. "You treated me as if I were in the way. A bother. Well, for tonight I won't bother you. We can discuss this again later when I'm not so angry."

I bustled about the room, picking up my nightgown and peignoir.

"Hannah, stop, please and—"

"No," I said firmly, rolling the pile of clothes in my arms, wrinkling everything horribly. "I can't. Not now. You abandoned me, Charles, when I needed you most. It would have been easier, I think, if you had simply stopped caring. But knowing you did and chose this... I can't. I need some space."

I stomped to Lou's door and knocked on it, firmly. When she opened it, already dressed for bed, I swept inside in a bubble of self-righteousness.

"Good heavens," she said, shutting the door behind me. "Whatever is the matter?"

"Men are the matter," I raged, flinging my clothes onto the smaller bed, creating a frothy pile of silk and lace. "May I sleep in your spare bed?" I asked.

"Of course you can. I heard your raised voices. I take it Charles did not react well to the news."

I gave her a succinct summary of our conversation, watched as her face grew more and more serious with each sentence. I began to wonder if I'd overreacted, though I couldn't quite see how. Everything I'd said was true. If Charles had talked to me, we might have been able to work through all this. Instead, he'd shoved me aside.

I perched on the edge of the bed as I ranted. When I ran out of steam, Lou helped me undress and I breathed a sigh of relief as the corset disappeared and I was able to slip into the soft comfort of my nightclothes. Then she sat on my bed with me, her hand rubbing little circles on my knee as we faced each other, sitting in a most undignified cross-legged posture, just like we had when we were girls in the dormitory. It was oddly comforting.

"Am I wrong to be angry, Lou?" I had a hard time speaking. My eyes were burning from exhaustion, and my throat was tight. I didn't want to cry, but tears were close, making it hard to swallow.

"Sweetheart," she said softly, her hand still making those soothing little circles, "you have held all this in for so long. You have tried to be the perfect daughter, the perfect wife, never angry, always smiling. Yes, you went through an extremely dark time, but good God, who wouldn't? And yet you came back with a desire to heal things in your marriage. You've been patient and kind and you always, always try to see things from someone else's perspective. Honestly, I don't know how you've gone this long. Imagine if one of those boilers below had no exhaust valve. The pressure would just build up and build up until it exploded."

I nodded, shivering a little. "I have spent so much of my life trying to make things all right for everyone else. And whenever I started to get angry, I'd talk myself out of it. I couldn't tonight, Lou. Why couldn't I?"

She smiled faintly. "Because while you wouldn't fight for yourself, you'll fight for your child. That's as plain as day to me."

"But the baby isn't even here yet."

"Does that really matter?" She gave a watery smile. "You are already a mother in your heart."

I shook my head. "You're right, you know. But Lou… I'm so scared. I'm terrified something will go wrong again and that it will be worse than before."

"Did you tell Charles that?"

"No. When he said he had stopped coming to my room to prevent us from having another baby, I got so angry. Clearly his resolve failed on the odd occasion." I put my hand to my slightly rounded stomach. "His withdrawal hurt me in so many ways and could have been so easily avoided. How do I forgive him for that?"

Lou nodded. "And let us not forget, your father did much the same thing after your mother died. I know that affected you profoundly. Of course this is going to hurt you, deeply." She sent me her "angry pout" face. "Men will say they are doing things out of concern for us, but the majority of the time they are doing it to avoid their own feelings. It would be much easier if they'd just come out with it and deal with things."

I couldn't disagree. "And they are supposed to be the stronger sex, but they are so afraid of their feelings, as if having them is like a disease."

Lou laughed a little, then slid over and put her arm around me. "I can't believe I'm going to say this, but I feel a bit sorry for them, when all is said and done. Think of what they miss out on by being so tough. Or, they'd say tough. We'd call it running away."

I had needed Lou's staunch support very badly, and she never let me down. I rested my head on her shoulder. "Thank you. For everything. I know I'll have to talk to Charles in the light of day, but tonight I just want to let everything settle. It'll be clearer after a good night's sleep."

"It will." Lou took my hands in hers. "It is all right for you to be furious tonight," she said firmly. "You have a right to be angry. Just as I know you will forgive him, because that is who you are. You are far more generous than I am."

"I'm not sure of that," I responded, looking down at our joined hands.

"I am." Her voice was firm. "Look, I don't know if you can fix this with Charles, or if, in the end, you'll want to. But if you ask me…"

She paused, as if waiting for me to give her the go ahead to dispense her advice.

"Go on," I urged.

"Well, if you ask me, it was never going to work until you got all this out in the open. You can't heal a wound until you cut out the infection that's inside, can you?"

It was a very good point.

"Sleep on it, darling. Come." She slid off the bed and pulled me with her, then turned down the covers. "Hop in. This will all look better in the morning, I promise."

I was too tired to do anything but obey. Lou tucked me in as if I were a child, with love and care. "Good night, and don't let the bedbugs bite," she said, something we'd laughed about at school and had been our usual ritual at lights out.

"Sleep tight," I replied, and despite the upheaval of the evening, I fell into a deep sleep within moments.

Chapter Fifteen

April 14, 1912
Titanic

LOUISA

Hannah had fallen fast asleep last night, but I'd laid awake a long time, trying to make sense of the roller coaster that had been the last few days. Hannah's marriage was crumbling, my plans were on shaky ground, and I was finding myself in uncharted territory: having actual, genuine feelings for a man that made me reconsider my life choices.

Hannah was having a bath, a calming indulgence after last night's upheaval. I was already up and dressed, and my current mission was to go next door and retrieve clothes for her to wear today. My stomach was in a knot; Charles and I were not on great terms as it was, and now I was in the middle. Firmly on Hannah's side, of course, but I couldn't be sure what Charles's attitude would be toward me when I knocked.

There was a splash from the bathroom, followed by a quiet "oops," and then another smaller splash and some humming.

I pinched my cheeks, bit my lips, smoothed my bodice, and gave three quiet knocks on the door between our cabins.

Charles opened it, anticipation on his face that dimmed when he saw it was me and not Hannah.

"Hannah's asked me to get her clothes for this morning," I said quietly. Charles, for his part, looked a wreck. Normally impeccably put together, his eyes had dark circles beneath them, his hair was puffed up on one side, he needed a shave, and his cravat was askew.

He stepped aside and I entered while he closed the door behind me.

"Is she all right?" he asked, his voice hoarse.

I went to the wardrobe room and stopped with my hands resting on her cotton and silk delicates. I picked up a set of combinations and then stockings to at least look busy. Charles did love her – I think we both knew that – and his concern was genuine. "She's fine," I answered, not unkindly. "She slept and she's having a bath right now." I looked over at him as I closed a drawer and moved to select a suit for Hannah. "All told, it looks like you had the worse night."

"I didn't really sleep," he confessed.

I chose a dark red suit with black trim, something elegant that would bring out the colour in Hannah's cheeks. "I won't betray her by getting into this with you, Charles. You have hurt her deeply." I met his miserable gaze. "But I also believe you love her. If you do, you need to make this right. She deserves nothing less than your total devotion and care. She has been through hell."

I expected him to puff up and say something short to put me in my place for interfering even this much, but he didn't. He simply nodded and said, "I know."

I couldn't help but soften. My problems with Charles had always been that he was uptight and dull, but I'd always known he was, deep down, a good man. "I know you've been through hell too, Charles. What happened was hard on everyone. When a tragedy occurs, it either brings people together or pushes them apart." I was involving myself even after I'd just said I wouldn't, but I discovered I had things to say, too. "I wanted to punch you last night, but that wouldn't solve anything. I will only say this: that woman in there means the world to me, and right now you must endeavour to deserve her."

"I'm not sure I ever will," he replied. "But I will try."

"Good," I said, heaping everything over my arm. "Now, go find some breakfast and get some coffee, for God's sake. You look like hell."

He smiled a little, as if amused. "You are so bossy."

"This is not news," I countered, but I smiled back, and a little peace was achieved.

Once Charles left, I managed to add shoes to Hannah's pile and I also grabbed the green mesh bag holding her jewellery. Last night's earrings sat on the dresser. I swept them into my palm to put in the bag later, and then I carted the entire armload into my cabin and put it down on the bed. Hannah called from the bathroom, so I dropped the earrings in my pocket while snagging a fresh towel for her.

"How are you feeling?" I asked, as she stepped from the tub and into the soft towel.

"A little wobbly," she admitted, "but good, really. I think you were right last night, Lou. Nothing was going to be fixed until everything was out in the open. I don't know what will happen next, but I do feel like less of a powder keg."

I darted back to the bed to retrieve her underthings. "I have never seen you so angry," I admitted, smiling to myself. "I didn't know you had it in you." Indeed, I was generally the fiery one, and she the more measured.

"Me either," she replied.

When I went back to her, she'd wrapped the towel around her

still-damp body. Little tendrils of hair fell softly around her face, curled by the steam of the bath water, and her skin glowed.

"You are so beautiful," I said. "You always have been. I can't believe I didn't guess about the baby. You're radiant when you're expecting, did you know that?"

She shook her head, but smiled. "I know I should be scared, and I am, sometimes. But deep down, I have this feeling that this time is different. That the baby – and I – are going to be all right. Is that foolish?"

"I think it's brave," I answered. "And I'm more than a little in awe of you. Now, start getting dressed. I'll help you with your buttons and things and then we're going to get a good breakfast."

"What about Charles?" Her face fell. "I'm afraid to cross paths with him. The first meeting is going to be so awkward."

"Charles has already gone for breakfast. And before you ask, I'll tell you: he looked like hell."

"Oh, dear—"

"Don't feel sorry for the man. After what he put you through, losing a night's sleep is not inappropriate. It also means he's been thinking about the error of his ways, in my view. So come. Let's make you look beautiful and strong and irresistible, and I'm sure that later the two of you will talk and start putting this marriage back together – if that's what you want."

"Of course it is. I am hurt and I'm furious, but only because I love him. I've always loved him, Lou. Maybe not with the blazing passion that you seem to have with Reid Grey, but one that suits me. Quieter, but no less strong."

Her mention of Reid sent my pulse racing. "I don't know if I love Reid. It could be nothing more than a case of being swept off my feet."

"Is that a bad thing? I have my misgivings, you know that. I don't quite trust him. But I do trust you, and while you are frequently impulsive and far more daring than I, you are not stupid,

Lou, nor are you foolish. Indeed, I think everything you do is calculated far more seriously than most people realize."

Her assessment left me a bit shaken. I responded by sending her a lopsided grin. "But if I act like the life of the party, no one suspects that my mind is always working." I winked as I made the confession. "And that's how I like it. There's value in being underestimated." Hannah really had no idea how much.

"See? Far more strategic. I, meanwhile, just muddle along. It's no wonder Reid is so taken with you."

"So you've abandoned the foolish notion that he's the *Titanic* jewel thief?" I quipped, holding up her coat as she slid her arms in and moved to button it over her blouse.

"If you believe he's innocent, I shall too. I only want you to be happy, Lou. I never would have bet on you falling for someone during the crossing, but now that I know there's some history between you..."

"He sees me for who I am. And it's not that he doesn't care that I'm occasionally a problem. He actually *likes* that about me. It's a rare thing, Han. I ran from it yesterday, and then last night he—"

I was transported back to dancing in his arms on the cold, dark deck. "He is very romantic. I didn't think I even liked being romanced until it happened. Would I be so very foolish to consider a life with him?"

"It's fast," she said, frowning a little as she reached for her gloves.

"I agree. I-I told him that I needed some time. That when we get back to England, perhaps..."

I wasn't sure what came after perhaps, but I did know for certain that I wanted Reid Grey in my life, and that in itself was a revelation. I gathered my gloves from the table and tried to settle the butterflies in my chest. "I've never been like this about anyone," I confessed, figuring if I couldn't be honest with Hannah, I couldn't be honest with anyone. "He makes me reconsider everything."

"That's not a bad thing, is it?" she asked, finally standing before me, ready to face the world.

"Probably not. But it is annoyingly disconcerting." I gave a light laugh, but inside my stomach churned. Things had been put in motion that I wasn't sure I could stop, or even wanted to. Mostly, I was reluctant to put my future in the hands of another person and not my own. I'd lived that way my entire life and loathed it. My desires, my wishes … none of it had mattered. My father was a cold autocrat that bullied my mother and at best, wanted me out of the way. I was a thing to be dealt with, shunted from place to place. The house in town, off to school. If we were in the same residence, I simply had to remain out of sight. The fact that I was inconveniently unmarried and still his "responsibility" galled him no end. I was useless. His words. I'd worked very hard not to make them mine.

I certainly wasn't about to leap into marriage with a man who knew how to charm a woman and say all the right things. Reid had a long way to go to prove to me that he meant what he said.

"Shall we go?" I asked, picking up my hat and placing it just so. "I am dying for some of the strawberries they've been serving."

"How you stay so slim when you are always eating, I'll never know," Hannah replied on a laugh. "But yes, I'm ready. I'm hungry."

We left the cabin and locked the door behind us.

I returned to the room shortly after ten. Our breakfast was slightly rushed as the dining saloon was being converted into a type of sanctuary for this morning's service, apparently presided over by Captain Smith. I had no interest in going. While Hannah had slept deeply, I'd lain awake long into the night, thinking about her, about Charles, about Reid. Thinking about my decisions and what I should do next. I was exhausted, and I desperately wanted a nap. I begged a headache, thinking Hannah would go back to her cabin as well. But she wanted to stay for the service, she said. Told me to get some sleep.

Which I was planning to do. But first...

I went to a small drawer and took out a silk bag that I'd hidden beneath my delicates. I poured the contents out on the small table, moving the bouquet of flowers aside as I considered the valuables before me.

A pocket watch. A lovely pearl-and-diamond necklace. A bracelet set with oval amethysts. A diamond-crusted cravat pin.

Guilt wound around my insides. It wasn't their value that caused hot shame to run through my veins. It was the personal value. Margaret Brown's bracelet in particular; Margaret had become a friend. And the pin ... that was Reid's. I'd swept it off a table that first afternoon we'd made love in his cabin.

The others were more a theft and less a betrayal, but as I sat there, running my fingers over the purple stones, I thought of the Gladstone bag in the purser's office one deck down. There was money in it certainly; I was going to be in New York, after all. But the real treasure inside was a variety of baubles that I had gathered over the past several months. A ring from my mother's jewel box; a giant Burma ruby she never wore and wouldn't miss. A jewelled hair clip that I'd pilfered during one of the raucous house parties I'd attended, the kind that got a little wild and that this guest in particular would assume she'd misplaced in her alcohol-fuelled haze. A bracelet belonging to a silly woman named Amelia, who had called me *Dahling* on every single occasion we'd met. I was rather adept at slipping clasps open now. All it had taken was an awkward bump and she'd dropped her bag right in the foyer of The Savoy. In my helpfulness, I gathered up the detritus that had scattered and handed it over, slipping the bracelet off her wrist and into my pocket with more ease than should have been possible. AMY, one would presume her nickname, was spelled out in diamonds. I rather thought it a childish-looking thing, but I added it to my growing collection.

Regardless of it being a Sunday morning, I went to a cabinet and pulled out a bottle of whisky, pouring myself what my Scottish aunt would call a "wee dram" that was really enough to make me definitively tipsy. I drank it in two gulps, looking at the items I now had to add to my bag of prizes.

I hadn't meant to become a thief. It had actually happened quite by accident.

It had been during one of those ridiculous house parties in the country. I was still with Royden at the time. Reid had been there and made eyes at me every chance he got. Cassandra Granville had been particularly tipsy on the Friday night, and I had been indulging far too much but had kept my wits. Or so I thought. Cassandra moaned the next day about losing a bracelet but bragged how she hadn't actually liked it and her significantly older and stuffy husband would simply buy her another, bigger one.

It wasn't until I was back in London and unpacking that I found it, hooked on the fringe of the wrap I'd worn when I'd disappeared with Royden for a moonlight rendezvous out in the garden.

I could have given it back. It would have been the right thing to do.

But then I'd thought, what would something like that cost? How much could that amount of money help someone less fortunate, give them some security or choices that Cassandra – and anyone in our set, really – would never have to think twice about?

I'd tucked it away, then at the next party, slipped something into my bag on purpose. I got a taste for it – the thrill, the danger of being caught – and then my father had dropped his ultimatum on me and I'd realized that in order to help other women, I first needed to help myself. It wasn't a legitimate way to earn a living, but at least I was doing something about it. I wasn't just sitting around, waiting for my circumstances to change.

The trip to New York had emerged as the perfect solution to the quandary in which I found myself. The jewels would fund my life once my father cut me off. I knew he was serious about it. He only cared about my brother and about passing the baronetcy on to him, which would have made me laugh if it weren't so pathetic. A baronet. We weren't even really nobility, but you would have thought Father was a duke, the way he pranced around, basking in his self-importance.

If I tried to pawn the jewels in London, there was a very good chance I'd be caught. I might have got away with a few of the more nondescript things, but a name in diamonds? Conspicuous. My solution to avoiding marriage did not include going to prison for theft.

Then Hannah had suggested the trip and a week in New York, and it was perfect. There were hundreds of places I could go to sell my collection, piece by piece, and the owners would never know because they were an ocean away. Well, except perhaps those whose trinkets I'd pilfered on the ship, but New York wasn't the final destination for most of them. Sell the gems for cash, return to England, set up my own life. It wouldn't be extravagant – I would need to be sensible – but my mother's ring alone would set me up for a few years. No more stealing. I'd be done with it.

I ran the tip of my finger over Reid's tie pin. Reid was a complication. But if I did decide to marry him, sometime in the future, I would have my own money. I could…

I reached for the bottle, poured another drink, and this time, sipped, albeit liberally.

If I kept my own money, I would never feel trapped. Reid wouldn't need to know.

Damn, but wasn't I a proficient liar. Here I was, lecturing Hannah about not keeping secrets while sitting on the biggest of them all. What a hypocrite I was.

I gathered up the items and put them back in the little bag. This afternoon I'd go to the purser's office, get my bag, and put these things in it. Nothing else, though. I was done with stealing and deception. There had to be a limit, hadn't there? Besides, every time I saw Hannah, my stomach twisted. If she knew... She'd already suspected Reid which would have been funny if it weren't so ironic. Reid's biggest flaw, if I could find one, was that he was too charming by half and I was afraid to fall for it.

Once the items were tucked away again, and I'd finished the second drink, I lay down on my bed, my head cushioned by the fluffy pillows. Hannah couldn't ever find out. She was the most moral person I knew. I couldn't bear her disappointment or censure. In fact, I knew what she would say: that I needn't have resorted to stealing because she would have given me the money. Charles certainly had enough of it.

But I would rather be a resourceful criminal than beg for my best friend's charity. If that was too much pride, then so be it. I hated my father, really, but one thing he said had stayed with me. *Never borrow money from friends*, he'd told my brother. *It never ends well, mark my words.*

"Well, Father, consider your words marked," I whispered, closing my eyes.

All things considered, I'd be glad when we docked and I was able to empty the bag of its cargo. Once I'd sold the lot of it, I'd be free to start my life anew.

Chapter Sixteen

April 14, 1912
Titanic

HANNAH

All things considered, I felt better than I'd expected as I re-entered the saloon for the Sunday morning service. I was surprised, too, when just before it began, Charles slid up beside me.

He said nothing, but he looked ragged round the edges, very unlike him. I didn't know what to say. What did one say after a flaming argument and a night spent apart? It ceased to matter, anyway, as the service started and conversation was silenced.

As we bowed our heads in prayer, I felt myself softening toward Charles. Oh, he'd been wrong, certainly. He absolutely should have talked to me about his feelings and there was no real excuse for refusing to discuss what had happened. He'd been a coward about it and no mistake. But at the same time, I could possibly forgive him because I also understood that it had come from a place of deep pain. Who was I to judge how a person dealt with grief and fear?

The service went on, but I barely listened. I sang along with the hymns from memory but cared little about them. During another prayer near the end Charles reached over and covered my hand with his, and when I whipped my head around to look at him, he was staring straight ahead but with the trail of a tear shining on his cheek. Oh, dear. My heart lurched knowing he was experiencing such pain.

Pain I understood.

The service ended and Charles discreetly dabbed his face with his handkerchief as I rose from my seat. I smiled at other passengers around me but had no appetite for socializing. Instead, I leaned toward Charles and whispered, "Can we talk?"

"I'd like that," he replied, and while we didn't exactly rush from the room, we did make our way to the door and the lifts that would take us back to B Deck. To our surprise – and to my relief, really – the lifeboat drill scheduled for eleven had been cancelled. Of course, the service had gone long so it would have been late anyway, but I was far happier being tugged along by Charles, who seemed intent on talking to me in private. Hope fluttered inside me.

My pulse rattled at my wrist and in my chest as we walked down the corridor toward our cabin. Lou had said she was going back for a nap, so I determined to keep this morning's chat on the less yell-y side. I went inside while Charles followed and shut the cabin door behind us. When we reached the main room of the cabin, I turned and opened my mouth to speak, but Charles was there, his hands on my upper arms, pulling me close, dipping his head beneath my ridiculous hat and kissing me.

All the words that had been sitting on my tongue for the past ten minutes fled as my shoulders dropped, my hands rested on his elbows, and I returned his kiss. Oh, it was glorious. Gone was the cool formality that had dominated our relationship for months and months. This was a surrender and a claiming all in one, and for the first time I felt real hope, not just the mirage of it, infusing my soul.

"Charles," I said, as the kiss tempered and he rested his forehead against mine, his chin tilted down while mine was up, seeking the sun that was *him*. "Charles, I'm so sorry, last night—"

"Hush," he whispered, lifting his hands to remove my hat. Oblivious to its fragility and, frankly, cost, he tossed it onto a chair and then cradled my head in his hands. "Last night was all my fault. So much has been my fault, and I'm sorry, Hannah. I'm so damned sorry." His hands cupped my jaws as he held my gaze. "You were so right. I'm a coward. But I don't want to lose you. I can't."

Tears flooded my eyes and blurred his image. "I don't want that either. I'm scared too, Charles, can't you see? But shouldn't we turn toward each other, rather than away?"

"Yes," he agreed. "I thought what I was doing was best. I truly did, Hannah. I thought never putting you through that again was the kindest thing I could do for both of us."

I nodded, and the tears slid down my cheeks. "What happened to us was horrible. I nearly died, and you had to witness that. But Charles, I'm still alive. We have another chance. Please, please let's take it."

"You're not still furious with me?" A half smile appeared on his sad face, and I truly thought about how to answer because we had to be completely honest with each other.

"I was furious. I'm still unhappy about it, too, but that doesn't mean I can't forgive you. It doesn't mean I don't want to try again. It's all I've ever wanted. Why else do you think I pushed you so hard? Why would I forsake that chance? Because of pride or anger?"

He pulled me close, resting his head against my hair as his arms wrapped around me. "I don't deserve you," he whispered. "I don't deserve you at all. You are so … so very good." He kissed my temple. "Thank God you walked out on me last night," he said, and I drew back, surprised.

"I'm sorry?"

His gaze plumbed mine. "If you hadn't had the strength to leave, I might not have stayed awake all night, coming to my senses."

"Lou was an absolute brick." I reached up and touched the stubble that still marked his face. He hadn't even shaved this morning.

"I'm sure—"

"No, Charles, she was." I had grown tired of defending Lou to Charles, trying to excuse her behaviour that was most often not quite proper but not so bad she couldn't get away with it. Indeed, sometimes her outrageousness amused me, though lately I'd started to wish she could be a little less … well … Lou. Not this time, though. Lou, despite her faults and our differences, was always there when it counted. "She wants us to be happy, I promise. Of course, she means that you're to treat me well and love me like mad or else you'll have her to answer to, but she has never tried to drive a wedge between us. I mean it, Charles. I know you two don't get on and you don't always approve, but she has always only ever wanted my happiness."

His face softened with tenderness. "Darling, Miss Phillips does not have to worry at all." A thumb grazed the skin of my temple, stroking softly. "I realized last night that I had kept you at arm's length because I was afraid of losing you, but because of it, I'd lost you anyway. I haven't protected you. I've hurt you. I cannot say that everything is fixed overnight, but I am going to try, dearest. For you, and God willing, for our family. You've been fighting for us, but it's not fair for it to be all on you. I need to fight for us, too."

He slid his hand down my arm and then rested his hand on my abdomen, where his child was growing.

I wasn't sure if I wanted to laugh or cry, but as his smile widened, I felt myself beaming, a flame of hope and happiness rising within me. And when he kissed me gently and said, "I love you," I knew that everything was going to be all right. Not perfect;

nothing ever was. And not all at once, either. But the one thing I'd needed to know was now a certainty. Charles loved me. We could work our way through anything now.

Not long and the bugle would sound for luncheon, but Charles and I needed something far more than food. We needed each other, so we ignored the schedule and instead found our way into each other's arms. Finally, finally the two of us curled up in the large bed, our bodies intimately twined together, clothing scattered on the floor haphazardly. I rolled onto my back with my head on my pillow and laughed, a low, slow chuckle that was relief and release and happiness all rolled into one. Charles rested on one elbow, gazing down at me, his hair standing up on one side in a most adorable way. I reached up and patted down a stubborn spot. "I think you should show up to all your meetings this way when you're in America," I suggested, feeling silly. "It's very becoming."

"Hush, you," he replied, then leaned over and kissed me lightly, before a shadow fell over his face. "Are you all right? Truly? I didn't hurt anything..."

"Right as rain," I replied. In fact, I was even better. It had been years since I'd been so thoroughly loved. Not since the early days of my first pregnancy.

His hand, under the covers now, slid up my thigh and then cradled the firm bump just below my navel. "And everything is all right here? How are you feeling?"

It was such a glorious relief to share this with him now. I wished that I'd told him before, for the news was what had finally prompted us to get everything out in the open. We'd wasted precious time, but I was just glad we had the chance to make up for it. "I feel mostly fine," I said. "Sometimes a little tired, which is to be expected, and once in a while my stomach will go off. Like with the oysters. I can't bear even the sight of them, Charles. For the love of all that is holy, please do not ask me if I want some at dinner again."

He grinned. "I shan't. But you shall have all the ice cream you want." He dropped another kiss on my shoulder. "Anything you want, really."

"All I need is just here." I rolled over to face him, and the coverlet slid down toward my waist, exposing my left breast. His gaze dropped; I knew they too had changed in pregnancy, growing larger, the nipples more florid. He looked at me and then lowered his gaze and then his mouth, while a sharp gasp came from my lips as delicious sensations rushed through me.

"Again?" I breathed, as his hand slid from my belly down to the juncture of my legs.

"We have time to make up for, darling," he murmured, kissing the soft spot between my breasts. "I have a lot to make up for, actually."

"Well, don't let me stop you," I replied, as another gasp rippled from my throat.

By late afternoon, we were starving. Charles rang for refreshments to be sent to our room, and while we waited, I pulled on a long, silk robe. Charles met the steward at the door when the knock came, and when he returned with the tray his cheeks were a delightful pink.

"You should have let him come in," I said, teasing. "He would have got an eye full."

"You sound like Miss Phillips," he replied, then held up a teacup. "Shall I pour?"

"That would be lovely."

After tea, Charles took some time to shave and tidy up, dressing for dinner. "I know you and Miss Phillips will want to start getting ready for the evening," he said. "I thought I might pop out for a bit. I'll come get you a half hour before the bugle?"

"Perfect." I already knew what I was going to wear. My peach dress – the Lucile design – with pearls in my hair. It was the most flattering frock I owned, and wouldn't it be fun if Lady Duff-Gordon recognized the design as one of hers?

When his cravat was perfect, his jawline flawless, and his jacket smoothed over his shoulders, he kissed me softly and then departed the cabin.

I floated over to the door to Lou's room, humming a little as I reached for the knob. I opened the door, saying, "Lou, you'll never guess wha—"

The thought fled as I stared at Lou, sitting at her table, her mouth open with shock and guilt written all over her face. Her bag, the ugly leather one she'd been so possessive about, was on the floor beside her chair. And on the table was the largest assortment of jewels and trinkets I'd ever seen.

Including my new earrings, the emeralds winking at me as I stared at the collection and then back at Lou.

"Let me explain—"

"You. It was you this whole time. Oh my God."

I rushed to the table, snatched back my earrings, and then swept out of the room, slamming the door behind me.

Chapter Seventeen

```
April 14, 1912
    Titanic
```

LOUISA

Panic raced like lightning through my body and down my extremities. I should have locked the damn door. Why had I not locked the door? Now Hannah was standing in her robe, staring at me with such shock and accusation that my neck and face flamed with shame.

Her eyes dropped to the collection in front of me and landed on her earrings. My heart sank. I hadn't stolen them; I wouldn't steal from her. I'd forgotten that I'd slipped them into my pocket and had taken them out to give them back to her. She'd never believe that now.

"Let me explain—" I began, the words strangling in my throat.

She shook her head, her eyes aflame with disgust. "You. It was you this whole time. Oh my God."

Then she grabbed her earrings and ran, slamming the door behind her.

I dropped my head onto my hand, a breath leaving my lungs in a mighty gust. Then I got up and went after her. I had to explain. I had to... God.

I tried the door and found it locked.

"Hannah, open the door, please. Let me explain."

There was silence, and I knocked again. "Hannah, please. You need to understand." A new fear took hold. What if Hannah called the... What was it on a ship, anyway? A Master at Arms? I had no idea. But if she turned me in ... would I be arrested? Denied entry into America? Be put in prison?

"Hannah, for the love of God, please. Please talk to me. Don't turn me in, please." I was crying now, more afraid than I'd ever been, except for when Hannah had been in early childbirth and I'd feared for her life. I'd taken part in protests and demonstrations and stared into the eyes of the police and had not been this frightened.

The lock snicked and she opened the door, but her face was a terrifying mask of fury.

"You're the jewel thief," she accused, stepping aside. "You took things that don't belong to you. There's not much to explain."

I actually thought I might throw up, I was so upset. "I know it seems that way. And you're not totally wrong. But if you knew why—"

"Stealing is wrong, Lou. No matter the reason." Her eyes were filled with fire. "Do you know, this afternoon I was defending you to Charles, yet again, and you were in here what, counting your money and thinking what a fool I am?"

"Yes, yes, you're right. I know it's wrong, Hannah, I—" I stepped into her cabin but did not know what to do with myself. Pace? Sit? I was too antsy to sit. Instead I gestured toward her hand, which still clenched the earrings. "I need you to know, I didn't take those. You left them on the dresser, and I grabbed them this morning with your other jewellery when you were getting dressed in my cabin. You called for me and I put them in my pocket, and totally forgot they were there until this afternoon. You have to believe me, Hannah."

While I remained in one spot, she'd started pacing the room, and she whirled on me as I said the last words. "*I* have to believe *you*?" She gave a short, humourless laugh. "You lectured me on keeping secrets from you, from my husband, and all the while you were sitting on this … deception. How can I possibly believe you? What have you done, Lou?" She glared at me. "Who are you? Because I don't know anymore."

I couldn't shake the panic squeezing my chest. "I'm someone with limited options, all right?" I didn't want to be overheard, so it came out in a violent hiss. "Marry Bulbous Balcombe or lose all financial support from my father. So I took a few things that most people will never miss. The plan was to sell them in New York, use the money to live my life. Perhaps a less pampered one than I've had thus far, but it would be mine. A little flat somewhere, money to fight for the causes I believe in."

She'd stopped and was staring at me with her mouth hanging open. "You're playing Robin Hood with yourself as the beneficiary. Unbelievable. As if that justifies anything."

"For God's sake," I snapped, "the people I stole from probably never even realized things were missing, they have so much."

"Oh, Louisa." Her voice dropped, and she used my full name, so I knew she was hugely upset and disappointed. "You know yourself that Margaret was particularly distressed at the loss of her bracelet. That was it, wasn't it? The amethyst one. Just because people are rich doesn't mean things don't hold sentimental value. You stole from your friends to pad your own pockets, rather than growing up and facing your father."

She was right about everything, except the growing up. I chewed the inside of my lip for a moment while my own anger grew at the same pace as my shame. "I knew you would be like this, you know," I retorted. "And that's why I didn't tell you. It's so easy for you to say how horrible and wrong this is. Hannah with her perfect morals and her perfect … I don't know, manners. You don't rock the boat, because you're perfectly happy to be exactly where you are. Charles would never throw you into the street without a shilling. You will never have to give up your comfortable life."

"There's nothing wrong with my life," she snapped back. "Whereas you … you've been flirting with the boundaries of propriety for as long as I've known you. I've overlooked a lot, Lou, to be your friend. But by God, there have been times when I've wished you could be a little less … you. All the times you deliberately provoked Charles out of sheer amusement. Antagonizing your father. Putting yourself in positions of danger for your causes, and I swear sometimes I think you hope to be arrested just to cause your family further aggravation and embarrassment."

"I'm an embarrassment," I said, my voice dangerously low. Yes, stealing was wrong, but Hannah was attacking all the things I held close to my heart as important. How long had she despised me, then?

"My life has never been comfortable, Hannah, and you know that. I've been kept out of my father's sight most of my life. And yes, perhaps this whole rights thing is my way of rebelling, but why shouldn't I? You, more than anyone, know what happened if I got in the way."

The only thing worse than being ignored was being disciplined. The pain and humiliation of it still stung. The marks on my skin had faded over time, but not the angry scar left on my heart. More than once I'd returned to school with a new bruise or scar. Father did not spare the rod.

"There had to be another way. Something legal." Hannah stared at me. "Something not … immoral."

"I'm a woman, Hannah. My choices came down to marrying someone I didn't love and subject myself to a life like my mother has, or rely on charity."

"I would have helped you a thousand times, rather than see you do this!"

"Perhaps." It cut me to the quick, this argument. Perhaps it had been coming for a long time, regardless of my latest questionable activities. Our lives – and how we wanted to live them – were so different. And perhaps judgment shouldn't have a place in this conversation, but it did. And not just from Hannah. I judged her, too, for thinking she needed Charles's approval, for tying her identity to his rather than owning her own.

I met her gaze evenly, trying desperately not to shrink in shame. "But Hannah, it wouldn't have been you helping me. It would have been Charles's charity. His money. Charles, who would tell me to just marry Balcombe and get on with it. Charles, who has never approved of me."

"Charles is fairer than that!" she insisted.

"Is he? He can't even bring himself to call me Louisa. He tolerates me because of you. And barely."

"Then what about Mr. Grey—"

"This was all put in motion months ago, when Reid was nothing more than a flirtation." I took a step forward, lifted a hand a little before dropping it again. "I care about him, Hannah. If I am going to be with Reid, I need him to know it's because I love him, not because I need his money. I won't marry him looking for an easy way out."

"I guess you're saying that's what I did when I married Charles, right?" Hannah whirled away again, the silk of her robe rippling at her heels. She went to the pitcher and poured herself some water, drank it. After she put down the glass, she turned back, her face impassive. "Lou, I have loved you like a sister for half my life. But this... We have our differences. More than I ever dreamed. Lou, you stole. From friends. You would rather do that than swallow a bit of your pride, but let me tell you, that pride is going to get you into a heap of trouble someday."

She'd said someday. As if today was not that day. Hope, relief, rushed over me in a cold wave. "You're not turning me in?"

Hannah swallowed and shook her head. "I am not. But you've betrayed me, Lou. Those earrings—"

"I told you that was an accident."

"I don't believe you. You were willing to take things not yours without a thought, and sell them for your own profit. I thought I knew you, but it's clear I really don't. Maybe I never did."

But she did. More than anyone in the world. That didn't change the fact that for months now, we'd kept things from each other out of fear of judgment and recriminations. And that was because deep down, our values weren't as aligned as we thought.

"Now, if you'll excuse me, I am going to call a stewardess to help me dress. It would be better if you didn't join us for dinner."

The rejection hit me like a slap. "But after that? What about New York?"

She stared at me a long moment, her face impassive. "I do believe I will take the train to Arizona with my husband instead. We've reconciled."

My heart withered in that moment. Nothing she might have said could have made it any clearer that she was distancing herself from me, that she loathed me. She didn't want me in her sight, and I knew, in her shoes, I would feel the same.

I did not deserve the goodness that was Hannah Martin. I might not want her life, but I could find nothing immoral about it. Unlike myself.

"You're really not going to turn me in?" I asked again, my voice cracking a little.

Hannah sighed. "No, I am not. But this... I... No."

What she meant by those halting words broke my heart, and that was exactly why I hadn't wanted her to ever discover my secret. If there had been any question of whether she could forgive me for what I'd done, it was erased when she said, more coldly than I had ever heard her speak, "Please leave."

I turned and went back to my cabin, pieces of me shattering as I went. I closed the door and locked it, though there was no purpose to it now, as something far stronger than a door lock separated us. My treasure still lay on the table: the bracelet, rings, a set of green cufflinks and studs, a bow brooch with a diamond in the middle, a couple of pocket watches ... a fortune.

A fortune that perhaps came at too great a cost.

I swept it all back into the bag and then tucked the bag into the bottom of my wardrobe, hidden behind my heavy coat. Then I sat at the table again, the bottle of whisky in front of me, deciding if I should get well and truly drunk or ... well, something else.

Hannah's words echoed in my head, telling me to grow up and face my father. I snorted, then blinked against tears. She couldn't know I had done just that, once, when I'd left our estate to go to Hannah when the baby was coming. He forbade me from going. He'd never considered Hannah to be in the same social sphere as we were, which was ridiculous. Nothing would have kept me from her side when she needed me, and I defied him to his face. All that had achieved was getting a slap on mine, one so forceful it dropped me to my knees. Then he'd forced me to get up by pulling my hair, an eye-watering pain that I could still feel when I thought about it. He'd pushed me away and said he had made his point.

Except it hadn't worked. I packed a bag, snuck out in the night, and once I got to the closest village, I hired someone to take me to Hannah and Charles's. I stayed over a month.

When I finally returned, I was informed that my father would be making a match for me and that if I did not comply, I would be cast out without any financial assistance. When I'd looked to my mother for help, she'd merely given a small shake of her head.

The entire reason I was in this predicament was because I'd defied my father at a time Hannah needed me most. I would not change that if my life depended on it. Not even now, not even knowing that it might lead to choices that one day could cost us our friendship.

Hannah knew nothing of this story, nor would I tell her and make her feel the least bit responsible. Truthfully, my father had only needed an excuse and would have found another one somewhere else. I never quite understood why he disliked me so, but now that I was grown, I realized it didn't matter. He treated everyone as disposable, everyone but my brother. So I tried to not take it personally, though some days were harder than others. To be turned away by my closest friend, though ... that caused a pain that stole my breath, and I had no one to blame but myself. Hadn't I known this would happen if Hannah ever found out what I was up to?

I had to choose what to do next. What I really wanted to do was get in bed and never come out, but Reid would be looking for me tonight and honestly, the thought of being held in his arms – and that's all – felt like a life preserver in a rough sea. I could go to dinner myself. I had enough "friends" that mingling wouldn't be an issue. I was very good at faking my emotions in public, and after tonight there were only a few more days until we docked in New York. Besides, I had to eat. I hadn't since breakfast. But I wasn't going to join Charles and Hannah in the dining saloon. I'd eat at the restaurant tonight. I was not so tight for money that I couldn't splurge a little and stay out of their orbit.

And so I decided to buck up, pick out a frock, and call for assistance. Just like every other time in my life, I would cover up my pain with gaiety, my sadness with fun. There were cocktails to be enjoyed, bright lights, rich people. I'd lose myself there for a few hours, and then come back and make some decisions. I doubted our friendship could come back from something like this, and while tonight I was going to ignore that fact and force myself to enjoy the evening, eventually I'd have to face up to the world without my dearest friend by my side.

Chapter Eighteen

April 14, 1912
Titanic

HANNAH

I did not tell Charles about what happened with Lou. When he came back precisely at the time he'd indicated, I was coiffed and ready for the evening. Seeing him come through the door and smiling at me – a genuine, open smile – warmed my heart and took away some of the aching pain nesting there. I had my marriage back. I probably could have had it all along if I'd stopped trying to cajole and had simply been honest.

Ha, honesty. Considering the revelation about Lou's activities, I was suddenly painfully aware of the absolute importance of honesty and how nothing good could come from lying.

That didn't mean I felt compelled to share what I knew. Charles was already not a huge fan of Lou, and I didn't want to shatter our new harmony by putting her in the middle of it. Indeed, after what she'd done, she didn't deserve to take up space in our lovely evening. The things she'd said still burned. That she thought so little of me, of the life I had chosen, stung.

Yes, I was still angry. And hurt, and disappointed, too. I never thought she was capable of something so devious and wrong, but what really had thrown me was realizing how much we had grown apart. Both of us had chosen to ignore it until it was impossible to do so any longer.

Charles bussed my cheek with his lips and stepped back. "You are a picture," he said approvingly. "That is such a lovely colour on you, and you have roses in your cheeks."

"You put them there," I replied, then turned in a circle. "I'll do, then?"

"You'll do," he said. He held out his hand. "Darling, are you truly all right? With the baby, I mean. After the last time—"

I put my fingers in his, wondering how many times he would ask, knowing he was completely entitled to his worry. "I am, Charles, I promise. I've seen a doctor; there's no cause for alarm." I didn't mention that Lou already knew. I'd admitted to her that I hadn't talked to the doctor about the risks. I was giving Charles assurances I wasn't quite qualified to give, other than what I felt in my heart to be true.

"I was walking the deck and thinking about you expecting and I —" He let out a breath and met my gaze, his eyes sincere. "Darling, I know you're looking forward to the week with Miss Phillips, but I wish you'd come with me. I also understand you don't want someone hovering over you all the time, but if anything *were* to happen and I was so far away…" Pain flitted across his face, pain that I now knew came from remembering our first tragedy.

"I was thinking the same thing and said so to Lou just this afternoon." Which was true, even if I made it sound like no more than a passing mention. "It might be nice to go with you, if you'll still have me."

He nodded. "Hannah, I'm so sorry about how I handled everything. I only wanted to save you pain, not cause you more. I hope you know that."

"I do," I said, lifting my hand to his face. "But don't do it again, Charles, no matter what life might bring us. We should be facing things together. That's what we promised to do when we married, do you remember?"

He smiled. "I do. We were so fragile back then. I loved you already, but wasn't sure if you really loved me. We got on so well, but everything felt … precious." His gaze roved over my face, admiration etched upon it. "You are such a strong woman," he said. "I'm honoured you're my wife, and I promise to do better."

"I promise that as well. Just don't shut me out again, Charles. I don't think I could bear that." Especially now, when I was feeling particularly alone.

"I won't," he vowed, and cleared his throat. "Now, I have good news. We've been invited to the restaurant for dinner. There's a party for Captain Smith and the Wideners are hosting."

I'd met the Wideners. They seemed like lovely people, and their son, Harry, had given Lou an appraising glance when we'd met. "Is it a large party?" I asked.

"I don't think so, but the company will be excellent and it's an honour to be asked. I accepted on our behalf; I hope that's all right?"

"Of course," I said, glad I'd saved my peach dress for tonight. My new earrings were tucked away – Lou wouldn't dare try to take anything of mine now – and I had pulled out my diamond necklace for the occasion.

"You should wear a wrap or a coat, darling. When I was on deck, I noticed a turn in the weather. It's gotten much colder."

I didn't want my heavy coat, so I chose instead a velvet opera coat in royal blue. I was immediately glad of it; my upper arms were already a little chilly even with the heater running in our room. The weather had been so nice thus far; it wasn't surprising we'd run out of luck in that regard. "At least it's not raining. Or snowing," I added.

I had to admit, the evening felt like a bit of a fairy tale. We joined the group in the restaurant where everything was absolutely perfect. Captain Smith was in his fine dress uniform, with the Wideners nearby. I noticed Major Butt and also the Carters. The Thayers were there as well, and when I looked around, I saw many familiar faces. It seemed that while the dining saloon was exceptional, the restaurant was *the* place to be seen.

Everything was beautiful. The food was delicious, the crystal sparkling, the lights twinkling, the conversation vigorous and entertaining. The Spode china sported a special pattern that had been reserved for the restaurant, and the attention to detail was staggering: moulded ceilings, carved walnut panelling, gilt brass accents.

I had no doubt, however, that my effervescence was due to the change in my marriage and my hope for the future, and not the elegant trappings around me. I watched as Charles spoke with the other men, sounding so smart and charming, and I was proud. Proud of him, proud to be his wife. Proud that we were going to have a baby, and I was determined that nothing should go wrong. Most of all, I was proud of myself for not giving up on us. Perhaps it had taken me a while to sort out the right approach, but I hadn't stopped trying. I wondered if my mama would be proud of me. If Father would. He had loved my mother so very much. My heart ached for him. I hadn't seen him in months. I resolved to schedule in a visit before the baby came, and see if I couldn't make some amends there, too.

The only dark mark on the evening was thinking about Lou. More than the rift in our friendship, I found I was still appalled by what she'd done, and I didn't believe for a moment the story she'd given me about my earrings and her pocket. I'd known she was desperate to find a way out of marrying Balcombe, and she'd mentioned having a plan of sorts, but not in a million years had I considered she would do anything illegal. I never thought she would betray her values, her friends ... her best friend. That hurt most of all. She had been there when Charles had given me the earrings. She knew how much they meant to me. Now I felt as if I didn't know her at all, and frankly, she'd been such a pillar of my life that the thought of doing without her had me feeling a bit adrift.

"Are you all right, darling?" Charles asked, leaning over. "You've hardly touched your filet."

"Perfectly well," I replied, smiling. "Just a little distracted. It's been a strange but wonderful day, don't you agree?"

"I do," he replied, and he touched my hand beneath the table.

My meal was further marred by the appearance of Lou and Reid Grey, who were seated at a table for two. She looked gorgeous as always, svelte and glamorous with her honey hair done up in an elegant style and a double strand of pearls around her neck, looking for all the world as if nothing had ever happened. Her dress was black but far from drab, shimmering beneath the lights as she moved with the innate grace I so envied. Even though we were seated on the starboard side and aft, I could hear her laugh from across the room. Reid Grey was clearly as in the dark as I had been. Fool.

"I do believe I'm getting full," I said quietly.

"You must have room for ice cream." Charles had been speaking to Major Butt and gave me his fleeting attention. It was past nine now, and I expected the captain would soon leave the party and return to his duties. Throughout the meal I'd heard some excited chatter about how the boilers had all been lit and we were making great speed. When someone mentioned the change in the air and asked if there was danger of icebergs, the captain waved it aside. There were always lookouts, he said. All in all, the mood was as jovial as could be. It was for me, too, with the exception of Lou. That was all right, I told myself. This was something that would take time to get over. I was entitled to be angry and hurt.

When the meal was over, I was exhausted. Last night had been emotionally draining and today had been up and down. I longed for our bed and to be held in Charles's arms, so after dinner we stayed for only two orchestra numbers, greeted Mrs. Brown and the Astors, and made our way to our cabin.

Tomorrow morning I would wake up in Charles's embrace and we would truly begin our lives anew.

Chapter Nineteen

April 14, 1912
Titanic

LOUISA

Dinner was an absolute torture, and I wished I'd never bothered.

I'd found Reid in the First-Class Lounge, enjoying a cocktail, and I'd joined him, looking for a friendly port in a storm. I tried not to think about the sheer force of relief I felt when I glimpsed his face, because I knew what it meant and it frightened me so. In the spirit of honesty, at least with myself, I needed to accept that I'd fallen in love with him on this voyage. There was far more to him than I'd realized. When he'd met my gaze across the room, it was as if the cold North Atlantic air disappeared and charged heat zapped between us.

And when he'd reached into his pocket and withdrawn the long strand of pearls I'd left in his room, dangling them from his fingers, I'd been nothing short of delighted. He'd given me a delicious, naughty wink as he'd put them in my hands, and I slipped them over my head, the creamy beads warm against my neck after being tucked into his pocket.

Since my "assigned" seating in the saloon was with Charles and Hannah, I suggested we dine together in the restaurant, an idea that Reid embraced heartily. He looked so dashing in his tuxedo. When we entered the restaurant, I caught a glimpse of us in the mirrors and saw we made a fine pair. I almost forgot about everything falling apart earlier, until we were led to a table and I saw Hannah and Charles seated at a table with the Wideners, the Carters, the Thayers, and Captain Smith.

My stomach knotted. Had Hannah told Charles about the stolen items? He leaned close to her and murmured something; she gazed up at him and smiled. It seemed that all was well there, then, and despite our falling out, I was glad of it. Patching up their marriage was what she wanted most in the world. But there was a chance I would not be there to witness her happiness. She wanted nothing to do with me and I couldn't even blame her. Nothing she had said today was wrong.

"Are you all right, darling?" asked Reid as we were seated.

I made myself smile. "Oh yes, of course. I didn't get much sleep last night. I'm sorry if I seem distracted."

"And what kept you up?" he asked, after ordering us a bottle of champagne.

He was teasing. I could tell by the sparkle in his eyes and the way one eyebrow gave the tiniest tweak.

I could flirt back, but tonight I felt different. Like keeping up the pretence of fun and games was suddenly too heavy, too much work. I was honest instead. "Hannah and Charles had a row, and she slept in my extra bed after we talked. She fell asleep, but I didn't, not really. I've had a lot on my mind."

Reid, bless him, took the hint. His flirtatious smile faded and his eyes softened with concern. "Are they all right? Are you? I know how much she means to you, Lou."

"I believe they are now. I'm actually very glad it happened, because once everything was out in the open, they finally dealt with it. Secrets, living a life of pretend … it doesn't work, does it?"

Our champagne arrived, followed by a first course, and for a time we chatted about lighter subjects. People we both knew, the attraction of New York City, what we hoped to do there. Now that Hannah was planning to go with Charles, perhaps I would spare some time to spend with Reid, though I kept that tidbit quiet for the moment. I made a point of not glancing over at Hannah's table and stayed focused on my dinner partner, smiling and laughing at appropriate times. But as the meal progressed, the more miserable I became. How could I say anything about Hannah living a life of pretend when here I was, doing the very same thing?

I was picking away at the perfectly grilled bream when Reid put his hand over mine. "What's wrong?" he asked, his voice low and soft with concern. "Something is bothering you, Lou, I can tell. Can I help? Is it what we talked about before? How…" He halted, as if searching for the right words. "I know you don't want to be rescued. You made that clear. But is it the Balcombe problem, or is there something else?"

I studied his face. He was so earnest, so kind. In fact, we were much alike. Until we'd got to know each other better during the voyage, I had considered him mostly flash and little substance. The fun but not forever type. He gave the impression of having money and a willingness to part with it at parties and such, but I had come to realize that, like me, it was a mask he wore to keep people from digging deeper. That was the man I wanted to get to know. The man I wanted to spend a lifetime discovering, bit by bit.

If that was what I truly wanted – and to my terror it seemed it was – I needed to come clean about my activities. I couldn't preach honesty and communication to my best friend and ignore it in my own relationship. Moreover, if this truly did go somewhere with Reid, I knew in my heart that beginning with a lie between us was a sure way to ruin everything.

The truth always came out, somehow. Today was proof enough of that.

"Darling, you're scaring me now. I have never known you to be so quiet. Whatever it is, you can tell me."

"Are you sure of that? You may hate me and never want to speak to me again."

He burst out laughing, then sobered as he realized I was serious. "That would never happen."

"It might." The very thought made me ill, and the bream was suddenly unappetizing. I put down my fork and dabbed my lips with my napkin.

"This is serious, then." Reid held my gaze. "Whatever it is, you don't need to tell me, Louisa. Everyone has a right to their own secrets."

He was giving me a reprieve and for five long seconds I considered taking it. I looked around me. I was strongly considering marrying Reid, if he'd have me. No one could be more surprised at that than I. As his wife, we could dine like this whenever we wanted. I'd never have to worry about where the money was coming from or how to make it stretch or if I could afford to help the women who worked to support their family on lower wages than the men who did the same job. I could keep my causes and my lifestyle. I could have it all.

More than that, I would have Reid. I would have the love and acceptance I'd always wanted and never found. With a wrench to my heart, I realized I'd thought I had that with Hannah, but even her love had limits. That's when I knew that I had to tell Reid everything. It would devastate me if he walked away, but far better to do it now than have him find out later and end things.

Ship of Dreams

I had to trust him. And this meant not just with the truth about the gems and money currently in my cabin. Marriage meant giving up my independence, the very thing I swore I would never do, and trusting he would not abuse that power. I wasn't sure I could go through with it.

"I need to tell you something," I said finally, my throat squeezing and my stomach heavy with dread. "Not here. If I'm even to consider reconsidering"—I gave a brief smile—"there are things you need to know. You may not want me after."

"Dear me." His brow furrowed. "This does sound serious. I'm sure there's nothing you have done or could do that would change my mind. But it does seem important to you, so if you need to unburden yourself, we can find a place to talk."

There were more courses and pudding as well, but I had lost my appetite and all desire to continue the charade of a carefree, happy dinner. "In my cabin," I said, putting my napkin on the table. "It needs to be there."

Reid's face took on a blank look of alarm. I knew I was being cryptic and we were in the middle of our meal, but I was exhausted and honestly wanted to get this over with. A glance told me that Charles and Hannah had already departed and the Widener party was coming to a close. In a flash, I pasted on a bright smile and faked my way through the restaurant.

Once we were outside, Reid took my hand and gave my fingers a squeeze. I tried to be reassured, but how would he react, seeing the evidence of what I'd done? I'd even stolen from him.

Neither of us spoke as we passed through the baized doors and down the hallway toward my cabin. It was quiet here, and our shoes were loud in the abrupt silence. I opened the door to my cabin and held it as he entered. Things were tidier than earlier; the stewardess had helped me straighten things a little, bless her, but it was certainly not pristine. "Have a seat." I gestured toward the settee, then swept a scarf off the nearby chair. "I'll get us a drink."

We were both going to need it.

Before long we were sitting side by side with generous glasses of whisky in our hands. Reid took a drink and then looked at me. "I have to admit, Lou, you're scaring me a little. If you tell me you have a body hidden in your wardrobe, we might be in trouble here."

He was attempting levity, but it hit a little too close. "Not a body," I answered, taking a fortifying sip. The alcohol burned down my throat and into my stomach, and I hastily took another drink for courage. "Let me explain this, please, Reid. Don't interrupt. Then you can decide if you really want to be with me or not."

His unease turned to downright fear, though a glint of curiosity sparked in his eyes.

I drained my glass and put it down on the floor beside me, then turned so I was angled toward him, our knees nearly touching, able to look at his face. I didn't want to. I was ashamed and afraid of watching his regard for me disappear, but if Hannah could be brave and confront her husband, I could be brave and confront … well, myself, really. That's what this really was, wasn't it? Facing my choices, wrong or right.

"When my father threatened to cut me off financially, he made me a deal. If I married, my dowry would go to my husband. If I didn't, I would be on my own without a farthing."

Reid's jaw tightened. "How could a father—"

"You agreed to let me explain," I interrupted, silencing him. "Anyway, I managed to avoid the first few men he threw at me, but then Balcombe came into the picture. Father likes him. Of course he does. And the threat suddenly became very real. Especially when he found out about my activities with the WSPU. He was livid about that. Anyway, there is no way I am going to marry Balcombe. And so I had to come up with a plan to secure my future. On my terms, you see."

Reid only nodded, bless him. He was allowing me to tell my story, and I loved him for it.

"My whole life, my father has giveth and he has taketh away," I continued. "I was sent away more often than not, a liability. I've never really trusted men, and my few relationships … well, I've started them and I've ended them, too, and that's been by design. Even when Charles seemed to be the exception to the rule, a good man, you see, I saw him withdraw from Hannah and break her heart after…" I hesitated here. This was Hannah's private business, but this was also the man I cared for deeply. "…after they lost their first baby. It changed everything."

"That's horrible," he murmured, but that was all. How he was exercising such restraint was beyond me, because Reid loved a bit of back and forth.

"I came up with a plan, but I told no one. I told no one because it involved something illegal. When Hannah told me about the trip to New York, I knew this was the perfect opportunity to complete my plan and return to England able to support myself and not have to marry Balcombe at all. It wasn't just to buy myself time."

Reid's face had paled. "Illegal," he repeated, and my stomach knotted.

"Wait here," I said, and though my knees were trembling, I went to the wardrobe, dug out the Gladstone bag, and brought it back to where we were sitting.

I placed it between us on the settee and opened it. Then I withdrew the items one by one, placing them in a pile on the firm cushion. "Mr. Weir's pocket watch. Margaret Brown's bracelet. Mrs. Allison's necklace." The other items, too: the brooch, the Amy bracelet, trinkets I'd lifted from house parties and events. It was quite a collection, and last of all, I took out two generous bundles of pound notes and Reid's diamond-studded tie pin.

He picked it up in his fingers, turning it around, then looking up at me.

"The plan was…"

"To sell the items in New York. Selling them in London would have been far riskier. I decided to come on this trip, sneak away and sell the items, and the cash would finance a modest but decent lifestyle without need of my father's money."

He put the tie pin on top of the rest of the items and looked into my eyes. "Is anyone else in on it?" he asked. "An accomplice?"

I shook my head. "No. Not even Hannah knew until this afternoon. She is no longer speaking to me." My voice hitched as I said it. I couldn't imagine a world without Hannah, and because of this plan I'd gone and ruined our friendship, though apparently it had been on tenuous footing anyway. "I do believe when we reach New York, she'll be going with Charles to Arizona and skipping the week with me. Which makes sense. She can't even look at me right now."

Reid sighed. He gazed at the sparkling pile of gold and gems and sighed again. Then he looked up at me.

"This is not a body in a wardrobe," he finally said, "but it's not good, Lou, and I can't believe you haven't been caught. You could go to prison for a long time. You'd never be able to show your face in society again if anyone knew."

"I know. The thing is, Reid, I'm trying to help people, too. Women who need better pay and working conditions, who need to escape horrible situations. The right to vote. Right now I have credibility. I have my good name. I wouldn't if this were to get out." I shook my head. "Believe me, I know the easiest way to get out of marrying Balcombe is to create a scandal. I considered it, but then I still wouldn't have the money, and my reputation would be in tatters. No one would take me seriously."

"And you couldn't ask for help? Surely Hannah… Even I—"

"Help always comes with conditions, Reid. Borrowing money, accepting charity … those are transactions. As a banker, you must understand that."

"You accept the money but give away the power," he said, and I nearly wept with relief at how completely he grasped the situation.

"It's why I refused to let you rescue me," I added. "I just didn't count on..."

This was the scariest part. Not showing him the evidence of my crimes but showing him my heart. "I didn't count on falling in love with you this week, Reid Grey. It's changed everything. I no longer know what to do. But what I do know is that no matter what, I cannot have this lie between us. If you walk away now, so be it. It's no less than I deserve. But if there's a chance you might love me too, I refuse to start our journey together on a lie."

Reid's glass had gone forgotten in his hand during my whole speech, but now he tossed the liquor back as if it were nothing. Then he, too, put his glass on the floor and stood, holding out his hand. When I took it, my heart clubbing away with fear and the tiniest bit of hope, he pulled me into the biggest hug I'd ever received.

How did he know that I didn't need kisses or lovemaking or promises at this moment, but the warmth and security of a hug? The ability to lay all my burdens down for a few moments and let him carry the weight of it all for me? Tears sprang into my eyes and I blinked, trying hard not to cry, wondering why it had taken twenty-six years to receive this kind of unconditional support and care. Wondering why I had never been worth it to those who should have loved me most. Instead I found it in a charming London banker who looked at my flaws and for some crazy reason, didn't seem to care.

"What do I do now?" I asked, my voice muffled in his jacket. "I had a clear way forward, and now it feels as if I know nothing at all."

He pushed me back a little and kept his hands on my shoulders before bending his knees a bit so we were eye to eye. "You might be able to return the items you stole on the ship, if your sleight of hand is as good in reverse. As far as the other things... Is there a way you can return them? At the very least, don't sell them. You'll be out the money, but there won't be a trail to you, either. And it's the right thing to do. If you don't profit off your crime—"

"Then what's the point?" I made a slight joke and gave a little laugh. "I know what you're saying, Reid. But ... aren't you furious with me? Aren't you angry? I mean, one of the things I stole was yours."

He pulled me into his arms again. "I'm shocked, I won't lie about that. And I'm disappointed, certainly. But I don't hate you. When people are cornered, they'll do all sorts of things."

"Hannah hates me."

"Hannah feels betrayed. She'll come around."

"I'm not sure she will. We've been friends for over a decade. We've never spoken a cross word to each other, and that's saying a lot because I'm very opinionated. It's not just this, either. We're ... different. In fundamental ways. We just spent a very long time ignoring it."

He smiled at me, a tender expression softening his face. "People can be very different and still love each other. Still be friends. The world would be a very boring place if we all thought and acted alike."

"Except Hannah is inherently good. It's a lot to try to live up to."

He led me to the bed and we sat on the edge, and then he gathered me into his arms until we were cuddled on top of the coverlet, a puddle of black wool and silk. "Lou, I thought for sure you were going to tell me you had a child hidden away in the country or something. Or that you were pregnant now with another man's child. This... This is definitely not what I expected, but darling, it's not unforgivable. I'll admit I don't understand the insistence to resort to stealing rather than accept help. That being said, I also admit that I do not know what it's like to be a woman and I can only try to imagine what I'd do if someone had issued such an ultimatum to me. In other words, darling, I try not to judge."

"How did you end up such a good man?" I asked, snuggling

into his chest. "I just know there must be a flaw in there somewhere."

"I have many," he replied, stroking the top of my head. "As I'm sure you'll discover if you finally say yes."

I sat up, stared at him. His dark eyes were serious, but his lips held a soft smile. "You still want to marry me."

"Someone needs to make an honest woman out of you. And a better man out of me. That's what you do, you know. Make me want to be better."

"If I say yes, can we go home and will you actually court me? Properly? I think I'd like that, Reid."

"How surprisingly traditional," he answered, then lowered his lips to kiss the crests of my cheeks. "I will absolutely court you. I will shower you with flowers and jewels – legal ones – and take you to soirées and dance with you in my arms and then we will have a grand wedding. Just wait and see. And then I will personally drive you to any protests and demonstrations – as long as they're safe, mind you – and—"

His declaration was cut short by my kisses, which I peppered all over his mouth, and before long we were sprawled over the bed, our breaths coming hot and fast. "Yes, then," I breathed, panting a little from anticipation. "I'll marry you, Reid Grey. God help us both. And I will never, ever, steal again."

He laughed and kissed me again, but then the room shuddered unexpectedly. We stopped and looked at each other, surprised and curious. When the vibration stopped, it stopped completely. The subtle sound that usually marked our movement was gone – undetectable in its presence but conspicuous in its absence. Reid got down off the bed and I did, too. "I think we've stopped," he said, frowning. "You felt that too, right?"

I nodded, disconcerted. "I'm sure it's nothing. The ship is so huge that anything else is dwarfed by it. We'll probably be on our way soon."

"I hope so," Reid replied, but I could tell by his face that he wasn't convinced.

Neither was I.

Chapter Twenty

```
April 14, 1912
   Titanic
```

HANNAH

The lingering strains of the violins followed us as we departed for our cabin. I was tired, I was sad, and all I wanted was a warm bed and my husband's embrace, which had been missing for so long. His hand was in mine now, and he let it go momentarily to open the door.

I stood just inside, admiring our cabin with new eyes. It wasn't just beautiful; it was where we had begun putting our marriage back together. It would always hold a special place in my heart for that reason.

"Darling, do you think we can have the same cabin on the return voyage?" I asked, plucking at the fingers of my gloves.

He gave a small smile as he shrugged off his jacket. "Perhaps. I can certainly request it, if that's what you wish."

"It's suddenly become very important to me," I replied, pulling off the gloves and laying them on the table. I went to him and wound my arms around his neck, lifting my face for a kiss, which he obliged. I smiled, then rested my cheek on his lapel. "Charles, are you still afraid?"

I didn't have to say of what. We both knew to what I was referring. "Yes," he whispered, resting his hands along the base of my spine. "I'm terrified. Losing our baby was horrible, but I almost lost you, too. There's a part of me that freezes when I think of it."

"Me, too," I admitted. "I'm afraid of how bad the grief was. I don't know if I could withstand that sort of pain again."

"You could," he murmured. "You're terribly strong. People just don't realize it because you're also awfully sweet." He kissed my temple. "Now that I know there's another baby on the way, there's no other real choice, is there? I must step up and be a better man, a stronger man. For you and for our child. I have to stop running away. But yes, Hannah. I'm scared to death. Please know, that while I did the wrong thing, I did it because I couldn't bear the thought of putting you through that again."

"Embracing this despite your fears is brave." I leaned back, looking up into his face. "I hope you know that. I'm afraid, too, but when I found out I was pregnant, I knew there was something stronger than my fear."

"Oh?"

I nodded. "Love."

"You are truly a forgiving woman," Charles said, twining his fingers with mine. "I can't promise that I won't ever let the fear get the best of me again. I might hold on too tightly, darling. Afraid to let you out of my sight, now that I know. I want to wrap you up in cotton wool and make sure nothing can hurt you, which of course is impossible. If you can just be patient with me—"

"And you with me," I replied. "The most important thing is that we keep talking to each other, don't you think?"

He nodded. "I wish I'd had the courage to do it months ago," he admitted, looking both sad and contrite. "I think sometimes people do the wrong things for the right reasons."

His words echoed through me as he helped me undress with tender care, sliding each button through its loop, untying ribbons, until I stood in the light of the cabin entirely naked. I shivered, and he carried me to the bed and placed me on it, and then made love to me before tucking me close to the warmth of his body.

Sometimes people do the wrong things for the right reasons.

Did that apply to Lou, too? Were her actions forgivable?

I was just falling asleep when it seemed as if the cabin shuddered, the glasses and pitcher rattling. I sat up, holding the sheet to my chest, when it ceased and everything went eerily quiet.

"We've stopped," Charles said beside me, also sitting. "I wonder what's happened."

Nerves skittered down my arms, tingling in my fingers. "It'll be all right." I said the words automatically, as if there were no other conceivable possibility. "I'm sure they'll fix what's gone wrong and we'll be on our way shortly."

We lay back down, but I could tell Charles was restless. The ever-present but subtle hum of vibration from the engines had not returned. Charles slid out of bed and placed a kiss on my lips. "I'm going to dress and see if I can find out what's happening," he said. "You wait here."

It was inky black in the cabin, without even moonlight to guide him, and I heard Charles rustling with his clothing. A few moments later, the click of the door told me he'd left.

I was not as comfortable in his absence. The quiet was disconcerting, and I got up and turned on the light, deciding to get dressed as well. If there was nothing to worry about, I could easily undress again and go back to bed. There was an urgency tapping on my shoulder, though, saying this was far from normal, and a horrible sense of foreboding I couldn't seem to shake. I told myself I was being ridiculous. Everyone said the ship was unsinkable.

There was no point in putting on an evening dress. Instead I grabbed one of my long, wool skirts with a cream blouse, and put on boots instead of my more delicate shoes. If we had to go outside for any reason, they'd be warmer. I had just finished struggling with buttons when there was a knock on the door, and I rushed to answer it. "Charles, I—"

It wasn't Charles standing there, but a steward, who smiled pleasantly. "Good evening, ma'am."

"What's happening?"

"Everything's all right, ma'am. Just a precaution. You're to take your lifebelt and go up on deck, if you please."

"My husband went to see what happened. I'll go up when he returns."

"You're requested to go now, ma'am. I'm sure he'll meet you up there."

"Thank you," I replied, and shut the door, the dread resting more heavily than before on my shoulders.

I did not rush to go up on deck, however. I didn't want Charles to come back and not find me here. He'd worry, certainly, and I did not want us to get separated. I did, however, locate our life vests and laid them on the bed, and then sat in a chair to wait.

It was just after midnight when he returned, not long in the scheme of things though it felt like hours. He came in, his hair standing on end, as if it had been blown about. "Oh, good. You're dressed. We need to go up on deck, dearest. They're saying it's just a precaution—"

"I know. A steward was by. I wanted to wait for you, though. I didn't want us to be separated."

"Thank God for that," he answered, then opened the wardrobe and began pulling out warm clothes. "It's very cold, so put on your coat. Gloves, too." He handed me my wool overcoat and I retrieved the warmest gloves I had. "I'm so glad you waited. We can go together. I would have been frantic if I'd had to look for you."

I stopped what I was doing and met his gaze. "I remembered what you said about worrying when I was out of your sight." I tried a small smile, though with each passing second, my dread multiplied. "Do you know what happened?"

"We hit an iceberg, on the starboard side. That's why we felt such a jolt."

A cold spear of panic sliced through me. "Are we going to sink?"

He smiled and shook his head, reassuring me with the tenderness on his face. "No, darling. The *Titanic* is built to withstand these things, and I'm sure we'll be on our way soon. But they are asking passengers to go to the decks, just in case. I think this is very much a 'better safe than sorry' thing. I see you got out our life vests. Good girl."

I wanted to believe him and his reassurances, but the surreal feeling taking over me was one of scepticism. "That's what we shall do then," I said, picking up one of the vests. I started to put it on, and he helped me get it over the bulk of my coat and then tightened the straps. Then he put on his own, and I helped as best I could, though I felt completely trussed up between the outerwear and the odd shape of the vest.

We left the cabin, and I didn't look back. I just took Charles's hand as we made our way down the hall, through the doors, and up the stairs toward the First-Class entrance to A Deck. Our cabins were in the section that was close to the bow, and a crowd had already begun to congregate up on the boat deck, where the lifeboats were. The cold hit me like a slap. Despite my coat, the bitterness of it seeped through the material and into my bones. Charles pulled me forward, out of the way of other passengers seeking to come out on deck as ordered. No one was panicking, thank goodness. In fact, most were acting as if it were a real lark to be out here as the clock turned to another day, looking up at the bright pinpoints of stars in the black sky.

"See? Nothing to worry about. Everyone is relaxed. As I said, just a precaution."

That was the third time I'd heard that word, and I didn't believe it. I looked around, and while there was a certain levity amongst the passengers, the crew looked far more serious, their faces grim and their actions brisk. A pair passed by – I couldn't tell their rank – but I heard the words "taking on water" before they disappeared into the gathering crowd.

"Mrs. Martin! Oh heavens, isn't this a to-do?" I looked over my shoulder and saw Helen Candee approaching, also wearing her lifebelt. "I was just getting ready for bed when the steward came knocking." She went to the railing and looked over the side. "Is it just me, or do we seem to be listing a little?"

I looked at Charles for answers. "It's possible that we might be taking on water," he said. "But you know, the bulkheads are watertight. I'm sure at the very worst, another ship will come sort everything or we'll limp our way to…"—he frowned, as if scouring his brain—"Canada, perhaps." He smiled. "This will undoubtedly keep Captain Smith from breaking any speed records, however."

I couldn't give a fig for any speed record. Now that Mrs. Candee had said it, I could feel that we were indeed listing to starboard. A thump grabbed my attention and I turned, realizing that the lifeboats were being readied. "Charles?" I said, my voice tremulous.

This did not feel like a precaution at all. It was far too real.

Chapter Twenty-One

April 15, 1912
Titanic

LOUISA

I wished now I had pulled on more than just my opera coat to come up on deck. The cold was sharp, icy fingers poking into my body, and the only part that seemed to be immune to the frosty bite was that part of me that wore the life vest.

I hadn't wanted to put it on, and had considered it nonsense, but when the minutes dragged on and the ship stayed still, Reid had insisted we see what was going on. We'd met a steward on our way out of the cabin, who brusquely ordered us to go up on deck. We'd headed for the lounge, instead, thinking it the most likely place to find someone who could tell us what had happened. The room was teeming with people, chatting gaily about the excitement. I let out a breath of relief. No one was acting as if there was anything horribly wrong. Someone had a flask of brandy and asked if we wanted a nip. I didn't say no; it had been a horribly long day. Normally I was up for a bit of adventure, but tonight I really wanted to hide away from the world and get some sleep and face everything tomorrow.

Reid, still dashing in his tuxedo, was asking around about what had happened to make us stop so suddenly. When he came back to my side, he was frowning. "Seems like we glanced off an iceberg, old thing," he said, keeping his voice casual. But I knew what Fun Reid sounded like, and this was not it. He was hiding his own concern, probably for my benefit.

"Oh, my God," I breathed, wondering what it all meant. "Are we all right? Can it be fixed?"

"One would hope. This crew is tip top and I'm sure they'll have us on our way in no time."

"I wonder if Charles and Hannah know." I glanced behind me at the stairs. I should go down and check—"

"I'm sure they do. Stewards have been going around, knocking on doors, telling people to come up on deck. The one we saw probably alerted them."

At that moment, a steward patted Reid on the arm. "Excuse me, sir, but you need to put on a life vest. You too, miss." He shoved two in Reid's arms, then moved on and handed out another few, his arms now empty as he rushed from the lounge.

"Reid..." I said, really starting to get anxious. "They wouldn't get us to do this if it weren't serious. Are we going to sink?" My heart froze. "Are we going to die, Reid?"

"Come now," he said, putting his arm around me. "That's quite a leap, darling. And I know you're not prone to panic. I'm sure this is all just standard procedure when there's an incident. Here, I'll help you."

Before long we were both in our bulky life vests, and with the entrance to A Deck open, the draft was making my feet cold. I turned my head to the left and right. There were some people standing about, laughing as though this were all a lark. Others, though, wore the same apprehensive expression I was sure was on my face. There was nothing right about this at all; I felt it deep in my bones and fear trickled in behind it.

Reid gave my wrist a shake. "Darling, they're calling for women and children for the lifeboats."

"No." The objection was out of my mouth before I could think about it. Filling the lifeboats meant we were going to sink. This was inconceivable. "No, Reid, that's ridiculous."

He stared at me, his face ashen, though his words belied his stricken appearance. "Listen, I'm sure it's a precautionary measure, and a wireless call would have gone out anyway, for assistance. We'll be all right. It's always women and children first, right? Standard procedure."

He took my hand and started guiding me toward the starboard side entrance, and I planted my feet and yanked back. "Can't I go back and get something warmer?"

"I'm sure there are blankets in the boats, darling, and it won't be for very long." He tugged again, but I refused to move.

"Reid Grey. You might be a charmer, but you have never, ever lied to me. Please do not lie to me now. We're in trouble, darling." I leaned closer. "I walked the boat deck, remember? I saw the boats. There is no way that everyone is getting off this ship. There simply aren't enough. I may not be a banker, but I can do simple multiplication."

His lips opened, but he said nothing, and then he gathered me in against his chest. "Damn you and your sharp brain," he murmured against my ear.

The truth smothered me until I could hardly breathe. If help didn't come, if this wasn't just a temporary measure, half the people on this ship could die. Tonight. In the space of a moment, I was standing on the A Deck at departure, looking down at those on the second- and third-class decks, waving goodbye to their families. First class would be boarded first. Those women and children below, their husbands, brothers, sons ... entire families could be erased this night. It was too much to bear. I wished my brain refused to understand. I wished my heart would cease to feel. Instead, the pain and shock of it nearly took me to my knees. That first day, when I'd turned from the railing and saw Reid there, looking so dashing, a teasing smile on his face as he tipped his hat...

"Louisa, I need you to look at me." I blinked and shifted my gaze to Reid's face, which was grim with steely determination. "You cannot fall apart, do you hear me? I need you to stay with me."

I nodded, my head bobbing up and down as I struggled to compose myself. I had never been one to lose my grip in a crisis and this would be the very worst time to falter. Instead, my mind shifted to Hannah. I had to find her. She would be with Charles, certainly, but in a moment like this, we couldn't leave things as they were. I had to beg for forgiveness. I needed her to know that I loved her, that she was my family in so many more ways than my own flesh had blood had ever been. I squeezed Reid's fingers and heaved a breath, steadying myself. "I need to find Hannah. I will get on a lifeboat, Reid, but not until I've found Hannah."

"Jesus Christ, woman." He ran his hand over his hair and shook his head in frustration. "You are the most difficult— All right. We must be quick about it. And when it's time to go, you need to promise me you'll go."

"You will go with me," I said, in a voice that brooked no argument. "We are both going to get on a boat and God willing this is all a false alarm and we'll be on our way by morning."

It was overly hopeful, but I didn't care. I needed to believe it in order to make my feet move.

"Starboard," I said sharply. "They'd go to the entrance closest the cabin."

"Then that's where we'll start," Reid agreed, and we pushed through the gathering crowd toward the entrance to the deck.

Chapter Twenty-Two

April 15, 1912
Titanic

HANNAH

They were calling for women and children.

I couldn't quite wrap my head around what was happening. Some people seemed horribly worried; others were pale and trembling, uncertain of what to do next. There was a bang and then my gaze followed a streak of light into the air. Flares. Distress flares. I looked at Charles, whose tight lips and clenched jaw were not comforting in the least. There were some women on deck still in their evening clothes; they must be horribly cold. How fortunate for me that Charles had insisted I put on my heaviest coat. Even so, the air was biting and each one of my breaths formed a frosty cloud. There was a constant scream from the stacks, which Charles explained was the boilers venting off steam. The howl of it set my nerves even further on edge.

I looked down into the water and saw the first lifeboat bobbing on the waves. A giant lump formed in my throat. "Charles," I said, loudly to be heard over the venting, "this doesn't feel like a precaution to me." It seemed as if the ship had levelled out somewhat, but it still felt off somehow. Like the front – the bow – was a little lower than the stern. Maybe I was just imagining it.

Charles stared at me, as if he didn't know how to respond, which only added to my certainty that this was not a drill or a small bump but something far more dire. I was jostled from behind; the starboard deck was crowded as the lifeboats were prepared to be lowered. I was pushed again, and Charles grabbed my arm. "Come," he said, "let's try the port side. It might not be as crowded."

We pushed our way back through the throng and through the entrance, into the blessed heat of the lounge, where the orchestra was still set up and playing. It struck me as incredibly odd, the soothing notes of music while something so worrisome, so dangerous, was happening all around them. For a moment I thought about Nero playing while Rome burned and I gave a short laugh, which earned me a quizzical look from Charles. I closed my mouth and held tight to his hand so we didn't get separated.

Over on the port side, boats were being readied. I spotted Margaret Brown and we immediately went to her. "Margaret! Margaret!"

"Well, hello," she said, turning around. "Bit chilly for a late evening stroll, ain't it?"

I choked out a laugh. Margaret had a way of taking a bad situation and defusing it with dry wit. "Women and children first, please!" came the shout. "Women and children!"

"Well, Mrs. Martin, shall we?" I looked in the boat. Helen Candee's face peered up at me, pale and pained. I snapped my head around to gaze at my husband.

"You're coming, aren't you Charles?"

"You heard him, darling. It's just women and children for now."

I gripped his hand. "I am not leaving you. Surely you know that."

Margaret stuck her head into our conversation. "Mrs. Martin, Hannah, come get in with me. I'm sure this will all be fine and we'll be back in our cabins in no time. It'll all go smoother if we do what we're told."

I laughed a little. "Mrs. Brown, you are not known for doing what you're told."

"You're right there. But I am known for doing what's smart. Come along now, the boat's filling and we don't have all night."

"Charles..." My heart lurched. I didn't want to get into the boat without him. Something told me it was so very wrong.

"Get in with Mrs. Brown, love," he said, holding both my hands. "I'll be in a later one, once they start boarding the men."

Just over an hour ago we had been lying together blissfully in our bed. Now I was being pushed toward a lifeboat in the middle of the frigid Atlantic. It didn't seem possible that this was all happening, so fast that I couldn't make sense of it at all. I had to trust him. "Do you promise?" I demanded. "That you'll be in another boat?"

"As soon as they say they're taking the men. I promise."

"Women and children, please!" The shout went up again, and I flinched.

"Please, darling. For the baby's sake, do as I ask. I'll see you later."

I nodded dumbly, and he walked me to the boat. "Only women now, sir," said the officer.

Charles nodded. "Yes, I know. I just want to help her aboard. She's with child, man."

I saw Margaret's face soften and for a moment she looked unbearably sad. I hesitated, turned toward Charles, who held my hand as if to help me inside. "Charles," I said, and my voice hitched.

I didn't want to cry but this felt so terribly wrong. "And Lou. Oh, Charles, I said horrible things. I didn't get a chance to say I'm sorry. Will you find her? Please? I can't do this. Oh Charles, I can't." I was crying now, not sure why, since he said he'd be along in another boat. The idea of being separated sent panic rushing through me.

He hauled me against his chest, kissed me soundly, and then set me back. "I love you, Hannah Martin. Now go with Mrs. Brown. I'll find Miss Phillips, I promise. And as soon as I can get a boat, I will. Go, darling."

And just like that I was in the boat, sitting on the hard, cold seat. I looked at him as the officers made the motions to lower away, and jolt by jolt I was inched away from him. "I love you, Charles," I called. I needed him to know. Right then and there, I swore that when we were reunited, I would never let him go again.

"I love you." I couldn't hear it, but I saw him mouth it as he looked over the railing. I held his gaze as long as I could, and then when he was beyond my sight, I turned my head and stared straight ahead.

It seemed we were under the care of Quartermaster Hichens, and we were partway down when he called out that he couldn't manage the boat on his own. To our surprise, it wasn't another seaman who climbed down the falls and into the boat, but one of our fellow first-class passengers, Major Peuchen.

I glared as he took a spot in our boat. It might have been Charles! There weren't supposed to be men right now! Then Peuchen looked at Hichens and said, "Yachtsman Major Arthur Peuchen at your service, sir," and my resentment lessened. Someone experienced with sailing was a good addition. I looked around. There seemed to be room for many more people, and again I wondered at leaving Charles behind. "Should we not have been full?" I asked.

Hichens glared at me. "The officers make those decisions, ma'am. You'd do well to remember that."

"Come now. There's no cause for rudeness." Despite the rocking

Ship of Dreams

of the boat as it settled on the waves, Margaret moved over and sat next to me. "You're quite right," she added. "But hopefully this is all temporary."

I looked around as Peuchen began rowing us away from the ship. There were some unfamiliar faces, some I recognized in passing, but also ones I considered friends, and I was glad of it. Not just Margaret, but Mrs. Candee and also Elsie Bowerman, Lou's friend. She was pale and in shock, I realized, and was huddled into herself against the cold. The water slapped against the hull of the boat and I shivered, wondering how long we'd have to be out here. Then I glanced up at the *Titanic*.

She was settling deeper into the water, by the ... what was the term? By the head. Lifeboats were being lowered, but there was an urgency now, frantic movements by passengers on deck. The sound of the boilers venting off steam still carried across the water, the scream of it mimicking the tension seizing my limbs. Margaret slid her arm around my shoulders in an awkward motion, difficult considering the bulk of our life vests. "You told him, then?"

I turned to her, saw kindness in her eyes. "Yes," I said. "You were so right. Things are fine. More than fine." Which sounded ridiculous considering the current circumstances.

"Well, now, isn't that grand?" She smiled. "Chin up, Mrs. Martin. That's a man who has a lot to live for."

But so did everyone else. Everyone aboard that ship had hopes and dreams and loved ones. I closed my eyes. Had I really blithely called this the ship of dreams when we boarded? More like ship of horrors. I opened my eyes again and stared at the vessel the papers had called unsinkable. A floating palace. There was no pretending this was a precaution. Now that we were moving further and further away, it was plain to see that she was sinking. There were over two thousand souls on board, and every single person's life would be changed tonight. Some would ... my lip quivered ... die. *Not Charles*, I said to myself. *Charles will find a way. Charles is a rich, important man. He'll get on a boat and come to us. He promised.*

At some point, the screaming of the stacks ceased, and the quiet was even more unsettling. In the absence of the noise, I could now pick up the strains of the orchestra, which seemed unbelievable. Music, as the ship sank lower and lower into the water. Shouts carried across the air as lifeboat after lifeboat was slowly lowered, the shape of them rising and falling with the gentle waves as they were rowed away from the hulking mass. There were more flares, but the light from them was cast over an empty, still ocean. Was anyone coming? Had anyone heard our calls?

Inside our boat it was eerily quiet, with only the odd sniffle and shudder and the wet dip of the oars in the water. I looked to my right and saw the propellers revealing themselves as the stern began to rise. Small dots slid down the deck, others dropped from the railings, and now the shouts turned to frantic cries. There were no more lifeboats to release, but so many people left on board. I stared, numb, paralyzed by the realization that those dots were human beings. So many people were about to perish in this icy water.

The lights went out, plunging the ship into darkness. For a moment they flashed on again, but then darkened as, to my horror, the ship rose almost vertical in the air, the massive propellers hanging aloft. Lifeboats were rushing away so they wouldn't be sucked down with the ship, and body after body, indiscernible, dropped into the waves. The orchestra no longer played. It was almost over.

There was a series of loud booms, and then the ship broke in half. The stern came slamming down on the water, waves rushing away as the bow disappeared completely. The stern remained for a few prolonged heartbeats, and then it, too, sank beneath the ocean.

Chapter Twenty-Three

April 15, 1912
Titanic

LOUISA

When we didn't find Hannah and Charles on the forward boat deck, Reid suggested we try further aft, where the rest of the boats were kept. I trotted after him as we wound our way through throngs of people all heading toward the lifeboats. I was tall, which gave me a slight advantage as I looked over the crowd, searching for Hannah's dark curls or the familiar coat and scarf I knew she wore. Nothing. Nor did I see Charles. I pushed further in, and a uniformed man grabbed my arms. "Women and children, miss, get in the boat!" He was rough and I fought against him, shoving his arms away.

"Don't make a time, now, get in the boat!"

"Get your hands off me!" I screamed, pushing at him.

He stepped back and was about to come toward me again

when Reid stepped forward. "Do not touch her again," he shouted, loud enough to be heard clearly over the horrible screeching sound coming from the stacks. Then he led me a bit away.

I put my hands over my ears. "My God, what is that?"

He looked up at the stacks and then to me. "Venting the steam. There's too much pressure in the boilers. It'll stop."

"Not soon enough," I grumbled, though he couldn't hear me over the racket. "I don't see her, Reid!"

"Will you please reconsider getting in a boat?" Reid's jaw tightened as he stared at me, nostrils flaring. "I would like to know you're safely away."

"If you think I'm leaving without you," I shouted, "you're sadly mistaken."

"Lower away!"

We turned toward the rail, where a lifeboat was being lowered. And that's when I understood what Reid wasn't explicitly saying. All the pieces came together in one horrible puzzle. He wanted me in a boat because he knew there wouldn't be one for him. If I refused to leave without him, there was a very strong chance I was going to die tonight, out here in the middle of the ocean.

Reid must have noticed the change in my face because he gave me a shake. "No," he shouted. "Do not give up, Lou. You've never been a quitter. Do not start now."

My breath started coming in hiccups. "I don't want to drown," I cried, fear taking over my body. The very thought of water over my head, of gulping it into my lungs, the pain, the torture... I gasped and gasped and couldn't breathe.

"Lou!" He grabbed my shoulders and shook me harder. "You're not going to drown."

"I'm not getting on a boat without you," I insisted. "Oh God, Reid..."

He looked at me, and didn't argue. "I love you," he said instead, speaking loudly because of the noise, but it took nothing away from the emotion.

"I love you, too," I replied, knowing it was so very true. It didn't matter that we had only truly been together a matter of days. I had known him – liked him – much longer. I had fooled myself into thinking the letters we'd exchanged were just friendly little missives, but men and women didn't do that unless there was a deeper connection. It had taken being together on a ship in the middle of the ocean with no escape to make me realize that a man I'd flirted with and treated in a most casual and flippant manner was actually someone whom I could love – and who loved me in return. Even after everything I'd done.

He cupped my face in his cold hand and looked into my eyes. "You won't drown, darling. If we go down together, the cold will get you first."

My lip wobbled. Was I really going to die tonight? I thought of all the things I wanted to do, all the fights I wanted to fight, the life I wanted with Reid, the way I wanted to hold Hannah's baby in my arms—

"Hannah," I said, grabbing his face. "I have to find Hannah. I can't go knowing we left things as we did. We can try the port side. Move forward…"

"Or the cabin. If you haven't seen her here, would she have gone back to the cabin?"

It seemed ridiculous, but we had passed lots of people going back inside to be warm or returning to their cabins for warmer clothing. In her condition, she should be bundled up. "Yes, the cabin first, let's try it!" I shouted, and we were off again.

We'd first noticed the ship listing to starboard, and now it seemed to be leaning to port and downward at the bow. My steps felt weird and slightly sideways as we fought our way back again, inside, and down the stairs to B Deck and our cabins. The hallway was eerily empty, though we passed a few of the ship's staff rushing about the open area at the bottom of the Grand Staircase. The staff ... so many would not make it off the ship tonight, either. My stomach did a sick roll, but I pushed on, Reid taking the lead and pounding through the hall doors and to Charles and Hannah's cabin.

I knocked with my fist, pounding four times. "Hannah? Charles? Are you in there?"

There was no answer, no sound, so I tried the door. It was open, and I rushed inside. The cabin was empty, and a quick check of the open wardrobe showed her heavy coat was gone, thank goodness. "They're not here, but she's warmly dressed," I said, then went to the drawer where I knew she kept her valuables. The bag was not in its usual place, but I did run my fingers over a pair of odd bumps. The earrings, the ones that Charles had given her in London. I needed to give them to her and let her know that I hadn't stolen them and I was so sorry for everything and that I loved her as a sister. I needed her forgiveness more than anything in the world. "Let's check the port side," I said. "But first, let me get my bag."

Reid's face hardened. "Lou, why the hell do you want that bag? If you're caught... If you..." He turned away, and I knew he was confused and angry.

"I want to put it in a lifeboat. I'll give it to someone and tell them to take it to the authorities in New York. It's not for me, Reid. If I'm going to die tonight, I need to make reparations."

He pulled me close and kissed me, his mouth mashing against mine in a desperate, rushed connection. "You have to be the most moral thief I've ever met," he said.

I laughed. "How many thieves do you know, Mr. Grey?"

He grinned, and I felt a little better. How odd, feeling a sudden peace and lightness in the face of death. That feeling told me I was doing the right thing, so we hurried next door to my room to grab the Gladstone bag.

"You should put on something warmer," Reid said, glancing at the velvet coat I wore.

"An extra layer of wool won't make any difference, darling," I replied, giving him a long, sober look. "It's all right, Reid. It really is. I'm where I want to be. I'm with who I want to be with."

He swore, then we took another moment to hold each other. Each time was more precious, more tenuous than the last. Time was not stopping. The way the ship was tilting meant she was still sinking. We just had to do what we could, so we headed back to the deck and the lifeboats.

We turned left down the hall, traversing the long corridor and making our way to the reception area by the aft staircase. The lifeboats at the bow had to be long gone; the best chance to find Hannah would be to the rear and on the port side. My heart lurched as I realized she might already be gone, and my opportunity lost, in which case I could be satisfied with her safety. Still, if there was the smallest chance I could see her once more, I had to try my hardest. That Reid was willing to go along with it only made him more precious to me.

We were just about to reach the bottom of the stairs when I heard a voice call my name. "Louisa! Lou!"

I spun around to see Charles barrelling toward me, sidestepping the few people left in first class who weren't already in boats or on deck. I halted, Reid's hand along my back.

Hannah was not with him.

I rushed to meet him. "Where's Hannah?"

"I put her in a lifeboat with Margaret Brown."

Relief and regret swept over me in equal measure. She was safe, at least for now. But I would not have the chance to tell her, to make things right. I saw the agony in Charles's face and knew that he had come to the same conclusion as I had, as Reid. There were not enough lifeboats. We were not going to make it off the ship.

"Oh, Charles, I'm so desperately sorry." I put down my bag and embraced him, a true, heartfelt hug. We'd had our differences, but we had our love for Hannah in common and that was the most important thing. He had just found out about his child, about getting a second chance for a family, and it was being cruelly ripped away from him.

"Me too, Lou," he murmured close to my ear.

I pulled back. "You called me Lou. This must be dire." I tried a smile, but we were both too sad to find any real levity.

"Well, let's get you to a boat, then," said Charles, making eye contact with Reid. "Grey," he said, holding out a hand for a brief handshake.

"Charles, I'm not going. I'm staying with Reid."

The men looked at each other, sharing matching expressions that I immediately resisted. "No. Reid, you promised. I love you. I can't — I won't—"

He put his hand on my shoulder. "And I love you. I can't let you die, darling. Surely you know that."

I pulled away, feeling my heart being ripped from my chest. "I only just found you," I said, squaring my shoulders. "No, I won't do it."

"Louisa," Charles said gently. "Do it for Hannah. She's going to be alone. She's going to need you."

One last denial. "Hannah hates me."

"She doesn't," Charles insisted. "I know she's angry at you about something, but she loves you fiercely. I won't be there for her, or for my child. I need you to be."

As emotional blackmail went, it was a humdinger. Charles kept on. "The ship is sinking, Lou. Water's been coming up the grand staircase for half an hour. You must do this."

"Maybe we can all get on." I waved my hand aimlessly. "Come, let's go then. There may be some boats left if we hurry."

If I had to go, so did they. Charles needed to see his child grow.

And I refused to leave without Reid. If anyone tried to stop me, I'd beat him senseless with an oar.

We dashed up the stairs and out the starboard side. Once on deck, I saw how low we were sitting in the water, how the stern was rising as the bow dipped lower and lower, and fear began to overtake me again. "Come!" shouted Charles, and Reid used his shoulders to make a path through the throng of people searching for a seat.

"Coming through! Coming through!" Charles led the way, and before I knew it, I was faced with the gunwale of a lifeboat and was unceremoniously shoved into it.

"No!" I cried, reaching back. "Reid! No! Not without you. Charles!" I looked around wildly. "Please, let them in."

"Women and children, ma'am, and crew to man the boat."

"Then let me out!"

I struggled to stand, and then I looked at Charles's face and sat heavily.

"She needs you."

"Take my place," I begged, crying, but he shook his head.

"I couldn't live with myself if I did." He reached over and gripped my hand. "Care for them for me. Love them."

I was sobbing now, looking through my tears at Reid just behind Charles. I couldn't hold him one last time, or kiss him… He and Charles were far too honourable by half, and in that moment I wished Reid were more of a scoundrel. Other men had found their way onto boats, I knew that for sure. But the men that Hannah and I loved would never take a seat meant for a woman or a child. How could I hate them for that?

"Reid! I love you, Reid!"

And just when I thought my heart wouldn't break anymore, I saw tears on his cheeks as he mouthed, "I love you, too."

The boat jerked downward. It was full, and some woman was

going on about her pig or some nonsense, but I heard none of it. My body jerked and rolled with the motion of the lifeboat as it moved inch by inch closer to the frigid waves. I welcomed the cold as some sort of odd punishment for surviving what was happening. The scream of the vents had ended minutes ago, but now I heard shouts and crying and people yelling out names. I registered nothing until the night seemed to grow suddenly darker, and I looked up to see that the lights on the *Titanic* had gone out. My mouth was open and tears were on my cheeks, but I didn't make a sound, rocking back and forth, imagining Charles and Reid standing on that sloping deck, waiting for their demise. I was not counting on a miracle, on their somehow finding room in a lifeboat. I didn't even know if we would survive out here; the horizon was black and endless, with no ship in sight.

A loud boom and crack and then I turned away from the ship as it broke apart and slipped beneath the black waves.

If only I could have turned away from the torturous minutes of listening to the cries of the people in the water. Or how, bit by bit, the screams grew softer, until they were silenced altogether.

Chapter Twenty-Four

```
April 15, 1912
On the North Atlantic
```

HANNAH

We spent the next few hours floating, freezing. I was incapable of doing much of anything, but marvelled at the fortitude of the women around me. Women like Margaret, who fought with Hichens to go back and pick up survivors since we had room in our boat. He refused and was downright abusive with her until she was forced to back down. I looked at him with loathing. He was the assigned captain of our little group, but he was no leader. It was Margaret and other women who all helped row the boat.

At one point we got some relief when another lifeboat came alongside, and we were lashed together. A few of the men from that boat came to ours. I could tell Margaret was livid, but I kept looking for other lifeboats in the dark, wondering which one held my husband.

He had promised. I knew other men had managed to find a seat in boats and I was angry all over again at how we'd been put in the water with over half our seats empty. Thirty lives, maybe more, that might have been saved. I understood the women and children first principle, but what truly made my life more valuable than a man's? Or if there were no more women about, why not fill it with men standing by? It was ridiculous! How many boats had been lowered with empty spaces?

No, Charles would be on one, I was certain. What I was less certain of was our rescue. Had anyone heard our distress calls? Seen our flares? It didn't seem likely, or else they'd be here already, wouldn't they? I vaguely remembered chatter about seeing ship's lights in the distance when we were rowing away – who had seen them? I couldn't recall. In those moments, there'd been a glimmer of hope that someone would come along and save us all.

As the night waned, hope died. My shivering was constant. My feet were freezing, my ears and face numb and stiff. At one point I must have drifted off because I jolted awake with a gasp, lifting my head abruptly and blinking, trying to sort my surroundings. There was nothing but ocean around us, the water making a *slap slap* sound on the side of the lifeboat. I don't know why I expected to see the *Titanic* still sitting on the water; I'd watched her go down hours ago. The vast emptiness surrounding me hollowed out my insides, leaving me empty and grief-stricken.

Margaret was still beside me, and at my movement, she too sat up straighter. She linked her arm with mine and patted it without saying a word. We were both shaking with cold.

The sky began to lighten as dawn approached, and when I looked around, I could make out other lifeboats dotting the waves. It struck me as unbelievable that something so incredibly catastrophic could happen on an ocean so calm and beautiful.

Shades of pink, peach, lilac spread on the horizon. My fingers didn't want to move, but I placed my hand over my belly, trying desperately to connect with my unborn child. *Hello, little one*, I said in my head. *I'm here. Don't worry.* Which was silly, because I was worried sick.

"A ship," came a voice, shaking with cold. "I think that's a ship."

I looked over at Margaret, then at the sea around me. There was something certainly, a dark shadow coming out of the grey dawn. "Praise God," said Helen in a thready voice, and I looked over at her. We both had tears in our eyes, moisture that felt sticky as I tried to blink it away. I shifted on the seat and looked again. It was growing larger, and I could see its stack now.

Help was here. We would be saved. Charles would be on another lifeboat, and we would be reunited.

For the first time since leaving the ship, I wept, great heaving sobs of grief and relief and something I couldn't quite put my finger on, that was somehow bigger than both of those emotions. I thought of Lou and wondered if she got off the ship – surely she must have. It felt horrible being separated from her, and our last words had been so harsh. At least … mine had. She'd betrayed me, horribly. She'd lied, she'd cheated … she had only been going to New York to sell her stolen goods and a week with me was just the icing on the cake. And yet I couldn't hate her. I was angry, but I could never hate Lou, no matter our differences. It might have been easier if I could.

The thought that I might never see her again opened a horrible, aching wound, one I could not possibly deal with at this moment which was already filled with such pain and misery.

We sat for a long time in the freezing morning before our lifeboat was brought aboard, and someone said that we waited as long to board what we now knew was the *Carpathia* as we had spent sitting on the endless ocean. That seemed unfathomable, but perhaps it was the hope and relief of being rescued that made the time feel shorter. Maybe it was the sunlight that now glinted off the roll of the waves.

All I knew was that when I went to leave the lifeboat, my fingers and feet wouldn't work properly and I couldn't climb the ladder. Instead, I was put in a bosun's chair and lifted aboard.

Margaret was already there, and she pointed toward me. "I'm fine, you see. But Mrs. Martin is pregnant and needs medical attention." She was still giving orders and I smiled faintly, even though this all felt like a dream. A nightmare, really. "And Mrs. Candee has hurt her ankle dreadfully. She'll need to be seen right away."

She had? I hadn't even noticed, and how awful was that of me? I had been in such a numb state that I hadn't noticed much about the other passengers. I should have been helping.

I was given a warm blanket, and I gave the crew member my name and class. Then I was checked over by a doctor, who to my great relief said there was nothing wrong with me except I needed warming up and rest, though to be sure to get attention immediately if I felt ill or experienced any bleeding. My heart stopped at that, briefly, but I straightened and told myself that his warning was a standard one. Instead, I followed the line of rescued passengers to the dining saloon, where we were given hot coffee and brandy. There was soup, too. The crew must have worked all night readying for our rescue, God bless them, but I couldn't eat. Not yet. Instead, once the worst of my chill was gone, I walked through the saloon, searching every face, looking for Charles.

There had still been boats being rescued when I was brought aboard. I slipped outside to the deck and squinted, peering into every pale, cold face, but I didn't see him anywhere.

It was now nearly seven o'clock and only a few lifeboats remained bobbing on the water, waiting their turn. I huddled in the blanket and stood watch, hoping against hope that he was there. That he hadn't... I swallowed against a massive lump that had formed in my throat. That he hadn't been one of those dots falling into the water. Oh God, I couldn't bear thinking of him that way. There was still hope. Still a chance…

I waited, until the last boat was brought on board. I had not seen his face. I went inside and studied each set of features, looking for that familiar jawline, the warm eyes, the soft wave to his hair.

He was not there.

I asked about him. Tried to find his name on a list somewhere, but he was not there.

I went to the infirmary, but there was no Charles Martin there.

And then I went back to the deck, huddled in my blanket, and sat on a bench, letting the truth sink in.

Charles was gone.

And with him, my hope and my future.

Chapter Twenty-Five

April 15, 1912
Carpathia

LOUISA

When I woke, I was on a bed, still completely clothed in my dress and velvet coat, but my shoes were gone and there was something warm tucked around my feet. A blanket, too, covered me, and I curled into it for just a moment, so utterly grateful for the warmth that I forgot everything else from the last eight hours. Was it eight? I didn't even know what time it was.

The *Titanic*. The lifeboat. The icy cold... Reid.

A cavern of pain opened up inside me. Reid. Reid was dead. Charles was dead. Dozens and dozens of people must be dead. I closed my eyes again, but all that did was give life to a nightmare, an image of blue-grey bodies floating in the water, crying out, then worse – silent. I put my hands over my ears but that didn't stop the screaming that was inside my head.

"Miss? Miss. I'm so glad you're awake."

Putting my hands over my ears only mildly muffled the noise around me. The voice was accented, and I struggled to understand the words as I drew my hands away. "I-I'm sorry?"

"No need to be sorry, miss. I'm Doctor Lengyel. How are you feeling?"

When I didn't answer, he sighed. "I'm sorry. That was a stupid question. May I examine you? You were quite chilled when you arrived."

Chilled? I'd been frozen.

"I don't remember coming aboard," I replied, feeling quite disoriented. "Where am I?"

"On the *Carpathia*, miss. When you stood to leave the lifeboat, you fainted. This is the first you've awakened."

"What time is it?"

"Just past two," he replied.

His face was kindly, and I tried to focus on it and say something appropriately thankful, but he shook his head. "It's all right, Miss…"

I stared up at him, wondering if I looked as wildly off-kilter as I felt. "Um, Phillips. My name is Louisa Phillips."

"You were in first class?"

I nodded, and he jotted it down on his notes.

"May I look at your feet, please, Miss Phillips? Your fingers and toes are a cause for worry."

I nodded, not having the wherewithal to care when he removed the blanket and the hot water bottle that had been placed at my feet. He probed each toe, and I told him I could feel everything, and no, nothing hurt. He looked at my hands, too, and asked me several questions that I answered easily. When he was done, I took a breath. "Please, Doctor," I said, coughing a little and then catching my breath. "How many…"

"I don't know for certain," he replied quietly. "I am guessing that around six hundred were saved, probably more."

He chose to give the number of passengers and crew that were alive, and I understood why, but as I had told Reid last night, I could do basic maths and there had been over two thousand people on the *Titanic*. I closed my eyes, then opened them again, afraid of the image that popped into my brain the moment my eyes were closed. "Thank you," I replied.

"Miss Phillips, if you go to the First-Class Dining Saloon, you'll find hot food and drink, and someone to help you get situated. I can't promise anything, but many of the passengers have given up their cabins for survivors. You'll be cared for. You're safe now."

I nodded. I didn't really care about being taken care of, but I had promised Charles I'd find Hannah. I should probably do that.

"Thank you," I answered. He helped me get to my feet. My shoes were dry now and uncomfortable, pinching my toes in an odd way that I supposed might be from the salt water and my close call with frostbite. I stepped gingerly, testing my legs. A kind stewardess took me to the dining saloon where the other first-class passengers were congregating. "Where can I check a list of survivors?" I asked.

"I'll find someone for you," she said. We passed by a window, and I caught a glimpse of my reflection, recoiling at the image that stared back at me. My hair was a rat's nest, my face pale, my eyes wide and sunken. The stewardess settled me in a chair and then left me, and I stared around feeling utterly discombobulated.

"Louisa! Oh! Louisa!"

I started at the sound of my name and snapped my head up to find Mabel Fortune headed my way. I was glad to see her, glad she'd survived, and yet had no clue what to say. It was as if my head was full of wool and I couldn't separate the strands into clear, coherent thoughts.

"Mabel," I said, rising and accepting her hug.

We clung for a few moments, a surprise. In that simple embrace was relief at being alive and grief at the losses, and a shared understanding of the horrors of the night. All in the space of ten seconds. When we drew back, tears were swimming in our eyes. "Your family?" I asked, hoarsely.

"All the women are fine. But Daddy and Charles…" Her face contorted with pain, and she gripped my hand as if it were a lifeline.

"I'm so sorry," I whispered.

"Have you seen Mrs. Martin yet?" she asked, brightening.

"She's here?"

"She is. I was so shocked you weren't together, but when I said so she got such a strange look." She lifted our clasped hands and patted the top of mine. "Charles didn't…" She let the sentence hang.

"I know," I whispered, but she didn't seem to hear me. Instead she guided me away. I wondered about the stewardess who was supposed to bring me the list, and if I disappeared she wouldn't know where to find me, but since Hannah was here, I didn't need to look for her name. The saloon was crowded with passengers I recognized – mostly women, though there were a handful of men. Ninette Aubart with her maid beside her, and the Duff-Gordons with Miss Francatelli nearby. I saw the entire Carter family, the children huddled close to their mother, looking much younger and unsure than the confident, happy children I'd met on deck. Eleanor Widener was next to them, but without George and Harry. I wondered how many women had suddenly become widowed overnight. I felt like one of them.

Then I saw Hannah, sitting at a table and cradling a cup of tea, staring into the cup while steam flickered up and out of the bowl. Mabel, who I had to admit was made of stern stuff, called out, "Mrs. Martin. Oh, Mrs. Martin. Look who I've found!"

Hannah looked up, saw my face, and hers crumpled as she rose from her chair, nearly knocking it over. "Lou!" she cried, and began nudging others out of the way in her haste. "Oh, Lou! I didn't know if you— if—" She couldn't say the words. Instead she gripped me by the shoulders and pulled me in for a hug. "Oh, thank you, Mabel," I heard Hannah say near my ear. "God bless you."

"I need to get back to my mother," Mabel said, "but I'll see you later, I'm sure."

Hannah released me, beaming through tears, then pulled me over to the table where she'd been sitting. "It's a bit crowded in here," she was saying, "but everyone is rallying together." She plunked me in a chair. I still hadn't said anything. She pushed over her plate, which held half a sandwich. "Have you eaten anything? You need tea. There's soup, too."

"Coffee," I said, the first word I'd spoken to her, and I knew I should feel badly about it but I couldn't somehow. How could she be so … proficient? For a woman who claimed to love her husband so much, she acted as if her world hadn't just ended. Anger roared up inside me, shaking me with its unexpected force. I was angry at her. Furious. "For God's sake," I hissed. "How can you act like this can all be fixed with tea and cake?"

She recoiled as if I'd slapped her, and then slowly her face relaxed, though her gaze remained wary. I felt as low as I'd ever felt, and that included the moment she'd glared at me when she'd realized I was no better than a common thief.

"It's what I need to do. It's how I'm dealing with it," she said, quieter. "But of course everyone handles things their own way."

That made me feel even worse. It would have been better if she'd just been mad at me instead of taking this gentle, careful tone.

"Charles—"

"Didn't make it," she interrupted calmly. "I know. I realized hours ago."

How was she not utterly devastated? I was so confused. "Is there a place I can lie down?" I asked. "I can't— There are too many people."

"I'll find out. And I'll find some coffee, too. Don't leave, Lou."

I stared at her. "Where could I possibly go?"

The answer, though, frightened me. In my head, I immediately considered throwing myself over the rail and into the water and just ending all this. How many miles away from the wreck were we now? Where was Reid? And Charles, too? Had it hurt? Or had it been like Reid had said, that it would be so cold that they would fall asleep before their hearts stopped?

I was terrified of what that might feel like, so I stayed in the hell I knew, sitting on a boat with hundreds of other survivors, listening to sounds of crying and hushed talking. It made me want to scream.

I did not want to talk to another soul, so I huddled in my chair, making myself seem small, and kept my head down to avoid eye contact. It worked, too, repelling anyone from approaching. Until Hannah came back after several minutes – I had no idea how many – and said she was taking me to a cabin where I could rest.

The first-class cabins on the *Carpathia* were not the equivalent of the *Titanic*'s, but they were well-appointed and there were two beds inside. "The occupants have volunteered to sleep elsewhere," said the steward who had led us to the cabin. "We won't reach New York for another few days, but you should be comfortable here."

I said nothing, just stared at the bed, wanting to crawl into it and never come out.

"I'll return as soon as I can with what you requested," the steward added.

"I know you're run off your feet, so I appreciate it." Hannah smiled at the steward. "I'm so sorry I have… I mean…" She halted, started again. "Your service is so appreciated, and I wish I had money to give you as a tip."

"Heavens. Not necessary, ma'am. It's the least I can do."

He shut the door behind him, leaving me alone with Hannah.

I flipped down the covers, unsure if the sheets had been changed, certain they had not, and caring even less. I peeled off my coat and removed my shoes and then got inside the cocoon of bedding.

Hannah sat on the edge of the bed. "Darling, I— I'm so sorry. About everything. About how we left things."

"It doesn't matter. I have nothing now. Just leave me alone, Hannah."

I had no idea why I was being so cruel. Hadn't I been desperate for her forgiveness? Now I was pushing her away.

"Charles … did you see him, Lou? Before you got on the lifeboat?"

See him? It was all I could see. He and Reid sharing that stupid look that said, "get Lou on the boat no matter what she says." Charles insisting that Hannah would need me, the one way he knew to get me to go. And now here she was, managing just fine.

"He should have been here, not me. But he refused. He made me get on the boat. I told him to take my place, but he wouldn't."

I heard her sniff, but I couldn't look at her.

"Of course he would do that. He… Oh my. I knew in my heart he would die with honour."

I flipped over and stared at her. She had this bittersweet, beatific expression glowing from her moist eyes and pink cheeks, idealizing the man she'd married. Well, hers wasn't the only good man who'd been lost. "Death is not honourable. It's just death," I replied, my voice harsh. "It's pain and suffering and then the end."

She hopped off the side of the bed as if I'd struck her. "Why are you so cruel? Why are you so angry?" She put her hand to her face, covering one eye and cheek. "I know you're hurting. We're all hurting! But Lou, you're my dearest friend!" Disaster had a way of making our differences small in comparison. I thought perhaps I was being unreasonable but I couldn't, for the life of me, respond otherwise. I was used to being in control not only of myself but of every situation. I wasn't right now, not even close.

"Why am I angry? It should be Charles here," I snapped. "He should be here, and I should have held Reid's hand and died with him, that's why."

"Lou!"

Anything else she might have said went unspoken as there was a knock on the door. She opened it and the steward came in with a tray consisting of a pot of strong-smelling coffee, a plate of sandwiches and little cakes, and a bottle of brandy.

He left it on the small table and departed.

"I thought you might like brandy in your coffee. It's been a horrific day." Hannah's voice was quieter again, and tentative, as if expecting me to snap at her again. Careful, while I was unpredictable. I knew it and hated it and yet seemed incapable of changing it. An apology stuck in my throat. My gaze stopped on the brandy.

"Thanks," I said, but nothing more. I was, I think, too scared to really say what was on my mind and in my heart, for fear I would not be able to stop. Maybe I was being hateful, or at the least, unkind. If I were to let down that wall, I would break wide open, and that terrified me.

"We've been given this cabin to share," she murmured. "I'll be back later. I'm going to see where I can be of help. If you need anything else, ring for a steward."

She sounded strong and rightfully piqued, but I saw beyond the cool response to the hurt beyond and hated myself for doing that to her. All I had done to her in the last twenty-four hours was hurt her. Some friend I was.

Hannah slipped out of the cabin and I finally got up, went to the table, and poured the coffee. It was hot but not overly so. I drank the first cup black and let the bitterness slide down my throat.

Then I filled the cup with brandy and followed the bitterness with the burn of straight liquor. And I filled it again. Finally, I got in bed and went back to sleep, wishing I might never wake.

Chapter Twenty-Six

April 15, 1912
Carpathia

HANNAH

When I'd looked up and seen Lou trailing behind Mabel Fortune, I'd felt pure happiness for a fleeting moment. Charles was gone, certainly, but knowing my best friend had survived, knowing that we would have a chance to make things right between us, was a spot of brilliant news on the darkest day I'd ever known. Yes, even darker than the day I'd lost our child. For I'd lost Charles, and more than that, hundreds of families had irrevocably changed overnight. This wasn't just my tragedy. The enormity of it was staggering, and the evidence of it was all around. Quiet weeping, open sobbing. The wail of pain as someone called out for their loved ones. Each scored my heart with a painful cut. I felt the weight of it because we were all sharing the same anguish.

But Lou was alive, hallelujah! It was the first ray of light since watching the *Titanic* sink beneath the black water.

Lou, however, was distant and even a little combative. I closed the cabin door behind me and let out a breath. I was thankful she'd made it, but it was clear that she was not all right. Until yesterday, we hadn't had a cross word between us, not in all the years we'd been friends. Yesterday, things festered between us, like a nagging splinter needing to be removed, but what were they at a time like this?

I was initially hurt she didn't see similarly pleased to see me, but then I looked in her eyes and I knew exactly what had happened.

She was grieving, but she didn't know how. I'd been here before, but Lou … she had no idea how to deal with the feelings bearing down on her.

I followed the hall to the doors and then, after a few wrong turns, found my way back up on deck. I stood at the rail a while, thinking about Charles, thinking about our baby, missing him horribly. I knew, however, that after the grief, he would want me to go on. Thinking about it now that the shock was just beginning to lose its edge, I realized that he had never meant to get another lifeboat. He was ensuring my safety… Our safety. The words Lou had hurled at me just now confirmed it. He had stayed behind and put her in a lifeboat instead. Was I still furious that the boats hadn't been filled? Yes. But did I understand his actions? Completely. I wiped a tear from my eye as I hoped he knew we were safe because of him.

Losing Charles wasn't something I thought I would get over, but what I did know was that I could survive it. Right now, I was horribly worried about Lou. I knew that look of fear and helplessness and most importantly, despair. I knew it because when our baby had come into the world without a single breath, I had felt the exact same way. Life was not worth living, and so I didn't live it. I existed, barely. A few times I seriously considered not existing. It was Lou who had pulled me out of that abyss, Lou who had been as patient as a saint with me, prodding me to eat, drink, bathe, take a walk in the garden. Charles didn't need me now, but my baby needed me and so did Lou, and I would not dishonour his memory by letting either of them down.

For a few hours this morning, we'd sailed past an ice field that had stretched as far as the eye could see. That was gone now, as the day waned, and we'd been told that we were headed to our original destination: New York. Not a single *Carpathia* passenger had complained about the delay to their trip, originally to Fiume. Indeed, it felt as if the passengers and crew had all agreed to put the survivors of the sinking first.

I, too, needed something to do and to find a way to help, while also caring for myself. Too often, when I found myself alone with my thoughts, I began slipping into that darkness of grief. Keeping busy was imperative, so I went inside to find something to eat; I knew that was important to keep up my strength.

The First-Class Saloon was teeming with women. Some were survivors, like me, but many were *Carpathia* passengers who had given up their comfortable quarters and had agreed to, quite miraculously, sleep in common areas for the next three days. It was said that Madeleine Astor, along with two friends, had been given Captain Rostron's personal cabin. The men, a group smaller in number, would take over the smoking rooms in first and second class. One man in particular had retreated to a cabin and I doubted he would ever come out: Mr. Ismay. Already there were rumblings about him climbing into a lifeboat, people calling him a coward when men like Astor, Guggenheim, Thomas Andrews – and Charles and Reid – had stayed behind. I gave a sniff. Ismay had been nothing but confident, perhaps even arrogant, the entire trip, and now he wouldn't show his face. That told me all I needed to know.

I could not imagine the sheer volume of work the crew would be putting in with nearly twice the number of passengers aboard, especially since everyone had only the clothes on their backs and were grief-stricken and in shock.

I had been through this particular fire before and survived. How terribly sad that the lessons I had learned in those darkest of days were now being put to use.

After a hurried dinner, I looked for ways to help, because more than anything I knew that people needed food, clothing, rest, and perhaps most of all, comfort. I ran into Mabel Fortune again, who was tending to her poor mother, Mary. Mary looked very lost, and my heart went out to her. She'd lost her husband and her only son; how devastated she must be.

"Mabel," I said quietly, putting my hand on her arm. "Good evening, Mrs. Fortune. It's Hannah, Hannah Martin. Do you remember me?"

She looked up, her eyes rimmed with red. "I do, dear, yes. I'm so glad you're safe. Your—" She broke off, as if saying the word would be such a horrible thing.

I knelt down before her, put my hand on her knee. "Yes, I lost my husband, Mrs. Fortune."

"I'm so sorry." Mary Fortune lifted her handkerchief again. "Oh, I don't know why I can't stop crying."

"Please," I said softly, "it's all right to cry. We've all had such a shock and so many losses. I'm sorry for yours, too. Is there anything I can do for you?"

She shook her head. "We've managed to get a cabin. I was just telling Mabel I'd like to go there. There's so much noise here, and yet…"

I knew what she meant. The silence could be even worse than the constant voices or the cacophony of clinking silverware.

"Margaret Brown is down in third class, helping the passengers there. I thought to help her after my mother is settled." Mabel kept her voice low and her gaze on me. "You'd be most welcome, Hannah. If you wish it. You also need your rest."

"No, I think I'd like that," I replied. "I was in the boat with Margaret. I'm not surprised she's digging in." I smiled a little. "We'd tied up to another boat, but then Margaret thought we should untie and row to keep warm. The women were rowing, can you believe it?" I gave a small snort. "And when Hichens gave her what for, she threatened to throw him overboard."

The memory came out of nowhere. I thought I'd been numb through most of the night, but bits and pieces revealed themselves about those long hours bobbing on the sea, my stomach churning from the rocking.

"She's an amazing woman," Mabel agreed. "Come find us when you're ready. A lot of it is seeing to comforts."

"I will."

"How is Louisa?"

I grimaced. "Sleeping. Everyone grieves in their own way. I need to do something. But Lou … she can't. I'll come see you when I'm certain she's all right."

Mabel squeezed my hand. When I looked into her face, tears came into her eyes. "I still can't believe they're gone," she whispered.

There was nothing to say that hadn't already been said so many times, so I squeezed her hand back, gave a small nod, and turned to her mother again.

"Would you like me to take you to your cabin?" I asked. "I want to check on my friend." I didn't say it, but everyone had to be exhausted. No one had really slept last night. It was as if everyone was in a fugue state, walking around in a daze.

"That would be very kind," she said. "My other girls are already sleeping, I think. I just couldn't face…" She gave a small sob.

"I'll be along soon, Mother," said Mabel, patting her mother's shoulder. "I promise."

"I don't like us being separated."

Mabel smiled indulgently. "Just keep your eye on Ethel."

That, at least, got a smile out of Mary. "All right. To be honest, a real bed sounds like heaven."

The Carpathia was much smaller than the *Titanic*, and while I was unfamiliar with the layout, it wasn't too difficult to find the correct corridor. The cabin was dark, and Ethel and Alice were in their beds, talking quietly when we entered. "Hello," I said softly. "I've brought your mother. Mabel is helping Mrs. Brown for a bit, but she'll be along."

Alice got out of bed and came to her mother. She wasn't wearing a nightgown, and the skirt she had on was a few inches too short, but it was serviceable and had no doubt been donated by another passenger. "Come, Mother. Let's get you settled." Alice looked at me. "Thank you, Mrs. Martin."

"You're welcome," I answered. "I'm about to check on Miss Phillips. I'm so very glad you girls are all right."

Alice nodded but said nothing else. They would be feeling the absence of their father and brother forever. Tonight it must be particularly sharp.

I looked in on Lou. The food was uneaten, but the coffee was gone and so was over a third of the brandy. She didn't even hear me come in, and I stood there, looking down at her, love and pain in my heart. She looked small in the bed, like a child, her hair hanging partly over her face.

I remembered that feeling. Wondering if I stayed in bed forever, if I would rot there, and not actually caring. I couldn't let that happen to Lou.

I went back out, closing the door quietly, and then made my way to the third-class saloon, where I met with Margaret and Mabel and together we tended to other survivors, some who had lost not only loved ones, but in some cases, everything they owned in the world.

I had just tucked a blanket around a young woman and turned away when Margaret appeared, her arms loaded with more blankets. "Darlin', you look run off your feet. You should go to bed. You have that little one to think of."

I sighed and had to admit I was starting to feel fatigue seep into my muscles. "I know." I met her gaze. "I've been avoiding being alone all day."

"You have Miss Phillips, don't you?" she asked.

I nodded, but then frowned. "She's not doing well at all. I'm worried."

"Give her time." Margaret looked at me so intently it felt as if she were trying to read my thoughts. "Girls like her, strong-willed and rebellious, tend to have very soft hearts. She will fight for those she loves and fight for her causes, but she does it from a place of care for others and an intolerance for injustice. I think she was quite enamoured of Mr. Grey. Probably more than any of us realize."

My eyes stung. Mrs. Brown had known Lou a short time but had seen all her best qualities. "I know. It hurts to see her like this."

"She has you."

"We quarrelled before the ship went down."

"So, now you have a chance to put things right." She bounced the blankets in her arms. "She can't hide forever, and you can't run forever. Go to bed, Mrs. Martin. And I'll welcome your help tomorrow, if you're inclined to give it."

"God bless you, Margaret Brown." Blankets and all, I gave her a hug, or at least tried to. We both gave a watery laugh. "I'll see you tomorrow."

I ventured back to the cabin, thinking that last night at this time I was on deck, holding Charles's hand, looking for a lifeboat. Holding tight to the promise that he would be in another and we would be reunited. Thinking that this was just procedure and the ship couldn't possibly sink. All of it wrong, except the love that had run between us. Tonight the entire world looked different.

I stopped by the women's lavatory and freshened up as best I could, then entered the cabin and sank into the second bed, utterly exhausted and afraid of my thoughts now that it was silent.

Chapter Twenty-Seven

```
April 16, 1912
  Carpathia
```

LOUISA

Hannah was being a royal pain in my behind.

This morning, while my head was pounding from too much brandy on an empty stomach, she made me get up and go to the lavatory to use the facilities and wash. When I came back, she sat me in a chair and, using a donated comb, painstakingly worked out the knots in my hair before pinning it into a simple roll. I didn't want to admit it, but it did feel better to clean up and have my hair combed. She also produced clothing from somewhere, which wasn't to my taste but was definitely my size. Then again, the drab grey skirt and plain blouse suited my mood. I certainly couldn't wander around the ship in my evening dress and light opera coat for … at least a few more days. I couldn't believe it was Tuesday already.

I didn't really fight her on anything. Instead, I just let her lead me around because it made her feel better. I couldn't have cared less. If I could have stayed in bed, I would have, but it would take more energy than I possessed to argue with Hannah when she was in one of her "take care of things" moods. I scowled; she responded with a chirpy smile. I was silent; she chatted about who we knew that she'd seen on board. I had seen this side of her in different incarnations over the past year, mostly when she'd tried to be happy and helpful while her marriage crumbled. It was how she coped. She wasn't fooling me a bit.

Now I had some understanding of how Charles had felt, however, and why he had refused to talk about the overwhelming grief and fear. It wasn't because he wouldn't; it was because he couldn't. It was simply too painful. I knew what Hannah wanted from me: she wanted me to talk about what had happened. Things had only got better with her marriage once they'd talked and got everything out in the open, and she thought it would fix us, too. But how could it, when I couldn't even think Reid's name without feeling ill and wanting to shrivel up into nothing? When I had so many regrets that were eating me up inside?

But God, I loved Hannah for trying.

She left for a bit and came back with coffee for me, tea for her, and a simple breakfast of bread and preserves. "The crew is worked off its feet," she said, putting down the tray. "I said I would bring it myself and spare a steward."

"How do you even know where to go?" The scent of the coffee pulled me out of the bed. I noticed the bottle of brandy had been removed. Pity.

"I asked around. And last night I was helping Margaret and Mabel with some of the second- and third-class survivors. It's helped me feel useful and made me appreciate what I have even though I've lost so much." Her voice faltered on the last three words.

"You're a good person," I offered quietly.

"You can't live on just coffee," Hannah said, sitting down. She selected a slice of bread and spread it thick with butter and preserves. "You haven't eaten since Sunday."

"I'm not hungry."

"Your heart is not hungry, but your stomach is." She put the slice in front of me. "Do you remember saying that to me, Lou?"

I stared at her.

"It was a week after … after the baby died. For days, I'd been in and out of sleep. I barely remember it. But when I finally woke, you were there, and I fully understood what had happened. I refused to eat a morsel, but you said that to me, and you fed me soup and tea. You fed me every day until I started eating on my own."

I couldn't forget those days. Of course I couldn't. I'd been terrified that Hannah would just let herself waste away and I would lose her, the person I was closest to in the world. "I remember." I took a nibble of the bread.

"Lou, I know you don't want to talk, and that's all right. Please let me say something, though. I am so sorry about our row. I was feeling hurt and betrayed and angry and I said horrible things to you. I love you, Lou. I would have calmed down eventually, but when I was in the lifeboat, I was thinking of you and Charles and my biggest regret was that I might not be able to make things right with you. I'm so, so glad you're here."

I felt the bubble around my feelings wobble, threatening to burst. "I'm scared," I whispered. "I hurt so much and I'm afraid of what will happen if I let it all out. I feel like it will consume me entirely. I… I can't abide not having control, you know that."

She nodded. "I know. Lou, I know what this feels like. You take the time you need. In the meantime, let me do what you did for me. Let me care for you. Let me make sure you're eating and getting fresh air and when we get to New York I'm going to have the hotel staff run you a bath and you can stay in until your fingers and toes shrivel. Let me make sure you're all right."

I shook my head, my lip wobbling. "No. I'm supposed to be doing that for you. I promised Charles."

She stared at me, her mouth open.

"I-I can't go through it all, but I did promise Charles I'd care for you. But I can't, Han. I can't even care for myself. I don't know how to... I wish..." My breath came in gasps as the seething mass of feelings collected behind my breastbone, fighting to be let out.

"Shhh." Hannah got up and came to me, put her arm around my shoulder.

"He... He called me Lou," I said, giving a half laugh. "First time he ever did that. That's when I knew it was really bad. And I couldn't say no. He and Reid ganged up on me. They knew—"

I stood up abruptly and swore.

"I'm sorry," Hannah whispered. "I didn't know you were so in love with him."

"I didn't either. Not until... I wasted so much time. And now—"

"I know."

She did know, too. She had lost Charles, just when they were on the verge of having everything they wanted.

Hannah had started this with an apology, and rather than make me feel better, it only made me feel worse. Those things that she'd said ... she'd been right. Why should she apologize for telling the truth?

I wanted to go back to bed again; the conversation had exhausted me completely. But first, she needed to hear me and believe me about something.

I went to the bed and retrieved my coat that I'd taken off when I'd changed clothes this morning. I reached into the pocket; the earrings were still there. I held them in my palm for a moment, then held my hand out to her.

"I did steal from people, Hannah, but not from you. It happened exactly as I said. I put them in my pocket and forgot about them when you called to me from the bath. I also meant what I said yesterday. I had decided to stay on board with Reid and we were going to go down together. We searched high and low for you, because I wanted to…" I stopped, breathed, regained control. "I did not want to die with such bad feelings between us. When I stopped in your cabin to see if you were there, I took these."

I put them in her palm and closed my hand around hers.

"I know how much these mean to you. I would never steal them, or from you. I'm not proud of a lot of things, Hannah. I came up with this plan and said nothing because you would have disapproved – and you would have been right. I wish I could have been with Reid at the end. I don't know how to do this; I've never loved anyone before. But I can at least give these back to you."

I pulled my hand away and went back to my bed.

Hannah stood there a long time, and when I glanced up, I saw tears streaking down her cheeks. "Thank you," she whispered, then a quick, shuddering, intake of breath. "Lou, what about the rest, that were in the bag?"

I gave a short, ironic laugh. "I had it with me. I was going to give it to someone in a lifeboat so that maybe things could be returned to their owners. But when Charles found us, I put it down, and when we went looking for a lifeboat, I forgot all about it. I didn't even think of it until I was off the ship. It's at the bottom of the ocean, with everything else."

She nodded. "It's going to be all right, Lou. Not for a long time, but it will be."

"Maybe for you," I said, my sharp tone making a reappearance. I was back where I started, but even worse. I had no money, no plan, and a father more than willing to push me off on the next man who would have me. I doubted my brush with death would change his mind that I should be married and having babies and forgetting all this women's rights nonsense. Maybe it was no more than I deserved.

I'd had a glimpse of a shining future for about five minutes, but it was enough to make me realize that what lay ahead was not much of a future at all.

She came and sat beside me, in that quiet way of hers that made it impossible for me to be angry. She was such a good person. Far better than I could ever aspire to be. For years we'd accepted our roles: I was the outrageous, outspoken one, and she balanced me out by being kind and thoughtful and gentle. The fact that she was not curled up in a ball right now shook me to the soles of my feet. The only thing more shocking was that I seemed unable to do anything at all.

I tried to tell myself that Reid and I had only truly been together for less than a week. I tried to pass it off as an affair, something that would have burned hot and fast. I couldn't make myself believe it in my heart, though. Reid Grey had seen exactly who I was and he didn't care. He loved me anyway. I didn't have to explain myself; I could just be Louisa Phillips. He was the first man to ever make me consider sharing a life with someone, and I'd seen it in all its sparkling, fun, sometimes frustrating glory. We would not have had a dull life. We would have lived it to the fullest, together.

How could I not be angry? How could I not be decimated after coming so close to touching that bright, shining dream, only to have it ripped away because of my selfishness?

"Lou," she said quietly, so close our arms were touching. "I forgive you for … well, really, for keeping this secret from me. I hope you can forgive me for the things I said."

I nodded. "There's nothing to forgive, Han. But if you're expecting me to, I don't know, be all right I suppose, I'm going to disappoint you. This has hit me so hard. I'm going to relive that night every day for the rest of my life."

She didn't say anything. I knew she was thinking of another night when things had gone horribly wrong. I was, too. I'd been so afraid for her, so heartbroken at the loss of the little one she wanted so badly. It wasn't fair for her to suffer yet another tragedy. Her activity and nurturing act didn't fool me. Inside she was a wreck. I was afraid of what would happen when she finally broke.

"Now, then," she said, patting my knee and rising. "I should have done this yesterday and never thought. I am going to send a wireless message to my father, telling him I'm alive." She looked down at me and lifted an eyebrow. "Do you want to come with me and send one to your parents, perhaps?"

I made a face.

"Shall I send one for you, then?"

"No, thank you. My name is on the lists here. It'll be printed on the survivor lists, I'm sure."

"Lou…"

"No, Hannah. I will have to contact them at some point. I have nothing to my name. No money, no clothing, no nothing."

"Surely they would wire you—"

"I don't want it. I know I'll have to, but I don't want to."

Hannah sighed. "All right. For now. I'll come back for you in a bit. I'm going to take you out on deck for some air and then lunch in the dining saloon."

"I'd rather stay here." I knew I was being obstinate, but the thought of seeing those people… I'd rather poke myself in the eye.

"It is not fair to ask a crew that is already struggling to serve twice as many passengers as they expected, to wait on you in your cabin. You are perfectly well and can walk to the saloon for your meals."

"You sound just like Sister Agatha," I replied, scowling.

"Good. That was my intent. I'll be back in an hour, Lou." She paused at the door. "We have a few days on this ship, time for us to rest and recover. But make no mistake, life will go on." She put her hand to her stomach. "I have a child I must think of. I need you, too, Lou. I don't have Charles, and I don't have my own mother. You're my family. We'll get through this together."

She departed, leaving me stunned by her speech. I pulled up the blanket, curled up, and stared at the wall. I didn't want to close my eyes and see the horror play out all over again.

Chapter Twenty-Eight

April 17, 1912
Carpathia

HANNAH

Lou was trying my patience. Plus, I was getting tired. I wasn't sleeping well; Lou was having nightmares and either woke herself or made distressing noises as she tossed and turned in her bed. Nighttime, too, was when I could no longer use the excuse of keeping busy to distract my mind. Exhausted as I was from helping where I could, the last two nights had seen me lying awake, picturing Charles's face and wiping away tears at what I'd lost. Lou had made the comment that it didn't even seem as if I were grieving, but I was. Just differently. She had no idea how much I relied on the baby to keep me going. What I wouldn't do for myself, I did for my child.

And for her. I might not understand it, for it seemed like a rather quick attachment, but it was clear as the nose on my face that Lou was absolutely gutted by the loss of Reid Grey. It had been bittersweet, knowing Charles had tasked her with caring for me, a final loving gesture. I didn't mind that it was me caring for her. She'd bolstered me in tough times before. It was right that I repaid that kindness.

That didn't mean it was easy.

I dragged myself out of bed and hastily dressed in the same skirt I'd been wearing since Sunday night, completely serviceable though I would be more than happy to exchange it for something else once we reached New York. I made a quick trip to the lavatory and then returned to find Lou staring at the ceiling.

"Sorry I woke you," I said, not unkindly.

"It's fine," she replied in a monotone voice. I tamped down my impatience.

"Did you hear the storm last night?" I asked. We'd sailed through a thunderstorm, and I'd found myself slightly seasick as well as unsettled by the flash of the lightning. Somehow it reminded me of the lights going out, then coming on again before going out for good before the *Titanic* sank, and each time the sky was illuminated I gave a little jolt.

"Not really. I think I slept through it."

I didn't mention the dreams, and instead simply said, "Lucky. It was a good one. Shall I help you dress? We can go for breakfast. You need your strength, dearest."

She turned her head and stared at me. "You're going to bother me until I agree, aren't you?"

"Yes," I chirped, smiling a smile I didn't feel. "And then we can take a walk."

"I'd rather stay in bed."

I held back a sigh and went to her. "I know. I know how everything feels so heavy right now you can't find the will to move. But it will get better, Lou."

"I don't want it to get better, because then I will have ... forgotten. I don't want to forget, Han. I just..."

"Your heart is broken," I said simply. "It mends. Slowly, but it does. And you won't forget, not ever. It just won't hurt so much."

She sighed, but the closed-off expression faded and she gazed into my face. "I know you've done this before. I watched it. It was awful to see, as your friend. Now that I'm on the other side, I understand. Oh, Hannah, how did you bear it?"

"I didn't, as you well know. Which is why, though you're trying my patience, I am trying to be both gentle and helpful. You do need to eat, and you do need to leave this bed and this room. You're not betraying Reid's memory by choosing not to torture yourself."

She nodded. "Thank you. For being patient. I know I can be a handful."

I patted her hand. "This is a Louisa Phillips I haven't met before. I'm adjusting. But I love her just as much as the person I've known half my life."

"You are so much stronger than any of us ever realized," she said, and I smiled, though I didn't quite believe her. She didn't know how close I was to breaking apart at any moment.

"Come, let's get you up and going. How are you with a needle and thread? Some ladies have been stitching emergency clothes."

A look of horror crossed her face. "I abhor stitching of any kind. Do I look like the embroidering type?"

I laughed, as I'd known that would be her response. I remembered her having very sore fingertips when we'd been required to do samplers and all sorts of ladylike pursuits. She had muttered something about sticking the nuns with pins...

Taking her out of the cabin was necessary but brought its own problems. We ate, but the crowding of so many passengers made us both claustrophobic. After breakfast we tried a walk on deck, but the lifeboats that had been brought on board were there and affected us both with the memories and the reminder of how many had never had a chance to be saved. Everywhere, too, were people talking, talking, talking. About their loved ones. Crying. Replaying the events that led to their own personal rescue. There was a handful of men, too: the *Titanic* crew, *Carpathia* passengers, the few survivors like Mr. Carter and Cosmo Duff-Gordon. Their presence only served as a reminder of the men we'd lost.

Truthfully, the only comforting presence was that of Margaret and her friends. "Let's get out of here," I murmured to Lou, when I couldn't stand the sound of one more sob. "You know what we need?"

"The half bottle of brandy you hid?" she asked, a little too hopefully.

"We need other women. We need to be with those who give us strength and comfort. Come with me. We're going to find Margaret and Renee and the others."

"Hannah..."

"I promise it will be fine. You avoided them all day yesterday, but they are good women, Lou. They'll offer you comfort without pity. You can rely on that."

She tugged on my hand. "I can't look Margaret Brown in the eye."

I had forgotten about the bracelet. "In light of all that's happened, she's probably forgotten all about her bracelet. What does it matter when everything else is at the bottom of the ocean, too?"

She hesitated, but didn't make a fuss, so we went in search of Mrs. Brown and the friends that always seemed to be in her orbit.

We found her in the first-class library, with a number of familiar faces from our journey. Mrs. Rothschild was there, as well as Margaret and Renee Harris. We were quickly introduced to a Mrs. Spencer and Mrs. Clark. I went to Renee and kissed her cheek, and she offered a wan smile. "Hello, you two. Oh, it's lovely to see you together."

Margaret came forward. "Miss Phillips. Hello, dear." She offered no platitudes, just folded Lou in a motherly hug which was certainly not the done thing but exactly what Lou needed. We both could use a little mothering, honestly, and I was slightly abashed but mostly thankful that Margaret Brown, with her no-nonsense ways and big heart was there to fill that space.

For over an hour, we sat and drew comfort from the others. Renee filled us in on her unfortunate slip earlier on Sunday which had broken her elbow when she'd fallen on the stairs. Margaret had taken the initiative to not only start a fund to help survivors – most of whom would arrive in New York with nothing – but to also honour the *Carpathia*'s crew for their heroic rescue. I had been so focused on helping those who'd been set adrift that I hadn't truly considered the crew, other than recognizing they were run off their feet. It was true, though. The captain and officers had, apparently, navigated through an iceberg-dotted sea at top speed to reach us, and while they were steaming ahead, the rest of the crew were up and preparing space for survivors as well as refreshments like coffee, brandy, and soup. As we spoke of their efforts, a feeling of gratitude stole over me.

I met Lou's gaze briefly and then added to the conversation. "They say times of strife can bring out the best in people. That's certainly true of the *Carpathia* crew and her passengers, too."

Everyone nodded.

"And you, Mrs. Brown," Lou said quietly. "You have apparently led the way with your generosity and organizational skills. We're very lucky to have you. To know you."

"Well, bless you for saying that." She smiled. "The truth is, I have a lot to be thankful for. I'm in a much better position than most who were rescued, so I will do what I can."

"Unlike a few others I could name," someone muttered, and while I wondered who they were talking about, I also knew of at least half a dozen first-class survivors who were keeping to themselves and not helping at all. I had always idolized Lady Duff-Gordon in a way, being a female businesswoman and a brilliant designer. But there was a rumour that there had only been twelve people in their lifeboat and that Cosmo had offered to pay the crew members to not go back for survivors. It was hard to hold someone like that in great esteem.

"I would like to contribute," I said, "once we're in New York. I've wired my father, who will contact my husband's man of business." I was thankful my father was a solicitor; he'd be able to guide me through the next several months and ensure I could navigate Charles's business interests. Right now the very thought was overwhelming.

"Remind me where you are staying?" Renee asked.

"The Belmont. Lou and I were to stay there a week."

Lou had gone even more quiet, if that were possible.

"Well, there is no need to rush. You have friends now, friends in New York and beyond."

Mrs. Rothschild piped up, "I always find it's helpful to think of things in steps. You only have to do one thing at a time."

It was oddly good advice from a woman who was rich enough to delegate all her tasks. Even though I had been brought up in slightly humbler circumstances, I'd got used to having the staff do it.

"So many of us are alone, but we're not truly alone," added Mrs. Spencer. "Oh, I can't tell you how much I needed this time this morning. I go from being unbearably sad to afraid and horribly overwhelmed. You ladies have been a balm to my battered soul."

I looked over at Lou. Tears were glimmering in her eyes and her lip was wobbling. Margaret noticed, too, and went to her, perching beside her on the sofa. "Oh, my dear," she murmured. "It's all right. If you need to have a good cry, you have it. I've an extra hanky and a strong shoulder."

Lou nodded, her tears splashing onto her cheeks, looking so much like a little girl I wanted to wrap her up myself. But I was battling my own tears. Seeing Lou so hurt... Had I ever seen her cry other than in frustration and anger? I couldn't remember. But I knew that seeing this strong, funny, outrageous woman cry broke my heart.

After a few minutes, Lou straightened. "I'm so sorry. I can't believe I—"

"Nonsense," said Mrs. Clark. "We've all been shedding tears off and on since we came aboard. Don't give it another thought, dear."

"We'll be in New York tomorrow night, I've heard." Renee spoke up. "For those of you remaining there, at least for a while, please stay in touch. I shall need to be near people who understand. People who were there, and women who are here right now." She coughed, an emotional clearing of her throat. "I had heard the *Titanic* called the Ship of Dreams. Do you know what I heard this morning? Someone called this the Ship of Widows. Isn't that sad? So many of us..."

"Except me," Lou said, her voice small.

I held her gaze. "You were in love. That counts."

Her lip wobbled again, but she held fast.

"I do believe I'd like a nap," Mrs. Rothschild said. "The thunderstorm last night kept me awake. I don't know about the rest of you, but it's nerve-wracking, still being at sea. I'll be so glad to have my feet on dry land again."

The group broke up after that, and Lou agreed that she'd also like to go back to the cabin. I agreed, because she'd been spectacularly good about the morning.

That afternoon, fog rolled in, making time out on deck impossible and casting an even darker spell over the ship as we steamed closer and closer to America and what would become the start of the rest of all our lives.

Chapter Twenty-Nine

April 18, 1912
Carpathia

LOUISA

The fog had finally lifted, and despite the weather still being bleak and grey, I found a few moments to go out on deck as we neared New York.

The journey was almost over, but nothing was as I'd planned. At times I caught myself feeling almost normal, but then another emotion would wash over me, leaving me dead inside, incapable of feeling much of anything at all. In those moments, the absence of feeling was the most frightening. It had been nearly four days since we'd struck the iceberg, and in those moments, I was so utterly overwhelmed that I simply shut down.

Right now, however, I felt like one of the boilers on the *Titanic* when we'd stopped: ready to blow unless I somehow managed to relieve some pressure.

The fresh air was helping, and I didn't care if I got wet. A foghorn sounded in the distance; goodness, were we that close to land, then? The idea was comforting. Since being rescued, there was no denying that having to spend another four days on the ocean had played with my head. Early on, someone had mentioned being too far south for icebergs, and that had offered a little relief for my worry, but Tuesday night's storm had set me off again, all thunder and lightning and lashing rain. I'd told Hannah I had slept through it, but really I'd been in my bed, frozen stiff with fear.

I would never be so glad as to be off this damned ship.

It would help if Hannah stopped hovering, too, though I understood why. She didn't trust me to care for myself, and maybe I resented her for it, but it did not mean she was wrong. I was tired. And not the "I didn't get enough sleep" tired, but the deep-in-the-bones weariness that comes from carrying too much for too long.

As far as what I was going to do next, I was avoiding thinking about it. What I needed – hoped for – were some answers. Perhaps if I understood what happened, I could make sense of it and leave it behind me.

Hannah found me shortly before five and begged me to come out of the rain. "We'll be docking this evening," she said. "Come inside. We can get ready together."

I snorted a laugh. "Get ready? I've been wearing the same clothes all week. I was given a spare set of combinations that I've hand-washed in the lavatory. Hannah, there's nothing to pack."

She looked hurt, so I added a meek, "Sorry."

"No, you're right. I just thought… I don't know. I do know I don't want you to catch a chill out here in the damp."

I didn't actually care about such a thing, which was also concerning. Never in my life had I suffered this sort of ennui. Not actually caring if I lived or died. I simply could not gather the wherewithal to do more than put one foot in front of the other. Or perform simple tasks that I was told to do. Eat this. Walk here. Get some sleep. Drink some tea. I did it to avoid having arguments. But I didn't *care*. I wasn't sure I would ever care again, not in the way I used to.

Still, I went in, because it was better than arguing.

It was still raining when we reached the pier, and we seemed to wait an interminable time to disembark. Hannah and I went together, me with my velvet coat over the horrid grey skirt and blouse, Hannah with her wool overcoat, both of us hatless. The continual flash of camera bulbs hurt my head, and even Hannah was pale and hesitant as we walked down the steep gangway. There had to be thousands of people, all getting a glimpse of our tragedy, for what? Entertainment? Morbid curiosity? There was crying and wailing and there were happy cheers when someone was welcomed and embraced. Voices calling out names as the rain fell. Reporters shouting out questions to get their story before deadline. My legs felt odd, being on solid, still ground after spending over a week on the ocean.

A kindly woman came up to us, wearing a heavy cloak and hat. "Hello," she said, her voice warm. "I'm Ada Townsend, with the Women's Relief Committee. I'm here to help."

I simply stared, but Hannah answered for both of us. "We have a booking at the Belmont Hotel. All we require is transportation, thank you."

"Are you sure? We have many resources available—"

"Just the hotel," I said, perhaps a little sharply. "And a warm bed that is not on the ocean."

Understanding softened her eyes. "Follow me. Are you to meet anyone here? Will there be family looking for you?"

Hannah shook her head. "No."

"Most are being taken to the hospital to be checked over. St. Vincent's."

"God, no," I interjected, my voice the strongest it had been in days. "We are perfectly well, as you can see. Neither of us needs poking or prodding."

Then I realized after I'd spoken that perhaps Hannah did need seeing to. She was pregnant, after all, and the whole time on the *Carpathia* I hadn't even asked if she was feeling all right, if everything was fine with the baby. I was such a rotten friend!

The woman led us expertly through the crowd to an area where several cars waited, and other organizations were set up to help. Ambulances formed a line as well, for those passengers who needed medical care. I was so thankful I was not one of them. I was not well, I knew that, but I could walk of my own volition and was not given to hysterics.

Though this was not my first time in New York, the commotion, mixed with the rain and darkness – it was around ten o'clock by my closest guess – made everything unfamiliar. We had docked at Pier 54; that was all I knew.

The woman – Townsend – got us into a taxi and gave instructions to take us to the Belmont. Once we were on our way and out of the horrific throng, I looked over at Hannah sitting on the back seat of the taxi beside me, and noticed she was utterly exhausted with dark circles under her eyes and a drawn look about her mouth. I was, too, but I was also so relieved to be on dry land again – even if it wasn't my own country. I never wanted to get on a boat again.

It was nearly midnight when we were finally in our suite at the Belmont. It was a gorgeous room, in cream and gold with a spread the colour of claret on top of the luxurious mattress. A maid brought us soft robes and we had our own bathroom, and the first thing Hannah did was run me a bath while she looked after details. I told her to go first, because she looked completely done in, but she insisted, saying that as soon as she had bathed, she was going to fall into bed and sleep for a solid twelve hours.

The hot water and scented soap did more for me in the first five minutes than anything had in days.

I heard Hannah's voice, speaking to the maid, thanking her, and the door shutting. Then nothing, not for a long while. I wondered if she'd fallen asleep, and though I could have stayed in the bath an hour, I got out and dried myself with the thick towel and pulled the robe on, feeling slightly more human. I wanted to burn that grey skirt if possible, though I was very grateful to the person who'd parted with it. Honestly, though, I wanted to wash every part of the disaster off my skin and not put anything back on that reminded me of it.

Hannah was not asleep; she was sitting at a little writing desk penning a letter. "Hello," I said, squeezing the towel over the ends of my hair.

"You look much better," she said, putting down her pen and rising. "I started a letter to my father. The emergency things I can send in a telegram, but there are others…"

Of course there were. "You're a rich woman," I commented. "You have concerns."

"I'd give it all up to have Charles back."

"I know you would." I waved a hand toward the bathroom. "I've started a fresh bath for you. I promise, you're going to feel so much better after a good soak."

"Thanks. And I ordered a pot of tea for me and a stiff brandy for you." There was one bed in the suite, and a plush sofa flanked by two well-cushioned chairs. "Do you want to flip a coin for the bed?"

Initially we had booked two rooms, but for reasons unknown to me, we'd been put in one big one. I didn't care. "You should have the bed," I said. "But truthfully, Hannah, I don't mind sharing. The bed is huge."

"It could be like school days when you'd visit me during the holidays. We always shared."

We had. We'd been typical schoolgirls, talking about horrible teachers and charming boys and the latest fashions, whispering long into the night. We were grown women now, and such things were trivial, really, but I yearned to go back there again, when it was simpler.

"It's settled then. Go, your water must be nearly ready. I'll bring you your tea."

She disappeared into the bathroom, and I wandered about in my bare feet, feeling the thick carpet under my toes, testing out the chairs and sofa for comfort. It was hard to believe we were here at last. Nothing seemed real. One moment I'd been dining in the most beautiful restaurant in the world with a gorgeous man I loved, and the next I was in a lifeboat with death all around me. How did a person make sense of all that?

I was lost in my thoughts when there was a faint knock at the door. The maid – goodness, it was late for her to be working – wheeled in a cart that held not just a pot of tea and the brandy, but food as well. "I wasn't sure if you'd eaten, ma'am. The kitchen sent up a selection of fruit and some sandwiches. We're all terribly sorry for your ordeal, ma'am."

I didn't correct her that it was miss, not ma'am. But I did thank her for the kindness. "This is very sweet, thank you…" I left the end hanging, prompting for her name.

"Ellen, ma'am. Goodnight, ma'am."

I picked up a strawberry and nibbled on it, then another. There were grapes, too, a real novelty, and then I tried a sandwich of minced ham and then a cucumber one, and before long I'd managed a full meal. There was a splash from the bathroom, and I wiped my hands on a napkin before pouring a cup of strong tea for Hannah and adding milk to it, just the way she preferred. I carried it into the bathroom, where I found her relaxing amid the steam and bubbles.

"Tea," I said, holding out the cup and saucer.

"Is it horrible that I feel like a new person?" she asked. "I feel guilty about it."

"It is not. And tomorrow we are going to get some proper clothes." I perched on the edge of the tub as she took her first sip of tea. "I suppose I shall have to telegram my father. I'll need money to ... well, to do whatever comes next. I have no idea what that is."

"Me either," Hannah said, sighing and closing her eyes. "I would like to spend a few days just getting my bearings." Her hair was damp and the dark strands curled around her face, her cheeks pink from the warmth of the water.

"I want a newspaper," I added. "We know what happened, but we don't really know why. Plus, people will have been interviewed now." Captain Rostron had kept the wireless communication restricted to notifying kin, not revealing details to the press, a fact that had raised him even another notch in my esteem. He was such a hero.

"Those reporters were horrid," Hannah said, giving a shudder. "They're likely not done, Lou. You can do what you want, but I have no intention of speaking to any of them."

"Nor I." The very idea was distasteful. "But those at the top, the crew, the White Star people, Ismay... they have answers. We deserve to know. The people we left behind deserve that."

She nodded. "You're right. But I meant what I said about falling into bed for twelve hours, Lou. I'm exhausted."

"Drink your tea. The maid, who is very sweet by the way, also brought up some food. I ate. Without you forcing me."

A faint smile touched her lips, then she held out her cup. "Will you take this? I think I'm done now."

I took the cup back to the cart and poured her a fresh cup, then added a splash of brandy from the crystal decanter to a glass and tossed it back. To be truthful, though I was also worn out, this was the most human I'd felt since everything had gone wrong. And with this humanity came acceptance of what my selfishness and self-absorption had cost.

She came out, dressed in a robe identical to mine, her hair down and curling around her shoulders. I handed her the full cup with one hand and a sandwich with the other.

"Hang on," she said, and she picked up the brandy decanter. She added the tiniest bit to her tea, then tipped up the cup and drank the entire thing. Then she devoured the sandwich, had a second, and, like me, went straight for the strawberries. "Do you know what I'd really like?" she said, chewing.

"What?"

"Mrs. Wilson's steak and kidney pie. My father would have a pint with it, and she always made some sort of veg, but her pastry and that rich gravy... I would like to be in my own home, and not in another ship's cabin or hotel room." She sniffed. "I want to be home, Lou." Her eyes were sad and weary, her lips turned down in defeat.

"I know," I soothed. I went to the bed and turned it down, then led her to it. "Get in. You need to rest." I had heard the homesickness in her voice, though, and it put me on edge. I had no desire to go back to Exminster. Honestly, I didn't have a home I was longing to return to. Where did that leave me? Never mind the fact the thought of crossing the ocean again made me want to throw up.

"I'll wire my father and have him send funds," I said, crawling into my side, both of us still cozied up in our robes in lieu of proper nightgowns. I turned off the lamp on the table next to me and waited for my eyes to adjust to the darkness. When they did, I turned to my side and saw Hannah looking at me, her eyes wide.

"You don't have to, if you don't want," she replied finally. "Ask your father for money, I mean. I have more than enough, Lou." After a moment, she added, "I know you don't want charity, but what we talked about on the *Titanic*... I would have helped you. You wouldn't have to marry Balcombe. Your happiness means more to me than pride."

"I thought it was my only option. It started by accident, really, a misplaced item among my things, but then the idea took hold until it became an actual plan. Now, though, well, what's the point of anything?"

It was quiet for a bit. The bed was exceptionally comfortable, the bedding thick and warm, and I was growing quite drowsy when Hannah's voice reached out to me in the darkness.

"I miss him, Lou. Oh God, I miss him. How shall I ever do without him?"

Her plea, so unexpected, reached out and pierced my heart, echoing my own pain so completely. "I don't know, Hannah. I don't know. At least you have something left of Charles. At least … you don't have to feel responsible for his death."

She sat up. "Responsible? What do you mean?"

I bit down on my lip, so afraid to give voice to the guilt and shame that had built inside me, hardening, sitting like a stone in my chest and making it hard to breathe.

"Lou?" She reached for my hand. "Dearest, what is it?"

I pushed myself up so I was sitting, the covers pooled around my hips, still wearing the robe as we had no nightgowns. I pulled my hand from hers and tugged the panels tighter around me. "I just… Oh Hannah, it's all my fault." I buried my face in my hands.

"What is your fault?"

"Reid dying. It's all because… Oh God, Hannah, you were so right. That day in my cabin, when we argued, you were right about everything. I am selfish and careless and now Reid has paid for it with his life."

She pulled my hands away from my face. In the shadows, I could see concern etched on her features, and confusion clouding her eyes. "I am sorry I said all those things," she said. "I was angry and I lashed out."

"No, you were right." I swallowed against hot tears, my throat tightening as I tried to keep from erupting in tears. "The only reason Reid was on that ship was because I was playing games. I wrote to him, telling him of my plans, hinting that he should come too. I didn't think he actually would, but he did. He came on board and he had the best of intentions. I was the one angling for a distraction, a fling. He came, he said, because he wanted a chance to win me, and he succeeded."

He certainly had. I'd lost my heart to him the first time we'd made love in his cabin. Our connection had been profound, even though I hadn't wanted to admit it at the time.

"He was only there because of me. He had no business in New York. I wanted him to come to keep me entertained while you were with Charles. A flirtation, a diversion. Games, Hannah. I'm so very good at playing games. But Reid is the one who lost. It is my fault he was on board and it's my fault he's dead."

My voice broke on the last word and the tears I had tried to hold back came streaming down my cheeks.

"Oh, Lou." Hannah pulled me into her arms. "Sweetheart, you couldn't have known. It's not your fault we hit an iceberg. It's not your fault the ship sank or that there weren't enough lifeboats. This is not your burden to bear."

"But it is," I cried, my heart breaking all over again. "He should have been back in London. I could have gone home and then met up with him at some party and started something up if I really wanted. He should be there now, with his family, with his friends. Not..." I couldn't finish. I didn't know where he was. A sick churning began in my stomach.

"Well, then," Hannah said firmly, "I guess I am to blame, too. I wanted you to come and insisted Charles pay for your ticket. You were only on the *Titanic* because of me, and if you hadn't come, Reid wouldn't have either."

"Don't be ridiculous."

"I'm not. If I follow your logic, there's lots of guilt to go around."

"Hannah—"

"I mean, we could blame Charles. He's the one who started this whole thing—"

"Now you're being daft." I wiped my face on the sleeve of the robe and stared at her in the gloom. "He was going for business—"

"Yes, but he could have booked different passage. A different ship, a different day."

"Why would he? No one knew this was going to happen."

"Exactly, darling. That's what I'm trying to tell you." She reached up and touched my face briefly. "No one could foresee this incident, or how tragic it would be. Not Charles, not Reid, certainly not you." She sniffled and ran her fingers beneath her eyes. "Believe me, you'll never win playing the what-if game. I have my own regrets."

I stared at her. "What do you have to regret? Hannah, in all of this, I compare my behaviour to yours. You are, and have always been, beyond reproach. I should not have criticized you for that."

She gave a harsh laugh. "Oh, I have regrets, and you were right about some of what you said, too. I do go along to get along. I won't apologize for wanting the life I had, but I should have spoken up more. I should have told him about the baby when I first realized. We might have had more time together … really together, as we were that last day. One day, Lou. We had one day of happiness."

She started to cry then. Maybe it was being safe, being here in New York and off the ship and away from everything that allowed our emotions to be set free. Maybe Hannah was tired of holding it all together, and holding me together, too. My heart had broken over and over again, every day since the sinking, and I had fought it. Ignored it or pushed it aside. Tonight, I let it happen. We both did, and I wasn't sure if I felt better or worse. But I did feel closer to my best friend than I had in months, so I reached over and pulled Hannah into a hug, and we cried together until we had no tears left.

Chapter Thirty

April 21, 1912
New York

HANNAH

If Lou and I had thought we could move freely in New York, we were mistaken. There were no shopping trips on Fifth Avenue, no evenings at the theatre or dinners at top restaurants, no walks in the park or tea at the Plaza, all things we'd planned for our week in the city. Instead, we were practically prisoners in our hotel, thanks to reporters waiting for any chance to pounce and get an exclusive from survivors. We had no desire to speak to the press and relive everything for public consumption.

This was our third day being cloistered in our suite. It wasn't exactly a hardship; the room was beautifully appointed and the staff attentive and kind. But after being stuck on a crowded ship for four days, and with so much to work through and plan, there was nothing I longed for more than a walk to exercise my legs and my brain.

Besides, I loved Lou, but we needed a break from each other.

We'd made our amends; we'd loved each other too long to not forgive. Our first-night confessional had cleared the air, and now it felt as if our hearts were open. The wounds were still raw and we were both fragile, but there was a new strength in having shared our deepest pain with each other. I was starting to realize how desperate she must have been to resort to theft to fund her independence, and the more I thought about it, the more I understood why she hadn't come to me. Lou had never been able to rely on anyone, and our friendship was a precious thing. Muddying the waters with financial dependence could threaten what we were. I didn't think it would, but as I pondered how things had unravelled, I put myself in her shoes and felt I was gaining some clarity. That she was automatically accepting my help now – I was paying for everything at the moment – was not the relief it might have been. I was worried that Lou had given up. By accepting defeat, the spark I so admired in her had dimmed.

"Lou, darling, what shall we do today?" I looked over at her across the table, where our breakfast sat, barely touched. I raised my eyebrow at her because it was a rhetorical question. Unless we wanted to be confronted with the press, we stayed put. Our days consisted of talking, sleeping, reading the papers.

"Well, I thought we'd start at the Bronx Zoo and then perhaps lunch, somewhere fancy and with lots and lots of people." Her response was dry, with a quirk of her lips. Then she sighed. "Hannah, I'm going crazy. I need to get out of here."

"I know." I had an idea that I thought she might go for. "Let's send a message to the Fortunes today." They were staying here as well, and to my knowledge, were in much the same situation. "Perhaps invite them to the suite for tea. At least see someone else. Not that I mind your face, I don't." I smiled at her. "Honestly, I have to do something other than sit with my grief and sadness, Lou. It's becoming unbearable."

"I know. I feel like I'm going a bit mad."

We'd both been following the papers, including reading a few of the older ones that had come out before the *Carpathia* had docked in New York. They were rife with speculation and misinformation. One had even said that the *Titanic* was on its way to Halifax, instead of sinking at all. In the absence of information, articles had been published with sheer speculation, all in order to "keep up" with other publications for the latest fantastical version of the story.

But the ones since our arrival were far more informative, in particular reports from the Senate investigation that had convened two days ago. No time had been wasted, and I had to limit how much I read, otherwise I grew too angry or anxious.

Lou gobbled it all up, absorbing the news until I took away the newspapers and told her to take a breath. The more she read, the more agitated she became. "Han, they're saying that the lookouts didn't have binoculars. How is that even possible? We might have had time to turn," she'd said. Then, "We were all joking at the betting for how many miles we could make in a day. But if there were really warnings about ice, shouldn't the captain have slowed us down, rather than lighting the last boilers?" She flipped the paper once more. "Also, I read that the *Californian* was only twenty miles away, but they didn't have a wireless operator on duty so didn't hear our distress call. Think how many lives might have been saved if they'd come straight away." She frowned. "It all makes me so furious."

They were all good points, and I was glad Lou didn't seem to be blaming herself anymore, but my head was ready to explode. Yes, answers were needed so this wouldn't happen again. But nothing could bring Charles back. I did not need to relive it over and over again. I already did that, thinking about my last moments with him, not realizing how final they were. Being afraid but also sure we'd both be all right in the end.

No, I couldn't stand another day locked up in this suite.

"We can message the Fortunes, but I have a better idea. I'm going to send a note to Renee Harris and see if we can sneak our way out of the hotel to see her."

Lou brightened. "Oh, that would be lovely. I'm so tired of seeing these four walls."

I set about writing a note and rang for someone to deliver it. My father had sent funds, so I was able to tip the messenger, and I hoped he would not betray us to the press. The Sunday morning paper had arrived, too, and Lou sat in one of the chairs, dressed in one of the new outfits we'd had delivered to the hotel on Friday from Bloomingdales.

"I think we should go to Halifax," she said suddenly, halting me in my tracks.

We hadn't made any solid plans. Lou had said she couldn't think of sailing again so soon, and I understood. We also didn't know if we would be called on to give any accounts of our experience. I knew I wanted to go home, but I, too, got a queasy feeling whenever I thought about stepping foot on a ship again.

"Halifax?" I asked, puzzled.

"In Nova Scotia," she continued. "Rescue boats were sent out on the seventeenth. Pardon me, of course they're not rescuing anyone." Her voice thickened but she persevered. "To recover any bodies."

It was a grim thought, and when I imagined Charles's body floating in the water I got a dizzy, sick feeling.

Did I want to see his face once more? I did and I didn't. The topic, though, took me back to thinking what he must have suffered in the end, which was unbearable. "Oh, Lou, why? It changes nothing."

She had lowered the paper and stared at me, but she'd shuttered away her emotions. "I need to know. If there's a chance to put Reid to rest, I must do it. Don't you feel the same way about Charles?"

I didn't. God help me, I didn't. Of course, if he were found he should be buried at home, in Devon, with his people. His parents were gone, his mother from influenza and his father from a heart affliction. He should be with them. But to go there, and find him, and see him... Was I a coward? Shouldn't I *want* to do this, as Lou did?

I just wanted to go home. To see the end of an English spring, to grow our baby, to leave all this behind.

"I want to go, Hannah. I'll go without you, if you can't, and I understand. But I want to. I need to do that for him, if it's possible."

I went to her, squatted down beside her chair. "I have been so worried about you. I've never seen you like you were on the *Carpathia*, caring for nothing, not even yourself. I don't want that to happen again, Lou. You're just starting to be more yourself. I'm afraid that if you see him..."

She met my gaze evenly. "I will never be 'myself' again, Hannah. Not like I was. This has changed me forever. Reid's love changed me, but losing it has destroyed me in ways I can't explain."

She said it so plainly, so matter-of-fact. Who was I to deny her what she needed at such a time? Hadn't I promised myself I would care for her just as she'd cared for me? I could not be selfish. She had got on the lifeboat for *me*. I was the only reason she hadn't given up and died with the man she loved. If she could bear that, I could go to Halifax.

"I'll ask about making arrangements," I said. "If that's what you truly want."

She nodded. "We are just sitting here, aren't we? Avoiding the press, wallowing. I need to do something, or I swear to God I'm going to go crazy. I know I was in a fog for days. I can't stay there forever. It'll kill me."

I stood again and took the other chair, tucking my skirt around me. "Well, it's a relief for me to hear you no longer want to die."

She folded the paper and placed it on her lap. "I'm too much of a coward, Hannah. So I must do *something*."

Lou had always been the kind of woman who chose action, and hadn't I confessed that I wished I had done something to restore my marriage sooner? I wouldn't deny her this.

A few hours later we received a note in return, asking us to Renee's for dinner. We enlisted the help of Alice Fortune's fiancé, Charles Allen, who had come to New York to meet the family, and he helped us sneak out of the hotel undetected. The evening was a welcome reprieve, and Renee was a lovely host, despite still suffering from her broken elbow. She also agreed completely with Lou. "You should go," she said, her eyes filling with tears. "In fact, my brother is going on my behalf. I find I'm not up to travel right now, but he'll ensure my Henry is brought home. I'll tell him to look out for you both, too."

It seemed we were to go, then, and when we got back to the Belmont that night, I agreed, with conditions.

"All right, Lou, I'll go. But first you must finally send a wire to your family. They must be frantic."

"Hardly," she muttered, but I shook my head.

"Regardless of whether you are close or not, seeing your name on a list is not the same as knowing you are alive and well."

"He'll tell me to come home."

"Perhaps. Only you can decide what to do about that." I gave her a little smile. "It wouldn't be the first time you defied your father."

"Fine."

My smile grew. I had heard that petulant tone before, and no matter what she said, I did see glimpses of the old Lou in there somewhere. She would find her way and be all right – eventually.

As would I. I did long to be home, but at the same time I dreaded crossing the threshold without Charles by my side, knowing he would never be there again. If there was a chance his body could be recovered, and sent back to England, wouldn't it be a comfort to have him close by?

"Also, we are going to brave the shops and purchase what we truly need to get us through several weeks, along with proper luggage. We could be in Halifax for several days, and then there's the voyage home. I need more than a few dresses and basic underthings."

"You're so practical," Lou remarked, but her eyes had taken on a light that heartened me. Now that I had agreed, she had a new energy.

"I am, rather. London was fun and I enjoyed buying my Lucile gowns and the Poiret and the rest, but I don't need that, do you?"

Lou shook her head. "Actually, no, I don't. Suddenly it all seems so frivolous, doesn't it?"

It did.

"But Hannah, if I might make a request?" She looked down at her dress, which was a dark grey with black lace trim, and then over at me, dressed in black. "I know you're in mourning, and I am too, but can we please buy something that isn't all black and grey? I'm gloomy enough on the inside. I don't need to be that way outside, too."

"We shall see," I said, but I knew what she meant. I was supposed to wear black, but I'd always hated it. The grey that Lou wore – the colour of the coal from Charles's mines – made her complexion wan and her hair seem drab. "Perhaps we can manage with subdued colours. No pastels."

And so we made plans to visit Fifth Avenue anyway, setting the day as the twenty-third. On the twenty-fifth, one week after arriving in New York, we boarded a train to Canada, leaving the city just as many other passengers had done in the days following our arrival. Those we had known and cared about were resuming their lives. Now we would, too. We just had to do this one last thing before putting the *Titanic* behind us.

Chapter Thirty-One

April 29, 1912
Halifax, Nova Scotia

LOUISA

I hadn't known what to expect when we arrived in Halifax, but seeing store windows draped in sombre black with pictures of Titanic displayed, took me by surprise. We settled at the Halifax Hotel on Hollis Street after a non-eventful but long train journey to Nova Scotia, and the following day we went to a meeting at our hotel held by Mayor Chisholm. All relatives and agents of missing passengers were required to register, and so we did. While I hated to do it, I had sent a telegram to my parents telling them where I was going and that I was with Hannah. Then I sent a second one to Reid's bank, requesting information about his parents. They should know that someone was here for him.

And then we waited, along with others who had arrived in the small city, for the boats to return.

I couldn't bear to stay locked in a hotel room any longer, so Hannah and I spent time each day walking the hilly city. The salty air restored me, reminded me of summer days at the seaside with the plaintive call of the gulls and even the morning fog, grey and mysterious. We stood at the clock tower at the top of the Citadel and looked down over what was Georges Island and then McNab's Island guarding the entrance to the harbour, and where we could see the ships coming and going, waiting for word of the return of the ships sent out to the area where the *Titanic* had gone down. But for the last three days, there was no *Mackay-Bennett*, the cable ship that was sent soon after the sinking. It was torturous, playing this waiting game.

I liked Halifax, though, which surprised me because I had always considered myself a "big city" girl. I loved living in London and the idea of returning to New York had excited me no end with its shopping and theatres and enterprise. Halifax, while a city, was rather provincial in comparison. Still, I quickly realized, by glancing in the papers, that there was a vibrant society here that, while perhaps not the pinnacle of fashion and exclusivity, still had its share of going concerns. In particular, I'd discovered there was a group called the Local Council of Women whose leaders worked on various projects, including campaigning for women to have the vote in Canada and collaborations with other local organizations like schools and hospitals to further women's causes.

Another time I might like to explore such a thing, but Hannah and I were constantly on edge, wondering when we'd be notified that the ships were returning. Vincent Astor was here, as apparently J. J.'s body had been found and the family notified, but Madeleine was sequestered at home. Maurice Rothschild had come, and of course, Renee's brother had made the journey as well and had checked in on us once or twice at his sister's request. Otherwise, though, we tried not to associate with others who were here for the same purpose. I simply couldn't abide the morbid fascination with the sinking over and over and over again. I relived it enough as it was. Some got relief from talking about it constantly, but others, like me, found it all too much. Thankfully Hannah and I were of one mind on that. We didn't need to speak of it all the time to know when the other was particularly suffering. We simply cared for each other, with a squeeze of the hand, or a cup of tea, or a little privacy to have a weep. Of the two of us, Hannah was the most self-possessed. "I can't go through grief the same way again," she told me, her eyes filling with tears. "I learned from my pain, Lou, and I have something precious to live for." She put her hand on her stomach and gave a wobbly smile. "I have a piece of Charles with me forever now. It's a comfort."

I had no such comfort. All I had was the demolished potential of happiness. It had hit me hard.

When the news came at half past eight, Hannah and I were just finishing our breakfast. The *Mackay-Bennett* was entering the harbour.

Neither of us could eat another bite. I put down my fork with a piece of egg stuck on it, my throat tightening and my stomach souring. We didn't know which bodies had been found; perhaps both Charles and Reid, most likely neither. I didn't know which I preferred, to be honest. The thought of seeing them again made my stomach roll with uncertainty and dread. And yet, if they had been retrieved, they deserved to have a proper burial.

"What do you want to do?" I asked Hannah. My stomach kept churning, as if there was a swarm of bees buzzing around inside me, looking for an exit. "Do you want to go to the pier?"

She stared at me, her face white. "No, I don't think so," she replied, having likewise dispensed with her silverware. "There'll be such crowds there, and we won't find out anything until later anyway."

I agreed with her. The activity in the lobby of the hotel told us that this was a main, morbid attraction, and we'd both had enough of that. "As much as being outside is usually calming for me," I said, "I think I'd rather just wait here for word to be sent."

"Me, too."

Word finally came that afternoon that all the bodies – nearly two hundred of them – had been unloaded and taken to the Mayflower Curling Club on Agricola Street, with the exception of ten bodies, which were taken to Snow's Mortuary on Argyle, including Astor's.

I sat in a chair in our room and stared at Hannah, wondering if I looked as pale and anxious as she did. We had been living in this alternate reality for exactly two weeks. We were tired, and I for one felt off balance all the time. I was on edge, needing normalcy desperately. A bed that was my own and not in yet another hotel would be a tremendous start. "Shall we go up there?" I asked, wanting to get this over with, but also afraid to take the next step. I was twenty-six and I had never actually seen a dead body. No, that wasn't true, of course. I had seen many on that horrible morning, white life jackets bobbing in the water. But not … laid out. Like for burial. Certainly no one I knew.

Hannah nodded. "I think we must."

A curling club was an odd place to view a body, cold and uninviting and certainly not comforting in the least, but it provided the things necessary for dealing with so many bodies all at once. Those of us who'd registered went to the observation room which had been set up as a waiting area. There was a wooden partition at the western end of the rink, and behind it were embalming benches. One of the dressing rooms was converted into a "hospital" of sorts, attended by a nurse, and I looked at Hannah. How was this our life right now? We were supposed to be carefree and happy and celebrating. We were supposed to be in love and planning our futures. "Why a hospital room?" I whispered, leaning toward her. "Everyone is dead."

Hannah met my gaze. "One would only assume it's for people overwhelmed with grief, darling."

I nodded, stared out at the converted rink, then looked at her again. "Hannah, I just feel numb. All the time. Like this is happening to someone else and I'm watching it from outside looking in."

"Me, too. I thought the shock was gone, but this feels like a different kind. Like I'm moving through time but not feeling any of it."

I held her hand. Since leaving New York, we'd truly started caring for each other. I tried very hard to not be a burden, to look after Hannah as I'd promised Charles I would. Hannah looked after me, too, when I faltered. I had nightmares, for one, and many nights I barely slept because I was afraid to close my eyes. Despite our conversation in New York, I still replayed "what if" in my head so many times I should have tired of it. Sometimes I was so exhausted I couldn't seem to do anything at all, and that was when Hannah stepped in.

She had forgiven me for my stupid plan, and I was relieved the evidence now lay at the bottom of the ocean. Tragedy had a way of putting things in perspective, and the fact that she valued our friendship so much gave me strength. The old me, though ... I missed her. My trademark snap and vigour and zest for life had abandoned me. I wasn't sure I'd ever get it back, or that I even deserved to. There was so much more to mourn than the people who'd died. Those of us on the *Titanic* had lost so much. Our protective bubble of innocence and safety had been shattered.

The bodies had to be embalmed before they could be viewed, and we waited for hours before they began calling out names. There were cubicles in the main part of the rink, with room for three coffins within each one. As names were called, people in the observation room rose and then were led to the designated space.

The wait was unbearable, and finally, as evening crept upon us, I turned to Hannah. "I can't sit here another minute. I'm going to go crazy. There's no way they'll get to everyone tonight."

She looked just as stricken as I felt. The entire building was shrouded in grief, dragging us even further down. "You're right. We can come back in the morning."

Neither of us slept much.

By nine the next morning we were back at the Mayflower, slightly refreshed. A check with an attendant showed that neither Charles Martin's nor Reid Grey's name had been called, and there were of course many unidentified passengers as well. I clasped my gloved hands together in my lap, biting my lower lip. I wasn't sure how I would manage if Hannah and I had to walk through those cubicles, looking at unidentified remains, searching for the faces that were so dear to us.

It was barely ten when I heard, "Reid Grey."

Something icy-cold ran through my body, from my head to my feet in the space of a heartbeat, and I felt Hannah grip my hand. "Oh, Lou," she murmured.

I stood, my knees like jelly. Reid. Reid. I kept hearing his name in my head. Heard it with each step I took, Hannah by my side, as we left the observation room and were guided toward the main floor, my feet moving mechanically. There was a buzzing in my ears and the room around me spun slightly. I would not pass out. I would not. I had to do this. For Reid. For us.

I was thankful for the bit of privacy afforded as we moved into the cubicle, and suddenly there he was, lifeless and pale, the red gone from his lips and his eyelids closed, as if he'd gone to sleep, somehow looking as if he'd been carved in stone. I remembered what he'd said about the cold getting us first and I automatically held out my hand, fingers trembling, toward his lashes. I drew them back; I did not want to touch him. I wanted my final memory of our touch to be a kiss, a held hand, an embrace, something warm and glowing and real. The way his skin felt against mine as we made love. The twinkle in his eyes as he teased me and then glanced a fingertip over some part of my body, letting me know he was there.

The earnestness in his face that night on the deck when he'd proposed.

That was the Reid I loved and how I wanted to remember him.

There was a sound of weeping and a long, drawn-out call of agony, and when Hannah's arm steadied mine, I realized the sounds were coming from me and that Hannah was crying along with me. My heart was utterly, utterly broken, seeing my future in front of me and forever unreachable, knowing I had finally allowed myself to fall in love only to have it ripped away so cruelly, and the innate knowledge that I would never love another man again.

"His personal possessions, ma'am," said the man who had guided us to the cubicle. His face didn't even register with me; I only had eyes for a plain canvas bag with a number stencilled on the outside of it. That was who Reid was now: a number. One of hundreds who'd died in a completely avoidable disaster.

"Thank you." Hannah answered on my behalf and pressed a handkerchief into my hand. I pressed it to my eyes with my right hand while holding the small bag with my left. I could not open it here. I gave it to Hannah while someone said something about burial arrangements and some other things that didn't register.

I couldn't take my eyes off Reid. When Hannah finished speaking to the gentleman, she went to lead me away, but I couldn't move. "I can't leave him," I said, my gaze glued to his still face. "I can't, Hannah. Oh God. When I walk away there is no more Reid. Nothing for me. It is the end and I'm not ready. I'm not ready for it to be the end."

Tears were streaming down her cheeks, too, and she pulled me into her arms. "I know, dearest, I know. It is such pain, saying goodbye. I'm so sorry, Lou. So desperately sorry. You should have had all the time in the world. You should have fallen in love and been romanced and had the most marvellous wedding and life together."

Perhaps it should have made me feel worse, though I wasn't sure there was a worse. Instead, though, Hannah's words gave me comfort. They were true, all of it, and after a few more minutes, I gave a nod. "All right," I said, pulling back and giving a sniff. "I can't stay here forever, even though—"

I didn't finish the sentence, as I didn't want to distress Hannah further. But the truth was, if I could be buried along with him I wasn't sure I'd say no. What did I have to live for?

Hannah stepped back, and I looked down at Reid once more. I was filled with such emotion in that moment – loss, certainly, but also so much love. Something I had never expected to feel, and God, how he had blessed me with that.

"I love you, Reid Grey, you silly, brave, noble man. I am so sorry, darling. So sorry for everything." I whispered it, wanting it to be between just us, and then, because I knew it had to be done some time, I lifted my chin and turned away.

The first step nearly broke me. But somehow I made it past the other cubicles and out of the rink, pausing to catch my breath in a sob from time to time but putting one foot in front of the other. "We need to go back," I said to Hannah. "To the waiting room. Because..."

"Oh, Lou ... how can you bear it?"

"I can because I must. And because you deserve to know if Charles is there and say goodbye just as I did. I'll be all right, Hannah. I will." I didn't feel that way, but this whole ordeal hadn't killed me yet and it probably wouldn't now, either.

We went back to wait. Hannah was given a cup of hot, bracing tea. I asked for some time and went to the next room where there were writing supplies set out and began writing a letter to Mr. and Mrs. Grey, whom I'd never met in person. There were things I just couldn't put in a wire, and putting them on paper was the most helpful and distracting thing I could do in this moment.

The day went on, and we never did hear Charles's name called. Together, we walked the rink floor, looking at each unidentified face.

Step after step, body after body, until the numbness I'd been feeling for days returned in full force. Not one face we recognized. No Mr. Harris. No Charles. We later learned that Frances Millet, Isidor Straus, and Alexander Holverson, all first-class men that we'd been familiar with, had been recovered on the *Mackay-Bennett* as well. So many others simply gone.

Neither of us had eaten a bite all day, and as we limped our way back to our hotel room, I knew neither of us felt like eating now, either. Hannah had to think of the baby, however, and I asked if we might have a tray of soup or something light – we didn't care what – sent to our room. I had the letter for the Greys tucked in my coat pocket. Hannah, I could tell, was completely worn out. I said little, not knowing which was better for her: seeing Charles and being able to say goodbye, as I had with Reid, or not seeing him and being spared the sight of what her husband looked like in death.

The tray arrived. I had a little soup, though I couldn't say what kind it was. Hannah managed half of hers before pushing it away. "I'm going to get ready for bed," she said weakly. "You don't have to yet if you don't want to."

I didn't. I wanted a chance to take out the mortuary bag and go through the contents, one by one, taking my time. These items did not belong to me, and I would be sending them back to Reid's family. But I could touch them, think of him. Remember.

Hannah fell asleep within five minutes of crawling beneath the covers; the poor woman was exhausted and not much wonder. Because I'd insisted, she'd seen a doctor once we'd arrived in Halifax, and he'd assured her everything was fine with her pregnancy, which considering what we'd been through, was a relief. I tucked the blankets up around her shoulders and looked down at her tenderly. I was used to being alone, but she … she shouldn't have to face the prospect of bringing up a child without her husband. I thought of Madeleine Astor, so young to be a widow, and all the other newlyweds on board. And I thought of Ida and Isidor

Straus. Stories said that she had refused to get on a boat and that they'd chosen to be together in the end, still utterly devoted after so many years of marriage.

Women, I thought, are stronger than men think. I never did buy this weaker sex bit. What we might lack in physical prowess we more than made up for in fortitude.

I went back to the chair next to the lamp, the rough fabric of the bag nestled in my hand. Upon opening it, I realized that a vibrant life had been reduced to a few meagre possessions. He'd had a little money in his pocket, the bills wrinkled from being wet and then drying, and a pocket watch that looked old and had perhaps belonged to a relative. There was a faded business card with Reid's bank and his name on it. And finally, there was the tie pin, the one I'd given back to him that last night on the ship when I'd confessed to everything.

It was a paltry collection with which to mark a life lived and lost.

I put everything back in the bag but the pin and put it aside. The pin I held in my fingertips, turning it over and over, running my nail over the diamond chips glinting dully in the lamplight. A watch, a little money, a card. I inhaled shakily as I thought about all the times we'd met, flirted across a room, smiled, raised a drink in a toast. The way he'd propositioned me at a house party and I'd left him wanting; the tip of his Homburg on the deck of the *Titanic* on that first day, and the knowing twist of his lips as he saw my surprise. The letters that had arrived in his distinctive scrawl, full of amusing anecdotes and insights.

Dancing on the promenade under the stars.

Drinking champagne from the bottle while relieving each other of our clothes.

Saying I love you.

Saying I love you for the last time.

I had promised Hannah that my thieving days were over, but I broke that promise as I took the tie pin and fastened it to my blouse, over my heart. I had nothing of Reid to take with me into the rest of my life. I was entitled to nothing but memories. But this pin... This pin meant something.

I sat up for a long time, remembering, thinking about what was waiting for me back in England, trying to sort out what was important to me now.

The answer that came back was so bleak that I turned out the lamp and joined Hannah in the bed, finally giving in to a dreamless sleep.

Chapter Thirty-Two

May 6, 1912
Halifax

HANNAH

On the third of May, several of the victims were buried in the Fairview cemetery, in plots paid for by the shipping company. Ismay had his private secretary buried at Fairview first. Sentiment against the White Star chairman was still extremely negative and understandably so, but he did seem to want to recognize his staffer. Lou and I attended the service out of respect for the unidentified victims who were being laid to rest with only a number to give any indication of their identity. The streets were packed as the bodies were transported from the curling rink to the cemetery.

Reid Grey was among the victims who were buried at Fairview on May sixth, along with thirty-three others. By now Lou and I had been staying at the Halifax Hotel for two weeks, and I'd been away from home for almost a month. We hadn't yet talked about the future, but we were going to have to soon. I was more than happy to take on the chore of booking us both passage back to England. The sooner the better. Every time I thought about stepping foot on another ship, the spectre of panic threatened to descend. Realistically, though, there was no other way to get home, and home was where I needed to be. I would get through it somehow, especially if Lou were there with me.

I also knew there was no question of leaving until Reid had been buried, so I'd not yet broached the topic.

Lou lingered by the grave for a long time, and I didn't rush her. She'd been subdued lately, so very unlike her, and one of the things I hated most about this tragedy was how this had changed my outrageous, fun friend. I wanted her back so badly. Yet I understood her grief, too. I missed Charles with every breath. There was no way a person could walk away from something like this unscathed.

Lou, for all her protests about wearing colourless garb, had forsaken any sort of pastels or cheering tones, opting for black, mauve, and navy. With her light hair and flawless skin, she was beautiful as ever, but I saw the sadness etched on her face. I could not deny that whatever she had felt for Reid – and it certainly appeared like love – had left her bereft. She would have married him; of that I was certain.

We might have been friends, all four of us, if we'd had time to heal the wounds of our pasts.

I stood back from the mourners at the graves, giving space. A woman approached Lou; she was dressed in black, and looked to be in her fifties, perhaps, and wasn't someone I recognized as one of the group of family members who'd travelled to Halifax for the same reason we had. I saw Lou nod, and the woman place a hand on her arm, before stepping away. Lou faced the grave again, then placed a single spring daisy on the fresh earth. When she turned and faced me, standing at the perimeter of the lines of graves, her face held a serenity I hadn't seen before.

When she reached me, she linked her elbow with mine, and we made the slow walk through the cemetery to the streets beyond, following the throng of mourners.

"Let's walk back," she said. It was a clear, spring day, and we had nothing but time. It was over now, everything but healing. Charles's body had not been recovered; the *Minia* had returned three days ago with a handful of bodies but not that of my husband. I had made peace with the fact that I would not glimpse upon his face again, or be able to repatriate him to Devon so he could be with his people – and with me. Reid's family had decided against having his body sent back to England, instead communicating with Lou about the details of a burial here in Halifax. Her parents had written, too, sending her money for a ticket home and promising a return to the life she'd left behind.

That made me uneasy, as did the look on Lou's face when she read the letter aloud to me.

"Left behind. Balcombe, they mean," she groused, her lips set in a firm line. "There is no way I am ever going to marry that man."

We were nearly to North Street – it really was quite a walk – when I broached the topic with Lou, gently, of course.

"Darling, now that we know … well, what we know, I think it's time we think about arrangements to go home."

Her arm tensed in mine, a warning.

"I know you don't want to marry Balcombe, and you shan't have to. I'm a wealthy woman, Lou." I had been thinking about this plan for days now, hesitant to bring it up after the row we'd had that last day on the *Titanic*. "I'll be lonely all by myself. I want you to come live with me. There's loads of room and it's large enough we won't be in each other's hair if we don't wish it. Or if you don't want to be at Lamerton, we can rent you a place in London. Perhaps not as grand as your father's house in Mayfair, but something suitable in a good location."

Our feet kept moving, which to my mind, was a good thing. If Lou had been totally against it, she would have stopped and told me no unequivocally. "That's a generous offer, Hannah, and a lovely one." She looked over at me and a faint smile turned up her lips. "I'm not totally sure what's next for me. I've been doing some thinking as well."

"I know you have. I've seen you with your scheming face on."

Her smile deepened, hinting at a dimple I hadn't seen in weeks. "I have not been scheming. But thank you for making me smile. I needed it today."

"If you live with me at Lamerton, in just under five months you'll have one big reason to smile, and that's because you'll be Auntie Lou. We'll get a couple of dogs and have tea in the garden and bask in the sunshine like a couple of turtles."

"It sounds idyllic, but you know that kind of life isn't for me," Lou replied, not unkindly.

"I know. Besides, it rains a lot." I jostled her arm. "What I'm really trying to say is, you do not have to worry if your father still insists on cutting you off. You're my family, Lou. In every way that possibly counts. I would do this for you a hundred times over. It wouldn't change our friendship a jot."

We were leaving the north end of the city now and my feet were starting to hurt a bit. We'd done a lot of walking during our time here, and I felt healthier than I had in a very long time, at least in body. The sea air, the hills rising up from the harbour, the hearty food … they had done me good. Today, though, I was ready to be off my feet and wishing we'd called for a carriage.

"Thank you, Hannah." Lou stopped, looked up at the sky, and squinted at the smattering of clouds before looking back at me again. "Could I have a day or two to think about it?"

"Of course." I agreed right away, but then bit my lip. "However,

I am itching to get home. By the time we find passage, and then the crossing ... my word, I'm ready for my own home and my own bed and my familiar things around me. Aren't you?"

She shrugged, as if she didn't care one way or the other. "In a sense. I promise I'll give you my answer day after tomorrow."

It wasn't too long to wait, not in the big scheme of things. I had said that I missed my own bed and my things, but truthfully, I needed to grieve. Not like I had when the baby had died. It was different, somehow, for various reasons. That being said, I truly felt like being home would offer me a kind of relief and security I missed, first in New York, now here in Halifax. It was at home that I would be able to truly say my goodbyes, where I could open my heart and finally set the pain inside free.

"Who was the woman who spoke to you at the cemetery?" I asked, changing the subject.

"Oh." Her cheeks flushed a little, and not just from the exercise. "Someone I met recently, that's all. She's a widow, active in a lot of charitable endeavours." We were getting closer to Hollis Street now, to my feet's relief. "When I went to see about Reid's arrangements, she gave me some assistance. Actually, we're meeting for tea tomorrow. I hope you don't mind."

It was good to see Lou taking the initiative to do something even a little bit normal, so I replied, "Not at all. I'll take the time to make some inquiries about possible passages home, that sort of thing."

Lou didn't talk about the woman further, and I was left wondering why someone volunteering to help the victims' families would invite one of them for tea. Then again, Lou had never had any problem making friends. I would not want to deprive her of an hour's distraction for the world.

Chapter Thirty-Three

```
May 7, 1912
Halifax
```

LOUISA

I met Lucinda Porter at a restaurant on Barrington Street at one in the afternoon. We ordered a hearty lunch instead of the elegant yet light teas I was so used to and secretly tired of. Mrs. Porter reminded me a little of Margaret Brown, actually. Perhaps it was the accent: different from the American, but with the same flat vowels and harsher r's, with something similar to an Irish lilt here and there. She had a ready smile, too, and an energy about her that told me she was the kind of woman to get things done.

"I'm so glad you agreed to meet," she said, putting down her glass of water and meeting my gaze directly. "How are you doing?"

I put my hands in my lap and considered. "Well. I mean, mostly well. I will go along for a while and it almost seems as if nothing's wrong. And then it's like I remember and my heart breaks all over again." I grimaced. "I'm sorry if that's too personal."

"Not at all, dear." Mrs. Porter gave an understanding smile. "It was that way for me in the days after my husband died. I'm a capable woman, but the feelings would come out of nowhere."

"Does it ever get better?" I asked.

She nodded. "It does. I still miss him. But it's softer now, if that makes sense. I have a good life, Miss Phillips. You will too. And you're so young. So much life ahead of you." She reached over and patted my hand. "Perhaps even the odd adventure."

I didn't feel much like having an adventure, but it was comforting to know that the pain would lessen while the memories stayed true.

"I feel odd, you know," I admitted. "Reid and I weren't even married. What right do I have to, I don't know, claim this much grief?"

"The heart doesn't know time, Miss Phillips. Your feelings are yours. I for one will not judge you for them. I'm just sorry his life was cut so tragically short."

Our meals arrived, and the scent was fabulous. I'd eaten in the finest restaurants with some of the top chefs in the world, but as I dipped my spoon in the rich chowder and took a first bite, I knew this simple, flavourful offering could stand side by side without shame. "Oh heavens. This is fantastic."

She smiled. "Isn't it? So, Miss Phillips, what did you want to discuss with me?"

I had told Hannah the truth: Mrs. Porter had invited me this afternoon. The invitation, however, had come after I'd asked her if I might get some advice. "I..." My throat tightened, but I swallowed and pressed forward. "I am considering not returning to England."

She put down her spoon and regarded me curiously. "I see. Well, no, I don't actually, but I suppose you have your reasons."

"A few, really. Reid is here, and perhaps it sounds silly, but I'm

Ship of Dreams

the only person here who will remember him, visit his grave. I-I find it comforting being near it."

Compassion softened Mrs. Porter's eyes. "Go on."

"I also cannot bring myself to consider getting on a ship again, especially not for the better part of a week to cross the ocean. I feel ill just thinking about it. If there were another way…" I sighed. "I haven't told any of this to my friend yet. I wanted to sort things first before broaching the subject, but she's ready to go home, for reasons I absolutely understand."

"You're wondering about building your own life here. As a single woman."

"A single woman without means," I corrected. "Mrs. Porter, my parents have already picked out a man I'm to marry, and if I don't go along with their wishes, my father has said the money will stop."

She lifted an eyebrow. "Pardon me, but that seems excessive."

"It is. I'm twenty-six. I honestly never cared to get married, but if I did, I absolutely think I should do the choosing. My love affair has been with my causes, actually. I have had a privileged life, that's true, but I'm passionate about women getting the vote, being appropriately paid for their labour, and everything that goes with living independently without a man. I hope you don't take this personally when I say a woman shouldn't have to be a widow to gain her independence."

Mrs. Porter smiled then. "I agree with you completely. I'm unsure how you think I can help, though." She dipped her spoon and ate a little bit more of her chowder. I did too. I wanted to enjoy it while it was hot. It was, I discovered, the first time I'd truly enjoyed a meal in days.

After two scrumptious spoonfuls, I took a sip of water and then put down my glass. "As a member of the Local Council," I began, "I thought you might have some ideas about what I might do to support myself here and where I might live."

"I hope you don't mind my honesty, Miss Phillips, but you're an

English lady. You have servants, you purchase from shops, but you have never done this work yourself, correct?"

"I have not. But I'm not too proud to. I'm a fast learner, and I have excellent organizational skills. I can read and write, of course, as my parents did see to my education. I..." I faltered. "I could be a companion to an older lady, perhaps. Or work in a shop. I don't mind living in humble lodgings if they are clean and safe. I just... I can't go back. There is nothing for me there but the movement, and that's here as well."

"There's your friend," she mentioned, her voice gentle.

Yes, there was Hannah. She had offered me a place to live, a place in her family, and to essentially fund my life. I loved her for it. But I couldn't accept it.

"I can't possibly let her bankroll the rest of my life," I replied. "I'd feel so beholden to her, a prison of a different sort. I still wouldn't be independent, you see?"

"I see you are a headstrong woman, and principled."

Oh, if she knew of my initial plan to gain my independence, we definitely would not be having this conversation.

"I need to give Hannah an answer tomorrow." I picked up the soft roll that had come with the chowder and broke off a piece. "If I knew I had a place to stay, I'm positive I could work out the rest."

Mrs. Porter considered for a few moments, tapping her fingers on the tabletop. "There is a project I've been thinking of starting," she said, pursing her lips. "I agree with your statement that you – and women like you – need safe and clean lodgings. I might be able to solve both our problems in one go."

I sat up straighter, intrigued. "I'm listening."

"I have a property that is sitting vacant up on Gladstone."

I blinked at the name. How ironic.

"My husband used it for some business interests, but it's been vacant for nearly a year now. It's a decent location, perhaps not a refined neighbourhood, but all right. I've considered renting it, but didn't necessarily want to be bothered with being a landlady. If I had someone who could manage it for me…"

She lifted an eyebrow and looked at me hopefully.

"You want me to be a landlady?"

"Of sorts. A property manager, I suppose. And probably more than that, when all is said and done. You'd lead a community, albeit a small one. Seven or eight women, at most, who, like you, need comfort and safety. Single, working women supporting themselves and perhaps even a family somewhere."

I gave a little laugh. "Good heavens. I would be Miss McDougall."

"Excuse me?"

"Hannah and I went to boarding school. A young woman from Aberdeen named Miss McDougall supervised our dormitory. We were lucky. Not every dormitory had someone as nice as she." I had fond memories, actually, of cozy chats whenever things seemed to be going wrong. She'd made hot chocolate and been kind and reassuring. I'd wondered at the time about her being unmarried and why that might be, and if she was lonely spending all her time at a girls' dormitory. For the first time in years, I wondered where she might be, and if she was still at St. Hilda's.

"I would pay you a wage, of course, and you would live there so your board would be included. There'd be a budget, and we would set very reasonable rents for the women. I don't see this as a money-making venture, Miss Phillips. The rents would pay for upkeep and food and staff such as yourself, with a little bit leftover for emergencies. I would like for it to be self-sufficient, but I don't need the income."

It was a different attitude from what I was used to. "Most men would sell the property and pocket the profit," I replied. "To be fair, most women I know would, too."

She smiled. "I am not most women, Miss Phillips, and I suspect neither are you. You'll find most in the council are focused on improving the lives of women here in Nova Scotia and across the country. If you wish to stay, I can offer you this. We will work together to set it up, and believe me, finding half a dozen working women in search of good lodgings will not be a problem."

"Mrs. Porter," I said, looking her square in the face, "I came for advice today, but I got so much more. I got something I never expected to feel, and that's hope. Thank you. I accept."

"Splendid. And I'm so glad, Miss Phillips. I'm happy to help. And I fully expect that one day you'll long to return home. In the meantime, you're most welcome here. I'm looking forward to this."

We lingered over lunch, and when I left to walk back to the hotel, I stopped a moment and gazed out over the Halifax harbour. This was to be my new home. I was either brave or foolish or both. Perhaps it would work out amazingly. Perhaps I would be homesick within a year and, as Mrs. Porter predicted, wish to return to England. But for now, I felt as if I were exactly where I was meant to be. If I couldn't be with Reid, I could remain close to him. And I could become the kind of woman he'd believed I was: smart, strong, principled. He'd seen all the best parts of me that had been so often overlooked.

It seemed odd to think this of a rich banker from London, but as I resumed my steps, I rather thought he'd be proud of me right now.

Chapter Thirty-Four

```
May 8, 1912
Halifax
```

HANNAH

Lou was up to something.

I'd felt the difference in her yesterday after she'd returned from her engagement with the woman I now knew to be a Mrs. Porter. At first I'd been thrilled at the change in her. The moroseness that had followed her for the past three weeks had shifted and she seemed lighter, more like the old Lou, but with a gravity that I understood was borne out of surviving a disaster as we had.

I hadn't questioned her about it beyond asking if she'd had a nice time. Instead, as we played a game of checkers in our room, I told her I had discovered we could sail back to England on a ship called the Victorian, which I took as a good sign as it was the month of the Queen's birthday. She seemed distracted as she made her play, setting herself up for me to take one of her markers, and I'd wondered if she was worried about going home.

We were back in our room after breakfast when she took a deep breath, meeting my gaze with a strained one of her own.

"I need to talk to you, Hannah," she said, as serious as I'd ever seen her, and I got the impression that I would not like whatever she was going to say. A sense of dread washed over me, and something else, too ... something dark and sharp that took me by surprise. I tamped it down and waved a hand at the chairs we'd sat in so often over the last ten days.

She sat, perched on the edge of the seat, and twisted her hands in her lap. "Hannah, what I'm about to say is very difficult, and you need to know before I say anything that I love you." Her eyes, so blue in the morning light coming through our window, were filled with apology. The nerves in my stomach tangled. What was going on? How much more could I stand? That last question weighed heavily. Lou had no idea how close I was to the breaking point. I was so very tired of holding it all together.

I wondered if she'd felt this way two years ago, when I'd been in such a dark place. Because of it, I exhaled slowly and told myself I owed her grace and understanding.

"You know I love you as a sister," I replied, trying unsuccessfully to keep a tremor out of my voice. "This has to do with Mrs. Porter, doesn't it?"

She nodded. "Hannah, I'm ... I'm not returning home with you."

It was not what I'd expected at all, and as it sank in, I sat dumbly in the chair, my mouth open. She waited. Where had Lou discovered all this patience? When I could finally speak, I said the words slowly. "What do you mean?"

Tears sprang into Lou's eyes. "I can't leave him here alone, Han. His parents chose to have him buried here, and there's no one to ... to visit him or remember him or make sure there are flowers on his grave. I can be close to him here, you see. I've decided to stay here in Halifax. There's nothing for me at home. Nothing except Arthur Balcombe." She said the name with distaste.

I wish I could say the anger came out of nowhere, but it didn't. It had been simmering for days, the fire of it stoked beneath the surface of my grief and pain and all the ways I'd kept myself busy and useful. Rage at being left behind and alone. Not necessarily directed at Charles, but rather at the situation in which I now found myself, fed by the wounds of the past, when I had come second to the grief my father had for my mother. "Nothing," I repeated, my voice shaking. *"I'm* there, Lou. My child will be there."

"That's not what I meant," she answered, which was followed by an awkward silence.

I didn't care what she meant, actually. Through our entire adult lives, even before that, we had looked out for each other and looked after each other. This made absolutely no sense. "Don't be ridiculous," I said. "I know you're upset, and you have every right to be, but be realistic, Lou. Your family is in England, and your friends. You don't have to marry Balcombe. I already offered you a home, or the means to have your own. What more do you want from me?"

I was shaking now. We'd been through something horrible, something that had changed us forever, but this made absolutely no sense. "Reid is dead and buried, Lou. He cannot care if you are close by or not. For God's sake, don't you know that cemeteries are for the living, not the dead?" My voice was rising and I seemed unable to quiet it. "At least you got to bury him. At least you got to say goodbye! Charles's grave is out in the ocean somewhere! He promised me he'd be on another lifeboat and we never even..." I thought back to that moment, just as I had every single day since boarding the *Carpathia*. "I said I love you. And that I'd see him later. And I never saw him again. And now you announce you're staying in this … this…" I couldn't think of how to describe Halifax. It was quite lovely, actually, and the people kind. But Lou was larger than life. "A girl like you will hate being in a town like this."

"A girl like me," she said slowly.

"Come on, Lou. You're a deb. You fit in first class because you *are* first class. For God's sake, you've never had to wash a dish in your life or press your own clothes. How on earth do you expect to survive here? Give up this ridiculous notion and come home."

I was nearly out of breath, and I popped up from my chair and strode to the window, full of a restless energy that was pressing against my skin from the inside out, as if I might explode if things got any worse.

Lou cleared her throat. "I knew you'd be upset. I didn't know you'd be so angry."

"I've spent the last three weeks holding myself together. Holding you together, or have you forgotten?" I turned to face her, unable to stop from speaking my feelings now that I'd begun. "I lost my husband, Louisa. The future that I'd just got back. I'm going to have a baby who no longer has a father. And my best friend in the world has just said she's staying half a world away, even though I've offered to build us a life where we both can thrive. Of course I'm angry! How many times do you think my heart can break? How can you do this to me, you of all people!"

Lou got up and came to me. She reached for my hands, but I pulled them back. I was too close to losing my tenuous grip and bursting into tears.

She dropped her hands to her sides and studied me sadly. "I know it probably feels as if I'm abandoning you," she said quietly, "and that's what makes this so hard. I don't mean to make you face your future alone, and I will always, always be your friend. I will always hold you in here"—she pressed a hand to her heart as her voice wobbled—"and hope you'll do the same. But Hannah, I cannot leave him. Nor can I stand the thought of setting foot on a ship again. Do you know I couldn't watch it go down? I had to turn away. Then it was the sound. The sound of all those people, calling out, getting quieter and quieter as they died one by one. I see Reid and Charles standing side by side as my lifeboat was lowered, knowing that they were going to die and that our happiness – yours and mine – would die with them. Now you want me to get back on a ship for a week to go back to an empty life?"

"We could face it together," I whispered. "Do you think I'm looking forward to the crossing? Do you?"

She shook her head. "Even if I could, my only option would be to live on your charity, at least for a while. I would resent it, Hannah, and I never want to live in such a way that I would resent you. Just as I hope you won't hate me for making this decision."

"You'll regret it," I snapped.

"Possibly. But I already regret so much. What's one more thing?"

The distant, sad expression on her face awakened a tiny bit of compassion. One of the things I'd always loved about Lou was her bravery, her willingness to defy expectations to seek her own happiness. The problem was, her current solution would affect my happiness, and that...

The truth slammed into me. That was selfish. Lou was being brutally honest with me and speaking from the heart. And I ... I was speaking from fear. Lou had always, from the first moment I'd known her, longed to make her own choices. How could I expect her to change simply because I was afraid of being alone? I had longed for her to be more "Lou" since the sinking. And now that she was, I was berating her for it? Using her regrets against her? That wasn't love. If I loved her, I had to let her be herself. I had to love her because of those things, not despite them.

"I don't know how to do this without you," I whispered, my anger extinguished as quickly as it had flared.

"I know. Oh Hannah, I know. This has not been an easy decision."

"What will you do?"

She gave a slight smile. "Mrs. Porter is part of the Local Council of Women. They're my kind of people, Han. They advocate for women's rights and try to make life better. Mrs. Porter is going to transform one of her properties into a boarding house for working women who need a safe, affordable place to live. I'm going to run it."

If she had said she was going to join the circus I wouldn't have been more surprised.

"I have strengths," she insisted. "I've organized marches and fundraisers. I've also done more budgeting that you might expect, since most of my allowance has been spent helping my causes. And yes, I'm a baronet's daughter. I may be able to lend a bit of refinement here and there. The position comes with a wage and with my room and board included at the house."

I thought of all the months she'd spent in London living in the Mayfair house. She'd had servants to do her bidding, but I also knew she'd managed her own time and was dedicated to her causes. A position helping other women was exactly the kind of thing she'd excel at. I cursed this Mrs. Porter for even suggesting it and taking her away from me.

I turned back to the window again so she wouldn't see the tears in my eyes. "I can't change your mind, can I?"

"I'm afraid not," she said. "Honestly, the worst part of all of this was telling you. I can't bear the thought of you hating me, or me hurting you. I've only done something that would cause you to hate me once before, and you forgave me. I hope you can do so again, especially since this is for much better reasons. And legal ones." I caught a bit of warmth in that last bit, some self-deprecation and humour.

"You're absolutely sure."

When she didn't answer, I turned around.

Lou was standing tall, her figure striking. She wore one of the suits we'd bought at Bloomingdales, a lovely navy one with a section of pleats in the front that added a touch of polish. White lace from her blouse peeked out from the neckline of the jacket, and I suddenly realized she wore Reid's tie pin at her throat instead of a customary brooch. She'd done her own hair this morning as well, the simple style flattering as it framed her face in a golden halo. Gone was the frivolous, impulsive girl I knew, and in her place was a strong, competent woman who could meet any challenge.

A woman who was still hurting so much and was moving forward despite it. That was who she'd always been, in the end. I needed to learn from her, to learn how to do that for myself. I would only accomplish it if I set her free.

"I shall miss you horribly. I will hate not having you near and I despise the fact that my child will not see their Auntie Lou at Christmases and birthdays and for summer picnics. But darling Lou, all you have ever wanted for as long as I've known you was the ability to make your own choices about your life. And so I say this: as much as I hate it for me, I want this for you, if it's what you truly desire."

She came forward, pulling me into a hug that lasted a long time. "I might be a fool," she whispered close to my ear. "I really don't know how I shall do without you. But this feels right, Hannah. For the first time in my life, it feels right. It means everything to me to have your support."

"Grudgingly given," I replied, unbearably sad at this turn of events. "I absolutely hate this for me."

We both gave a short laugh.

"When does the ship sail?"

I told her the date.

"Then we have a little more time together before you must go."

I nodded. We sat after that and talked about the future and our plans and reminisced about our younger days at St. Hilda's, the summer picnics and the antics we'd got up to.

For the better part of a week, we crammed in as much time as we could, quality time of building memories that would have to sustain us in the months and years to come.

In the end, I realized it would never be long enough.

Chapter Thirty-Five

```
May 13, 1912
Halifax
```

LOUISA

Saying goodbye was harder than I'd imagined.

Hannah was going home with far less than she'd left with. In a week's time, she'd be back at Lamerton, in her own bed, as she wanted, sitting at her own table, walking in her garden. But it would be without Charles, and I could only imagine she was both looking forward to being home but also dreading the emptiness at the same time. It was nearly time for her to go aboard the RMS Victorian, and I had gone to the pier with her to say our final goodbye.

I tried not to think of it as final. We were both young. Surely, sometime, we would meet again. We had a lot of life left to live.

"You must promise me to have regular appointments with the

doctor when you're home," I commanded, giving her a stern look. "Don't take any chances with this one."

"I won't," she said, a sad smile on her lips.

I stepped forward and pressed a hand to the small mound at her belly. "You be good for your mother, wee one," I said softly. "She's going to love you so much."

"Oh, Lou..." Hannah sounded as if she were going to cry again.

"It's going to be all right," I said, sounding far braver than I felt. Not that I would admit it out loud, but several times over the last week I'd caught myself wondering if I was doing the right thing. If I was being selfish or a coward. If I could even do the job that was ahead of me.

Then I visited the Gladstone House with Mrs. Porter and the excitement I felt as we walked through the empty rooms told me this was where my future lay.

I'd also written a letter to my parents, which Hannah was going to deliver on my behalf. I fully expected a reply that would cut me off completely, which surprisingly hurt to think about. I was their child, but their regard had always been conditional, based on me doing what they demanded. I knew now I'd inherited my father's stubbornness, but I hoped that I could put it to good use to make the world a better place, rather than trying to keep those different from me in theirs.

"You are going to make a fantastic mother," I said, holding her gloved hands in mine. "You are strong and loving and any child would be lucky to have you as its mum. And don't be afraid to lean on your father." I gave her fingers a squeeze. "Maybe he didn't handle his grief well after your mother died, but you have another chance to bridge the gap between you."

"Maybe yours will come around, too," she said hopefully, smiling a little, but we both knew that was unlikely.

There was a loud blast from the horn and we both started, then

Hannah let out a deep sigh. "I can't believe this is it. This is not how any of this was supposed to turn out." Her lower lip quivered as she fought not to cry.

"Maybe it is," I answered. "Maybe this is exactly how it was supposed to unfold. You're going to have a brilliant life, Hannah, with your baby and maybe one day you'll find love again."

"I can't imagine that."

"Of course not. It's too soon. All I know is that falling for Reid showed me that life can have unexpected blessings and turns in the road. I will never regret falling for him, no matter how short our time or how much it hurts in here." I put my hand to my heart.

Hannah sniffed, blinking back tears. "And I had Charles. I am thankful every day that we managed to find the love between us again. I know in my heart he loved me, and that he wanted our life together as much as I did. It hurts, but it gives me some peace, too."

"We were loved," I replied, and the warmth of it settled around me, around us both, I thought, as if Charles and Reid were somehow there, wrapping us in it.

Another blast from the ship and our eyes caught, inevitability and finality there. "This is it," Hannah said. "Lou, if for any reason you change your mind, you can always, always come to me. I will always be there."

My throat tightened painfully, and my heart ached. "And if you need me, Hannah, all you have to do is ask."

"Don't say that. I'll be apt to write you every week, begging you to save me from something or other."

We gave sad smiles, and then suddenly we caught each other in a hug, desperate and loving.

"No one could have a better friend than you," I whispered in her ear. "No one."

"Be happy," she said back. "Fight the good fight, but for heaven's sake, stay out of prison."

I choked out a laugh as I released her, and then we couldn't put it off any longer. She picked up the small bag that held a few precious items and a bit of money, and stepped back. "Goodbye, Lou."

I lifted my hand in farewell. "God bless you, Hannah."

Epilogue

May 31, 1912

 Dear Lou,

 I hope this finds you well and settling in at Gladstone House. I missed you horribly on the journey home, but now I'm here, and while I'm relieved and thankful to be home, it seems so very empty without Charles... I have done as you commanded and seen the doctor, and everything is just fine. I also spent two days at my father's, which was the nicest visit I've had in several years.

 I delivered your letter to your family, though they were not home at the time, and so I left it with the butler...

June 22, 1912

Dear Hannah,

I miss you dreadfully, but I'm so glad I made this decision. Of course it feels empty at Lamerton, but soon you will have a little one to dote on. I can only imagine how splendid the gardens are now that summer is in full swing.

The women are settling in and after one minor dust-up we seem to be getting along just fine. I have hired a new housekeeper and cook to care for the common areas and keep things tidy (as we both know, domestic chores are not my forte) and I was right: all those years of planning marches and protests have come in handy. I have drawn up charts for cleaning duties so that everyone pitches in. We have a music night on Fridays and the women have been planning some entertainments, too. It's not the social life I'm used to, but I don't miss the fast set like I thought I would...

November 3, 1912

Dear Lou,

I'm pleased to announce the arrival of Charles Louis Martin (Louis after you, dearest) born yesterday at just after two in the morning. We are both doing fine, though I am missing his father horribly and keep thinking how proud he would be at this moment and how in love he would be with his son. I shall call him Charlie and he is perfect...

November 26, 1912

Dear Hannah,

Congratulations, dearest, and give that sweet little head a kiss from Auntie Lou. Does he have Charles's fair hair or is it dark like yours?

Now that the boarding house is in full swing and the flies are out of the ointment, as Mrs. Jessome likes to say, I have begun working in earnest with the Local Council of Women. Do you know, we never met George Wright on the ship, but he left his house to the council? The space is lovely, and ever so helpful to have a place of our own...

December 15, 1912

Dear Lou,

Thank you for the gorgeous blanket and the rattle! You didn't knit that yourself, did you? I seem to remember you cursing your way through any sort of sewing or stitching classes, with lots of pricked fingers and cursing under your breath...

August 5, 1914

Dear Hannah,

I cannot believe I am writing the words "we're at war." It was official yesterday and today I signed up to be a VAD - a worker with the Voluntary Aid Detachment. I do not know where I'll be assigned yet, but with Halifax being a navy town, we're sure to see soldiers coming and going on their way to the front, poor lads. I still go to Reid's grave each week, and yesterday I went and wondered if, had he lived, he would have signed up to fight and then lost his life anyway. It all seems so wrong and futile, doesn't it? And yet I would have given anything to have even two years together...

December 7, 1917

Dear Lou,

I hope to heavens that you are all right. We got the horrible news about the explosion and the devastation seems too much to be real. Please let me know you are safe.

Love
Hannah and Charlie

December 16, 1917

Dear Hannah,

I am safe. The house suffered a little damage but nothing that can't be put right. I thought nothing could ever be as bad as April of 1912, but I was wrong. I have been at the hospital every waking hour and it is horrific… Some of the soldiers are saying it's worse here than they ever saw at the front. This bloody war needs to end. I hope you're bearing up all right…

November 12, 1918

Dear Lou,

Hosanna, the war is over! I found such purpose in helping the war effort that I have volunteered to help with the boys coming home. Some of them are horribly wounded, others exhausted and have that haunted look in their eyes that you and I know so well. When you have seen tragedy on such a scale you are changed forever, are you not?

Charlie has just turned six and he is learning to read. I cannot tell you what a joy he is. Do you think you will ever marry? I can highly recommend motherhood; Charlie keeps me on my toes and makes me laugh. Life is not boring.

I was sorry to hear about your father. I suppose this

means your brother is the new baronet. I do miss you and wish you would come home... Do you think you might?

July 27, 1920

    Dear Hannah,

    Guess what I just did? I voted! This is the first election where all women could vote, and I marched down there and made sure to put my ballot in the box. It felt like a very sweet victory and made all the protests and troubles worth it... Imagine me with my fist in the air! I expect Mr. Murray of the Liberal party will win...

April 15, 1922

    Dear Hannah,

    Ten years ago today everything changed, and I am sitting here wondering if you are remembering it all as I am. Mrs. Porter was right in that the grief changes and softens, and when I think of Reid now the sharp edges are gone and I remember him with love, as I'm sure you do with Charles.

    I do hope you know how much I miss you and continue to cherish our friendship. I have nearly booked a ticket to visit a half a dozen times, but I still can't bear the thought of getting on a boat and making that journey, which seems silly when I think about what others have endured, especially during the war. Please know, though, that you are always in my thoughts and heart, my dearest friend. Thank you for forgiving me. Thank you for letting me be me unconditionally. A sister could not be dearer to me than you...

July 19, 1936

Dear Lou,

Happy Birthday! I am trying to imagine you at fifty and cannot. To me you will always be twenty (something), with your gorgeous blond curls and without the wrinkles I see at the corners of my own eyes.

The news from around the world is so troubling. There was apparently an attempt on the king's life and can you imagine who sent him a "congratulations" on escaping the gun? Hitler himself. That little man is very dangerous, I think. I don't like the idea of Edward being pals with him. Then we heard about Spain and the uprising there... What is happening to the world, Lou? It's all so unsettling.

I wish you were here...

March 20, 1938

Dear Hannah,

In sad news, Mrs. Porter has passed on and has left Gladstone House to me. She has been a wonderful mentor and friend, and I'm going to miss her wisdom tremendously.

And speaking of sad (and alarming) news, that odious little man in Berlin has annexed Austria. I'm so afraid of what is happening over there, and do not understand why Chamberlain isn't taking a stronger stance. This violates the Treaty of Versailles...

Let's talk of brighter things, shall we? Please tell me how that brilliant and strapping son of yours is doing. It is hard to believe that he is the same age now as we were on the Titanic. May he never see that sort of tragedy in his lifetime...

September 3, 1939

Dear Lou,

Once, a very long time ago, you said that if I ever needed you, you would come.

England declared war on Germany today. I remember the last war and how devastating it was, and I was already on edge after the announcement, when Charlie informed me over dinner that he had joined up and was going to be a pilot and "bomb the hell out of Hitler."

I'm so afraid, Lou. For the world, for Britain, for myself. I lost Charles, but having Charlie kept me going. I don't know what I shall do if I lose him, too.

Oh Lou. Please come home.

Hannah

October 1, 1939

Dear Hannah,

I'm coming. Hold on, dearest.

Lou

Author's Note

Sometimes books seem to trip off the fingers as if sprinkled with fairy dust.

This was not one of those books.

I've been writing for many years, and occasionally a story will simply not play nicely. The reason, I've learned, is most often because I have somehow approached it in the wrong way. And such was the case with the first half of *Ship of Dreams*, which is now sitting in my file folder and bears little resemblance to the story on these pages. In fact, when I realized (with my editor's help) that I needed to start over, I think I used perhaps three or four thousand words from the original, all description of the ship. Everything else was new and fresh.

As a result, though, the words started flowing, and I fell utterly in love with Hannah and Lou. I love Hannah's gentle, steadfast determination and her desire to make a happy home and family as a way of healing from her own pain of losing her mother at a young age. Conversely, I love the sometimes outrageous Lou, who consistently surprised me as I was writing and showed me that there were depths upon depths of feeling beneath her feisty exterior. That these two women were the closest of friends felt very right. And that their friendship is tested in so many ways is a testament to their devotion to each other and their capacity for acceptance and forgiveness – things the world could certainly use more of.

I learn something with every manuscript. Sometimes I remember lessons I've forgotten along the way, and in this case I had to relearn that there must always be light to balance out the darkness. The sinking of the *Titanic* was a horrible tragedy and incredibly traumatic for those who survived. Some talked about it as a way to heal; others never spoke of it again. What was missing in the first version was hope and love, and to be honest, we need reminders of those two things today as we navigate an increasingly chaotic world. I'm so thankful to my editor for being honest about the first version not working, because I felt a rush of relief when I put it aside and began again with two unlikely best friends, Hannah and Louisa – young women with hope for the future and the determination to make their dreams happen. These bright ladies injected an infectious energy that was just what the story needed. Of course, they're also harbouring some secrets, and that friendship is severely tested in more ways than one. I knew that each must have the ending that would give them the greatest fulfillment and hope for the future – even after, or perhaps especially because, they'd been through so much. I do hope I've achieved that.

I was happy to discover most of the research I'd already done still applied to the new story, and there was a lot of information! If I struggled to find some details about 1917 Halifax in *When the World Fell Silent*, there was no shortage of information in researching the *Titanic*. That, in fact, created its own problem: so much information, so many details, and a massive community that is spectacularly knowledgeable and passionate. Talk about being worried about getting something wrong! I found deck plans and photos and YouTube videos to help with visuals, countless websites and wikis, and the "Big Daddy" of all information, *Encyclopedia Titanica*, which was first brought to my attention by Rebecca Connolly after she wrote her book, *A Brilliant Night of Stars and Ice*, about the *Carpathia*. (Thank you, Rebecca, for the rec!)

Then there was reading, reading, and more reading. I read some first-hand accounts, and I wasn't surprised to find that versions of what happened that night varied from one person to the next.

Several of my sources also contained contradictory information, such as the order of lifeboats as they entered the water or even who was in those lifeboats.

I have tried my best to be true to my sources, and in cases where there were discrepancies, I went with the version that is both most common and most likely. I tried to take as little creative license with facts as possible, but this *is* a fiction novel. Scenes and how they played out come from my own imagination. As always, I try to avoid rewriting any sort of history by staying true to dates, times, places, etc. and if I take any sort of liberties, it is with minutiae. The course of history will not be altered if passengers dined on duck on a night for which no recorded menu exists.

I also drew upon a real-life mystery surrounding some items recovered from the wreckage, in particular the Gladstone bag and the Amy bracelet. There isn't really a consensus on the ownership of the bracelet, which made it perfect for constructing an alternate, fictional narrative.

Hannah and Lou are completely fictional, as are Charles Martin and Reid Grey. I have inserted them into the story and placed them in cabins on B-deck (with Reid on A). Those with whom they interacted, however, were real passengers. Of course, those conversations never happened, but I read about each person I included and tried to construct those meetings as true to who they were as much as possible. In particular, I came to adore Margaret Brown (not Molly; I still hear Eric Braeden/J.J. Astor say "Well hello, Molly" in the 1997 movie and cringe), Renee Harris, and Helen Churchill Candee – such fabulous examples of strong, independent women for Lou! Mrs. Porter is fictional, but the Local Council of Women does exist in Halifax, even to this day. George Wright, a passenger on the *Titanic*, bequeathed his house on Young Avenue to them, and it is still there at https://lcwhalifax.ca/the-george-wright-house/. Having Lou become part of that organization seemed a perfect fit for her character's values and passions.

And let's not forget Hannah. I chose Devon as her home purposefully. In 2024 I visited the area for a conference and spent three glorious days touring the countryside with my good friend and author, Fiona Lucas, and fell in love with its rolling hills and colourful charm. Lamerton is a real village near Tavistock, though Hannah and Charles's house is fictional, of course. Lou's family's baronetcy in Exminster is also fictional.

Halifax, Nova Scotia is where I currently live and is a beautiful port city steeped in history. It was a joy to revisit it even for a small part of the story. Snow's, the mortuary and funeral home on Argyle, went on to perform that grim function again during the Halifax Explosion, the event at the heart of *When the World Fell Silent*. J. H. Barnstead, the Registrar of Vital Statistics in Halifax at that time, devised the system of identification for the *Titanic* victims and their belongings that was used again in 1917 after the explosion and is still used in today's forensics.

Snow's is now a restaurant named The Five Fishermen and is rumoured to be haunted. I've celebrated both my historical fiction novels there in some way. When I sold *When the World Fell Silent*, I had celebratory drinks there with friends visiting from Boston and Oregon. And as I worked on *Ship of Dreams*, I was able to introduce this marvelous building and piece of history to fellow authors Madeline Martin and Kate Quinn. If you are ever in our fair city, it's worth a visit. While you're here, make sure you check out the Maritime Museum of the Atlantic, which has incredible permanent exhibits on both the explosion and the Titanic disaster.

I also need to say some thank yous, because so many have been working behind the scenes and supporting me while I floundered along (or at least felt like it).

Top of the list is my editor, Charlotte Ledger, and the editorial team at One More Chapter: Jennie Rothwell, Sofia Salazar Studer, Lydia Mason, Federica Leonardis, and Caroline Scott-Bowden. Thank you for the care and professionalism you bring to my stories, and for sending me emails that tell me how much you cried – sorry not sorry! I always know my books are in capable hands and your feedback and expertise always make them better – and usually make me wonder why I hadn't done things that way from the beginning! You always seem to be able to look at a story and envision what it should be, and thankfully, how to get me there.

The Art Department in the UK and Canada. Lucy Bennett and co., you guys knocked it out of the park again. I especially appreciate being a part of the process of bringing a visual of the story to life. It's ridiculously exciting to watch you craft what becomes the first impression of my book in the world. And to Kara Daniel, who does such a great job on interior design and coordinating the audiobook details. Thank you, Kara!

Massive thank yous (yes, multiple!) to my publicist in Toronto, Dave Knox. At almost every event, I say the phrase "Everyone needs a Dave." You are indispensable, and always an absolute joy to work with. No matter my question, you'll find me an answer, and I appreciate all the work you and the team do on my behalf.

HarperCollins Canada has been nothing short of amazing, start to finish, since before *When the World Fell Silent* came out in 2024. I would be remiss if I didn't give a shout out to the sales and marketing teams and in particular Colleen Simpson, Peter Borcsok, Cory Beatty, and Brenann Francis here in Canada. Your support has been tremendous! Likewise the sales team in the US and UK: Emily Gerbner, Sophia Wilhelm, emma sullivan, Chloe Cummings, and Grace Edwards.

The group at Adventures by the Book, especially Susan and Sara: thank you for all that you do to help me reach new readers! Your organizational skills and professionalism are top notch, and the joy you take in your jobs is so easy to see. From Pitchfest to Bingo and scheduling book club appearances, everything goes without a hitch.

Booksellers – I SEE YOU! From handselling my last book like crazy to letting me know you're anxiously waiting for what's next, you are the ones out there getting my books into readers' hands one by one. I am so appreciative of your support and enthusiasm. In particular, thanks to Indigo for getting behind *When the World Fell Silent* in such a big way and introducing me to a whole new readership. Indies: you have embraced this book and hand-sold it like a boss, and I cannot thank you enough! I also cannot move on without a massive thank you to Sue Slade and the staff at my local Dartmouth Book Exchange. There has never been a bigger champion of my work and I am so thankful for all that you do, from handselling to hosting events to being my bookseller off-site, sometimes even on short notice. You are THE BEST.

A huge thank you to my agent, Carolyn Forde. The day we zoomed for the first time was the beginning of a something special. I'm so very happy you're on my team! To big things ahead!

And then there's my fam, because boy do they put up with a lot. 2024 was *a year*, was it not? But we're still here, and you've endured both the famine and the feast of my writing over the past several months, not to mention some dubious cooking fails and things being a little more ragged around the edges. I got a little pouty when I wanted a breakfast date and was told to finish my book, and I know I didn't always take plot and character advice well (sorry, Ash) but it is truly a group effort because I couldn't do this without you all behind me. Darrell, Kate, and Ash – you're everything. And CJ – what a light you've brought into all our lives. Your smile is the bestest treat at the end of my day.

One of the best new things about writing historical fiction, in particular historical fiction in Canada, is making new friends. Jen, Rachel, Bryn, Janie… it has been so great getting to know you better. Thank you all for taking me under your oh-so capable wings and making me feel I belong there. Tom, Bethany, Charlene… thank you for the DMs and coffee dates. They keep me sane.

Now to you readers, the entire reason I do this job (for otherwise I would be an author with no audience!) – I hope you have enjoyed this book. You can always find out what's happening on my website at www.donnajonesalward.com; there are book club resources there, too, and a link to schedule a book club appearance if you'd like me to pop in and say hi – I'm almost always up for a zoom! Thank you for embracing my stories and to those of you who have taken the time to drop me a note, you have no idea how much that makes my day.

With my best wishes and a see you next time,

Donna

Suggested Reading

A few of the reading resources I recommend:

FICTION

The Girl Who Came Home, Hazel Gaynor
A Brilliant Night of Stars and Ice, Rebecca Connolly
A Dress of Violet Taffeta, Tessa Arlen
The Second Mrs. Astor, Shana Abe
The Girl in the Lifeboat, Eileen Enright Hodgetts
On a Cold Dark Sea, Elizabeth Blackwell
The Girl on the Carpathia, Eileen Enright Hodgetts
Women and Children First, Gill Paul
Unsinkable, Jenni Walsh

NON FICTION

Titanic: The Tragedy that Shook the World, LIFE
Secrets of the Titanic: The Truth about the Tragedy, Centennial Books
Titanic Remembered, Alan Ruffman
Titanic Victims in Halifax Graveyards, Blair Beed
Titanic Style, Grace Evans
Titanic: True Stories of the Passengers, Crew, and Legacy, Nicola Pierce
Halifax and Titanic, John Boileau
Wrecking and Sinking of the Titanic, Jay Henry Mowbray
Voices from the Carpathia, George Behe

Book Club Questions

1. *Ship of Dreams* is set on the iconic *Titanic*. Did you know a lot about the tragedy before you read the book? How true do you feel the author was to the time period?

2. Hannah and Louisa are best friends, yet they are very different women. Do you think their personalities complemented each other? Which character did you relate to more, and why?

3. Both Hannah and Louisa are keeping a secret from the other. How do you feel about secrets? Are people entitled to their own secrets, or is honesty really the best policy?

4. Do you think Hannah has a right to feel betrayed when she discovers the truth about Louisa? Do you think Louisa is in the wrong?

5. The characters in *Ship of Dreams* experience trauma from the sinking. What do you think about the way Hannah and Louisa responded to that trauma? Did anything surprise you?

6. In addition to themes of secrets and betrayal and friendship, there's also an underlying theme of women helping other women. We see this in characters like Margaret Brown, Helen Churchill Candee, Mabel Fortune, Renee Harris, and the fictional Mrs. Porter. What are your

thoughts on this theme, and how might this idea play out in today's world?

7. Many of the women in the story were outliers, trailblazers, and in some cases, troublemakers. How much did you know about the women's movement in the early 20th century? Can you think of other women doing the same thing today?

8. Hannah and Louisa find different ways of coping with their grief. Why do you think Hannah's feelings were so different from Louisa's? What did you think of their decisions in the end?

'Alward tells this story of the wounded survivors and the people who cared for them with affecting grace' - *Toronto Star*

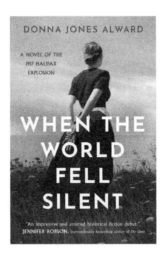

1917. Halifax, Nova Scotia.
Nora Crowell wants more than her sister's life as a wife and mother. As WWI rages across the Atlantic, she becomes a lieutenant in the Canadian Army Nursing Corps. But trouble is looming and it won't be long before the truth comes to light.

Having lost her beloved husband in the trenches, Charlotte Campbell now lives with his haughty relations who treat her like the help. It is baby Aileen, the joy and light of her life, who spurs her to dream of a better life.

When tragedy strikes in Halifax Harbour, these two women's paths will cross in the most unexpected way, trailing both heartbreak and joy its wake...

Available in paperback, ebook and audio!

The author and One More Chapter would like to thank everyone who contributed to the publication of this story…

Analytics
Abigail Fryer

Audio
Fionnuala Barrett
Ciara Briggs

Contracts
Laura Amos
Inigo Vyvyan

Design
Lucy Bennett
Fiona Greenway
Liane Payne
Dean Russell

Digital Sales
Laura Daley
Lydia Grainge
Hannah Lismore

eCommerce
Laura Carpenter
Madeline ODonovan
Charlotte Stevens
Christina Storey
Jo Surman
Rachel Ward

Editorial
Kara Daniel
Charlotte Ledger
Federica Leonardis
Lydia Mason
Jennie Rothwell
Sofia Salazar Studer
Caroline Scott-Bowden
Helen Williams

Harper360
Emily Gerbner
Ariana Juarez
Jean Marie Kelly
emma sullivan
Sophia Wilhelm

International Sales
Peter Borcsok
Ruth Burrow
Colleen Simpson
Ben Wright

Inventory
Sarah Callaghan
Kirsty Norman

Marketing & Publicity
Chloe Cummings
Grace Edwards

Operations
Melissa Okusanya
Hannah Stamp

Production
Denis Manson
Simon Moore
Francesca Tuzzeo

Rights
Ashton Mucha
Alisah Saghir
Zoe Shine
Aisling Smyth
Lucy Vanderbilt

Trade Marketing
Ben Hurd
Eleanor Slater

The HarperCollins Distribution Team

The HarperCollins Finance & Royalties Team

The HarperCollins Legal Team

The HarperCollins Technology Team

UK Sales
Isabel Coburn
Jay Cochrane
Sabina Lewis
Holly Martin
Harriet Williams
Leah Woods

And every other essential link in the chain from delivery drivers to booksellers to librarians and beyond!

One More Chapter is an award-winning global division of HarperCollins.

Subscribe to our newsletter to get our latest eBook deals and stay up to date with all our new releases!

signup.harpercollins.co.uk/
join/signup-omc

Meet the team at
www.onemorechapter.com

Follow us!

@onemorechapterhc

Do you write unputdownable fiction? We love to hear from new voices. Find out how to submit your novel at
www.onemorechapter.com/submissions